DAVID WILLIAMS

The Umbra Signal

First published by Cipherlock Press 2026

Second edition

ISBN (print): 979-8-9946844-0-5
ISBN (digital): 979-8-9946844-2-9

This book was professionally typeset on Reedsy.
Find out more at reedsy.com

Contents

I

Act I: Awakening the Echo (Initiation Layer)

It starts with a flicker.

A forgotten pattern buried in the static.

An echo that doesn't belong to the present.

As clues surface, from a desert transmission to buried Cold War files, a deeper pattern begins to emerge.

Not a coincidence. Not random. A signal.

Something has been trying to speak across time.

And now, someone is finally listening.

1

Cipher: Breach in Time

Groom Lake, Nevada – June 14, 1955, 0200 Hours

Stars blinked above the Nevada desert, timeless and unreadable. Moonlight washed over Hangar 18 at Area 51, its silhouette rising like a fortress chiseled from silence.

Static hung thick in the air as Private Timothy Rustand sat alone in the guard shack on the facility's outer edge. He hunched in his chair and took a swig of lukewarm coffee from a tin military-issue cup.

"Just once I'd like it to stay hot," he muttered.

He wiped his mouth on his sleeve and tapped the Morse key. Nothing, only an annoying hiss. Just his luck. Then, a sharp metallic thunk. Somewhere behind the wall. Or below it. Or inside it.

Rustand froze mid-blink.

His eyes tracked left. Then right. Then up. He leaned back, stared hard at the ceiling tile with the old brown stain, squinting like it might blink first.

Then he ducked and looked under the desk.

Nothing.

He stood up. Kicked the empty chair like it owed him money.

Still nothing.

Getting more spooked, he lifted the garbage can, looked inside. He even opened the supply locker and poked his head in.

"Mice, maybe," he muttered. "Or a jackrabbit. Radioactive jackrabbits."

Another pause. He finally looked at the Morse set. Like it had personally betrayed him.

He took a step toward it. Then two. Real slow.

"Gonna be the first man in history taken out by a haunted filing cabinet."

He sat down again, picked up his coffee. Didn't drink it. Just held it like a nervous habit. His eyes never left the wall. Rustand then tried the Morse key again, which, thankfully, decided to work this time.

He began logging his hourly check-in with Central HQ:

—. .-. —- —- — / ... - .- - .. —- -. / .- .-.. .—. .... .- .-.-.- /
.- .-.. .-.. / -.-. .-.. . .- .-. .-.-.- / .. / ... .- -.— / .- —. .- .. -.
—-... / .- .-.. .-.. / -.-. .-.. . .- .-. —..—

"Groom Station Alpha. All clear. I say again: all clear," he sent, while repeating the words aloud, an old habit from tech school.

Each *dit* and *dah* drilled into the silence. More reflex than thought now. Each chirp reminded him of everything he wasn't cleared to know.

And he felt extra jumpy tonight.

He paused, massaging his shoulder to ease his tension. Through the window, the black and diamond-studded sky implied eternity.

Dit-dah-dit, dah-ditty-dit, dah dit-dit.

Another series of taps echoed through the shack. This time, no reply came. The silence stretched. Too precise, too sterile. Not human.

"HQ? You CC?" Rustand clattered back. "Did you RX that last MSG?"

The radio crackled, then flatlined into static, as if the silence had swallowed the reply.

Rustand frowned and reached for the antenna tuner. The moment he twisted the dial, the radio spat out a sharp burst of static, followed by an odd pattern.

Dah. Dit-dit. Dah-dah.

He froze, recognizing the letters. But this wasn't standard protocol. The signal repeated, deliberate, almost... patient.

A calibration error perhaps, or someone having fun. But unease prickled the back of his neck.

Curiosity got the better of him. He tapped out a response, mimicking the pattern he'd heard. The words didn't get verbalized this time. He couldn't bring himself to say them aloud.

Dit-dah-dah ditty-dit-dit dah-dah-dah, Dit-dit ditty-dit, Dah ditty-dit-dit dit-dit ditty-dit?

Another pause, longer this time. The radio snapped alive with a piercing tone, sharp enough to cut bone, followed by a string of rapid, high-speed Morse. The dots and dashes blurred into an incomprehensible rush, far too fast for any human hand to send.

The lights flickered.

The hum deepened. Low, resonant, and unnatural. It rolled through the floor like distant machinery waking up. Rustand stiffened, hand hovering near the console, as the desk shook beneath his wrist.

It stopped.

Abrupt and absolute. One moment a scream of code. The next, only the soft hiss of static, like nothing had ever happened.

"HQ this is Alpha," Rustand keyed. "Confirm ur RX."

"RX Alpha. All clear," Control keyed back.

Rustand rubbed the back of his neck, forcing a shaky laugh. "Gotta be these old lines," he said nervously. He reached for the logbook. But the taps had sounded almost rhythmic. It was as if the interference knew exactly what he was listening for. An echo he couldn't shake, familiar but impossible. He scribbled a note:

"Unexpected transmission. Non-standard code? Logged and archived."

He didn't think about it again.

But out there, somewhere across the cold vastness of space, the first ripple had been sent.

* * *

He scanned the horizon. The hangar loomed behind him like

an impenetrable monolith, its heavy doors closed tight in silent vigil.

Rustand stepped out of the shack and made his way toward his partner. He shifted his weight. The rifle rested loosely in his grip as he approached Sergeant Frank Carter.

Carter flicked ash from his dying cigarette without looking up. "You check in, kid?"

"Yeah," Rustand muttered. "Got some weird chatter back. Didn't sound normal to me." His curiosity weighed on him like the rifle strap on his shoulder. "I've got to ask," Rustand ventured in a low, thoughtful tone, glancing toward his partner who was leaning on a weathered crate. "You ever think about what they've got sealed up in there?" Carter, his sharp features softened only by the flicker of a match as he re-lit his stubborn cigarette, raised a skeptical eyebrow. He took another long drag. "Nope. And I plan to keep it that way."

Tim Rustand's lips twitched, but he couldn't keep his gaze from drifting toward the hangar. "Come on, Sarge. The security, the way they act so cagey... it's not just aircraft in there, is it?" His tone carried the echoes of stories passed down among privates in hushed voices.

Carter's expression hardened, and he exhaled a stream of smoke, his tone clipped and matter-of-fact. "You keep asking questions like that, and you're going to find yourself guarding the back end of a supply depot. They'd assign you to watch paint dry if they thought you were too curious." His voice, though light with humor, carried an undercurrent of caution. A warning borne of years of following orders without question.

Rustand hesitated, shifting on his feet weighing the gravity of the conversation. "I don't know. My dad swore there were stories. You know, about things we pulled out of the sky. Machines that don't belong here." His words were soft, laced with an almost childlike wonder. A wonder that recalled evenings spent around a crackling radio, listening to tall tales of strange happenings.

Carter chuckled, his expression softening as he crushed his cigarette under his boot. "Stories are for people with time on their hands. Out here, you've got a job. Keep your eyes open and your mouth shut. The only thing flying around tonight is your imagination." His laugh was low and knowing, as if he'd heard a thousand such questions and learned to dismiss them with practiced ease.

Before Rustand could reply, a faint metallic sound, sharp and deliberate, interrupted them. It was a click that split the night's silence with uncanny precision.

Both men froze. Tim's knuckles went white on the rifle. "Did you hear that?" Carter scanned the dark. "Could be a coyote... but that didn't sound like teeth on wire." Rustand's heart hammered, and a wave of nausea mixed with disbelief overtook him as he staggered backward, unable to process the surreal split-second vision.

Carter straightened, his focus intensifying as his eyes scanned the dark horizon. "Stay alert. Could be nothing. Could be trouble." His words were clipped.

The wind whispered softly through the sand, carrying with it secrets of distant times and places. And then, time stuttered.

Rustand steadied himself. Something sharp and unseen scraped across his nerves, gone in an instant but real. It was as if the world had skipped a frame, like a film reel that jumped, distorting reality. The distant buzz of the generators, a constant presence in the night, skipped a beat. A sudden, jarring break in the familiar background noise that made both men's skin prickle.

Rustand turned toward Carter, and what he saw defied logic. Carter was there, but he was not alone. In that split second, Rustand saw two Carters: one standing as he had been moments before, his fingers brushing the holster of his sidearm; the other, a ghostly, fractionally ahead version of Carter, who had already drawn his weapon, his mouth open as if to issue a silent, urgent warning.

Then: snap. In the blink of an eye, only one Carter remained.

But the moment lingered, like a scene replaying itself out of sync.

Rustand blinked rapidly, the sensation different from déjà vu, more like an intentional reset, as though reality had deliberately stuttered. As if something wanted the moment to repeat, until someone noticed. He swallowed, uncertain whether the signal was watching him, or simply waiting.

It felt like reality stalled and vibrated. Like something a professor once called 'spooky action,' only this wasn't theory. In that instant, Carter's inexplicable duplication and sudden erasure felt like a ripple in one stretched fabric of reality. Distance and time no longer followed the rules.

Rustand froze. The hum of the generators faltered. Not only in sound, but in pressure. The air felt impossibly thick. It pressed around him as if he were moving underwater. Carter looked directly at him. His eyes were sharp, full of concern, as if he too had experienced something indescribable.

"Rustand, you all right?" Carter called out. The words reached him a second too late, like an echo from a half-remembered dream.

A low hum, deep and resonant, vibrated through the ground beneath him. Tim's breath caught in his throat. The hum intensified, and the metal desk shuddered beside him. He noted with a mix of fear and incredulity that Carter's posture had shifted, his fingers now brushing the grip of his sidearm. But Rustand swore he had already seen that exact moment unfold before his eyes. A cold, static-like sensation electrified his spine, feeling as though his body had skipped forward while he struggled to catch up. It was as if time itself had faltered, leaving him stranded between two seconds.

Rustand's boots crunched once on the gravel, then stilled.

He hadn't taken another step, but the world around him had shifted, like a room that had been rearranged in the dark. The air didn't shift. It bent. Ever so slightly. Like something had leaned in too close and pulled the world with it. He froze. The wind had been steady. Now it pushed back in tiny bursts, like it couldn't make up its mind. There was a shimmer, like the blinking of stars. And yet, not light. Not heat. Something else. Like space forgot what shape it was supposed to be. He looked at Carter, but Carter was still scanning forward, unaware. How was he not feeling this? Rustand's fingers curled tighter on the rifle grip.

"Something's... not right," he intoned. He wasn't sure who he was talking to.

His helmet buzzed and then... cold silence.

His left foot twitched. Not because he moved it. It had shifted forward, like someone had spliced out a frame of time and dropped him into the next.

He held his breath. Waited.

Then the shimmer passed again. This time, he felt it in his teeth.

His balance swayed. Not from motion, but from the weight of what he couldn't see.

Whatever this was, it hadn't merely touched him. It had folded reality around him. And it wasn't done yet.

The wind that had been a constant, gentle breeze, became a carrier of a strange echo of sounds that had not yet happened, the future and present intertwined. Then, in that eerie silence, Rustand heard Carter's voice again. Not once, but twice. "Stay alert. Could be nothing. Could be trouble."

Carter's voice was first heard during the real-time conversation, but a second, nearly identical version of the message was received immediately after the first one, as if it had been sent as a ghost echo, as if someone had recorded it onto an audio tape and put it out of sync, poorly, yet in a rather chilling manner. Rustand stopped breathing, the panic was intense. He looked, expecting Carter to react with visible alarm, but the sergeant remained unfazed. He flicked his cigarette away and rubbed his temple as if nothing unusual had happened. "You hear that?" Rustand whispered, his voice trembling with a mixture of disbelief and fear.

"Hear what?" Carter replied with a scowl, his tone clipped and full of uncertainty.

Rustand's boots betrayed him. The ground beneath his feet felt unsteady, not as if the earth was shifting or moving, but as if he was standing on a memory of the present and not the present itself. He blinked in rapid fire, confused, and found himself 10 feet in front of where he was moments before.

The sensation was surreal. The rifle strap dug into his shoulder. Rustand blinked, but the moment held still, as if reality hadn't reloaded. His brain hit a wall. It wasn't confusion, it was more like the whole world had been tilted and no one warned him.

His foot was forward. He hadn't stepped.

"I... what?" he whispered.

His voice came out strained, like it belonged to someone else. He turned toward Carter, but Carter stood frozen in a way that didn't look natural. Not stillness, but suspension. Like time had hiccuped.

Rustand reached for the ground to steady himself. His palm scraped the gravel as he caught himself, the pain snapping him back into the moment.

Then he was back. The same position. Same breath. Rifle clenched. A sharp pulse drummed behind his eyes. Something had snapped him into place; something other than gravity.

"Carter," he croaked. "I was..."

The words broke apart as another ripple passed through the air.

Carter's head lifted. He straightened fast, boots shifting back. His eyes locked on Rustand.

"You..." Carter forced out words. "You moved."

"I didn't," Rustand muttered. "But I wasn't here either."

He heard it. It sounded absurd, even to him. But Carter didn't question it. He had already drawn his sidearm.

Rustand didn't move. He couldn't trust the ground beneath him.

Carter's face tightened. "You blinked. One second you were five feet ahead."

Rustand gave a small nod. "Felt like both. Like I stepped out of sync."

Then came a sound. A clean, deliberate click.

Not boots. Not gravel. Something cleaner. Intentional.

Carter turned sharply. His voice lowered. "That wasn't us."

Rustand stayed still. His mouth was dry.

A second click followed. Closer this time.

Their eyes met. No one spoke.

Then the shadows shifted.

Carter's voice was low, almost hushed. "Tell me you saw that."

Rustand didn't answer right away. "I saw it... I just don't know what I saw."

Carter shook his head, eyes scanning the horizon. "No time to process it. Not now."

Rustand exhaled shakily. "That was plain wrong."

"Keep it together," Carter said, though his voice betrayed a crack of unease. "We'll deal with this nightmare later."

Rustand nodded, trying to push the moment down, deep. "If there's a later."

* * *

Beyond the fence perimeter and shadowed depths of the hangar, five intruders, dressed in black, moved with unnerving precision like predators. Each step exact, like they'd rehearsed this breach a hundred times before. Each step was planned. Every movement sharp, efficient, and cold.

In an instant, Carter and Rustand were on their weapons, their rifles up and level, with a primitive urge to survive erasing any of the confusion that might otherwise have clouded their minds. Rustand backed up against the wall. Carter offered a two-finger salute, a quiet, unspoken gesture that hinted at battle scars buried deep beneath the surface, earned in the heat of active combat. Rustand exhaled through his nose, slow and planned. Whatever the anomaly was, he decided for the time being it could wait. The present danger required attention. The hangar was massive, shadowy, and threatening, sitting right there in the darkness with its doors shut tight. And now, there was no question of it: they were not alone.

* * *

The first of the intruders, a wiry man with piercing blue eyes and whose actions communicated that he was clearly the leader, moved as though he had already memorized every inch of the terrain. In his hand he held a small, smooth cylinder, its edges worn and pitted as if it had seen countless secret operations before. The device was from a forgotten era, from the future.

Right behind him, a squat, stocky man shifted restlessly, his burly hands flexing against the grip of his weapon. "I don't like this," he muttered, his voice barely rising above a breath. "Feels off."

A slender woman with a scar across her cheek shot him a piercing look. "Shut up and move," she ordered curtly, her delicate fingers twitching in a familiar, soldier-like habit. The reflex of someone who constantly checked her weapon even in moments of relative calm.

The fourth member of the group, a tall, broad-shouldered man, remained silent. He did not need words. His inscrutable expression and the confident set of his jaw spoke volumes. Clad in gear that blended with the surrounding shadows, he looked as though he already knew secrets that the others could only guess at. In a measured, almost ritualistic manner, he pressed a switch on a compact device strapped to his arm.

A soft, deliberate vibration pulsed outward in an unseen wave; a signal of readiness or a warning to unseen watchers. The entire team paused for a full second, collectively holding their breath as if waiting for fate to decide their next move. Nothing happened.

The leader exhaled slowly, breaking the silence. "Clear. We're good." His tone was smooth, confident; a stark contrast to the palpable tension that still vibrated in the air.

The youngest member of the team, a man with a perpetual look of nervous energy, let out a shaky breath. "Did you feel it outside?" he croaked, his voice tight with apprehension.

The woman with the scar nodded as she adjusted the strap of her pack. "Yeah. Like a misfire." Her fingers fidgeted with the edge of the pack, a reflex that betrayed more unease than her voice did.

"Too close," the leader muttered, his gaze flicking toward the distant perimeter where Carter and Rustand continued their patrol, looking intently for the silent intrusion unfolding beyond the hangar's shadow.

"Lucky for them," the leader added under his breath, a wry smile tugging at the corners of his lips as he contemplated the situation.

The tall, silent man tilted his head, brow furrowed. "They didn't register it?" His tenor-pitched voice was almost a murmur. Too calm for the weight behind the question.

The leader shook his head. "No, but they felt it. That's the edge of the radius. The scientists at the facility call it 'localized chronal shear.'" His explanation was brief, yet ominous. It implied the intruders were operating on the fringes of a temporal anomaly.

The tall man shifted his weight, visibly uncomfortable. "If they'd been closer...?" he ventured, his voice trailing off in uncertainty.

The leader snapped his fingers. Perhaps too sharply. His confidence was strained. "Then we'd have a bigger problem." He growled sharply. "Move. Now."

"Still too unstable," the scarred woman shook her head and muttered, a note of frustration creeping into her tone.

The leader's knuckles tightened around the worn cylinder. He hesitated briefly, then signaled the others to move. "Enough. Move out." With that, the intruders dispersed, merging with the deep shadows of the hangar as they advanced steadily toward their target.

Behind them, in the warm, starlit Nevada night, the last wisps of a mysterious time ripple dissipated silently into the desert air, unseen, unfelt.

The five intruders moved rapidly, the lead figure raising the cylindrical device already humming with restrained energy. The beam slipped out, and the fence vanished. Not burned, not cut, but erased, as if edited out of the present. One by one, they crossed the threshold, not so much entering as resuming something already set in motion. They carried with them an assortment of advanced equipment and communication tools that defied the technology of the era, and weaponry modified for stealth and rapid action. Their target: a spacecraft, a vessel of mystery and enigma, shrouded in its own secrets.

"Eyes sharp," muttered the wiry leader, his piercing blue eyes scanning the surroundings with calculated intensity. He gestured silently for the others to fan out.

The intruders approached the hangar. The wiry leader held up the cylindrical device and pressed a small button on its surface. A faint, almost imperceptible purr filled the air, followed by a sudden ripple; an invisible shockwave of energy that spread outward in a perfect circle, bending the moment around it. A two-meter section of the hangar door vanished into mist. The four armed guards at the entrance froze mid-step, eyes wide with confusion, before collapsing where they stood, dropped cold by the silent force.

* * *

Carter and Rustand were on high alert as they made their

way around the outer hangar perimeter. Something was definitely off, and nothing made sense anymore.

On the far side of the complex, Rustand staggered slightly and gripped a wooden crate to stable himself. "What the... did you feel that?"

Carter had already turned toward the hangar. "Yeah. Like a punch without the sound."

"That wasn't wind," Rustand said, adjusting his grip on the rifle. "That was... something else."

Carter took off towards the distant hanger at a sprint. "Let's move. Now."

They ran.

* * *

"*GO*," the leader ordered, his voice low but carrying the weight of command.

With that single word, the team surged forward, their boots making barely a crunch on the cold concrete as they slipped through the breach and swept into the hangar.

And there it was: hovering low, silent and ominous.

The spacecraft was bathed in an eerie green light. Its hull was etched with shifting symbols and appeared otherworldly; a fantastical blend of futuristic design and enigmatic antiquity. The details were as mesmerizing as they were perplexing.

Eyes wide with wonder, the youngest stared up at the hovering craft, mesmerized, until his knee slammed into a jagged crate edge. Pain flared. He bit back a cry as blood soaked through the tear. Limping forward, he cursed the ship and himself in the same breath.

Nearby, a small desk cluttered with papers and outdated equipment caught the leader's eye. "Bingo," he murmured, his voice low and conspiratorial as his eyes caught the faded gleam of an American-made Morse code keyboard lying incongruously among the clutter. "We've found it, as they said. This goes with us." Swiftly and without hesitation, he unplugged the device and tucked it under his arm. A precious relic that held the key to secrets long buried.

"Control panel's here," the scarred woman said, motioning toward a section of the spacecraft's hull that appeared less uniform than the rest. The leader stepped forward, placing the cylindrical device against the surface. Almost immediately, it emitted a soft, rhythmic buzz, and with a subtle mechanical click, a hidden panel slid open. Inside, rows of strange, glowing symbols pulsed with a steady rhythm, reminiscent of a human heartbeat. A silent, mesmerizing cadence that hinted at a language older than time.

"Here goes nothing," the leader muttered, his voice a blend

of determination and excitement as he manipulated the interface with a deft combination of instinct and memorized instructions. The symbols shifted and reorganized on the screen, their glow intensifying in a hypnotic dance of light and shadow.

"What do we need that old World War Two souvenir for?" the burly assailant grumbled, his tone laced with incredulity. "Let's dump it and get out of here. It's slowing us down!"

The wiry leader shot him a withering glare. "Do you think we're the first ones to touch this technology? This thing wasn't built. It was recovered. The military's been sitting on it for decades without realizing what they had."

The scarred woman ran her slender fingers reverently over the device, studying the worn symbols beneath its surface. "This thing," she hesitated, "It doesn't just translate signals. It interfaces with the other technology."

The leader's grip on the device tightened imperceptibly as he responded in a near-whisper, "*YES*. The Morse Code Unit is the cipher key, and it must go with us!"

* * *

Groom Lake, Nevada – June 14, 1955, 0205 Hours

At a control panel near the vessel, the leader unlatched his pack and then carefully removed the unassuming Morse code device. The metal box, weathered and marked with the faded insignia of the U.S. Military, held an aura of enigmatic history.

Wincing as his knee throbbed, the young assailant tapped the device with gloved fingers. "I still don't get it... why this thing? Shouldn't we be using something more modern?" he muttered, equal parts confused and frustrated.

The scarred woman beside him shot him a sideways glance. "You think this ship works on 'modern' tech?" she replied angrily.

"Enough," barked the leader. He knelt beside the spacecraft's control interface and placed the Morse code unit carefully on a flat surface, below a seam in the metal. With deft, precise movements, he twisted a dial on the side of the device. The brief respite allowed the young operative to steal a quick, bitter espresso shot from his hidden flask and tend to his bleeding, gashed knee. His eyes snapped upward as a sharp tone sliced through the air.

The ship stirred.

A thin blue light scanned the Morse unit, its wavering glow dancing across the weathered exterior before disappearing into the hull. A series of vibrations cascaded outward from the control panel, each one matching the exact rhythm of a coded transmission.

The leader's jaw tightened as he observed, "It's recognizing the frequency."

The tall, broad-shouldered man, silent and imposing, finally broke his silence. "This is much more than a code unit," he stated.

The youngest member of the team glared in confusion. "What do you mean?" he demanded, gesturing toward the alien, intricate surface of the spacecraft.

The leader's eyes never left the vessel as he tapped the device again. "This thing isn't what it appears to be," he blurted in frustration. "The military had no idea what they were dealing with when they recovered it." With a click of a small toggle switch, another pulse of energy raced up the spacecraft's hull, causing a section to slide open with a quiet, almost reverent hiss.

"Repurposed," he muttered under his breath.

The youngest's brow furrowed with urgency. "Repurposed from what?" he pressed, his voice trembling with both curiosity and concern.

A heavy silence hung between them before the tall intruder spoke again, his tone imbued with reverence. "Older than radio. Maybe older than us," he said quietly.

* * *

Behind them, the unconscious guards stirred, the quiet murmur of movement a stark reminder of the narrow margin between success and failure. Carter and Rustand reached the opening right as two of the guards were shaking off the hit, eyes wide with residual shock.

"You all right?" Carter asked, crouching beside one.

"I think so," the man said, voice groggy. "What... what did they hit us with?"

"No idea," Carter said, helping another guard to his feet. "But they're inside... and they've got something big."

They stepped through the hole, weapons raised, breath catching as their eyes locked on the ship.

"Holy cats..." one of the guards muttered. "That thing real?"

Rustand stared, wide-eyed. "I used to laugh at the alien stories." He swallowed. "Ain't laughing now."

* * *

The youngest assailant cast a nervous glance over his shoulder. "We're out of time," he yelped.

"Almost there," the leader barked, his voice edged with tension as he aggressively pressed on.

The hangar doors groaned open, and a flood of pale light spilled in; headlights from an approaching vehicle flared through the haze, and the unmistakable sound of boots striking the ground echoed through the cavernous space.

"We've got company," hissed the scarred woman, her tone laced with concern.

The leader muttered under his breath, "Prepare to defend the ship. This doesn't end here."

* * *

A gunshot shattered the tense silence. A bullet ricocheted off the spacecraft's hull with a metallic clang, fired by a guard who hadn't waited for orders.

A second shot followed. Then a third.

And then something went wrong.

One of the guards near the bay entrance, a young man barely more than a recruit, staggered backward without being hit. His rifle clattered to the floor. For a split second, he looked confused, as if his body no longer matched the instructions his brain was giving it. His mouth opened, but no words came. His skin drained to a gray pallor.

His veins darkened. Not bruised, not broken. Darkened,

visibly, like ink being drawn up through invisible threads.

He reached for his face, but his hands twitched mid-air and locked in place. The air around him wavered. There was no light, no noise, but space itself rippled inward toward his chest.

The soldier let out a choking sound that didn't match pain. It sounded like something being unwritten. His entire form jittered like a poor video signal. Then he folded in on himself, not bending or falling, but compressing into a narrow column of distortion, like a person being pulled through the wrong end of a telescope.

And then he was gone.

No body. No blood. Just a half-second image of where he had been.

The nearest guard screamed in terror. The tall intruder gasped and fell to one knee, staring in utter shock.

Even the leader hesitated.

No one spoke. No one could grasp the horror they had just witnessed.

Then another round slammed into the side of the vessel, and the standoff shattered, giving way to chaos once more.

"Cease fire!" Carter shouted, but the spell was broken.

The intruders responded with lethal precision. No hesitation. No wasted motion. In seconds, two more guards were down, their bodies crumpling before they hit the floor. Carter turned to shout again. A flash of light, and then a round caught him square in the chest, and he dropped without a sound.

Rustand dove behind a support beam, heart hammering, ears ringing.

* * *

The intruders moved like machines.

Another guard went down with a short cry, a pattern of red sprayed against a stack of wooden crates, his weapon clattering uselessly to the ground.

The youngest member of the team ducked behind a nearby rusting diesel fuel tank, clenching the Morse code unit tightly as if it were a lifeline. "What now?" he shouted over the dissonant clamor of gunfire.

"We finish what we started," the leader commanded with fierce resolve.

With a sudden, explosive motion, he slammed his hand against the Morse unit's interface, and the spacecraft responded as it shuddered to life. Lights along its surface undulated erratically, casting eerie, shifting shadows that danced across the hangar's walls. The subtle vibrations of the machinery grew louder, resonating in their chests as the ship's surface distorted in a subtle liquefaction. An effect so fleeting it defied comprehension.

A seam split open across the side of the craft, unveiling a darkened passage illuminated by a low, internal glow. Vapor hissed outward in serpentine coils as the hatch widened, revealing a mechano-organic interior that pulsed with a faint, rhythmic thrum. Walls that breathed softly, their surfaces threaded with bio-luminescent veins and metallic tendons. The leader didn't hesitate. He sprinted and then vaulted into the opening, swallowed by the living glow. The others followed, boots pounding the deck as tracer fire stitched the ground behind them, ricochets flaring like fireflies. As the last figure dove through, the hatch irised shut with a hiss, sealing them inside as the vessel slowly rose from the concrete.

* * *

Amid a sudden burst of muffled gunfire outside the craft, the leader climbed into the command chair and brought the control panel to life. His fingers deftly moved over the glowing interface panel, with a grace that defied a 1950's understanding of keyboards and computer interfaces. With a series of rapid keystrokes that suggested a rehearsed instinct, he entered a sequence as if guided by a force beyond human will. The spacecraft's engines roared to life, sending a searing wave of heat cascading through the hangar. The guards outside, momentarily overwhelmed by the spectacle, fell back and shielded their faces as the ship levitated in a silent, surreal defiance of gravity as it hovered mere inches off the ground.

"Next stop... Andromeda!" the youngest intruder quipped nervously, the tremor in his voice belying the gravity of their mission.

The spacecraft tilted; its imposing nose aimed directly toward the hangar's ceiling. A burst of energy tore through the roof as the engines fired, sending a cascade of debris raining down like confetti. The vessel rocketed upward, its view through the fractured roof warping and bending, as if reality were being stretched, distorted, and reassembled as the Alcubierre warp drive engaged.

* * *

Outside, the remaining guards stood in stunned silence, their eyes fixed upward as the spacecraft vanished into the vast night. Only a trail of distorted light remained; a ghostly fingerprint against the backdrop of an indifferent universe. The stars wavered, like even they weren't sure what had happened when the ship departed. The smoldering remnants of the hangar warped and bent, caught in a liminal space between what had been and what was yet to come.

Rustand also watched as the craft vanished into the sky. Gone in a blink, no more than a glimmer against the stars. He stumbled through the breach, boots skidding across loose concrete, lungs burning as he sucked wind. Gunfire still echoed in his ears.

"Carter?" he called. Nothing.

He saw him.

Slumped.

Rustand dropped to his knees beside the sergeant, *his sergeant*, and reached out, hands fumbling and numb. Carter's body was still warm. His eyes halfway open, staring at nothing.

"Come on, Sarge," Rustand breathed, voice frayed. "Don't do this to me. Don't... you hear me?" He gripped the front of Carter's jacket, shook him lightly. "Hey... *hey*! You can't just punch out without warning. You said we were grabbing chow after shift. You..."

His voice cracked. He looked down. Blood soaked Carter's left side, but not from anything he recognized. There was no hole, no tear. Just gone, like something had scooped reality out of him.

Then the thought came.

His shot.

He'd aimed at the shimmer. The flicker. He swore it wasn't Carter.

"No. No-no-no. That wasn't you. I didn't hit you. I was shooting at..." He stopped, couldn't finish.

Rustand yanked the tin out of Carter's vest. It had a few Ohio Blue Tip matches. And two smokes left.

Rustand sat there in the wreckage, one hand still resting on the older man's shoulder.

"I'm sorry," he whispered. "I didn't know. I didn't know what I was even lookin' at."

Above him, the night sky was silent again.

He looked up, eyes straining toward the empty space where the craft had torn through the roof and become a dot in the sky in a blink. Not even a vapor trail remained. Only a trace of ruptured metal on the ground and a hum that still rang in his bones.

His gaze caught on the wall-mounted clock across the hangar. Its hands were frozen at 02:17.

He blinked hard. Looked again. Still 02:17.

"What just happened?" he hissed, voice raw, barely there. "What was that thing?"

No one answered. No one could.

He was alone.

The hangar was a black wound in the desert, its metal still hissing under a blank sky.

Rustand walked until the wind stopped biting and the smoke cleared from his throat. He crouched near the fence, boots in the dust, and pulled the tin from his jacket. It felt heavier now.

He took one of the cigarettes and lit up. Same rhythm: Flick, flame. Familiar.

He hadn't smoked in two years. Not since the doc said ulcers. Carter always called him a quitter.

The cigarette tasted like cardboard. Like paper and guilt.

The smoke hit hard. He didn't cough.

He didn't cry either.

He just sat, eyes locked on the break in the sky where the ship had punched through. The stars hadn't settled yet. Some still twitched. He inhaled deeply, and after a contemplative pause, blew out a long puff of smoke.

Nearby, the surviving guards quietly tended to the wounded and covered the fallen, their movements solemn and mechanical. Rustand barely registered their presence, lost in his own daze.

“You were supposed to outlast us all, Frank,” he muttered.

He flicked ash into the dirt and held the smoke steady in his fingers the way Carter always had, between the knuckles, not the tips.

“I think I saw you die twice,” he said. “And neither one made sense.”

He drew another breath in. Held it. Let it go.

The wind moved past him. Nothing else did.

2

Cipher: Cold War Convergence

Geneva, Switzerland – November 19, 1985, 0200 Hours

The room was unassuming at first glance, an ordinary conference hall with paneled walls, a long polished table, and faintly glowing lights. But for Ronald Reagan and Mikhail Gorbachev, it was anything but ordinary. The two leaders sat at opposite ends of the table, their faces lit by the soft glow of dim lighting that shimmered across the air between them.

Despite their political differences, an uneasy camaraderie hung in the air. Both men knew the gravity of the moment and the rare convergence of circumstances that had brought them here. Outside the perception of their respective governments, away from advisors and diplomatic scripts, this meeting had been orchestrated by forces greater than either of their nations, a select, unseen group whose influence spanned continents and ideologies.

Reagan adjusted his suit jacket and leaned forward, his

characteristic Hollywood charm momentarily replaced by the sober demeanor of a man grappling with a reality he could barely fathom. "Mikhail," he began, his voice steady, "it's not merely about the Strategic Defense Initiative. We're talking about something far larger than our nations. Larger than anything humanity's ever faced."

Reagan nodded, gesturing to the projections between them. Images flickered between grainy aerial photos, propulsion schematics, and ancient symbols mixed with modern code.

Gorbachev's sharp eyes studied Reagan, his expression inscrutable. "I'm not convinced. This sounds too fantastical even for our times. We must be missing something," he said, his voice tinged with skepticism. His accent, heavy yet precise, filled the otherwise quiet room.

"These aren't stories or figments of imagination," Reagan said. "They've been here long before us. And they're tied to something we've only begun to understand." He hesitated, his words catching on the weight of their proposition. "We're talking about a force that's embedded itself in human history. Technological, manipulative, and beyond our grasp."

Gorbachev leaned back, folding his hands in his lap. He exuded calm, but the slight furrow in his brow betrayed his unease. "And what is this force? Aliens? Beings from another world?"

Reagan smiled faintly, though the expression lacked humor. "That's the convenient explanation, isn't it? UFOs. Extraterrestrials. They keep people distracted, always looking up at the stars while the real threat is right here on Earth."

The room fell silent. The glow of artificial light cast long shadows across the walls.

"Da. Almost like the diversion our two countries created back in the fall of '83, eh, Mr. President?"

"Yes," said Reagan. "And I felt horrible that the KAL007 plane had to be the decoy. But it worked."

"It couldn't be avoided, dear comrade," the Soviet President said softly. He paused, then continued, "So you're saying it's not aliens?" His voice was quiet, but deliberate. "Then what?"

"The others... they've all seen it," Reagan said, his voice lower now. "Bits and pieces. Enough to know this thing didn't start with us. It's been nudging us forward. Maybe forever. The Tower of Babel. The printing press. Railroads. It leaves fingerprints."

Gorbachev's lips pressed into a thin line. "And now it's accelerating," he said. "These 'fingerprints,' they've become more frequent. More visible."

Reagan nodded. "Precisely. And our Strategic Defense Initiative? It's not about defending against missiles. It's about preparing for a force we barely comprehend."

Gorbachev stood, pacing slowly as he processed Reagan's words. "Why bring me here? Why tell me this? We are adversaries, Mr. President. The Cold War..."

"That's a smokescreen," Reagan cut in. "C'mon, Mikhail... you know it, I know it. They pulled us in because we're the only ones who won't choke on red tape when the truth gets ugly."

"And what is the truth, Ronald?" Gorbachev asked, his gaze piercing.

Reagan exhaled slowly. The pause wasn't hesitation. It was calibration. He traced a finger along the edge of a manila folder, unopened between them. "There's a compartmentalized archive," he said, "one even our own defense establishment barely touches. Artifacts recovered in the fifties, officially labeled as misidentified weather experiments or misattributed Soviet prototypes."

Gorbachev arched an eyebrow but stayed quiet.

"They weren't," Reagan continued. "We ran materials testing across multiple defense labs. No match to known alloys, no match to foreign designs. One sample was completely resistant to corrosion. No oxidation, no wear. It was as if it hadn't aged a day since it was retrieved."

Gorbachev folded his hands. "Nyet. That could be fabrication. Misinformation planted to sow panic or provoke escalation."

Reagan's tone flattened. "That's what some thought. Until we saw similar reports surface during your campaign in Afghanistan. The British encountered something similar during their Cyprus entanglement in '54. Even the French buried findings from a crash site near Dien Bien Phu. Different continents, same inconsistencies."

Gorbachev didn't blink. "And what do you think it means?"

Reagan let the question hang. He tapped once on the folder. "The real surprise wasn't the material. It was the data attached. Locations cross-referenced with intercepted transmissions. Some of the dates didn't align with reality. Not errors... anomalies."

"In what sense?"

"They carried embedded metadata with inconsistent timestamps. One packet claimed a signal was received in Nevada two days before the sender was born. Another indicated a relay from East Berlin that hadn't been constructed yet."

Gorbachev stiffened slightly, but said nothing.

Reagan leaned in. "We dismissed most of it. Blamed clerical mistakes or Soviet disinformation. But some of us started asking the wrong kinds of questions. Questions about the past. About causality."

The silence between them thickened, no longer diplomatic, but philosophical.

"Whatever's guiding these incidents," Reagan added, "it's more than who holds the bigger arsenal. It's about who understands the pattern."

Gorbachev asked incredulously, "You mean who understands that history might not only repeat itself ... it might already be repeating right now?"

"Right now," Reagan said pensively, "I'm not sure that either of us have a clue."

Reagan looked at the table, where a glowing artifact entirely out of place in 1985 sat. The artifact lay on the table between Reagan and Gorbachev, its crystalline lattice shimmering faintly under the dim overhead lights. The object, a blend of quartz-like organic material and nanotech design, appeared to breathe; its translucent surface demonstrating liquefaction. Glyphs and mathematical symbols danced momentarily across its structure, disappearing as quickly as they appeared, leaving only the impression of something ancient yet far beyond human understanding.

"This," Reagan said, his voice almost reverent, "is one of the artifacts. It was found decades ago, buried beneath layers of Arctic ice. It's not man-made. And it's not from beyond our world, either."

Gorbachev stared at the projection, his jaw tightening. "Then where did it come from?"

Reagan's gaze dropped to the pulsing crystal.

"That's what scares me," he said. "What if it wasn't from out there?" He leaned forward. "What if it was born here, then sent back? What if it's not from anywhere at all, but from time itself?"

* * *

A shared memory passed between them. An unsolved breach at Groom Lake decades earlier. Whispers of a vanished craft that neither superpower could fully explain. Each had files on it, fragments pointing to a larger puzzle beyond any Cold War rivalry. Even the best intelligence hinted that what happened in 1955 might be the key to what they faced now.

* * *

The weight of the memory hung in the air, filling the silence with an almost tangible tension. Gorbachev finally broke the quiet. "If this is true, then the others are more a collective of power brokers. They are something else entirely."

"They see themselves as guardians," Reagan said, his tone skeptical. "But even they admit that what's happening now is beyond their control."

Gorbachev returned to his seat, folding his hands atop the table. "And if this force cannot be controlled? What then?"

Reagan's face darkened. "Then humanity is playing a game it doesn't even realize it's losing."

"This meeting," Gorbachev said finally, his voice low, "will it change anything?"

"It has to," Reagan replied. "Because if we fail to understand what's really at stake, it won't be nations that fall. It will be everything."

The two men finished staring at each other and got up from the table. Silently.

President Reagan continued, "Mr. Gorbachev, to be clear: we will meet back here in two days as we have been instructed. The others have requested our presence and wish to include the two of us in their plans. Our countries may be opposed, but this is far bigger than the Cold War. They will explain the expansion plans and more about the technology we're using... even now, in this meeting spot."

Gorbachev slowly nodded in agreement, and the two of them broke their gaze, pivoted, and headed to opposite walls of the room. They both dematerialized into the blackness, with an almost imperceptible glimmer of light.

In the empty room, the shadowy walls hummed faintly, as though bearing witness to truths too vast for any one moment, or one generation, to contain.

3

Cipher: The Signal in the Static

SETI Outpost near Groom Lake, Nevada – Present Day, Wednesday, 0215 Hours

Officially, the Search for Extraterrestrial Intelligence, or SETI, was a decentralized scientific effort. Dozens of connected universities and research centers were quietly listening to the stars for any hint of intelligent life.

But tucked deep in the Nevada desert, behind barbed wire and satellite-blind zones, existed a facility not listed on any organizational chart. Known to its few occupants as the Listening Glass, the SETI outpost near Groom Lake operated under a different charter; one sanctioned, denied, and classified all at once.

Outside, Franklin, the ancient security guard (rumored to have come with the original construction), grumbled about "weird hours" as he fumbled with his ring of mismatched keys. It was his third attempt at locking up that night, and he was no closer to finding the right key than he was to understanding the researchers' odd habits. A thermos of stale coffee dangled from his free hand.

Inside, the control room pulsed with an almost hypnotic glow. The electrostatic hum of machinery set Liam's teeth gently on edge, a constant reminder of humanity's obsession with the unknown. The air was cool and sterile, with the acrid scent of ozone and burnt circuitry. Occasionally, the speakers spat out a faint hiss, data pouring out into the digital void. Liam Mills hunched his lean frame over a cluster of glowing monitors, fingers tapping a quiet rhythm on the desk. For him, this wasn't just a job. It was a quiet refuge, a place where obsession was the default, a solace for anyone who still believed that something extraordinary might be waiting in the static.

Tonight, though, felt as uneventful as the thousands of nights before it.

Then, the pulse arrived.

At first, it blended into the noise; a click, faint and erratic. Liam leaned closer. His eyes locked on the meter, then the scope. The second burst was sharper, planned. His heart picked up pace.

He adjusted the gain manually, bypassing the digital noise suppression. Another click, longer this time. Then more.

Ditty-dit-dah.

He blinked. Morse.

It couldn't be. He rerouted the audio through the analog monitor line and closed his eyes, isolating the timing.

Ditty-dit-dit ditty-dah dah-dah

He uttered aloud, "H... U... M..."

Dit-dah dah-dit, dit-dit dah-dit, dah

A second wave came. Liam sat forward. "A... N... I... N... T..."

He mouthed the rhythm as the signal finished.

HUMAN IN THE DESERT.

He leaned back, the words hanging in the dim blue light. The clicks continued. "HUMAN IN THE DESERT," he whispered.

Liam frowned. "It's more than Morse. It's efficient. Way too efficient."

He looked over at the screen again. "This doesn't feel alien. It feels... familiar." He paused. "It's almost like it was left here, like it's always been part of the noise, waiting for the right ears to hear it." To anyone else, it would sound like random pulse train noise. But not to him. Not with his grandfather's training. Not after years of decoding Morse by ear.

He knew what it was.

He recognized the signal immediately. But how? Why him?

His dark brown eyes, framed by the faint lines of too many sleepless shifts, scanned the endless streams of data. His notebook lay open beside him, its pages filled with transcriptions of static and blips that had led to nowhere.

Across the room, the empty desk of Gina Alvarez was a bitter reminder that not everyone had to endure this monotony. He stared at his half-empty mug of European coffee, a lifeline to keep his focus sharp.

"Lucky Gina," he muttered.

The clock ticked to 2:17 a.m., and then the monotony shattered.

* * *

A faint anomaly glimmered on the spectrum analyzer; a sharp, rhythmic pulse threading through the usual static. Liam froze, his head snapping toward the nearest monitor. As the numbers scrolled by, Liam's hands trembled. Not only from the cold, but from the realization that this wasn't mere interference. His mind reeled, and his eyes flicked to Gina's empty workstation, silently hoping for an explanation from a human colleague, who had taken the night off, to ease the chaos. The signal continued, gaining strength and cadence. Liam's eyes widened, and for a moment, he forgot the equations as his heart pounded with the thrill of discovery.

As the decrypted sequence glowed on the monitor, Liam's vision blurred and shifted. In a seamless overlay of memory and reality, the lab's sterile light gave way to a warm, amber glow of a long-ago study. Sitting at his grandfather's knee in a room filled with the soft clatter of an old typewriter, the scent of stale tobacco, and the gentle murmur of secret lessons, he recalled the last of those nights.

The shortwave radio sputtered with distant storms while Grandpa Rustand, cheeks sunken from chemo, tapped a single, shaky string of Morse: DIT-DIT-DIT DAH. "Means 'Victory,' my boy, and to keep listening," the old man wheezed, closing Liam's tiny fist over the brass code key. An old tin was there on the vintage military desk, tucked in the corner of the top cubby. Two smokes and a few Ohio Blue Tip matches inside. As if he'd meant to quit. Again.

Liam remembered, as his fingers absentmindedly moved over imaginary keys. He muttered, "ditty-dit-dah, this-is-a-vee, Victor," in his best "grandpa voice."

The ICU phone rang. A nurse's voice said the doctors could do no more. In the hallway's antiseptic glare, Liam watched his father crumple to the floor and felt his world narrow to the pulse beating in his palm. The key, still warm from his grandfather's grip, became a vow: decode every mystery the universe dared whisper, and never quit or back down.

This is a *VEE.*

DITTY-DIT-DAH.

BE A *VICTOR.*

Whenever the lab lights dimmed and the mingled scents of disinfectant and ozone filled the air, Liam was pulled back to that corridor, frantic to translate a dying man's last transmission before it vanished forever. In that memory, his grandfather leaned close and whispered, "Remember, every number is a secret, every pause a doorway." The memory spliced into the present, blending the timeless cadence of his grandfather's voice with the cold precision of the terminal. As the vision receded, Liam's hand hovered over the keyboard, the moment's significance crystallized around those echoing words.

* * *

Liam was pulled back to the present with a start.

"Fascinating... it seems we have eliminated all conventional sources," he muttered, leaning in.

He sat back again, cracking his knuckles. The cold air in the lab clung to his fingers. Something about the signal's clarity unsettled him. It was eerily clinical. Unlike the erratic bursts of radio chatter he was used to tracking, this one moved with purpose. Liam keyed in a secondary diagnostic, an old script from grad school that visualized harmonic overlays. It wasn't elegant, but it had never failed him.

The program launched. The signal blossomed on his monitor, unnervingly precise; each vibration stacked like whispers exploding into a primal scream. Each beat carried a subtle echo, faintly behind the original, as if something were reflecting the message before it finished sending. He leaned in, the tension in his jaw saying what words didn't.

His fingers reached toward the brass code key on his desk. The metal was cold, familiar. His grandfather's old tool, polished smooth by years of use, now sat beside state-of-the-art signal software. He pressed a thumb against it, grounding himself. "Listen between the clicks," the old man had once said. "That's where the secrets live."

Liam pulled up a thirty-day archive sweep, cross-referencing the signal against other SETI detections. There was nothing. No matching pulsar, no repeating fast radio burst, no signal artifact. This was new. Not merely in content. In presence. It didn't blend with cosmic noise; it cut through it.

He ran a quick spatial check. Strangely, the signal matched a forgotten Cold War satellite path. The scan had been redacted for decades. Only some parts had been declassified in recent years. Most of the data was still blacked out. Liam was at a complete loss.

The overlay flickered. The signal's angle of origin aligned

with a classified surveillance pass from 1983. He checked it again; the telemetry was solid. The odds of this signal intersecting that specific, archived corridor were impossibly small.

He stood and crossed the room to the physical logbook. SETI protocol demanded manual documentation for all primary anomalies. Liam flipped to a clean page and began writing. Halfway through the entry, he stopped. The spacing of his notes mirrored the signal cadence; his pen strokes, the same intervals. He looked back at the monitor. The pulse continued. Unchanged, but somehow watching.

He said aloud, "Every time I think I understand the rules, the universe changes the question." Liam's smile faded as he stared blankly at his cold European-style espresso. "That's it, I'm switching to decaf," he muttered, running a hand through his hair. Out of habit, he tapped a pencil twice on the desk, a nervous tick his old Air Force buddy Sparky used to call "the Morse for trouble."

Behind him, the signal blinked again. One beat.

Everything felt oddly distant. Liam stepped back to the terminal and hovered his hand over the keyboard. The screen flashed, once, as if reacting.

The pulse held steady, but something in the silence had shifted. He reached out and tapped the side of the monitor. No reaction. Still, the unease remained.

One of Liam's sideband diagnostics stalled mid-sweep, freezing for less than a second. An overflow flag triggered, and a low-level debug window flickered to life on his console.

Liam didn't move. "What the...?"

A chunk of plaintext buffer scrolled across in quick pulses, too fast to register, then snapped shut. He caught only the final line before the system auto-cleared it:

/// GROOM.ALPHA.PROTOCOL /// 1954.07.19 // LINKED::TR/LM>BL // RA.PATH ECHO MARKED // HOLD CONT.STAT: MA // AR.FLAG PENDING //

The log reset to green. No errors reported.

"Weird," Liam muttered, rubbing his temple. "Archive artifact, maybe..."

He dismissively shook his head, and turned back to the waveform.

The signal pulsed again, steady, waiting.

The key remained in his grip, his thumb tracing its edge while his other hand hovered over the desk, unsure of its purpose. He didn't know why the signal had chosen this moment, this sky, or his voice. But it had. With intent. And it was far from over.

His fingers flew across the keys, isolating the frequency and stripping away layers of interference. "I've systematically ruled out any terrestrial origin. The anomaly appears genuine."

The rhythm repeated. Precise, methodical, it was intentional. A successive barrage of dits and dahs flooded his ears as he leapt to a keyboard and intercepted the ancient code. As he typed, he became more excited than he had ever been at the outpost. The code paused, and he stared at what he had just intercepted:

HUMAN IN THE DESERT

His heartbeat hammered. Disbelief tangled sharply with fear. Maybe he was slipping into madness. Memories of childhood nightmares mingled with the stark reality of the hangar.

The message alone shook him to his core. However, the precision of the cadence was truly disturbing. It was a sequence that matched something buried deep in his memory, too exact and impossible.

"No... that can't be right," he whispered, staring at the screen.

He ran diagnostics. Checked for interference. Scanned local and satellite transmissions. There was no rational source, no earthly origin. The signal pulsed again, steady, waiting.

Liam swallowed hard and forced himself to think methodically. He initiated a series of diagnostic tests, determined to prove the signal was nothing more than a fluke.

First, he scanned nearby aircraft frequencies, cross-referencing them with the signal's timing. Nothing matched.

"Okay," he muttered, adjusting the spectrogram. "What about satellites?"

He pulled up satellite telemetry, overlaying orbital paths with the timestamp of the signal. The spectrogram pulsed steadily, but no satellite aligned with the signal's origin.

"Not a satellite either," he said, his voice tinged with growing curiosity.

Next, he applied ionospheric filters to account for atmospheric distortion. The signal emerged clean and undistorted.

Finally, he triangulated the source. His breath caught as the coordinates resolved on his monitor:

RA 00h 42m 44.3s | DEC +41° 16′ 9″

He stared at the numbers, feeling totally numb and in shock. "No friggin' way..."

"Andromeda," he intoned, "...the Andromeda Galaxy."

* * *

As the signal repeated, Liam began noticing subtle irregularities in the structure. Faint distortions between the bursts of transmission, too deliberate to ignore.

"C'mon... this is too unreal."

Liam refocused. "Just amazing... a signal within a signal," he murmured to himself. "It's got to be there. Only thing that makes sense and aligns with the data."

He thought back to his grandfather's lessons about pattern recognition. Hidden messages often lay in the gaps, in the shifts between the obvious. But even as he scrutinized the spectrogram, he couldn't make out a discernible pattern.

"It's there," he mused, his frustration mounting. "I can't quite see it yet."

4

Cipher: The Voice in the Void

SETI Outpost near Groom Lake, Nevada – Present Day, 0227 Hours

Gina Alvarez's phone buzzed on her nightstand, shattering the quiet of her bedroom. She groaned, fumbling blindly for the device while burying her head under a pillow. The glow from the screen illuminated the name Liam Mills.

She exhaled sharply. This better be good.

Eyes still closed, she pressed the phone to her ear. "If this isn't a spaceship landing, I'm hanging up," she muttered. Her voice was still groggy.

Liam's voice hit her with a jolt of urgency. "Gina, I need your help, like ASAP. I found a weird signal and need you here, pronto."

Gina rubbed her eyes, already irritated. "Liam, it's two in the morning. Whatever it is, it can...." She hesitated, rubbing her eyes and yawning. "Dios mío," she groaned softly, "not another false alarm, por favor."

The last time she had chased an anomaly, it had nearly cost her career. The deep-space FRB incident haunted her; a pattern she thought had been an alien signal, only for it to be dismissed as a malfunctioning microwave at Arecibo.

"Liam, this can wait until..."

"No. It can't." His words were clipped, his tone carrying an edge that made her sit up. "The signal is Morse code."

She hesitated, still shaking sleep away from her brain. "Morse? So? That's a hundred-year-old system."

"I know, Gina, which is why you need to get over here. It isn't about *what* the signal is but *where* it was broadcast from."

She swung her legs over the side of the bed. Barely awake at 2:28 AM, she snatched a half-eaten granola bar from her bedside, took a small bite, chewed pensively, and continued. "Liam, enough. What is this, the Cold War? Did some ham radio geek bounce a signal off a satellite? Who cares *where* a Morse signal broadcasts from?"

There was a beat of silence, like he was bracing himself for her reaction.

"*You* will. It's coming from the Andromeda galaxy."

* * *

Gina's pulse ticked up. That was impossible. The odds of a signal from that deep in space were virtually nonexistent. The Morse part was even more unbelievable and fantastical.

And the last time she had let herself believe in something fantastic, she had become a joke to her colleagues.

She laughed, hard and long. But Liam wasn't backing down. "Gina... I know it's your day off, but I need you to come in and go through this."

It was far-fetched and fantastic.

However, Liam wasn't usually the type to fall for hoaxes.

"Please. I would not call you and wake you up out of a sound sleep if I hadn't been over every inch of the data multiple times."

"This had better not be another one of your sleep-deprived theories," she continued, rubbing her temples, "Liam, I..."

"It is legit, I swear. Andromeda."

A long pause as Gina's brain caught up. "Andromeda? The only thing that could be...." She hesitated, then waved it off. "No. That's crazy." She ran a hand through her dark hair, her mind racing. "Last month you yanked me out of bed for a phantom signal that ended up being a loose cable. Now you're saying Morse code... from the Andromeda galaxy? Liam, are you hearing yourself?"

"I know, I know... sounds crazy," he said quietly. "But it's real. And there's something else. A pattern hiding in the pauses. Like someone wanted it buried."

Gina sat on the edge of her bed, shaking her head, her skepticism warring with curiosity. "Okay, I am on my way in. You are a dead man if this is a wild goose chase."

* * *

Liam's next thought was to call Sig, but he decided against it, for now. He did not want to poke that particular bear, but he knew that if anyone would have a good idea of what to do next, it would be him.

Sig always seemed to have his back, even if he had ulterior motives. Liam hadn't asked too many questions when the SETI posting came through. Graveyard shift in a dusty outpost didn't exactly scream career move, but it came with perks. No oversight. No faculty meetings. Just a quiet room and the stars.

He noticed the name when he signed the transfer form.

Assigned by Special Directive / D.M.M. Berry.

Sig.

Only a few people called him that. Officially, it was Commander David M. M. Berry, a legend in military intel circles and an unrepentant genius who could dismantle a surveillance net in his sleep. The nickname had stuck after a mission years ago when he cracked a quantum-layered encryption set left behind in a crashed stealth drone.

"The only one who could read the signal," they said.

After that, everyone on the inside started calling him "Sig." Short for Signal. Though some joked it really stood for "Significant Pain," depending on the day.

He and Liam had served together, briefly. Sig had the kind of brilliance that made superiors nervous. Some loved him. Some wanted to throttle him.

He'd never explained why he put Liam here. But now, with the signal humming in the dark and weird pieces moving, it didn't feel random anymore. Sig may have done this on purpose.

Of course.

* * *

SETI Outpost near Groom Lake, Nevada – Present Day, 0242

Hours

The door to the control room hissed open. Gina Alvarez strode in, her sweatpants and hoodie a testament to her reluctant departure from bed. Her dark hair was tied back in a loose ponytail. The stubborn crease on her forehead made it clear this had better be worth it.

Liam glanced up from his workstation. "That was fast!"

"I only broke one traffic law, and at this time of the morning, who's gonna pull me over?" she muttered, dropping her bag onto a chair. "Now, before anything else, let's confirm where this signal is coming from."

Liam smirked. "You don't believe me?"

"It's not about *belief,*" Gina said, walking briskly toward a nearby console. "It's about *verification.* If this is real, we need to nail down the origin beyond a shadow of a doubt. Otherwise, it's only *noise.*"

Liam nodded, stepping aside as she pulled up the triangulation software.

Gina Alvarez folded her arms, leaning against the workstation, her expression set like stone. "This doesn't make sense," she said, shaking her head. "None of it." As she worked, her fingers instinctively found the old Montblanc pen she kept clipped to her collar. It had once belonged to her brother Mateo, tucked into the margins of his final notebook.

She didn't write with it often, but she held it. Spun it. Clicked it. The rhythm steadied her, even when nothing else did.

Liam, still locked on the incoming data, barely glanced up. "Okay... which part doesn't make sense to you?"

"All of it." She pushed off the console and started pacing. "Morse code, Liam. A hundred-year-old obsolete communication system. But somehow, we're picking it up from Andromeda?" She stopped, turning to him. "Does that sound even remotely plausible to you?"

Liam tapped on his keyboard, replaying the transmission. The precise rhythm of the signal echoed softly through the room.

"Mathematically?" he said. "No."

"Exactly." She gestured to the screen. "Then why are you so convinced?"

Liam exhaled, swiveling in his chair. "Because it's happening. Right in front of us. And dismissing it won't make it go away." Gina shook her head. "Look, Liam. If this is real, then it's not communication. It's instruction."

"What do you mean?"

Her sixth sense alarm was going off as loud as ever as her bloodshot eyes stared at the screen. "Code set up like this. Liam, it's not for communicating. It's for executing."

* * *

Across the Pacific, a technician at the FAST array in China flagged a narrow-band anomaly; strong enough to register but with no clear structure. It was logged under "unclassified galactic emissions" and dismissed for later review.

At the Giant Metrewave Radio Telescope in India, a junior astronomer noted a burst in the high-precision feed. He marked the pattern as "persistent, non-random" but admitted the pulse spacing was too uneven to match known astrophysical events. Also flagged and kicked to an upstairs office.

In Chile, at the Atacama site, a similar pulse train was received. This time, it was cataloged as an atmospheric interference candidate due to the lack of clear origin. Stamped with an official "WEATHER EVENT ANOMALY" it was sure to never get a second look, ever again.

All three put out the anomaly to the late-night community, but in a skeptical fashion.

* * *

Back in Nevada, Liam cross-referenced the feeds. "The other listening posts are all getting something," he said, "but no one sees the structure."

Gina glanced at the overlays. "It's the same timing, but flat. No interpretation."

"I don't get it... they're hearing sound," Liam replied, "but not the message."

She narrowed her eyes. "Then why you?"

Liam's voice was quiet. "I can't figure that out... maybe because I know how to listen for it. My grandfather trained me to hear Morse by ear. By patterns. Not just read it."

She looked at the data again. "So the signal isn't encoded by language. It's encoded by method. By rhythm... not only symbols. A pattern you feel, not just read."

"Exactly," Liam said. "Anyone can receive it. But only someone trained to hear the rhythm can translate it."

"And that makes you the message."

She clenched her jaw. Words burned behind her teeth, but she held them in.

Not because Liam was careless with data; he wasn't. But accepting his conclusion meant opening the door to something she had spent two years trying to bury.

She stared at the screen. The signal pulsed with digital certainty, clean edges, uniform timing. No distortion, though her stomach tightened. She had seen something like this before.

* * *

At Arecibo, the night had been unremarkable. She had stayed late to re-calibrate the north array. Then the burst came. A repeating pattern. Tight intervals. Crisp rise and decay. She logged it. Verified it. Submitted the anomaly.

By morning, it had been labeled microwave interference from the breakroom. A security camera had caught someone warming soup during the detection window. That became the explanation.

It didn't matter that her analysis was clean. The story stuck. The fallout was quiet. Private emails stopped arriving. Invitations to panel reviews dried up. A colleague from the NSF told her over drinks that her name was now on a "pause list." No one wanted another public misstep.

* * *

She shook off the memory and crossed to Liam's console. "Run the signal. Raw feed. No suppression or noise shaping."

Liam nodded. The spectrogram refreshed. The pulse repeated as before.

"Freeze it," she said. "Zoom to five-millisecond intervals. Hold gain steady."

The waveform expanded. Still clean. Still sharp. No echoes. No scatter.

She turned to her own terminal and started pulling orbital telemetry.

"Overlay known satellite paths. Cross-check with recent high-altitude balloon traffic. Add weather radar logs from the last six hours."

The system processed the data. No matches appeared.

"No correlation," she said.

Liam stepped closer. "Same result I got earlier."

Gina leaned in, frowning. "Wait... why isn't the cache saving?"

Liam tilted the screen slightly. Not enough to be rude, only enough to reclaim a margin of solitude.

"I've got it," he said without looking up.

Gina didn't move. "That's not what I asked."

He hesitated, then angled it back toward her. Not everything needed to be hidden. Just most things.

Liam checked another tab. "It's not just missing. It's gone. The log's been overwritten." Gina nodded slowly as she took it all in. "Not erased by accident. Erased on purpose."

She drew in a breath. "Try Doppler analysis. If the source is moving, it'll stretch."

Liam entered the command. The pulse held steady.

"No velocity skew," she said. "Which means it's either stationary or compensating for movement with precision."

Gina didn't want to finish that thought. She backed away from the screen.

Her eyes drifted toward the notebook on the far table. She picked it up, opened a clean page, and began sketching the rhythm from memory. Jotting down ideas from deep recesses of her mind that synced up with the current signal pattern. Something was familiar to her.

She had done this before.

* * *

Gina's brother Mateo used to call her with strange recordings. She surveyed the battered leather notebook, edges fraying, cover worn smooth. Inside, Mateo's looping handwriting still bled through the margins. One entry caught her eye:

"The rhythm isn't for hearing; it's for seeing." She stared at the scrawl, heart caught somewhere between awe and ache.

Mateo had chased this too. Right up until they found him. She flipped to a clean page and began copying Liam's signal data beside her brother's notes, one glyph at a time. Right before his death, he had left her a voicemail. "It's not coming from the sky," he had said. "It's underneath us." He believed in patterns no one else took seriously. The message was mysteriously wiped days later. Only the memory remained.

* * *

Now, the signal was here. Clean. Familiar. Silent.

She stared at the waveform again. Then she capped the pen.

"I'm not saying you're right," she said to Liam. "But I'm not ignoring it either."

Because the alternative, the idea that this signal was real, was too big.

And far too dangerous.

She exhaled, rubbing her temples. "You remember what happened with the deep-space FRB signals?"

Liam's brow furrowed. "That was different."

"Was it?" Gina shot back. "That discovery almost ruined my career."

Liam hesitated.

She never talked about it. But now, it was boiling over.

"When I was working at Arecibo," she continued, her voice quieter, "I found an anomaly in the deep-space fast radio bursts. A pattern, repeating, structured. Like this one." She motioned to the screen. "I was so sure we had something big. A signal, maybe even proof of something out there."

Liam listened, silent.

Gina let out a humorless chuckle. "Turns out, I'd picked up the interference pattern of a malfunctioning microwave in the break room." She looked away. "You know how long it took to recover from that? I almost left the field."

Liam watched her carefully.

"This isn't a microwave, Gina."

"I know that." She pinched the bridge of her nose and took a breath. "But that's exactly why I couldn't afford to jump at shadows again." She turned back to him and crossed her arms. "So forgive me if I wasn't ready to call NASA and tell them Andromeda was sending us SOS messages."

* * *

Gina's eyes darkened as memories of her lost brother and the career-shattering fallout flooded back. In that heavy silence, she wondered whether pursuing this truth would finally honor his legacy or drag her into a vortex of secrets and heartbreak from which there was no escape. It became a silent vow: no matter how deep the conspiracy, she would uncover the truth, even if it meant confronting the ghosts of her past.

Most people assumed Gina was all intellect. Equations, theories, precise logic. What they didn't see was the other layer, shaped years earlier in the streets of San Juan, where she had to protect her younger brother Mateo. He was gentle and artistic, and he had no way to defend himself when things turned violent.

Gina took a few hits before she learned how to hit back. She developed quick feet, sharper instincts, and a hardwired refusal to back down. For an instant, she re-lived a humid San Juan alleyway where it came to a head.

Yellow crime-scene lamps pooled over rain-slick cobble-stones. Hours earlier, Mateo had called her, voice crackling with excitement: "Hermana, the signal isn't up in the sky, it's under our feet." She had mocked him for chasing ghosts. Now, pressing her fingertips against his cooling wrist, she tasted iron and regret.

The detective labeled it a mugging. His notebook vanished into evidence. Throughout the funeral she replayed his last voicemail, promising herself she would never again dismiss a pattern because it sounded impossible. Each anomalous data point on a spectrogram became Mateo breathing in her ear, urging, "Keep digging, before someone buries the truth and you with it."

She never planned on becoming a fighter. It was just something she had to become. Later, those habits followed her into the lab. She didn't mention it, and nobody asked. Most people saw the brain and stopped there. That was fine with her.

* * *

The weight of her past, mingled with her relentless need for proof, drove her to balance skepticism with a quiet determination to expose the hidden machinations at work. Liam didn't answer right away. Instead, he pulled up the spectrogram, highlighting the hidden layer beneath the Morse code.

"Then explain this," he said, his voice steady. "You see those timing irregularities? That wasn't just static. There was a second pattern buried in the gaps."

Gina's eyes flicked to the screen. Her resistance wavered. Liam pressed on. "I ran a probability test to see if these pauses could be random. You know what came up?"

Gina stayed silent.

"Zero-point-one percent probability of randomness," he said. "The gaps, clicks, and elongated sections aren't interference. They're intentional."

She glared, stepping closer.

"The signal isn't only transmitting," Liam continued. "It appears the transmission is multi-layered. The primary sequence conceals an additional, structured message. There is not only straightforward Morse, there are also encoded bits that suggest lines, curls, circles, and highlights."

Gina struggled with this.

She hesitated, glancing away. Her jaw tightened.

Liam leaned forward. "You don't have to believe in aliens. You don't have to believe in anything supernatural. But tell me, scientifically," he pointed to the screen, "what's the explanation for that?"

Gina stared at the data, her mind racing.

There wasn't an explanation.

Not a logical one.

For the first time, she felt something in her soul shift. Not belief. Not yet, but a fracture in her recent certainty. Her face lost some of its hard edge.

Liam smirked. "Anything?"

Gina sat down beside him, cracking her knuckles. "Alright, mi querido amigo, let's tear this thing apart."

"Fantastic," Liam said, his voice quieter now. "If I'm wrong, I'll buy you coffee for a year."

She glanced at the clock. 2:59 AM.

5

Cipherlock: Echoes from Andromeda

SETI Outpost near Groom Lake, Nevada – Present Day, 0301 Hours

Gina's fingers flew over the keyboard, cross-checking coordinates, isolating the frequency. A holographic map winked to life on the main screen, the origin point flashing in a pulsing blue dot.

Gina squinted, reading aloud: **"RA 00h 42m 44.3s | DEC +41° 16′ 9″..."**

"Absolutamente increíble..." she muttered. Absolutely incredible. She stopped. Looked at Liam. "I, I... think... you're right, Liam. That's... Andromeda."

"Told you," Liam said, his grin widening.

Her thumb flicked Mateo's Montblanc pen clipped to her collar. She rarely wrote with it. She leaned back, her arms crossed. "And the timing? The arrival patterns?"

"They're consistent across all measurements," Liam said, pulling up the logs. "There's no way this is terrestrial."

Gina frowned. "This still makes no sense. Aliens... using Morse? It's like expecting them to speak Spanglish." She shook her head, sarcasm creeping in. "Next thing you'll tell me, they're sending us salsa recipes." She leaned in. "How could an entirely separate civilization land on the exact same system? And why Morse, of all things?"

"The simplest stuff tends to travel best," Liam said, shrugging. "Dots and dashes, it's binary. Anyone out there would get the pattern."

"But an identical communication form?" Gina challenged. "What are the odds of that? It seems way too coincidental to me, Liam. It's like writing Shakespeare with crayons. But fine. Let's hear it."

Liam tapped a command on his keyboard. The rhythmic clicks of Morse code filled the room, their intentional cadence cutting through the quiet.

"It sure sounds like something straight out of an old war movie," Gina admitted, despite herself. "What's the message?"

Liam exhaled. "'Human in the desert.'"

Gina's brow furrowed. "That's cryptic." She uncapped the pen unconsciously, twirling it once between her fingers as she stared at the screen. Same rhythm. Same stillness.

She stared at the waveform. It didn't shift. No taper. No spread. Just clean symmetry that defied every model she had trusted since grad school.

She walked to the side console and opened a new frequency pane. "Drop the gain by three percent. I want to see if we're amplifying a ghost artifact."

Liam adjusted the settings. The signal held.

"Now strip the harmonics above one gigahertz," she added.

Again, no change. The pattern remained stable. Clear as a pulse. Steady as breath.

Gina crossed her arms. "How far out was the last confirm?"

"Triangulated with three stations. Australia, Chile, and Mauna Kea," Liam said. "They all resolved the same coordinates."

She turned to the main monitor. "Re-run the coordinate plot."

The star field zoomed into view. A repeating blue point locked into place.

"Right ascension zero hours, forty-two arcminutes. Declination forty-one degrees, sixteen arcminutes." Liam read aloud.

Gina exhaled. "Andromeda."

She didn't say it with wonder. She said it with weight.

"I thought it might be a false return from orbital clutter," she said. "But the frequency isn't distorted. And there's no delay curve."

Liam pulled up the log. "We're reading a flat propagation rate with no fringe noise. Not even minor atmospheric scatter."

"That makes no sense," she replied. "A signal coming that far should have decay. At least some particle shift."

"It doesn't." Liam didn't look up. "I even cross-checked every burst from the last decade. Nothing comes close."

They stood in silence for a moment. Liam had already been poking at the waveform for an hour. Too long. He was tired, riding the high of a discovery that hadn't fully landed.

He ran a batch script meant to isolate frequency shifts. It had worked before.

This time, something twitched. A blip on the side display. A spike, then... gone.

Liam frowned. He backtracked the log. A handshake request had pinged from an outbound monitoring node.

"No..." he muttered. "That shouldn't have triggered anything."

He tapped a few more keys, isolating the server path. It didn't show external traffic. But it had sent out a brief location echo.

If someone was listening...

"Agh. Sloppy," he muttered to himself, jaw tight. "That was dumb."

Gina tapped a pencil against her pad and silently shook her head. "Have you checked the negative space?"

"You mean the gaps between the dits and the dahs?"

"Yes. Look at the duration variance. It's intentional. If it wasn't, the spacing would randomize slightly under cosmic drift."

Liam pulled up the timing data. The gaps repeated. Not perfectly, but with an internal rhythm. A faint vibration rattled Liam's mug as the signal repeated, low, rhythmic, like a heartbeat trapped in wire. He glanced at the timestamp again. Still perfect. Still impossible.

Liam adjusted the graph. "As I thought, Gina. Every fourth pulse is followed by a wider gap. Then two narrow ones. Then another wide."

She nodded. "It's structured. Whoever sent it wanted it read a certain way."

Liam stepped back from the console. "This confirms my hunch. It IS an embedded message." He hesitated for a beat, fingers hovering above the waveform controls.

"Last time I trusted my gut," he muttered, "it torched my career."

Gina glanced over. "Wait... what happened? I haven't heard this story about you."

Liam forced a tight smile, eyes still on the screen. Embarrassment flushed through him, but saying it out loud, finally, loosened something inside. "Aah, so... there was this anomaly. A precursor burst signal that we caught in the tertiary band. Buried deep. I thought it was intentional interference, kinda like someone was jamming the signal from inside our own system."

"And?"

"And... I, ...I published a redacted extract on a fringe forum. Thought it would force the truth out. Thought I was doing the right thing."

He exhaled, feeling the burden lift off his shoulders, but worried that Gina would lose faith in him. He finished his story. "The truth was a lot less exciting. Turned out it was only corrupted calibration data. But the real fallout? Nobody trusted me after that. Got booted to backroom projects for two years."

Gina didn't say anything, just studied his profile in the dim light.

Liam broke the silence with a half-laugh. "So yeah, you'll understand if I double-check the math before crying *alien* again."

Gina didn't respond right away. She picked up a notebook and began sketching the sequence by hand.

Liam looked tired and defeated. "Hey Liam, I understand. More than you may realize," she said softly.

Their eyes met and communicated everything that still needed to be said. They were good.

Gina continued working on her sketch, Liam's honesty triggering her own struggles. The shapes emerged in columns. Narrow gaps. Wide gaps. Pauses. She had done this kind of plotting before. Years ago, with her brother. He used to say that some messages hide better in silence than in sound.

Her eyes followed the marks across the page. Something about the spacing stirred a memory she didn't want to revisit. Mateo had once called her in the middle of the night, excited and agitated. "They're not reaching out," he told her.

"They're reflecting back."

She had dismissed it at the time.

Now she wasn't so sure.

"We need to catalog every element," she said. "And we don't tell anyone until we've confirmed it four different ways."

Liam gave a slow nod. "You think they'll shut us down?"

"I think they'll bury it. Like they buried everything else."

A low tone emanated from the side display; another pulse had arrived. Still clean. Still measured.

Gina closed the notebook and rested her hand on the edge of the console.

"Whatever this is," she said, "it isn't a coincidence."

"That's not all," Liam said, his fingers moving rapidly across the keyboard. He highlighted faint distortions in the waveform. "See the spacing? It's not uniform. There are additional layers hidden in the pauses."

Gina leaned in. "Wait... you're saying it's coded inside the code?" Liam nodded. "Exactly."

Gina's skepticism warred with her growing intrigue. She crossed her arms, tilting her head. "And when you decoded the other layers?"

Liam's expression darkened as he pulled up a fresh stream of numbers.

Gina leaned in. "What are we looking at?"

He scribbled them into his notebook; same old habit. "Co-ordinates." His pulse quickened as he wrote. Gina leaned closer, squinting at his notes. "Wait, what kind of pen is that?"

Liam blinked. "Huh?"

"That thing," she said, already picking it up. "Air Force issue?"

"Yeah. Writes smooth, doesn't it?"

She scribbled a quick doodle in the margin and nodded approvingly. "Dangerously smooth. I'm keeping it."

Liam raised an eyebrow. "You're stealing my pen?"

"Rescuing," she corrected. "You left it unguarded. Rookie move."

He shook his head. "You seriously collect pens?"

She reached to her workstation, grabbing a ceramic mug packed with mismatched pens. Sleek, vintage, half-dismantled. "I like tools that don't crash. These are my tiny loyal friends."

"You have a real problem, Gina." Liam said. "Mental note: guard all writing utensils around Dr. Alvarez."

She gave him a playful smirk. "Relax. I only take the good ones." Gina then refocused her gaze on Liam's writings. She read them aloud, her voice slowing. "Thirty-seven, twenty-three, fourteen north... one fifteen, forty-eight, oh-two west."

She looked up, eyes wide. "That's here. The other side of the Groom Lake compound. Area 51."

Liam stared at the screen. "Same spot as '55," he murmured. Gina turned sharply. "Wait. 1955? What are you talking about?"

"It was classified," Liam admitted reluctantly, eyes distant. "But Groom Lake wasn't only an experimental facility. Decades ago, as legend has it, a craft allegedly disappeared. Stolen by people never identified. The craft supposedly emitted an unexplained signal before it vanished."

Gina tensed. Not at the data, but at the ghost of a memory that clung to her like ash. Arecibo.

* * *

The night she stayed late, recalibrating the north array. The screen had flared green with a crisp, repeating pattern. She'd gasped aloud. Thought it was *the* moment.

By morning, it was a soup sandwich, as Liam liked to say.

A grainy security tape showed a technician microwaving lunch during the detection window. That became the explanation. The paper was buried. Her funding withdrawn. Colleagues stopped making eye contact. Mateo tried to defend her, but even he had fallen silent after a while. That silence had hurt more than the skepticism.

* * *

Now, standing in this dull fluorescent chamber, watching the real pattern unfold before her, she clenched her jaw.

This time, she wouldn't walk away. She'd chase it down, to the edge of reason, to the edge of the signal, and prove she'd been right all along. Now, as she stared at the display confirming the location, the past and present collided. Gina stared at the spectral data, blinking twice as the waveform held steady. "No dejaré que la historia se repita," she said softly, barely louder than the console's hum. She didn't look at Liam. She didn't need to. Her hand drifted to the Montblanc still clipped at her collar. She didn't write. She tapped it once against her thigh. Then again. The weight of it, his pen, made the moment feel real.

Silence filled the room, heavy and charged.

Without another word, Gina reached for one of the stored Kingston DataTraveler Max USB drives, plugged it into the console, and initiated a recording.

Liam glanced at her. "What are you doing?"

"Recording everything," Gina replied, her voice brisk. "If this is real, we're going to need every second of it. This is more than a discovery, it's proof. If we're going to convince anyone, we need hard data."

Liam nodded, a flash of pride in his expression. "Good thinking." Liam paused.

* * *

He was awash with the weight of decisions made long ago. In that fleeting moment, the sterile hum of the lab was replaced by memories of a night filled with dark secrets. A night when his mentor, a figure as enigmatic as fate itself, had confided in him, "Your path was chosen before you even knew it." The recollection was vivid: a dim corridor of an abandoned military archive, footsteps on cold concrete, and a single conversation that had sealed his destiny.

As the coordinates on the screen aligned with his past and his future, Liam's expression hardened with a resigned determination. "I can't run from what I was meant to do," he murmured, the words whispered over the buzzing monitors. As if accepting that every step forward was a step back into the legacy that defined him. In that silent declaration, it was as if the act of observation itself had forced the hidden layers of the signal into a single, tangible reality. Like in quantum theory, just observing the signal seemed to force it into reality.

His thoughts drifted briefly to Grandpa Rustand, the elusive figure whose shadow he'd unknowingly chased his entire life. Grandpa's face, captured in yellowed, grainy photographs from decades past, now haunted Liam's every waking hour. The reality that he was walking a path set long before his own birth was both a comfort and an unbearable weight.

* * *

Gina smirked, "Liam? Are you still with me? I said, if this turns out to be nothing, I'm still billing you for my sleep deprivation." Her earlier skepticism melted into cautious excitement.

"I can live with that," Liam said. "But you have to admit... this signal is going to make history."

Gina exhaled, shaking her head. "Or make us infamous," she muttered. Her gaze softened as the spectrogram wavered, thoughts drifting to her brother. So passionate, so driven.

"No te volveré a fallar", she thought. The scandal at Arecibo had haunted her for years, but maybe this was her chance at redemption, her opportunity to finally bring meaning to his loss. "No matter how this turns out," she said softly, almost too low for Liam to hear, "at least I'll know I didn't fail you again." She crouched behind the lab's overturned console, eyes locked on the glowing drive in her palm. A second later, she closed her eyes and whispered into the dark: "Ayúdame, Mateo... haz que valga la pena." Her voice caught on the last word, but she didn't let herself break. Her slender fingers found comfort in her brother's pen as she forced herself to move. Grief and grit forged into purpose. Her voice was thick with lingering sadness. "I won't make the same mistake twice."

The room fell silent as the signal pulsed on, its rhythmic beat filling the air with a mystery too vast to comprehend. At that moment, the low hum of the SETI control room was interrupted by a sharp chime from Liam Mills' workstation.

Liam froze, the stale coffee he had just sipped turning bitter in his mouth as he glanced at the screen.

Another alert.

He swallowed hard, eyes wide. Not possible.

"What now?" Gina Alvarez's voice cut through the tension, sharper than before. She was still trying to process the Andromeda signal, but she straightened instinctively, moving toward his workstation.

Liam's fingers moved with practiced ease, isolating the frequency. A familiar rhythmic pattern emerged from the speakers. The hair on the back of his neck stood up.

His voice came out in a whisper. "Morse code... again."

Gina quickly opened her own console. "No way."

She keyed in a sequence to trace the source, her brows knitting together as the results appeared on her screen. "Virgo Cluster," she muttered, her voice losing some of its usual skepticism. "Fifty-three million light-years away."

Then, another chime.

And another.

II

Act II: Signals Beneath the Surface (Pattern Emergence)

The deeper they dig, the stranger it gets.
Languages no one remembers. Numbers that don't quite behave.
Familiar things start to feel... retooled.
What looked like coincidence begins to resemble intent,
and the signal that brought them together refuses to play by any rules.
Meaning isn't just in the message.
It's buried in them.

6

Cipher: The Fourth Whisper

SETI Outpost near Groom Lake, Nevada – Present Day, 0313 Hours

The room filled with the cascading chimes of more signals arriving in rapid succession. The same deliberate rhythm over and over.

Dah-dit-dit-dah ... dit-dit-dit dah-dah-dah.

Liam's pulse quickened. "They're identical."

Gina's fingers flew across her keyboard. "Coma Cluster, 300 million light-years." Another entry flashed. "Perseus Cluster, 100 million light-years." She stopped, her expression tightening.

"Liam, they're all transmitting the exact same message at the exact same time. Galactically speaking."

Liam exhaled sharply, raking a hand through his short-cropped brown hair. A faint thread of Bach's Invention No. 13 hummed under his breath, steady and looping. Gina glanced over, unsure if it was the signal… or him. His mind raced as he tried to reconcile the impossibility of what they were seeing.

"That doesn't make sense. In fact, it's impossible," he muttered, pacing, as he tried to piece things together. "How does an identical signal… staggered by millions of light-years… get sent from the distant past? Different galaxies… at different times in history… all end up hitting earth at the same time?"

Gina, her sharp brown eyes locked onto the display, muttered more Spanish under her breath.

"Unless something's bending the rules," she said softly.

Liam stopped mid-step, staring at the holographic map now glowing on the main display. Points of light, representing the origins of the signals, shimmered against the dark backdrop of the cosmos.

He gestured toward the map. "Four signals. From multiple galaxies. All transmitting Morse code. Simultaneously."

* * *

Liam turned back to his console, his expression a mix of wonder and disbelief. His pulse thundered in his ears.

"Something's happening, Gina," he said, voice tight with excitement. "Something big. Do you realize what this could mean?"

Terror and wonder warred beneath the surface. Neither wanted to say it aloud yet, but they both felt it. A coping mechanism of sorts began to set in.

"Right now, I'm realizing how much coffee it's going to take to get through this," Gina deadpanned. Despite the exhaustion evident in her voice, a small, unwilling smile tugged at the corner of her lips.

Liam ignored the jab, too wired to let it bother him. He paced the small space between the consoles while probing the possibilities.

"Think about it! We're the first to detect this. The first. Do you know what this could do for our careers? We could be the modern-day Jerry Ehman."

Gina frowned. "Jerry Ehman?"

"The Wow! signal," Liam said, animatedly gesturing toward the holographic display. "Ohio State, 1977. He was analyzing data from a radio telescope when he found a signal so strong, so unusual, that he wrote 'Wow!' in the margins of the printout." He turned to Gina, eyes glinting. "It became a legend. A one-off signal we've never been able to explain. But this?" He pointed at the four glowing galaxies. "This blows the Wow! signal out of the water."

Gina leaned back in her chair, arms crossed. "Yeah, and Ehman didn't exactly get a talk show out of it. He got headaches, skepticism, and decades of unanswered questions." She tilted her head, studying Liam. "You sure you're ready for that kind of fame?"

Liam smirked, undeterred. "You're missing the point. This isn't a one-off. It's happening now. And we're capturing it."

He started rattling off potential headlines, eyes flicking between the map and Gina.

"'The Scientists Who Heard the Stars Speak.' Or, if you want something snappier ... 'Dittyboppers from the Sands of Time.'"

Gina snorted. "That's terrible, Liam."

"Okay, fine," he said, grinning. "How about 'A Signal Across the Ages: Humanity's First Cosmic Conversation'?" He snapped his fingers. "Or 'The Stars Speak, and We're Listening.' That's a good one, right?"

Gina rolled her eyes. "Sure," she said with mock seriousness. "And the subtitle can be: 'How Two Sleep-Deprived Scientists Lost Their Minds and Invented an Intergalactic Mystery.'"

Liam laughed.

"Come on, admit it. You're excited." He leaned closer, eyes locking with hers. "This is the kind of thing that defines a career. Forget coffee... this is the kind of discovery that gets you written into history books."

Gina sighed, shaking her head, but there was something new in her expression.

"I'll give you that, Mills," she admitted. "But I'm still vetoing 'Dittyboppers from the Sands of Time.'"

Liam mock-gasped. "You wound me."

Gina smirked. "And I want Jenna Ortega to play me."

"Not if I get Tom Cruise first and he does his own stunts," Liam shot back.

Gina rolled her eyes again but couldn't hide her grin. "Dios mío, Liam, your enthusiasm is going to be the death of me, or at least my sleep schedule. You're impossible. We don't even know what we're looking at yet. And anyway, no one's going to take us seriously if we don't have the data to back this up as proof." She gestured toward the recorder.

Liam nodded, the earlier humor giving way to something sharper, more focused. "Fair. The recording will help. I'll analyze some of the underlying signals at higher gain and resolution in playback."

He gazed at his console. "But you must admit. Four signals. Multiple galaxies. All at once." He met Gina's gaze, his voice quiet but charged with meaning. "You can't tell me you're not even a little bit thrilled."

Gina crossed her arms, her skepticism warring with her growing curiosity. "Thrilled? Sure. Baffled? Absolutely." She exhaled, running a hand through her hair. "But I am also a bit freaked out on the coincidence."

Liam stopped, his expression thoughtful. He turned back to the display, watching the strobe flashes synchronize. He focused, laser-like, on a portion of the code they had recorded and put up on the screen. Something about the rhythm bothered him. He scribbled the pattern onto his yellow pad, overlaying crude symbols with a portion of the Morse transcription.

His mind snapped back to a cryptography conference in Washington D.C., years ago. Dr. Benjamin Abram Levinson, brilliant cryptologist, mathematician, and rabbi, explaining hidden codes embedded within codes, all the while keeping everyone's attention with his morose and sarcastic Yiddish sense of humor.

Could this be that same principle?

His stomach twisted. This was acting more like a layered language.

He then grabbed his Scripto pen and a yellow pad and

translated the mysterious stutters, taps, and subtle pattern changes into his own variation of a code picture. He created his own squiggles and lines to represent the secondary information based on something he remembered from the discussion from Rabbi Ben's lecture.

Number values embedded in... letters?

Some of the symbols echoed patterns he'd seen before. But where? What was it called?

Then he took the Morse Code and overlaid it onto his own creation. Vague pictures emerged on his yellow pad and continued to nag at his brain.

After the conference in Washington, D.C., a conversation unfolded between Liam and Dr. Benjamin Levinson about Liam's grandfather's lifelong fixation on Morse code, a passion intertwined with a secret message he claimed to have been a part of during the Cold War.

He kept scribbling, his pen tracing restless doodles that merged the intricate patterns of the secondary layer with a raw composite of the code. The shapes took on new life, evolving into a crude but intentional arrangement, each one inspired by his own evolving glyph formations.

He kept drawing, fusing the stutters and pauses into abstract glyphs, rough but deliberate, overlaying them into a composite that hinted at a hidden language.

The fact that Dr. Levinson was also a Rabbi explained the cryptological fascination with Hebrew letters, numbers, and codes.

More doodles and scribbles.

Gina turned toward him, her voice quiet but firm. "Liam, where did you go? Did you hear what I asked you?"

Liam barely processed her words, as he tracked an impossible conclusion.

Gina's voice sharpened. "Liam."

He snapped out of it. "What?"

She pointed at the screen. "Why the heck is the Morse code in *English*?"

Liam swallowed hard. That question sent a fresh wave of unease through him. Not only did it make no sense, it shouldn't even be possible.

"LIAM, why is the Morse code in *ENGLISH*?"

"I don't know, and it doesn't make sense," Liam slowly responded, "But it also appears to include a hidden code of letters and numbers."

Gina was aghast. "What does that mean?"

Liam shook his head and said, “I need to call a rabbi.”

7

Cipher: The Rabbi's Code

SETI Outpost near Groom Lake, Nevada – Present Day, 0321 Hours

"I didn't know you were Jewish." Gina snorted. She smiled wryly and added, "Not that I'm judging. Mi abuela always says wisdom crosses every border."

The faint electrical noises of the computer cooling units filled the room as Liam dialed the number. "I'm not," Liam replied. He glanced at the clock: 3:21 a.m. in Nevada, 6:21 a.m. in New York. He winced, knowing this was hardly an ideal time to call anyone, much less Rabbi Ben Levinson.

Gina asked with concern, "Aren't you jumping the gun? How can you be sure that the code is that complicated?" Liam ignored her, mostly because he was focused on getting an answer.

The phone rang several times before a gruff, distinctly Bronxaccented voice answered.

"This better be important," Ben grumbled, the rustling of sheets and a creaking bed audible in the background.

"Rabbi Levinson? It's Liam Mills." Liam's grip tightened on the edge of the desk.

A long pause. Ben muttered, "Oy gevalt, you've got the timing of a meshugener rooster." Ben fumbled for his glasses on the nightstand and wiped them absently with the corner of his blanket before sitting up.

Then, with the sharpness of a man who never appreciated surprises, Ben replied, "Mills. The cryptography guy from that conference in D.C. years ago?" There was an edge of suspicion in his voice, as if he were pulling a memory from a locked drawer.

Liam hesitated, then forced a dry chuckle. "That's me."

Ben let out a tired sigh. "Yeah, I remember you. You're the one who kept pestering me about military encryption projects. Thought you were another spook."

"I was," Liam admitted. "Sort of. Not anymore. I'm at the SETI site in Nevada now."

Ben snorted. "Nobody's ever 'not anymore.' Nevada is a good place to be a nobody doing something 'not anymore.'"

Liam ignored the jab. "Listen, I know it's early, but this is big, Rabbi Levinson. Really big."

Ben shifted, and Liam could hear the faint click of a bedside lamp. "Big like, 'I found the lost pages of the Torah'? Or big like, 'I went down a conspiracy rabbit hole and decided I need a rabbi'?"

Liam ran a hand through his hair, took a deep breath, and continued. "Big as in, a signal from the Andromeda galaxy transmitting in Morse code that seems to match patterns found in ancient texts big."

Another pause. Then the sound of sheets being thrown aside.

"From Andromeda, a galaxy far, far away? Mills, what in heaven's name are you tangled up in?" Ben's voice sharpened, no longer thick with sleep.

Liam knew he had him now. Ben wasn't laughing anymore.

He pressed forward. "It's coming through in Morse," he said, pulling up the spectrogram. "But there's more, patterns inside the gaps. At first I thought it was background noise. Then I ran a check against old cryptographic archives, and that's when I found something. Something impossible."

Silence.

Then, in a voice calculating and more cautious, Ben asked, "You cross-referenced it against wartime encryption, didn't you?" Ben pressed. "Let me guess... some deeply classified Cold War transmission. Maybe from an old Numbers Station? Mills, I've seen my share of cryptographic oddities, and they always end up being something mundane with a scary-looking wrapper."

Liam's grip on the desk tightened. "Not this time."

Ben paused, frowning. "Fine. Let's hear it."

Liam exhaled slowly. "Okay, yeah. So I used some of the details you covered at the conference regarding layered codes and some of the patterns reminded me of the military ciphers that you covered."

A pause. Ben's tone sharpened. "And you found a match."

"Yes."

Another beat of silence, then a harsh breath on the other end of the line. Liam added "And the dataset fits exactly with your universal cipher theorem."

Ben muttered something in Yiddish under his breath. When he spoke again, his voice had lost any trace of grogginess.

"That's impossible," he said. "From what you are implying... such a pattern seems to have similarities from a classified World War Two-era project I saw years ago, buried in intelligence archives. No one outside those circles should even know about it. You're telling me an alien signal, from another galaxy, is using a code the US and allies developed in the 1940s?"

"That's exactly what I'm telling you." Liam's pulse was pounding now. "I'm sending you a sample of the signal."

He tapped a few keys, transferring a segment of the spectrogram to Ben's email. The file zipped away into cyberspace, carrying with it a truth neither of them could yet explain.

Ben was quiet for a long time. Then came the clacking of keys, a few muttered Yiddish curse words, more furious clacking, and the faint creak of an old wooden floor being accosted by an energetic rabbi bouncing in his chair. Ben paused again, hands resting over the worn keys. His eyes weren't on the screen anymore; they had drifted across the room to the shelf where a photograph leaned between an old volume of Maimonides and a radio receiver casing from 1957.

* * *

The photo was cracked near the edges. A young boy stood next to Ben in a cluttered garage; wires draped over a pegboard, a soldering iron perched on the edge of a metal stool. The boy's face was lit with excitement, holding up a homemade volcano science project like he had uncovered a secret no one else had seen.

Jacob.

Ben leaned back slightly. He hadn't spoken to his son in over six years. The last real conversation ended with slammed doors and silence. Jacob had called his father's worldview outdated, a relic from Cold War paranoia and old books filled with symbols no one used anymore. Ben had called his son naïve, too trusting of data scraped from servers and algorithms written by corporations with no memory.

The fight was about a government project, classified enough that Ben couldn't explain the full truth. Jacob thought it involved unethical bio-tracking. He wasn't wrong, but he didn't know the full extent. Ben had tried to protect him by keeping him out of it. That had been a mistake.

Jacob had once wanted to be a physicist. He had ended up in biotech. Still brilliant, still burning to uncover something meaningful. But when he got caught up in a leak investigation at his company, Ben had stepped in behind the scenes. A few favors called in, a few conversations steered. No charges were ever filed. But Jacob had known. He told his father that protecting him wasn't the same as trusting him.

Ben hadn't heard his voice since.

* * *

He rubbed his temple, breathing out slowly. There had been dozens of times he had picked up the phone. To apologize. To explain. To ask how he was doing. But each time, something stopped him. Pride, maybe. Or fear that the damage couldn't be undone.

Now this.

A signal from another galaxy. Encoded in a structure that mirrored wartime cipher theory. A pattern that should not have existed, but did. And the person calling about it was the same kid from the conference years ago. The one who took notes in the margins and asked questions two steps ahead of the room.

Ben looked back at the screen. His fingers hovered over the keyboard again.

He thought about the last voicemail Jacob had left; months after their fallout.

"Do not contact me again unless you're ready to tell the whole truth."

That message had replayed in his head more than once. He never deleted it. Never answered it either.

Ben stood up and walked across the room to the shelf. He picked up the photograph, brushing his thumb over the boy's face.

There were things he had spent his entire career burying. Files burned, evidence erased, people moved or silenced. All under the illusion of protection, that keeping certain knowledge confined served the greater good.

But maybe the greater good was no longer in safe hands.

He returned to the desk and sat down slowly. The Morse transcription still flashed in the window, waiting for review. He highlighted the spacing between segments. The microsecond delays matched the ones used in a classified Allied encoding protocol from 1944; something buried so deeply that only four people had ever seen the field application.

It couldn't be a coincidence.

* * *

Ben tapped a few keys, pulling up a schematic from an old archive. Layered frequency hopping. Noise shaping. Symbol compression through timing gaps. It all aligned.

He shook his head.

There was no possible way anyone outside of the Manhattan-era archives could have known how to mimic that format. It had been developed before digital memory. Passed by hand and spoken aloud in guarded rooms. The last person who had used it in the field had died over thirty years ago.

And yet here it was.

The signal hadn't merely copied the structure. It had replicated the fingerprint of the men who made it.

His hand moved again, not toward the keyboard but to a drawer beneath the desk. He pulled it open and reached for the old coin. A smooth bronze disc etched with Kabbalistic symbols and a cipher wheel nested along its edge. A gift from his mentor, once upon a time. A reminder that meaning required interpretation, and that interpretation was always rooted in time, culture, and context.

Ben held the coin in his palm, closed his eyes, and muttered a short prayer under his breath. Not for protection. For clarity.

He opened his eyes and looked again at the waveform.

Maybe it was time to stop guarding the past and start decoding the future.

He set the coin beside the keyboard.

* * *

Finally, Ben let out a long sigh.

"Mazal tov, kid," he muttered. "You may have opened Pandora's Ark."

Ben leaned back in his chair, but his mind didn't rest. He

rubbed the coin between his fingers, the one from his mentor, worn smooth by years of anxious thinking, and stared through the screen as if it might blink first. He wasn't afraid of the data. He was afraid of what it meant. A few weeks ago, he was deciphering wedding blessings and giving lectures on Kabbalistic metaphor. Now he was fielding calls from classified SETI labs and reviewing Morse code laced with divine fingerprints. The old him, the quiet scholar behind stained glass and coffee-stained notes, would've laughed this all off.

But Jacob's words echoed in his skull.

"Do not contact me again unless you're ready to tell the whole truth." Ben exhaled slowly. He hadn't told the whole truth. Not to his son. Not even to himself. What if this really was part of something larger; not cryptographic coincidence but a pattern? A plan? The kind you don't stumble into... unless you were meant to? His hand trembled slightly as he gripped his phone.

* * *

Liam's breath came fast. He knew what Ben's tone meant. He wasn't dismissing this anymore. He believed it.

But that wasn't enough. He needed Ben to come.

"Rabbi Ben, listen... this isn't a mathematical anomaly. It's bigger than that. I need you here."

Ben snorted, and attempted to convince himself. "Kid, do you have any idea what you're asking? I'm seventy-three years old. I've got a full schedule, two lectures this week, and a congregation that expects me to be a functioning human being. You think I can pick up and go gallivanting off to a SETI site in 'nowhere Nevada' that listens for aliens all because you found some old numbers dressed up in a fancy alien costume?"

"I wouldn't ask if it wasn't important," Liam countered.

Ben was still grumbling, but Liam could hear the subtle shift in his voice; he was thinking.

"The sequences, Ben. They're not similar. They're the same."

"You sure?"

"Positive."

Ben clicked his tongue. "That's statistically impossible. Send me more. This is too fantastic to believe at 6:30 in the morning. And without my coffee, no less."

Liam scrambled to compose the email, his fingers flying over the keyboard. He attached the spectrogram, the decoded sequences, and the comparisons with the World War Two encryption project. Then he hit send.

Others also silently received it.

"I just sent it," he said, gripping the phone tightly. "Check your inbox."

Ben didn't respond immediately. There was a muffled thud, followed by grumbling as he presumably fumbled for his glasses. Then, "Alright. Got it."

The line went silent except for the faint hum of static.

Then, a chair creaked on the other end of the line. Liam could hear the faint tapping of fingers drumming against a desk, the sound of a man doing mental gymnastics at 6 a.m.

"Okay, let's say you're right," Ben muttered. He took off his glasses and rubbed his eyes, then let the frames dangle from one hand like a pendulum of hesitation. "Let's say the patterns match. Then there's still the big question hanging over all this."

Liam leaned forward. "Why bury it like that?"

"Exactly." Ben's voice was tight now, focused. "If this thing, whatever it is, has been transmitting information using a code from our history... then one of two things is true. Either..."

"...either someone fed them our code," Liam cut in, feeling a chill creep up his spine.

"Or," Ben said darkly, "they've been using it long before we even invented it."

Liam swallowed. "That's what I'm afraid of."

Gina, sitting nearby, leaned closer, whispering, "He talks so loud I can hear him from here. Who is this guy?"

"A genius," Liam responded, "And a bit of a handful."

On the phone, Ben went quiet. Then, in a tone Liam had never heard from him before, a mixture of awe and dread, Ben muttered, "Well, I'll be..."

Liam sat up straighter. "Do you see it?"

"I see... something," Ben admitted begrudgingly. "There's intent here. The timing, the alignment; it's too precise to ignore."

Liam hesitated before asking, "So you'll come?"

Ben huffed. "I'm an old man with a congregation and a life, right? And I don't hop on planes for the thrill of it."

Liam tightened his grip on the phone. "I know, Ben. Please. And I wouldn't ask if it weren't necessary."

"Necessary," Ben repeated, voice dripping with skepticism. "I feel for you, kid, but this is your problem. I am not taking a red-eye to Nevada because an alien signal is broadcasting in a weird Morse code variation. Oy! Even saying it out loud makes me sound like a crazy person needing a long-sleeved white jacket."

Liam sighed. "Yes. But you admitted it's not arbitrary."

Ben groaned. "I said it was interesting. This doesn't mean I buy a plane ticket."

Liam forced himself to stay calm. "Ben, listen to me. If the timing of this signal is what we think it is, then this isn't about curiosity anymore. It's about who knew what and when."

A beat of silence.

Liam pressed forward. "You worked in classified intelligence projects, right? You've seen things buried in archives that never made it to the public. What if this is one of them?"

Ben exhaled sharply. "That's a massive what-if, kid."

Liam softened his voice. "Then come prove me wrong."

A long pause.

Then, finally, Ben sighed again, but this time, there was no sarcasm in it. Only reluctant acceptance.

"Fine," he sputtered. "But if this turns out to be an elaborate prank, I'm making you sit through a four-hour Talmudic lecture. And believe me," he added with a sardonic severity, "I'll make sure it's as riveting as my bubbe's gefilte fish recipe."

Liam chuckled. "Deal. And I will take care of all of your arrangements to get you here."

"I know. You think I'm made of money? Besides, this is your schtick, kid, and your nickel."

Liam exhaled. "It will be. I'll get you travel confirmations and details in your inbox asap."

* * *

As soon as the call ended, Liam pulled up his browser, searching for flights.

"JFK to McCarran," he muttered under his breath, scanning the options. Most flights were hours away, but he found a direct flight leaving in three hours.

"Got it," he said, booking the ticket.

"What about getting him from Vegas to here?" Gina asked.

Liam groaned. "There's no Uber that'll go all the way to Groom Lake. I'll have to arrange a private car from the SETI garage."

"Better hurry," Gina said, smirking. "Your genius rabbi won't wait forever."

Liam grabbed his phone and dialed a local car service, juggling the arrangements while finalizing the flight. By the time he hung up, his face was flushed with relief and exhaustion.

"It's done," he said. "Ben's flight is booked, and a car will meet him in Vegas."

"Great," Gina said dryly. "Now we have to hope he doesn't hate us before he even gets here."

Liam sank into his chair, the weight of the night pressing on him. "He won't hate us," he said, almost to himself. "He'll see what I see. And then we'll finally have the help we need."

Gina had the last word. "I swear, if he spends the entire time lecturing us about divine intervention, I'm out."

Each recognized that the collision of skepticism and wonder was not only inevitable but vital.

What was missing was context.

* * *

Before Liam had a chance to digest the call with Rabbi Ben,

his secure comm monitor chirped once. A green static bar crawled across the top of Liam's screen.

SECURE LINK: DSIGBERRY-ECHO-7 — handshake received.

"Seriously?" Liam muttered.

The screen locked, then cleared. Sig's face appeared with his traditional unkempt hair, his screen backlit by harsh white fluorescents and what looked like stacked files in chaos behind him. His shirt collar was half-buttoned, and he tapped his knuckles three times.

"Finally," Sig said. "You pick up slower than you used to."

"I didn't know I was on standby for secret calls from the basement of the Pentagon."

"That's adorable," Sig replied dryly. "This isn't Pentagon. It's worse. It's compartmented."

Liam leaned closer. "Are you alright?"

"No. But I'm working on it."

Sig rubbed his forehead with the back of his hand. "That signal you just intercepted... your activity's being monitored. Whoever or whatever is doing the monitoring is a ghost entity, but they are leaving a slight digital vapor trail."

"You mean they're watching us?"

"Not us, buddy. You. The second you processed that signal, you painted yourself into the pattern. That's how they hunt. You're now a data point with a name."

Liam stared at the screen. "And you're just telling me this now? Is this why you put me here?"

"I needed to be sure. I also needed to keep you clean. If you'd known more, they would've triggered early. Trust me, ignorance was safer."

"Sig, are you saying this thing is... what, radioactive?"

Sig hesitated. That alone was alarming.

"Not in so many words, but there's something off about what we have learned," he said finally. "We don't have all the pieces. The software algorithm we have profiled doing the heavy lifting doesn't appear to only process. It anticipates. It's modifying predictive behavior into causality. And the more you try to decode it, the more it adapts to you. It learns by reshaping its observers, and I think it may be a software program developed by... potential bad actors."

He pinched the bridge of his nose, then tapped his knuckles three times on his desk as he went into deep thought. A tic Liam remembered from long ago. Sig's silent punctuation mark.

"Listen, buddy. You must go dark. Pull *ALL* your analog backups. Disconnect from SETI cloud. Don't let the central net get wind of your analysis. That whole pipeline's been mirrored since day one. You must be extra careful."

"By who?"

"No idea," Sig said. "That's the scary part. We're running blind against an adversary that is a phantom."

He leaned forward, voice low now. "Liam. If this gets into the main data stream, if I'm right, this... computer program... won't just interpret the signal you discovered. It'll *leverage* it. And then everything changes."

"Leverage it?"

"Yeah," Sig said, and for the first time, Liam noticed a crack in his voice. "It'll fold it into its operating model like it's always been there. And nobody will even know the baseline changed."

A pause. Sig's mouth twitched.

"And for the record," he added, quieter now, "I never stopped backing you. I hope you know that. Even when you were burning every bridge you had. You're not wrong, Liam. You just jumped the gun."

The screen flickered.

"Sig..."

"Stay deep in the shadows, buddy. And whatever you do... *do not* finish decoding the second layer alone. That's not a message. It's a door."

He smiled faintly, as if he was about to say something more. Then the line dropped.

8

Cipherlock: The Hidden Interpreter

Undisclosed Continuum Complex, Undisclosed Time

Across the dimly lit Continuum operations center, a low murmur of voices punctuated the quiet hum of high-speed servers. Agents hunched over terminals; their faces illuminated by the glow of classified data feeds. One analyst scrolled through a dossier marked LEVINSON, BENJAMIN – PRIORITY WATCHLIST.

"Social media presence is minimal," the analyst reported in a measured tone. "A few mentions of sermons and charity events at his synagogue. No political activism, no flagged activity. But he's sharp; he maintained his DoD clearance until 2004 despite having left official advisory roles years earlier."

Elias Keller, the Continuum's second-in-command, smirked. "We don't need dirt. We need someone he'd bleed for. What's his weakness?"

The analyst continued, "Nothing obvious, except his son, Jacob Levinson, estranged for over a decade and now working as a research lead at a Boston biotech firm. There's definite tension there. Levinson once pulled favors to help Jacob out of a sealed court case. It was significant enough for him to risk burning bridges."

Keller nodded slowly. "That'll do. If Levinson starts to push back, we'll use that."

Ramos, one of Keller's field operatives, then inquired, "What about the flight itself?"

Keller tapped a finger against his chin. "We'll assign an agent on the same plane. Once he's in Vegas, we'll tail him to the SETI facility. Keep your distance, but don't lose him."

* * *

Within the hour, assets were mobilized. A plainclothes operative was dispatched to JFK to monitor Levinson's departure. Another agent, already embedded on the flight headed for McCarran, would sit three rows behind the rabbi. A third team in Vegas prepared for discreet tailing.

* * *

Back in Brooklyn, Ben Levinson methodically packed his worn leather suitcase in his modest apartment. Early morning light filtered through the blinds onto stacks of books and ancient texts. Pausing to thumb through a weathered leather-bound journal dense with ancient languages, codes, and cryptographic sequences, he murmured, "A signal from Andromeda," a wry smile tugging at his lips as memories of cosmic patterns surfaced. His mind, alight with theories that danced on the edge of conventional science, brimmed with ideas hinting at worlds where cause and effect twisted in unforeseen ways; mysteries he preferred to leave partly unsolved.

Then Liam Mills' call cut through his reverie. "Ben, everything's set. Your flight leaves in three hours. A SETI SUV will pick you up in Vegas and take you straight to the SETI facility."

Ben replied dryly, "Great. Just what I need, a science road trip." He exhaled, pinching the bridge of his nose and pushing his glasses back into place. "You're lucky I'm too curious for my own good." Ben hung up and stared at the dead line for a long second. He had told himself this was merely another puzzle. But the truth gnawed deeper.

Curiosity didn't drive him. This was a promise, one made to a younger version of himself. A vow never to look away when the signal finally arrived.

That brief exchange mingled anticipation with caution. The journey ahead promised revelations that might rewrite the boundaries of his carefully constructed theories.

* * *

As he gathered his belongings, Ben's thoughts wandered to his mentor: a brilliant yet elusive figure who had vanished under as-mysterious circumstances as the puzzles he now chased. The mentor's parting gift: a small metal coin etched with a Kabbalistic symbol, now resting in his briefcase, meticulously preserved notes, serving as a talisman that some secrets must be safeguarded as much as sought. With deliberate care, he closed the suitcase then paused to retrieve the coin, palming it tightly as if seeking a spark of wisdom or luck. He had a feeling he would need it.

* * *

Almost like a waking dream, he arrived without incident at JFK. Ben shuffled through security while suffering modern traveler indecencies and muttering, "Centuries of advancement, and this is where air travel lands us. Socks on linoleum." In the bustling terminal, he moved with the practiced efficiency of a man navigating both scholarly puzzles and the shadowy intricacies of hidden networks. As he complied with security procedures, his thoughts drifted to the cryptic notes in his journal, an ever-growing tapestry of symbols, coded sequences, and half-remembered lore from his vanished mentor.

Nearby, a plainclothes operative in an unremarkable suit feigned casual phone scrolling while his keen eyes tracked every specific movement Ben made. Through a discreet earpiece, the operative's quiet report came through: "Subject is clear. Proceeding to Gate 42."

After checking in and collecting his boarding pass, Ben found a quiet seat near his gate and indulged in a small morning ritual; a bagel and black coffee from a familiar vendor. He pulled out his notebook, its pages teeming with insights and enigmatic theories that had both fascinated and confounded him over the years. Across the terminal, the operative settled a few rows away, blending into the ambient hum of airport life.

Ben adjusted his glasses as he examined his boarding pass. The airport was nearly silent at this hour, punctuated only by soft intercom announcements and the occasional clatter of rolling suitcases. Then he moved toward the security checkpoint, tightening the strap on his shoulder bag. As he passed through, he noticed a figure standing near a vending machine beyond the scanners. The man wasn't looking directly at him, but Ben felt that unmistakable, instinctual awareness of being watched. Moments later, the figure pivoted: tall, clad in an expensive gray overcoat with polished military-black shoes, and holding no briefcase or luggage; an aura of quiet purpose. Ben hesitated, and then the man strode toward him.

"Mr. Levinson," the man said in a smooth, neutral tone; no accent, no fluctuation. "A word?"

"I'm catching a flight," Ben replied, fighting the urge to swallow nervously.

The man's expression remained impassive. "You don't have to take it."

Ben furrowed his brow. "Excuse me?"

"You could go home right now. Forget about all of this. You are stepping too far into the unknown."

Ben exhaled slowly, meditatively controlling the waves of paranoia rolling over him. This wasn't a random encounter; it was a warning. "Are you with the government?" he asked cautiously.

Without answering, the man produced a folded slip of paper from his pocket, gripped Ben's forearm, and pressed it into Ben's hand. "Whatever you think you're looking for," he said in a lowered voice, "it's already been found." Then, without hesitation, he turned and walked away.

Ben clenched his jaw and unfolded the paper. Printed in block letters was a single sentence:

YOU WERE NOT SUPPOSED TO SEE THIS.

A wave of heat rose in Ben's chest; part fear, part anger. He could still hear Jacob's voice from that courtroom hallway. "You taught me to decode secrets, Abba. And now you've buried mine." Ben's fingers curled around the slip of paper. It was barely thicker than tissue, but it felt like a weight pressing down on his ribs. There had been so many moments when he could have reached out. After the trial. After the fallout. Even after that last voicemail. "Do not contact me again unless you're ready to tell the whole truth."

And now, staring down a mystery threaded through time and ethics, he wondered whether Jacob had been more right than he wanted to admit. The truth wasn't data. It was sacrifice. Regret. The bruises you don't show. He'd kept his son in the dark thinking it was protection. But maybe, just maybe, that darkness had made Jacob easier to manipulate.

Ben exhaled slowly and pressed the paper flat before folding it into the pages of his journal. No more buried truths. Not this time. A dizzying mix of confusion and regret washed over him; he was in way over his head, yet he couldn't turn back now. Tucking his journal securely under his arm, he stepped toward the boarding area. The operative, positioned a few spots away, adjusted his comm device and reported quietly, "He's boarding. No indication he's aware of the tail."

* * *

Once on the plane, Ben settled into his assigned seat after stowing his carry-on, then allowed himself a moment of deep concentration. The cramped space of the aircraft became a cocoon for his thoughts.

He pulled out his notebook, a personal lexicon of symbols, intricate equations, and ancient Hebrew letters that hinted at mysteries woven into the fabric of existence, as his mind wandered. Ben could still smell the stale courthouse coffee. Jacob, brilliant and impatient, had stood trembling as the judge sealed the biotech-theft indictment at Ben's hush-money request. Outside, the boy's rage cut deeper than any verdict: "You taught me codes, Abba, then coded my life away." Weeks later, Jacob had emailed a single sentence: "Do not contact me again unless you're ready to tell the whole truth." Ben never replied; he was too busy safeguarding truths for governments that would never bleed for him. Even now, every encrypted line he cracked echoed with Jacob's absence; the son who had once spliced glow-in-the-dark plasmids from dumpster-bound lab scraps, convinced that DNA was another cipher waiting to be solved.

Ben's private heresy was this: he would collapse every cryptic code and hidden intel to hear Jacob say "Dad" without anger one more time.

* * *

Though the operative behind him pretended to peruse an in-flight magazine, his intermittent glances betrayed relentless vigilance. The unspoken orders were clear: observe, report, and ensure nothing in Ben's methodical exploration disrupted the Continuum's carefully plotted agenda.

* * *

The flight landed on time, a comfortable flight that took off at 11:45 AM EST and landed at 2:37 PM PST. Ben disembarked. The pull of unanswered questions propelled him forward. Outside, the afternoon heat was oppressive as the SUV driver, already briefed on Liam's instructions, pulled up to the arrivals queue at Harry Reid airport.

Ben stepped off the plane into a twilight that blurred the line between day and night; a liminal space where secrets felt palpable in the cool desert air. The terminal's bustle faded behind him as he navigated a maze of corridors leading to a waiting curb. Outside, the landscape was painted in the soft hues of dusk, each shadow hinting at the mysteries that lay beyond the familiar airport grounds.

As he made his way toward the waiting SUV, Ben's thoughts drifted to the intricate web of clues he'd spent years untangling. His grandfather's lessons in subtle observation and deciphering hidden messages echoed mentally. Every instinct told him that this journey was far more than a simple ride to a SETI facility. It was a descent into a world where the past and the present intermingled and where the weight of suppressed secrets pressed on every inch of his being.

At the curb, an older driver in a weathered SUV greeted him with a nod and a warm, if tired, smile. "Evening, sir. I'm your driver," the man said, his tone devoid of unnecessary chatter. The vehicle, its interior softly lit and quietly comfortable, stood as a moving sanctuary against the encroaching desert chill.

Ben glanced up as he slid into the back of the SUV and noticed a black vehicle parked in the distance. His survival instincts kicked in. He settled into the back seat, briefcase clutched tightly in his hand, while the driver engaged the navigation system with a few practiced taps.

The black vehicle eased into motion and slipped in behind them.

Liam's instructions were clear: the route would take them along a lesser-known stretch of highway, one that would cloak their movement away from prying eyes.

The SETI driver merged onto the highway and a subtle disquiet stirred within Ben; a sensation of years spent deciphering the cryptic and the concealed. In an attempt to keep himself distracted, Ben glanced at his glowing phone and checked emails. The driver had barely spoken since picking him up at Harry Reid Airport. That suited Ben just fine. He needed time to think.

The sleek black sedan maintained a measured distance behind, its silent presence communicating over a secure line, "He's en route."

Ben adjusted his glasses and exhaled slowly as he watched the endless ribbon of blacktop disappear into the desert night, each mile carrying him closer to the secrets waiting to be unraveled.

He glanced into the side mirror.

He noticed the sedan for the second time.

Trailing. Not too close, not too far. Barely keeping pace. Watching. Ben's fingers tensed on his bag. Paranoia didn't apply, not when someone actually was following him.

Then, it happened.

The dashboard flickered.

Not a small glitch; the entire digital display blinked out for two full seconds, then snapped back online. The speedometer dropped to zero, even though the car was still moving.

Ben sat up straighter. "Did you see that?"

The driver didn't react. He kept his eyes on the road, hands steady on the wheel.

Then Ben saw the dust outside.

Or rather, he saw it stop.

For a fraction of a second, the particles kicked up by the tires froze in midair, as if trapped inside a paused video. The road itself appeared to elongate and collapse at the same time, stretching too far while somehow pulling back.

Ben's stomach lurched.

Then: a snap.

The dust settled. The road was smooth again. The headlights painted the terrain in an unnatural stillness.

But something was wrong.

The desert around them hadn't changed, but the road?

The road was different.

Ben turned his head sharply, scanning the surroundings. This wasn't Interstate 15. It wasn't the road they had been driving on mere moments ago.

The asphalt was older, cracked and worn, like something untouched for decades. The lane markings were faded, barely visible.

A battered road sign stood crooked on the shoulder.

Ben squinted, adjusting his glasses as he read it.

U.S. ROUTE 91

MILE MARKER 54

Ben frowned. Route 91? That sounded wrong.

He knew the major highways leading to Groom Lake: Interstate 15, State Route 375, the Extraterrestrial Highway. He had researched them in preparation for the trip. But this one?

The name nagged at him, pulling something from memory.

Then it hit him.

Ben might not be from Nevada, but he knew history.

Route 91 hadn't existed in decades.

It was an old U.S. highway, one of the original routes through Nevada, before the interstates were built. It had been decommissioned in the 1970s, replaced, rerouted, erased from modern maps.

And yet, here he was.

His pulse pounded in his ears as stared at the driver. "Where in heaven's name are we?"

The man finally glanced at him through the rearview mirror.

But he didn't look surprised.

He looked like he'd seen it before. Without a word, the driver simply kept driving.

A detail, a memory stirred; fluorescent light on warped linoleum, the stale drift of cigarette smoke clinging to everything. Ben had been there; silent, unreadable. Across the table, two men in government-issue lab coats spoke in lowered voices. A map with no legend. A warning he hadn't understood at the time.

Then it was gone again.

The tension in the air grew palpable as traffic thickened near a construction zone. The blacked-out sedan maneuvered aggressively into their lane, its driver emitting a string of indignant grumbles before swerving dangerously close to another vehicle. The black sedan then decelerated abruptly, forcing the SETI driver to apply sudden, forceful brakes.

Ben's grip on his briefcase tightened as he murmured, "That wasn't accidental." His driver offered a quiet word of concern, "Some foolhardy driver. You alright, sir?"

His fingers twitched near his briefcase. Years of decrypting intelligence reports had given him an instinct for misdirection, when something looked like an accident but wasn't.

The SETI driver glanced at him in the rearview mirror. "Sir, you want me to call the police?"

Ben shook his head. "No cops."

"Why not?"

Because, Ben thought grimly, the people behind this are the cops. Or something worse. "I can't be late for my meeting," he concluded.

Ben's eyes remained fixed on the mirror, noting that while the SUV had disappeared into a side street, the black sedan lingered persistently. For a fraction of a second, the reflections in the side mirror doubled. Ben saw the sedan ahead of them, then behind again, as if the vehicle had momentarily jumped in time. His pulse quickened. He turned to the driver, but the man remained focused on the road, oblivious to what had happened. The hairs on his arms stood on end. He had felt this before; the eerie sensation of time stumbling over itself, like in the old war documents he once studied.

Then the sedan's brake lights winked before it actually braked.

Ben's mouth went dry. "Drive faster," he muttered. "Now."

The road itself blurred.

For a fraction of a second, he saw it; two versions of the highway overlapping, one slightly ahead of the other. The sedan was behind them, then ahead, then behind again.

The SETI driver didn't react. His hands remained steady on the wheel. The GPS display glowed, momentarily showing an arrival time that hadn't happened yet but was listed as passed.

Ben forced himself to breathe. His mind was sharp enough to recognize what had happened: the trip had glitched. The car had moved, but time had slipped out of order.

He stared in the mirror. The sedan was still there, its driver's expression unreadable behind dark-tinted glass.

"This isn't just a tail," Ben muttered. "They're using something."

The driver glanced at him. "What's that?"

With mounting urgency, Ben called out, "Driver, don't slow down." The driver's reply was resolute, "I don't plan to." As the sedan pulled alongside, the passenger window descended enough for a shadowed figure, with an impassive expression and dark glasses, to be seen. In a split second, a small, unmarked device was hurled toward their car.

"Go!" Ben barked, his voice a blend of command and alarm, as the object struck the pavement and erupted in a sharp, dazzling flash. The car swerved violently as the driver struggled to maintain control amid the chaos, horns blaring in the surrounding traffic. Ben's gaze darted backward. The sedan had vanished, and the harsh gleam of the device's burst was already receding.

The SETI driver exhaled shakily once calm had returned. "What in the world was that? I don't get paid enough for doing stunt driving." Ben slowly nodded and agreed.

9

Lock: Shadow Protocols

Continuum Black-Ops Site, Washington, D.C. Undisclosed time and place

The room was cold, not physically, but in presence.

Elias Keller stood at the head of the long, polished table, the overhead light slicing shadows across the sharp lines of his face. The room carried that familiar scent of performance and polish: cherrywood gloss, plastic-cased tech humming softly, the bite of industrial cleaners, and the faint, lingering breath of long-buried secrets.

He was a man with many skeletons in numerous closets.

Each one buried not for protection but for power, not for safety but for utility. Elias Keller didn't merely keep secrets. He organized them, labeled them, knew exactly when to use one. And never suspected that his skeletons may be talking to other skeletons.

The monitors along the walls hummed with silent data feeds, endless strings of numbers, and intercepted communications scrolling in tight, efficient lines.

Across from him, Director Rourke leaned back in his chair, fingers steepled, his expression unreadable.

"You failed to contain Levinson," Rourke said, his voice quiet but edged with authority.

Keller didn't flinch. "He was never meant to be contained," he replied evenly. "We needed to see what he does next. He's not a threat."

Rourke's fingers tapped against the table once. "That remains to be seen."

A third voice entered the discussion: Dr. Milena Vostarev, head of the Continuum's Theoretical Signal Analysis Division. She adjusted her glasses, her expression betraying none of her thoughts.

"With all due respect, Director, I think we're looking at this the wrong way."

Rourke gazed at her. "Enlighten me."

Vostarev glanced at Keller, then back to Rourke. "The assumption has been that this signal, this multi-galaxy transmission, is something external. That it's an outside force acting upon us." Vostarev tilted her head slightly, an adjustment, not a choice. “But what if it’s not?” she said, her tone devoid of surprise. “What if the signal isn’t contact... but calibration?”

Keller tilted his head. “Meaning?”

“What if this isn’t a message to us,” Vostarev said, “but a message from us?”

The room fell silent.

Keller’s expression darkened. “Impossible.” He continued, but it felt less like opinion, more like alignment. “If this is a mirror, then it reflects only what we’ve permitted.”

“Is it?” Vostarev leaned forward, activating one of the screens. The waveform of the Andromeda signal appeared, its layers carefully dissected, as well as the reinforcing signals from the other galaxies. “Look at the embedded pattern in the transmission pauses.” She tapped a section of the display, zooming in.

“We assumed it was an encoded frequency, but I ran a different test.” She clicked, shifting the visualization. The screen now displayed an old, grainy document.

Faded ink. Military classification stamps.

Rourke’s jaw tightened.

“That,” Vostarev said, pointing, “is a transmission recorded in 1955, intercepted from a downed aircraft over Arctic waters. It was dismissed as corrupted data at the time." She tapped again. "But it's an exact match for the signal we're receiving now."

Rourke's gaze flicked to Keller. "Did you know about this?"

Keller didn't answer immediately. His silence was its own kind of answer.

Rourke turned back to Vostarev. "What are you saying?"

She folded her hands. "I'm saying we're seeing echoes of something that already happened. Or something that's going to happen."

Another beat of silence.

Then Keller spoke. "If this is true, we're dealing with something far more complicated than an alien transmission." Keller ran a hand down his face, staring at the screen. The timeline wasn't adding up. A signal from multiple galaxies, simultaneously, using a 1940s encryption pattern? Even if he didn't believe in ghosts, this was something close to one.

"Then we're looking at something looping," he muttered, half to himself. "A message not only sent, but re-sent, through time itself." Keller had believed in a fixed, controlled timeline; a world where every deviation could be smoothed out. Now, doubt gnawed at him. Was he merely a pawn in a far grander design, forced to choose between following orders and questioning a destiny that wasn't entirely his own? In that silent reckoning, Keller understood that the pursuit of control was as much an internal battle as it was a mission.

Vostarev nodded. "And we have no idea who's truly behind it."

Keller hesitated, then shook his head. "Or when."

Vostarev agreed. "Yes. And that's why I'm recommending we stop interfering... for now."

Rourke's expression hardened. "That's not an option."

Keller's jaw clenched as he reviewed the ambiguous orders. Questions lingered, casting a long shadow over his every decision. Very troubling.

"With all due respect, Director," Vostarev said, "if we keep pushing against this without understanding it, we might end up accelerating something we can't control."

Rourke exhaled slowly. "And if we do nothing?"

Vostarev hesitated. Then she closed the file and met his eyes.

"Then we see what plays out."

* * *

Ben couldn't be sure, but one fact was undeniable: the top government agencies were not merely observing; its agents were actively sending a message and also aggressively pursuing him, while trying to remain in the shadows. He would not be surprised if that government list included the ultra black-op group known only as "Continuum."

A few minutes later, the car pulled up to the secure gates of the SETI facility. Ben thanked the driver for taking care of him during their little adventure, and stepped out into the cool evening air, adrenaline still pulsing through his veins. He cast one last glance back along the road. No sign of his tail.

For now.

* * *

SETI Outpost - Groom Lake, Nevada, same day, 1751 Hours

Inside the dimly lit SETI desert lab, the steady hum of equipment provided a backdrop to Liam Mills' restless pacing. His lean frame cut sharp shadows against the glowing monitors as he ran a hand through his already-mussed hair.

"That guy, Berry, seems... intense, and paranoid." Gina shared. "Can you trust him?" She had seen and heard the whole thing unfold, but had kept silent.

“Yeah, he helped me out of a dark place. Confident guy. Knows his stuff. We need to follow his lead.”

“Maybe so, but let’s be cautious with what we do, eh? Measure twice and cut once is a good approach, Liam.”

“I’m okay with that. But I’m also glad we have some help with the next step, Gina. Dr. Levinson is amazing.” He continued to pace, and to think. Sig’s words had him deeply worried about what was coming.

Liam’s anticipation was built from months of meticulous research; preparation that had led him to this singular moment. The signal, a transmission so intricate it defied conventional explanation, pulsed on the large screen with an almost hypnotic regularity. Its layers were structured yet imbued with an enigmatic depth that made every flash of light seem deliberate.

Then came David ‘Sig’ Berry’s urgent warning: spycraft embedded in the heart of the growing signal enigma.

Perched casually against a console, Gina observed Liam’s fervent pacing and classical humming with a blend of curiosity and concern. The message from Berry had her on edge as well. Her dark eyes flicked over his animated gestures, and though her tone dripped with gentle skepticism, she couldn’t hide the spark of intrigue. “You’re acting like this Ben guy’s the president,” she quipped, her remark light yet laced with a challenge.

Liam shot her a sidelong glance. "He's not just any regular person, Gina. He's the kind of person who sees connections the rest of us miss. And this is what Sig was referring to with getting some help."

* * *

Rabbi Ben Levinson stepped up to the front doors of the SETI Research Facility, shaking off the lingering fatigue from his cross-country journey as well as the harrowing event that occurred enroute. He was shaken, to be sure.

The cool desert night carried a crisp edge, but inside, the sterile glow of fluorescent lights cast a clinical, almost detached, atmosphere.

He adjusted his glasses and approached the security desk, where a young officer in a SETI-issued polo was scrolling through a monitor. At the sight of Ben's arrival, the officer straightened.

"Dr. Levinson?"

Ben nodded, absently polishing his glasses on the hem of his shirt before setting his well-worn leather briefcase down with a faint thud. "That's me. And call me Ben, please. A stuffed shirt I'm not."

The officer smiled and glanced at the screen, scanning the

pre-approved clearance file Liam Mills had forwarded hours earlier. He tapped a few keys, then reached for a visitor's badge. "Dr. Mills arranged for your access. I need a quick signature here, and I'll have someone escort you to Section C, Ben."

Ben returned the officer's smile and replied, "So I guess that this place has a lot of stuffed shirts, eh? I didn't know that 'Dr. Mills' was a big shot now." They both chuckled. Ben added with a playful shrug, "Ah, but what do I know from big shots? Back in Brooklyn, I'm just a schmendrick with books." Ben took the offered pen, signing the log with practiced efficiency. As he handed it back, the officer motioned toward a waiting escort; a woman with sharp features and a no-nonsense demeanor, her ID badge clipped neatly to her belt.

"This way, sir," she said, already turning toward the corridor. As they walked away, the officer at the desk heard the Rabbi attempt to make conversation. "So, are you a doctor? Are there good places around here to get a coffee and a New York bagel?" A confused stare from the officer, followed by deafening silence, meant that the conversation was over. They proceeded down the hall. Ben kept pace, his sharp eyes flicking over his surroundings as they moved deeper into the facility.

As they neared Section C, the low noise of equipment grew more distinct, the quiet murmur of voices filtering through the air. Ben caught sight of a large display screen through a half-open door, its contents shimmering with spectral analyses and waveform sequences. His escort stopped at a reinforced door with a security panel, swiping her card through the reader.

"They're expecting you," she said, stepping aside as the door unlocked with a soft beep.

Ben took a breath, adjusted his grip on his briefcase, then pushed the door open.

* * *

SETI Research Facility – Section C, 1808 Hours

Gina was still attempting to have Liam explain how a rabbi from the Bronx could possibly help when the main doors slid open with a quiet hiss.

Rabbi Ben Levinson stepped inside, adjusting his shirt and tucking his well-worn leather-bound notebook securely under one arm. His eyes swept the room with the awareness of a man accustomed to deciphering hidden meanings, whether in texts or in human expressions. The soft murmur of distant researchers and the ambient drone of machines filled the space, but it was the rhythmic pulse of the Morse transmission on the main screen that caught his immediate attention.

Liam rose from his chair. "Dr. Levinson." His tone was polite, but measured, each word carrying the weight of what they were about to uncover.

Ben offered a brief nod, setting his notebook and case on the nearest table. His gaze moved from Gina to Liam, his expression revealing equal parts curiosity and amusement. "No need for titles, kid. Just call me Ben."

Liam nodded.

Ben smirked. "I don't usually get summoned for interstellar puzzles."

He set his bag down. "So what's this about a signal?"

Liam gestured toward the expansive screen, where rhythmic Morse code pulsed like the steady beat of a distant heart. "That's what we're trying to figure out. It isn't a simple transmission, it's structured, layered, as if another language is woven beneath the surface."

Liam's eyes locked on the terminal as he watched streams of glowing coordinates dance across the screen. Each number and symbol pulsing like the beat of a distant, cosmic heart. In that moment, the room blurred around him; he could almost feel the electric hum of data flowing like water through an unseen conduit. The air was thick with anticipation as he recalled snippets of ancient texts, where the faintest whisper of a code held the power to unlock mysteries long buried.

Gina's fingers moved over the keyboard with a deliberate precision, each keystroke sparking an internal flash of light in her mind, an image of electromagnetic waves sweeping silently across a star-pocked sky, carrying secrets from the farthest reaches of the universe. In the background, the soft, steady rhythm of the lab equipment provided a counterpoint to the unfolding spectacle on the monitor. For a few long, suspended moments, the three of them inhabited a space where the past and future converged. The air shimmered with the weight of history, as if every flicker of light on the screen was a message from a bygone era.

Ben leaned in, squinting at the shifting patterns, adjusting his glasses as if to bring the hidden details into sharper focus. "Ah. Interesting." He paused over his notes, eyes reflecting the glow of the oscilloscope. "You see that drop in the waveform?" He traced a jagged trough on the screen. "This is the signal's umbra. It's a deliberate shadow cast over the final gematria cluster."

He tapped his leather-bound book of notes absentmindedly, as if harnessing the details directly through his index finger. "Umbra wasn't only Latin for shadow. Back in the 1980s and '90s, the NSA and USAF ran a TOP SECRET program called UMBRA out of the X- and Y-stations in the UK, intercepting every code on every wavelength they could. They chose that name for its principle: hide your eyes in darkness to see more clearly."

Gina exchanged a glance with Liam, realization dawning.

"So this code... conceals as much as it reveals." She hated to admit it, but this rabbi's insights were cutting deeper than most PhDs she'd met.

Ben shook his head slightly and mumbled under his breath, "Such tsuris... every cosmic mystery turns into a headache sooner or later."

He continued. "Thanks for all that," he added with a faint smirk directed at Liam, "now, how about a proper introduction? You remember we're not exactly old friends."

Liam blinked, a hint of chagrin crossing his features. "Oops! Right! Apologies. Ben, this is Dr. Gina Alvarez, my colleague here at SETI. Gina, Rabbi Ben Levinson. He's an expert in... well, in a multitude of disciplines."

Gina extended her hand with a skeptical arch of her brow. "Nice to meet you, Rabbi. Liam's mentioned you can be a wildcard."

Ben chuckled as he shook her hand. "Oy... direct, aren't we. I'll take it." He gestured toward the room. "Call me Ben. I've got a reputation for stirring the chicken soup just enough to keep things interesting." He glanced around the high-tech room with feigned seriousness, adding, "Though judging by all this fancy shmancy equipment, maybe you already have enough chaos, eh?"

Gina smirked faintly. "Perfect. We're short on chaos this week."

Ben turned back to Liam, his expression shifting to something more serious. Ben nudged his glasses up the bridge of his nose and gestured toward the monitors. “Alright, let’s continue. You’ve introduced me to the signal. Now impress me. What kind of cosmic mess did you two drag me into?”

10

Lock: Unseen in the Umbra

SETI Research Facility – Section C, 1828 Hours

Liam wasted no time, flipping open his battered notebook filled with frantic scribbles, sketches, and numeric sequences. "It's coming from Andromeda. That part checks out." Liam gestured to the waveform. "The surface message is all Morse... structured phrases, clear enough. But something about it didn't sit right."

Ben tilted his head. "Off how? Like noise? Or something worse?"

Liam tapped the monitor. "The pauses."

Ben's eyebrows lifted. "The pauses... hmmmm..."

He let the silence hang for a moment.

"Umbra. Latin for shadow. From an old Indo-European root,

meaning shade or darkness. Funny thing... the NSA blackops program in the eighties wasn't listening for what was said, but for what wasn't. Silence as signal."

He gestured toward the screen.

"What we're seeing here isn't about radio bursts or light signatures. It's in the rhythm itself. The gaps, the intentional absences. Engineered nulls between pulses. Intelligence through omission. That's our Umbra Signal. But why... why are they there, and why so intentional?"

Liam nodded. "Yeah, I agree. It's odd. The bursts vary, but they repeat at a rhythmic and structured interval. The nulls are not only obscuring details but hiding key information critical to seeing, and understanding, the entire message. I ran a probability test using statistical analysis models... and, the odds they're accidental?"

He pulled up the analysis.

Ben squinted at the screen.

"Zero-point-one percent," Liam finished. "They're not only pauses. They're data."

Ben inhaled, rubbing his chin. "That's... interesting."

Liam met his gaze. "Interesting enough that I needed your expertise."

He tapped a few keys, eyes focused.

"I started isolating the timing differences. That's when I noticed something else. When I mapped the pauses as numbers instead of blanks... some of them lined up with Hebrew letters."

Gina took a sharp step forward, then froze. "I've seen something like this before. Military timing codes," she said. "Only they weren't measuring sound. They were measuring silence intervals between sonar pulses."

She hesitated. "This... this code... is anticipating interpretation."

Ben nodded in full agreement. He turned to Liam. "You mapped them to Hebrew?"

Liam hesitated. "Sort of. I recognized some of them from a conference you spoke at years ago. That cryptography symposium in Washington. You talked about how Hebrew was more than a language; it was a mathematical system. Every letter has a numerical value. That stuck with me."

Ben's eyes widened slightly in surprise. "My lectures, you actually listened to?"

Liam smirked. "Some of it."

Ben pinched the bridge of his nose. "So, you're telling me a Jewish ghost from another galaxy has your number? Oy.

Just once I'd like a mystery that doesn't end in existential crisis." He exhaled, then rolled up his sleeves. "Alright, let's see what you've got."

Liam flipped through his notes, stopping at a hastily sketched table. "These are the first sequences of numbers I pulled from the pauses."

Ben took his own notebook and ran his fingers over the calculations, murmuring under his breath. He cross-referenced Liam's handiwork with notes he'd compiled during the flight. He stared at the scrawled finished product in disbelief:

IAM → ינא (Ani) → 1+50+10 = 61

THE → אה (Ha) → 5+1 = 6

TRANSMISSION → תרודשת (Tashdorot) → 400+300+4+6+200+400 = 1310

Ben stiffened as he pulled off his glasses and pressed his fingers to his eyes. "Liam, do you realize what you've done here?"

Liam frowned. "What do you mean?"

Ben tapped the page "Morse code is binary on and off It relies on dots and dashes. Hebrew, however, is the original binary system. It's alphanumeric, meaning every letter has a numerical value. You cross-referenced two completely different linguistic structures. One based on pure signal logic, the other on mathematical relationships hidden in text. And it worked."

Gina, who had been quietly listening, folded her arms. "Alright, but how does that help us? Morse code is a basic communication method. What's so special about Hebrew?"

Ben paused, glancing at the stack of notes with a crooked smile. "Trust me, Gina, I'm only about three cups of coffee ahead of total confusion myself."

Gina shot Liam a look. "See, I told you this was going to turn into some cosmic word jumble." Liam shrugged, half-grinning, "If I start quoting the Torah, someone unplug me, okay?"

Ben smirked. "Morse... binary. Hebrew... free-form. Put them together? You're not just sending a message, you're hiding it inside a prayer." He flipped back through Liam's notes. "The pauses in the Morse are doing much more than breaking up words. They're hiding an additional message, embedded numerically."

Liam nodded. "That's what I suspected, but I didn't understand the why."

Ben pointed to the numbers again, his glasses sliding forward slightly with the motion. He pushed them back without looking, eyes locked on the cipher. "Look at these values... sixty-one corresponds to the Hebrew word Ayin, which means 'nothingness' or 'the unseen.' Six? That represents 'man' in Kabbalistic numerology; the bridge between the divine and the earthly. And thirteen-ten?" His finger traced over the symbols. "That's the numerical equivalent of two key phrases: Etz HaDaat, 'The Tree of Knowledge;' and Messer Nistar; 'a hidden message.'"

Gina leaned in.

"I'm confused. How does this all tie into Hebrew letters? And how did Liam know where to start?"

Ben and Liam glanced at each other, and Ben cleared his throat as if preparing for a lecture.

"Alright, let's keep this simple. The Hebrew letter 'Aleph' (א) is one of the most ancient symbols in written language. Originally, it was a pictograph..."

He picked up a marker and drew on a nearby notepad.

"...this."

On the page, a simple shape appeared; a symbol that looked like the head of an ox, with two horns pointing upward.

"Aleph comes from an early pictograph of an ox, a symbol of strength and leadership. Over time, it evolved into the modern Hebrew letter you see today. Kind of a slanted 'X' with a middle bar cutting through it."

Gina squinted at the drawing. "Okay, but how does this connect to the layers in the Morse code?"

Ben next drew a slanted figure on the page. "Okay class, pay attention. Now... Aleph doesn't look like much, right? But it's built from three parts."

He marked each one as he spoke. "Yud here at the top right. Another Yud down left. And this line through the middle, that's a Vav."

Gina leaned in, frowning. "So what? It's stylized?"

"No," Ben shook his head, tapping the page. "In Hebrew, letters aren't merely sounds. They're also numbers."

He pointed again, slower this time. "Yud is ten. Vav is six. Another Yud... ten again. You add them up..."

"Twenty-six," Liam finished, already seeing it.

Gina sat back. "And 26 is significant because...?"

Ben smiled. "It's the same numerical value as the Tetragrammaton," YHWH (הוהי) he scribbled furiously on the notepad, "the unspoken name of God in Hebrew."

He continued, sketching the stylized Aleph again, slower this time. "Now here's the genius of Hebrew. Aleph isn't just a letter. It's built from two Yuds and a Vav, the slanted X with the line through it. Every stroke means something."

He tapped the Vav.

"Sixth in the sequence. Vav, the letter 'V,' means a hook,

a connector, a bridge. The sacred nail that holds past and future together."

Liam murmured, "That's what my grandfather taught me. Said it was just Morse code. The letter V. Three dots and a dash."

Ben glanced at him, then nodded. "Exactly. And that's where it gets interesting."

He flipped the page and wrote:

...-

Ditty-dit dah. Three dots and a dash.

"A V in Morse. But as Liam knows, if you shift the break just a little, you get..."

Liam leaned in, eyes narrowing. "It's layered Morse. Subtle. You get an I and an A, dot-dot, then dot-dash."

Ben grinned. "Precisely. It's the spark and the source. Yud, Aleph. י א. Creation before cognition. Meaning before mechanism. A divine inversion."

He tapped the Vav again.

"Shaped like a funnel, pulling meaning through time. Between Aleph, the breath of origin, and Yud, the seed of self, Vav binds them. In Morse, it signals victory. Less about conquest, more about convergence."

The silence hung as Ben's lesson settled in.

This Vee, Victor, is something more, thought Liam. Rustand didn't give him a random letter. He planted a fragment of divine logic in a boy's memory, hidden in a rhythm.

Gina squinted at the page. "So... Hebrew math circles back to God's name?"

Ben nodded. "It's not a coincidence. It's embedded. The form and the number lead to the same place."

Liam's eyes lit up. "And now layer that into Morse... dot, dash. The shape of the letter echoed in signal form."

Ben gave a slow nod, impressed. "Not a translation, but a resonance. That kind of symmetry doesn't happen by accident."

Liam grinned. "Exactly. Aleph doesn't make a sound, but it still carries meaning. The message works the same way. Quiet on the surface. Loud underneath."

Ben underlined the Aleph again. "This is why Hebrew's so fascinating. The letters are more than sounds or pictures. They're equations. Layers stacked inside a single shape."

Liam leaned in, lips pursed, as the connection clicked. "Wait... wasn't this part of your talk in D.C.? The cryptographic structure of sacred language?"

Ben glanced at him, respect breaking through his usual sarcasm. "Now you're tracking."

Liam tapped the Vav. "So this isn't just tradition. It's by design." Liam got even more animated. "So, now... imagine you layer that stuff into Morse code, dots and dashes matching the structure of the letter."

Ben picked up the idea. "Ahhhhh... that's how the hidden code was embedded. The Morse Liam pulled out? Similar framework of Hebrew letters and Gematria. Same scaffolding. Same pulse."

As he spoke, the glow from his laptop flickered, just once, then flared into a sharp blue-white glimmer. The camera light on the top of the console blinked red for half a second, then went dark again. Not a system crash. More like a deliberate action.

Gina stopped pacing. Her voice dropped. "That wasn't you?"

Ben's brow furrowed, but he didn't take his eyes off the screen. "No," he said slowly. "But something... recognized the message sequence, it appears. And then stopped. Like it didn't want us to know it had."

* * *

Liam stepped back from the desk and squinted through the high window. "You see that?" Gina joined him. A small object drifted low and slow above the ridge. "Drone?" she asked. "Possibly. But it veered when we got the last echo." She studied the sky. "That's not coincidence. It's interest."

The paranoia in the room was palpable. However, the rising stakes required them to deliberately shake off their unease and refocus on the task at hand.

Gina folded her arms. "So let me get this straight: Aleph stands for God's name, it's connected to the number 26, and now you're saying it can be buried inside Morse code?"

Ben smirked. "Oy, now you're getting it. Well done!" His eyes gleamed. "It's what's missing. The spaces."

Gina leaned back. "So it's not only what they said. It's how they shaped the silence around it. Like folding meaning into form. Digital origami." She exhaled, rubbing her temples. "So, whoever sent this didn't just want us to read it. They wanted us to decode it."

Silence filled the room.

Liam's fingers hovered over the keyboard, pulse drumming. "Let's assume this second layer isn't random. What's it actually say?"

Ben flipped through his notebook, matching sequences to Hebrew terms. "They appear to be coordinates."

Liam looked up, breath caught. "Coordinates?"

Ben scribbled quickly, cross-referencing locations. His face darkened. "They point to Groom Lake."

Gina's head snapped up. "Area 51?"

Ben nodded, jaw tight. "And not any old section. A precise point inside the restricted zone."

Liam was pensive. "If this is where it's leading us, then the signal isn't only reaching out." His voice was barely above a whisper.

"It isn't noise," Ben continued, "it's the white space that leads. Or in our case, the umbra shadow."

The weight of the revelation settled over them like a tangible force.

Gina crossed her arms. "Alright, let's say this isn't some fluke. Let's say it was meant for us. Then what... are we just supposed to follow it?"

Liam's fingers hovered over the keyboard, his pulse pounding.

He exhaled slowly. "We follow it."

Ben and Gina agreed, but they needed to do more work on the signal to refine the details. Liam was feeling overwhelmed;

something was off, and he couldn't quite place his sense of unease.

"Hey guys," Liam offered, "I need to do a deeper dive on this first." Ben and Gina silently nodded as they processed the details, and Liam shuffled towards a vacant desk. He needed to work out a few ideas with a pen and paper, old school. He slipped away from the intense discussions in the control room, seeking a quiet corner where the chaos of the night might finally give way to reflection.

* * *

He found himself alone in a cramped, dimly lit corner of the SETI facility; a temporary refuge from the chaos of their unraveling investigation. In the soft glow of a single desk lamp, he pulled out the yellow legal pad his grandfather once used to scribble Morse code lessons, and with a reverent sigh, started writing. He paused, pen hovering. Grandpa's stories had once felt like bedtime tales. Now they read like blueprints. He wasn't that wide-eyed kid anymore. The shadows had weight. And he had responsibilities.

Every scratch of the black Scripto Finepoint on the paper sketched a legacy that had been both a gift and a burden. There, in the margins between meticulous calculations and frantic diagrams, he noted the intimate details that had shaped him: his secret Morse code bracelet that pulsed with a message known only to him, and the static-filled radio transmissions he listened to before sleep that provided the tactile comfort he found in the cold, rough surface of antique military radio equipment.

In those solitary hours, Liam allowed himself to remember the stories his grandfather had spun under the veil of night; tales of spaceships that defied reason and encounters that skirted the edges of human understanding. He recalled the man's trembling hands as he operated the ancient Morse box during the chaos of the breach and how those same hands had passed on a secret code that now resonated in every line of the Andromeda signal he painstakingly decoded.

As his pen moved over the page, Liam's thoughts drifted to his own journey: a journey forged in the chaos of duty and regret. His time in Air Force Intelligence, where he had once concealed truths to protect national secrets, now felt like a shadow he could no longer ignore. Liam's grip tightened around the pen. For a moment, his hand hovered mid-sentence. He thought of the secrets he'd buried, the missions gone sideways. But instead of retreating, he pressed the tip to paper again. This time with clarity, not doubt.

His hands paused over the page. The childhood awe had long faded, replaced by the cold weight of what he now knew. He wasn't chasing stories anymore. He was chasing ghosts, his own among them.

He wrote about the non-repeating segment of Morse code, a signal meant solely for him, its cadence a private language that bound him to his lineage, whispering that every moment of his life had been meticulously prepared for this intersection of fate and discovery. In the quiet solitude, Liam admitted that the logical world he so desperately trusted was now unmoored by inexplicable phenomena, leaving him to wonder if the unknown was not a void to be feared, but a legacy to be embraced.

He didn't write to remember.

He wrote because the signal had already started to forget.

It was a moment of raw confession, a chapter of his life that had been hidden between the coded messages and the classified files, waiting for the right time to be spoken aloud. And as the desert night deepened outside, Liam's thoughts promised that someday, in time, the truth would not only set him free, but also illuminate the hidden destiny that had been his all along.

* * *

He snapped out of his deep thoughts when a loud voice interrupted his train of thoughts. "Hey all," said Gina, "let's pack it in and get some sleep. Tomorrow's going to be a busy day of analysis, and the Rabbi looks tired after a long day of travel and science abuse." Ben chuckled. "I don't mind explaining codes and ancient languages. Not getting my daily supply of coffee and bagels, I mind." Liam agreed, and they all plodded down to the overnight quarters where they each took a small room and retired.

11

Cipher: Global Powers Take Notice

Continuum Black-Ops Site, Washington, D.C. Undisclosed time and place

In the dimly lit government facility on the outskirts of Washington, D.C., three intelligence agents sat in tense silence. Rows of monitors illuminated the room, each screen streaming live feeds of SETI's activities and the encrypted communications of its lead researchers. Agent Keller, a grizzled veteran with a perpetually furrowed brow, leaned against the console, arms crossed. His sharp eyes flicked to the largest screen, which displayed a scrambled feed from the SETI computer.

Agent Patel, a middle-aged woman with a no-nonsense demeanor, interjected. "That's an overstatement. They don't even know what they're looking at. This is simply academic curiosity spiraling out of control." Ramos echoed, seconds later, voice flat: "They don't even know." The room went still, as if the echo hadn't been repetition, but confirmation.

"Maybe," Keller replied, his voice low. "Or maybe they're closer than we think."

Patel shook her head, frustration evident in her voice. "You're jumping at shadows, Keller. SETI isn't equipped to handle something like this. They're not us; they're scientists, not operatives."

"Exactly," Keller snapped, his tone icy. "And that's what makes them dangerous. They'll broadcast this to the world if we don't stop them."

Ramos hesitated, then added, "We've been monitoring their communications. Mills hasn't contacted anyone outside the team yet, but they're clearly collaborating; cross-referencing historical data, scanning for patterns."

"What about Levinson?" Keller asked, turning to Patel.

Patel grimaced. "He's the wild card. A rabbi with a knack for cryptography. He's feeding them connections we don't need anyone else seeing."

Keller exhaled sharply, rubbing a hand over his face. The room smelled of stale coffee and perspiration. He wasn't prone to hesitation, but something about this case gnawed at him.

He'd overseen countless suppression operations: silencing whistleblowers, rerouting classified research, ensuring breakthroughs never saw the light of day if they threatened global stability. This was different. This wasn't about keeping another military project under wraps. This was something older.

Something even Drexler hadn't told him everything about.

"We've been playing defense for too long," Keller muttered, half to himself. "They're pushing boundaries we can't afford to let them cross."

"So what's the move?" Ramos asked, his fingers hovering over the keyboard.

Patel's voice was steady, but there was a hint of concern. "Before we escalate, we need clearance. This isn't about watching anymore. If we step in, it's a whole new ballgame. That could elevate things to Phase Two."

"I've seen those words before," Keller murmured. "Phase Two. It's not protocol. It's scorched-earth doctrine."

Ramos raised an eyebrow. "Thought that was decommissioned."

"That's the thing," Keller replied. "It was never written down to begin with."

Keller stopped pacing, his gaze hard. He thought about Liam Mills: brilliant, relentless, but reckless. He wouldn't stop. Neither would Gina Alvarez. And Levinson? That old man was deciphering something Keller himself didn't fully understand.

The last time Keller had felt like this, like he was one step behind forces far greater than him, was when he'd first learned of the true nature of the Continuum.

"No choice. We call the boss."

The secure feed blinked to life, then darkened again as the uplink cycled. Keller said nothing. His shoulders were square, but his eyes betrayed the creeping realization: this wasn't a decoding issue. This was about control. And something else, something older, was already writing the rules.

* * *

Elias Keller's life was shaped by the quiet currents of control that ran beneath the surface of power. Born into a family steeped in military intelligence, Keller's earliest memories weren't of playgrounds or schoolyards but of the cold, sterile halls of government facilities, places where classified documents outnumbered bedtime stories. His father, Nathaniel Keller, was a respected strategist within a shadowy intelligence division, a stern man who believed that control—over information, people, and outcomes—was the bedrock of stability.

Growing up under Nathaniel's watchful eye, Elias was groomed to see the world not as a web of chaotic events, but as a series of cause-and-effect chains, each one controllable if you understood the right leverage points. His father's lessons were never delivered with warmth, but with precision. "Free will is a myth," Nathaniel once told him. "History is shaped by the ones who understand where to apply pressure."

Elias excelled in cryptography and behavioral psychology, blending the science of codes with the study of human nature. He learned that controlling people was often easier than cracking ciphers; because people followed patterns. By the time he entered military intelligence, Keller had mastered the art of quiet manipulation, using a soft-spoken authority that unnerved his peers.

But it wasn't until his induction into the Continuum that Keller found his true calling. The Continuum was much more than a shadow organization; it was the architect behind the scaffolding of global events. Wars, economic collapses, technological leaps; all subtly guided to maintain balance and prevent societal collapse. Or so they claimed.

Keller's work within the Continuum wasn't overt espionage or battlefield strategy; it was the control of information streams, guiding narratives at a macro level. His primary role was in "pattern forecasting," using cryptographic data combined with social modeling to predict future outcomes. If a certain innovation posed a risk to the delicate global balance, it was suppressed. If a government teetered too close to collapse, its fall was accelerated to avoid a more catastrophic implosion later.

The tipping point in Keller's belief system came during an operation code named Project Meridian. The mission focused on identifying "Keystone Individuals"—people who, through their actions, could dramatically alter the course of history. Keller's assignment was clear: identify, monitor, and, if necessary, eliminate these individuals before they disrupted the Continuum's carefully orchestrated designs.

But as the operation unfolded, Keller began to notice something unsettling. These "Keystones" weren't random outliers. They appeared to be part of a sequence, almost as if someone had placed them in history deliberately. Their lives overlapped across generations, and their actions converged on precise technological and social flashpoints.

The more Keller studied them, the more he saw patterns repeating, cycles that defied statistical chance or human chaos.

He didn't dismiss it. He couldn't. It felt like proof of something deeper—a guiding force older than the Continuum, and possibly above it. He reported his findings. The reaction was immediate. The project was sealed. His data wiped. He was reassigned to lower-priority oversight.

Still, Keller wouldn't stop. It wasn't about a crusade. That instinct had been buried long ago. This was compulsion, because if the patterns were real, then everything the Continuum had done was mostly noise. All the favors, all the compromises, all the carefully phrased lies used to keep bigger lies in motion—they meant nothing.

So he went quiet. Off-book. And he started tracing the overlooked. People, places, moments dismissed as irrelevant—yet, when overlaid, they formed a hidden structure beneath the accepted narrative.

What emerged disturbed him. Centuries of anomalies. Sudden jumps in technology. Cultural shifts that landed with eerie precision. And worst of all—erasures. People surgically removed from history, as if they had never existed.

His obsession deepened until one realization hit him with a clarity he couldn't ignore. He wasn't studying the system anymore. He had become part of it.

And once that thought rooted itself, the world around him shifted. Decisions were made before he made them. Files pre-flagged before he even opened them. Messages arrived before he requested them.

It wasn't a malfunction.

It was momentum.

And whatever had started it had already moved far beyond him.

* * *

In the dim light of the operations center, Keller stood motionless, his thoughts catching up to the weight of what had been said. The Continuum had always portrayed itself as the invisible hand on the wheel of history, but Keller had started to suspect they were following a script rather than writing it.

Buried deep in restricted archives were scattered references to something predating even the earliest roots of the Continuum. Not an organization, but a presence—something that moved beneath the surface of events, guiding outcomes under the illusion of human control.

The Andromeda signal was more than an anomaly. It was a signal pattern Keller had seen before: in older files, in redacted transmissions, in the quiet unease that sometimes passed between senior analysts who knew not to ask questions. This wasn't new. It was returning.

The voice on the secure uplink had spoken with calm authority. One phrase—no debate, no elaboration.

"Phase Two is greenlit."

Keller's mind raced as the words echoed inside him. There was no confusion about what they meant.

Preserve the timeline.

The voice had added only four more words before the connection dropped.

"Containment. At all costs."

The line went dark, and silence reclaimed the room.

Ramos glanced at Patel. No one spoke. They didn't have to.

Keller swallowed, his throat dry. He stared at the monitors, then at the untouched files on his screen. This wasn't about analysis anymore. It was about action—precise, untraceable, final.

And the clock had started ticking.

* * *

Back at SETI, Liam's laptop pinged, pulling him from his thoughts. He frowned at the screen as a new message appeared. The text was brief, chilling in its simplicity:

"Cease your investigation. This is not your domain."

He felt his pulse quicken. No sender. No digital footprint. Whoever sent this had bypassed every security measure on the system without leaving a trace. That wasn't hacking. It was precision.

Liam called Gina and Ben over, his voice tight. "You need to see this."

Gina leaned over the screen, her sharp brown eyes not blinking as she read the message aloud. "Anonymous? No contact trace?"

Liam shook his head. "Nothing. It's like it appeared out of thin air."

Ben set his coffee down with intentional care, his fingers tightening around the ceramic mug. His usually brash demeanor was subdued, his voice quieter than usual. "You dig into something ancient and coded, and you think no one's watching?" He exhaled sharply. "The real question is, what are they willing to do to make sure we stop?"

Gina's fingers moved to the Montblanc on the console, the feel of it steadied her voice. "Either way, the message is clear: we're being watched."

* * *

Inside the secure Continuum operations facility, Keller watched the screen. The live feed displayed Liam's computer, the warning still blinking in stark white letters.

He exhaled through his nose. "They saw it."

Agent Ramos adjusted his headset. "Message delivered. You think they'll back off?"

Keller didn't answer immediately. Instead, he studied Liam's reaction on the screen; the way his brow furrowed, the way Gina stepped closer, as if bracing for impact.

No. They wouldn't back off.

"They won't," Keller muttered, rubbing his jaw. "Mills is too stubborn, and Levinson; he's already seeing patterns."

Agent Patel folded her arms, watching the same feed. "So what's the next move? If they ignore the warning, Drexler won't give them a second chance."

Keller didn't respond right away. His gut twisted. He'd delivered warnings before, but this one felt different. Not silence. Erasure.

Drexler wasn't planning to scare them off. He was planning to make them disappear.

Keller's fists tightened.

This wasn't a mission to maintain order anymore. It was a purge.

* * *

The desert wind howled outside the SETI facility, swirling sand against the metal siding.

The laptop screen cast a cold glow across the room. Liam tapped his pencil once, twice, then stopped.

“No breach. No log. That message didn’t come from outside.”

Ben squinted. “So it manifested out of nowhere? Like a ghost with admin privileges?”

Gina stayed focused on the console. “It wasn’t a hack. More like it was already in the system, waiting.”

Ben gave a slow exhale. “Delightful.”

Liam leaned back. “It wanted to be seen.”

Gina turned, arms folded. “Not only seen. It’s looking for a reaction.”

Ben tilted his head. “So the universe left a note and is peeking to see if we noticed.”

“No,” Liam said. “It’s checking if we flinch.”

Ben shot back. “Then we don’t.”

Gina stepped forward. “Isolate the signal. Kill every connection. Local only.”

Ben gave a small nod. “Manual mode. Finally, something I trust.”

Liam resumed typing, quieter now. “This wasn’t a warning.”

Ben raised an eyebrow. “What, then?”

“A signal,” Liam said. “A kind of trigger, waiting for us to reach this point.”

Ben smiled faintly. “Well. Consider us reached.”

* * *

Ben paced near the doorway, tapping the arm of his glasses against his lip in thought before slipping them back on. He had been reading through the translated cipher for nearly an hour, occasionally muttering to himself, periodically shaking his head in disbelief.

The air inside was thick; not from the heat, but from the weight of the moment. They had been chasing ghosts in the code for almost two days, decrypting and reassembling fragments of the signal. But now, at last, the patterns were emerging.

They were inside the SETI mainframe. Illegally, permanently, irreversibly inside.

Gina exhaled, rubbing her temples. "We shouldn't even be seeing this."

Liam's fingers moved over the keyboard with mechanical precision, filtering out interference, aligning frequency timestamps, stripping encryption layers. What lay beneath the surface of the transmission was planned. And structured.

A whisper of intelligence buried within the static.

"We've been reading this wrong the whole time," Liam muttered.

Gina leaned in. "What are you seeing?"

Liam tapped a sequence into the command line. The spectrogram reassembled; an overlaid waveform, faint but undeniable.

A second message.

Not in the primary transmission. Not even in the secondary layer. Deeper. Beneath the noise and under the static. Beneath the pauses.

The screen blinked, and the decoded symbols snapped into place.

Gina's breath caught.

Liam didn't need to look at her to know what she was

thinking.

A set of coordinates buried inside a deep-space signal from Andromeda.

12

Cipherlock: Unlocking the Sands of Time

SETI Outpost near Groom Lake, Nevada – Thursday, 0718 Hours

Liam wandered back to the control room the next morning, with more resolve and clarity. The others were already working through the data; they did not seem to have missed him. Gina made eye contact with Liam as she waited patiently for the Rabbi to respond to her last question.

"Gina," Ben finished, "Hebrew letters are embedded into every alphabet and language in every country. Even our English word 'Alphabet' is from the first two letters of Hebrew 'Aleph' and 'Biet,' so you are incorrect, dear maidele." Gina glared and let out a Spanish curse word.

Liam retreated and went back to his workstation, and resumed activity. His fingers hovered over the keyboard, his jaw set with determination. "Ben, if we follow this trail, we're stepping into territory guarded by those who don't welcome unexpected visitors."

Ben turned to him with a resolute expression. "Then we prepare. Whoever sent this message knew we'd decipher it, and I doubt we're the only ones keeping watch."

As Liam prepared to key in the sequence, his hand paused, then tapped out a rhythm: ditty-dit-dah, "V for Victory."

Gina glanced over, brow furrowed. "That your Morse code again?"

He gave a quiet half-smile. "Yeah. My grandfather always said it meant more than just a letter. It was a promise not to quit. Especially when things get weird."

* * *

Outside, the desert stretched endlessly, its sands etched with long, shifting shadows. Inside the lab, the rhythmic pulse of the lab equipment persisted, its intensity deepening with every second.

They had uncovered a real key. The lock, whatever it was, hadn't shown itself yet.

Gina paused, her arms slowly unfolding as she stared at the drawings and texts. "Coordinates," she murmured. "That reminds me of something..."

Liam turned to her. "What?"

She hesitated, then grabbed her tablet and began typing furiously. "Back when I first joined SETI, there was a rumor about a piece of classified intel. A few of the staff had mentioned it, but it didn't seem legit to us. Something retrieved from the Arctic in 1955. It was labeled 'Artifact'—Top Secret UMBRA. The details were vague, but... some of them were eerily similar to this."

Liam's curiosity was piqued. "Do you think it's connected?"

"Only one way to find out," Gina said, already pulling up SETI's secured archives. The terminal screen wavered as she bypassed layers of encryption. In moments, a collection of heavily redacted files appeared. The terse summaries and fragmented data hinted at a secret history, locked away in classified vaults for decades.

Together, the three of them delved into the documents. Grainy black-and-white photographs accompanied reports from decades past. One image stood out: a crystalline object, angular and alien in design, recovered from deep within the Arctic ice. Gina excitedly continued, "The reports described it as '...emitting faint electromagnetic distortions, almost imperceptible, but enough to disrupt nearby equipment.' Its surface was '...etched with fluid symbols that defied traditional linguistic or mathematical analysis.'"

Gina leaned closer to the screen, squinting at the images. "Wait a minute... this isn't only a relic. Look at the symbols on the device in the photo. They seem almost identical to what you two are describing coming from the four galaxies."

Ben and Liam looked at each other with a knowing look. Ben sat back, pensively. Something was nagging at him. Rabbi Ben Levinson let his thoughts drift back to the early days when the mysteries of sacred texts first revealed themselves to him. SETI's white corridors were colder than usual, and something about those symbols pulled him back, not just to ancient scrolls or Yiddish phrases, but to a feeling he hadn't touched in years.

Every coded inscription and numerical pattern in the Andromeda signal stirred a deep, familiar longing. A reminder that the secrets of the past were not lost but carefully veiled beneath layers of time. Sipping bitter black coffee from a paper cup, his thoughts traveled to a long-ago mentor's solemn warning: that some knowledge, once liberated, could never be reburied.

In that solitary moment, Ben felt the weight of his duty intensify. Translating cryptic messages was only part of it. The real weight, the one he barely spoke aloud, was guarding a kind of wisdom that could twist too easily, and fall into the wrong hands. With a quiet resolve tempered by both sorrow and determination, he vowed to protect these ancient secrets, even as he wondered whether the act of revealing them might unmoor the balance he had spent his life striving to preserve.

Liam, hit with a thought, tapped on another file, his analytical mind working at full throttle. "These symbols... they're not random markings. There's a structure here—patterns that could align with quantum entanglement principles."

Ben, who had been observing quietly, leaned in, his expression alight with recognition. "Wait, let me see that." He pointed to a line buried in the report, his voice growing more animated. "Sequence noted: 'Aleph, Tav, Yud.' Referred to as the 'Chronos Lattice.'"

Liam hunched over the corner of the table, sketchpad in his lap, flipping slowly through older logs.

"Probably nothing," he said. "But when I sort the intervals instead of the data points, there's something layered. Not symmetrical, but not noise either."

Ben stepped beside him. "Are they forming anything?"

"No," Liam said. "Not exactly. It feels like something trying to remember how to form a shape. It seems like X, Y, and Z coordinates; like a three-D puzzle only partially assembled."

Ben's eyes lingered on the familiar symbols, and in that silent pause, memories of a long-ago cryptography conference resurfaced. He recalled his mentor's quiet, urgent words—how, amidst murmurs of ancient texts and modern enigmas, his mentor had confided that certain secrets were destined to shape history itself. That day, the mentor had revealed that the interplay between numerical symbolism and language was not merely academic, but a map to the forces governing time and fate. The weight of that revelation, coupled with personal loss and the burning need to uncover hidden truths, had set Ben on a lifelong quest. Now, as he stared at the Chronos Lattice, he felt that same profound connection—a reminder that these symbols were not relics of a forgotten past, but beacons guiding the course of human progress. He turned to the others, his tone urgent. "Schmegegge, this is *not*."

Liam raised an eyebrow, but remained silent.

Ben paused, a heaviness settling over him as he considered the forbidden truths locked within those ancient numbers. The cost of unveiling such secrets was not merely intellectual. It was deeply personal. He remembered the warnings of his mentor and the sacrifices made in the name of preserving certain knowledge. In that moment, he silently resolved that some truths, however tantalizing, might come at too steep a price for humanity to bear.

Ben continued. "Aleph and Tav—first and last letters of the Hebrew alphabet. They signify the beginning and the end. Add Yud, and you have a connection to creation and divine essence."

Gina frowned. "Creation? This is starting to sound mystical."

"It's not mysticism," Ben insisted. "It's symbolic logic; mathematics encoded in language. And if these symbols are linked to quantum fields as Liam suggests, it might mean this artifact operates on principles we barely understand—principles tied to time and existence itself."

Liam leaned back in his chair, staring at the screen as if the artifact might leap out at him. "So this 'Chronos Lattice' isn't a random find. It's a bridge between ancient knowledge and modern science."

Ben nodded, his excitement tempered by a growing unease. "Exactly. The sequence Aleph, Tav, Yud points to time, while embodying connection. It's a phrase that resonates with the idea of continuity across all things." Ben leaned over the cluttered worktable, his eyes alight with excitement as he traced his finger along a faded section of Morse code Liam had transcribed on a scrap of paper.

Gina scrolled slowly through the backscatter logs, her fingers hovering above the keys, waiting for a signal.

"Look here," Ben interrupted, still in his own thought pattern. "We've always assumed these dots and dashes were a mere puzzle. But when I cross-reference them with our ancient texts, something extraordinary emerges. These Hebrew letters—Aleph, Tav, and Yud, in the simplest Gematria, are assigned 1, 400, and 10 respectively. When you add them up, you get 411. It's not a coincidence; it's as if the Morse code itself was hinting at this hidden total."

Gina leaned in, eyebrows raised in a skeptical arch. "Just wait, Ben. You're telling us it was intentionally designed to evoke these Hebrew letters and the number 411?"

Liam took Ben's concept at face value, intrigued but not entirely certain. Still, he understood where Gina was coming from.

Ben, too caught up in the moment to notice Gina's need for hard data, pressed on with enthusiasm. "Exactly! Aleph signifies beginning. Tav marks completion. Yud, small but powerful, is the divine spark that bridges the two. When you combine them, it's more than a number. You get a narrative. Morse code is a language in its own right. The Morse sequence we intercepted had those numbers embedded in the string... the 411. It's a call to look beyond the surface, to recognize that every signal and symbol is part of a design."

"It's not a prophecy," Liam snapped. "It's data."

Ben raised an eyebrow. "Sometimes data carries intention."

Liam turned away. He trusted patterns. Not people trying to explain them.

Gina rubbed her temples, trying to make room for the idea. "C'mon, Rabbi. That sounds a little too on the nose for an alien transmission."

She leaned against the opposite table and plunged back into the business at hand: cross-checking the signal log with the last triangulated pulse. She didn't speak right away. Her brow furrowed.

"There's something off in the ID trace," she said. "It's not just bounce-back echo. It's tuned... almost like a radar sweep looking for a target."

Liam looked up from the corner. "Us?"

She gave the slightest nod. "Or someone who was here before us."

The room fell silent as the implications settled over them. Outside, the faint hum of equipment filled the air, a reminder of the relentless search for meaning.

Gina broke the quiet, her voice measured but charged. "If all this is real, and if the government locked it away for decades... what exactly were they afraid of?"

* * *

Ben continued to intently probe the Hebrew letters in his notebook, cross-referencing them with the decoded phrases from the Andromeda signal. "There's something deeper here. The numerical values of the letters: Aleph - one, Tav - four-hundred, and Yud - ten, align with another profound concept in Gematria... Kesher shel Zman: an artifact to a 'Bond of Time.'"

Ben's voice trembled with barely contained excitement. "It's about time itself. This phrase, these numbers; they symbolize interconnectedness... nodes forming bonds across eras."

Liam leaned in, his brow furrowed. "Nodes? What kind of nodes?"

Ben pointed to a redacted line in the classified document spread across the desk. "Look here. The 'time artifact' is described as a 'stabilizing unit' for temporal anomalies. Now look at the multi-galaxy signal's embedded sequence—the phrase 'a hand that shapes.' Together, they suggest a framework, connections through time. Maybe even space."

Gina hovered over Ben's shoulder, squinting at the text. "So you're saying these artifacts or 'nodes' are... what? Some kind of time-machine puzzle pieces?"

Ben shook his head rapidly. "No, no, I'm not saying that..."

Gina cut him off, her voice sharp. "Because that sounds insane, Ben. Nodes across time? Do you hear how that sounds?"

"Of course I do!" Ben shot back, his voice sharp. "But the numbers don't lie. You think I'm just pulling this out of thin air?"

"Or somewhere much darker, and it wouldn't be your first attempt." Gina snapped, crossing her arms tightly. "You've been jumping to conclusions since the moment you walked in here. What if you're wrong? What if..."

Liam stepped between them, raising a hand to cut through the growing tension. "Enough. Both of you." His voice was firm but calm, commanding their attention. "Gina, let him finish. Ben, dial it down. We need facts, not a shouting match."

Ben exhaled sharply, his hands gripping the edges of the notebook. "Fine," he said, his tone softening. "Look, I'm not saying I know exactly what this is. But the combination of the Andromeda signal and this redacted text strongly suggests that these 'nodes' aren't unique. There could be others. If that's true, then these 'nodes' might form a kind of network."

Liam nodded slowly, glancing at the terminal, the signal still scrolling in its steady rhythm. "It's like you said earlier, Ben. The Morse gives structure, but the deeper meaning... it's in the layers. They're tied together at every level."

Gina's skepticism didn't fade entirely, but her expression shifted as she leaned over the desk again. "A network? What kind of network are we even talking about here? For what? Communication? Time travel?"

Ben shook his head, his fingers tapping nervously on the notebook. "I don't know. But think about it... 'a bond of time.' That phrase isn't random. In Hebrew, 'Kesher' implies a unique connection, like threads tied together. These nodes, if there are more of them, might be stabilizing something. A timeline? A sequence of events? It's like they're anchoring history itself."

* * *

Without warning, the screen on the far wall flickered. Sig's face appeared, grainy and motionless, as if the link had activated itself.

"Buddy, heard you tagged a node lattice point," he said, eyes slightly off-screen.

Liam stepped closer. "Yeah. Not just signal data... it's spatial."

"I know," Sig replied. "That's why I called. There are more of them."

He glanced down, as if reading something outside the frame, then shifted abruptly, eyes sharp now, but his posture tighter than usual. Sig looked tired and jumpy, simultaneously.

"This isn't only communication," he said quietly, yawning. "It's... insistence."

Gina tilted her head. "Meaning what?"

"Meaning," Sig replied, "whatever's sending the signal doesn't adapt. It doesn't hesitate. It just... continues. Even when we don't respond. Especially when we don't."

A short pause. Sig blinked slower than normal, jaw tight.

"I used to think it was looking for someone," he added. "Now I'm not so sure. Might be... waiting."

Then, almost as an afterthought, barely above a sigh:

"And if it is watching... then this call's already too long. Be careful, buddy. Watch your back."

The feed cut.

* * *

Liam's jaw tightened as the implications settled over him. He reached for the document, scanning the redacted phrases again. "Sig is on to something. Look. 'Hand that shapes.' 'Stabilizing unit.'" he said, his voice low. "This matches up with what Sig described. A system."

The room fell silent, the hum of the equipment the only sound as the three of them processed the enormity of the idea.

Gina finally broke the quiet, her voice steadier now but no less wary. "So let's say you and Sig are right. There are more of these node things. Why? What's the purpose?"

Liam leaned against the table, his hands pressing into its surface as if grounding himself. "If this is a network, then someone, or something, put it in place. The question is, what are they trying to achieve?"

Ben's voice softened, his hands trembled as if the truth itself pressed down on his shoulders, settling into his words. "I don't know. But this much is clear: this is older than we've ever imagined. Using an ancient language tells us this. And, it's bigger than we can conceive."

Gina paced for a moment, running a hand through her hair. "What I don't get is why it feels like everything is converging now. If this system is ancient, why is it waking up? And why involve us?"

Liam turned his gaze to the glowing terminal, the galactic signals still pulsing in quiet rhythm, the thumb drive silently recording everything. "Maybe it's been guiding us all along," he said, almost to himself. "And now that we're here, maybe we're finally ready to see it."

Liam's voice trailed off, caught between awe and dread. The others said nothing. Outside, the desert wind kicked up dust across the dry expanse, silent, as if waiting for them to catch up with something already set in motion.

13

Cipherlock: The Chronos Lattice

SETI Outpost near Groom Lake, Nevada – Thursday, 1237 Hours

The terminal's glow intensified as Ben removed his glasses. "Let's keep going," he said softly. "If this signal is what I think it is, we've only started scratching the surface."

Gina leaned forward, her skepticism cracking under the weight of too much coincidence. "Fine. But no more metaphors until we hit something with real data."

Ben glanced at Gina, his nervousness tempered by an unshakable sense of wonder. "Another thought. Maybe it's the opposite," he said with a shiver, "maybe we're only seeing it because the system is breaking."

"So let's do more digging and see what we can find," said Liam. Ben agreed, and Gina, though reluctant, was intrigued too.

Ben's fingers traced the faded ink on the scattered papers, his brow furrowed in concentration. The bunker was dimly lit, the glow from Liam's monitors casting long shadows across the piles of files, maps, and cryptographic charts they had assembled. Gina stood at the whiteboard, cross-referencing historical timelines with numerical sequences that Liam had extracted from the Andromeda signal.

"I've got something," Liam announced, his voice edged with excitement and unease. "A sequence that matches a date when converted from Morse to numeric format. It translates to 150 BCE."

Ben looked up, his eyes sharp with recognition. "That corresponds with what some historians believe was the construction of the 'Sacred Mechanism.'"

Gina tilted her head. "Sacred what?"

"The Antikythera device," Ben explained. "An ancient Greek astronomical computer. But more than an analog calculator—it was centuries ahead of its time, a device so precise that its existence didn't make sense for the era."

Liam frowned, scribbling the translation onto his legal pad. "So, the signal points us to the sudden emergence of an impossibly advanced machine?"

Gina, flipping through one of the old files they liberated from the archival records, nodded. "It fits with the pattern. What's next?"

Liam continued decoding, his fingers tapping rapidly against the keyboard. Another sequence appeared. "1250 AD."

Ben inhaled sharply. "That's the 'Time's Covenant.' The year European clockmakers produced the first true mechanical escapement, the foundation of modern timekeeping."

Gina crossed her arms, glancing between them. "You're saying the same signal that pointed us to an ancient analog computer also aligns with the birth of precision timekeeping?"

Liam's pulse quickened. "It doesn't stop there." He entered another fragment of the transmission, isolating the embedded patterns. "1969 AD."

Ben didn't need to think long. "Digital Dawn," he murmured. "That's the year ARPANET launched: the predecessor to the internet."

Gina interrupted, her skepticism wavering as she stared at the collected data. "Okay, I don't like this," she muttered. "These aren't random dates. These are the major shifts in human technology. The multi galactic code isn't just historical... it's predictive."

Liam sat back, staring at the screen as the final lines of code settled. His mind raced, assembling fragments faster than he could speak. "These signal patterns align with moments of massive change, not only technology, but political upheavals and cultural shifts."

Gina pressed forward, her voice low. "You're saying the signal influenced history?"

"More than influenced," Liam said. "Directed it. There are records, buried and classified, that describe sudden surges in human development. Moments where something seemed to accelerate progress without any clear origin."

Ben's brow tightened. "I've seen those reports. They never made sense. No root cause. Nothing to trace."

Liam nodded. "Because the cause was upstream. This signal, or something like it, might be designed to appear at critical points, seeding information, shaping events before they unfold."

Gina looked from Liam to Ben. "You mean it's been here before. This isn't a one-time contact."

"It's recurring," Liam said. "Cyclical, maybe even predictive. And if that's the case, it changes everything."

Ben crossed his arms. "So we've been walking a path we didn't choose. Mapped by something we don't understand."

"More like guided," Liam replied. "Quantum entanglement, time symmetry, we've seen particles respond to measurements that haven't happened yet. That principle might extend beyond particles. It might shape cognition, discovery, even society."

Gina's voice was careful. "A message encoded through time. Designed to appear only when humanity reaches a certain threshold."

Liam met her eyes. "It's not random. It's structured. This could be a blueprint—one meant to steer us."

The room fell quiet.

Ben exhaled slowly. "Then past, present, and future aren't separate. They're synchronized."

"And someone," Gina said, "intends to keep them that way."

No one spoke after that. The idea didn't feel abstract anymore. It felt close.

Liam hesitated before translating the final encoded sequence. His breath caught.

"2001 AD."

Ben rubbed his temples. "Cyber Threshold," he murmured. "The birth of quantum computing theory. The moment artificial intelligence stopped being a theory and started shaping the future."

The implications were unsettling. Every event had guided humanity's progress—mechanics, time, computation, and now... something more.

Gina, unable to resist the nagging feeling in her gut, accessed the computer console. "We need to verify. I'm checking the historical records."

She accessed multiple databases, her fingers flying across the screen as she searched for context on each date. The more she read, the more her expression darkened.

"Liam," she said slowly, turning the tablet toward him. "Look at this."

On the screen were records of technological breakthroughs as well as shifts in global power. Each event had been accompanied by political upheaval, unexplained financial disruptions, or scientific anomalies.

Ben exhaled sharply. "It's not only guiding us toward progress. It's engineering history."

Liam scanned through yet another classified file from the old Cold War archives. With every sentence, the picture grew darker.

Most of it was standard declassified noise: military reports, intercepted transmissions, nonsense about UFO sightings. But then he saw the memo.

His head started to spin as the facts solidified.

It was dated 1954.

It contained his name.

Liam Mills.

Right there, in a decades-old government document.

Gina noticed him freeze. "What is it?"

Liam had the look of a man who had seen a ghost. Only this time, he *was* the ghost. He didn't answer. He flipped the document toward her.

She frowned, scanning it quickly—then froze. "Liam... this isn't possible."

The memo was short and direct.

TOP SECRET – PROJECT ECHO

INTERCEPTED MESSAGE – 1954

"LIAM MILLS MUST FOLLOW THE PATH."

"BEN LEVINSON HOLDS THE KEY."

"DO NOT INTERFERE."

Ben also read the memo.

As he absorbed the weight of those chilling words, he involuntarily slipped back to a night long past—a night in the cold, forgotten corridors of a government archive. He remembered the dim glow of a single desk lamp illuminating rows of classified files of his mentor as he methodically erased documents that threatened to upend the balance of power. "Some truths are too dangerous to bear," his mentor had murmured, the sorrow in his voice etched permanently into Ben's soul. In that moment, the cost of forbidden knowledge had been made painfully clear.

Now, staring at the directive that intertwined his destiny with Mills', Ben felt that old burden resurface with a new urgency. His hardened features softened for a fraction of a second as he silently vowed, *"I will carry this weight, even if it means facing the darkness again."*

"Gina," Liam said firmly. "I want to check something." He grabbed the headset. "I'm going back to the records archive room. I'll let you know what I find. I have an idea." Liam set off to the archival files again with a renewed determination. Something was there. He had to find it.

Dust hung thick as Liam Mills navigated the dimly lit corridors of the old SETI archive. The odor of aged books, moldy paper, and the sour edge of mildew clung to every surface, undercut by the damp chill rising from the stone floor. Upon inception, SETI had access to the US military's 'Project Blue Book' files of unexplained phenomena. Rows of metal filing cabinets stretched endlessly in both directions, their surfaces coated in decades of neglect. He found what he was looking for in one of the old cabinets, almost as if he was being guided. He pulled open the rusty drawer with a protesting squeal. He paused, brushing away grime from a faded stencil on the metal frame: *RAF Chicksands – Signal Archive Transfer, 1962.* The name meant little to him at first, but something about it stirred an echo—like a half-remembered whisper from one of Ben's late-night briefings.

The faint hum of fluorescent lights buzzed overhead as he scanned a clipboard filled with handwritten codes and old project numbers. "Gina, I've got nothing in the digital logs," Liam muttered into his headset. "But there's a mention of analog transmissions from the 1950s—coded as 'Anomalous Morse.'"

Gina's voice crackled through the headset. "That's decades before the Andromeda signal. Why would it be flagged?"

"Exactly why I'm looking," Liam replied, stopping at a dusty filing cabinet labeled 'Morse Intercepts—1950-1960.' He yanked the drawer open, coughing as a cloud of dust billowed out.

He flipped through brittle folders until his fingers stopped on a log sheet marked 'Groom Lake—1955.'

Liam sat cross-legged on the cold floor, spreading the documents before him. The faded transcript included standard military check-ins—routine exchanges in Morse code—until an odd note in the margin caught his eye:

"Anomalous transmission. Interference?"

He scanned the transcribed dots and dashes. At first glance, it looked like noise—random bursts—but something about it tugged at his subconscious. He recognized the pattern.

His heart pounded as he pulled up a modern transcript of the Andromeda signal on his tablet and overlaid it with the 1955 code. The alignment wasn't chance. Something had been encoded across time.

The two patterns aligned—imperfectly, but unmistakably.

"Gina, you're not going to believe this," Liam croaked. "The Andromeda signal—it's connected to a 1955 Groom Lake transmission."

Gina hesitated before answering. "That's impossible. That would mean..."

"...Someone initiated the signal from Earth," Liam cut in, "before we ever picked it up."

There was a long pause. Then Gina asked, "Whose call sign was on the 1955 log?"

Liam squinted at the fading ink.

Rustand, T.

His stomach dropped.

"Tim Rustand," Liam whispered. "My grandfather."

A cold shiver ran down Liam's spine.

Gina swallowed. "Someone knew we'd be here. Seventy years ago."

Liam responded. "Yeah, maybe. But it raises another huge question: how did an answer to a seventy-year old signal get responded to in the ancient past, from another galaxy?"

* * *

Liam sat alone in the SETI archive's dusty backroom, the old 1955 transmission logs spread around him like the shards of a broken mirror. His head was spinning as he replayed the realization over and over: His grandfather was part of this. He triggered it.

The old transmission had to be a starting point.

Liam closed his eyes, overwhelmed by the weight of legacy and inevitability. "He didn't trigger the loop. The loop triggered him."

A cold shiver ran through Liam as he stared at the old notebook. The clue—etched decades ago—was not merely a bureaucratic anomaly but a silent directive woven into his lineage. He recalled secrets from his youth, stories his grandfather had once imparted about hidden paths and cryptic signals. Every clandestine conversation, every coded instruction from those formative days converged into a singular, inescapable truth. Liam stared down at the memo, its typewritten ink half-faded but unmistakable. The paper felt too warm in his hand. He hadn't stumbled here by chance. That much was clear now. Each step, each signal, each echo from his grandfather's stories, all of it had led him to this file.

Not fate. Design.

Liam made his way back to the group as he pondered these details.

This was no random document. It was a forewarning, a carefully laid cornerstone of destiny, confirming that his life had been meticulously guided from before he even knew it.

But the circular logic of his grandfather's 1955 trigger being responded to in the ancient past made his mind reel.

He entered the room, where he saw Gina and Ben in a heated debate.

"You know that MIT confirmed quantum time-reflection, right?" Gina added. "They bounced particles backward in time, like a mirror, but for causality. If waves can do it, so can messages."

Ben was coming around in agreement. "Yes, I read that study. Even the physicists now admit time can fold back on itself.

So truth, also, doesn't move in one direction. It reflects, like memory."

Liam cleared his throat, and they both looked up. Gina was spinning the Montblanc slowly between her fingers, its cap clicking softly as if keeping time with her breath. It was a quiet tic she didn't even notice anymore. Mildly annoying but in a cute way, thought Liam, as he settled at his workstation and joined the discussion.

"That's what MIT's time-reflection experiment showed. They reversed particle trajectories like mirrors in time. If that's possible, it may explain the echo patterns we're seeing."

Before they could process and further discuss the full extent of their discovery, Liam's screen stuttered. His heart sank as an alert flashed across his terminal.

Unauthorized Query Detected.

Remote Monitoring Initiated.

They weren't searching alone. Somewhere, without notice, in the hidden corridors of power, the Continuum was watching.

Gina gripped the Montblanc still clipped to her collar, thumb tapping the barrel. Once. Twice. Then she stepped back. She stared at the screen and slowly backed away, as if it was a dangerous animal ready to pounce. She decided a hot cup of tea was the best way to regroup. "Guys, I need a break." And with that, Gina opened her top drawer and gingerly extracted a chamomile teabag, placed it in her NASA mug, and headed to the breakroom to heat some water.

Liam and Ben nodded and resumed their code breaking efforts.

* * *

Still shaken from the night's chaos, Gina moved toward a broad window overlooking the Nevada desert, seeking comfort in the silent language of the stars. She held the hot cup of chamomile tea, the steam carrying a soft scent of flowers and herbs. It mixed with the faint smell of old paper and dust. She opened her battered notebook, the one that had belonged to her brother Mateo. Inside were star maps, equations, and rushed notes, each one holding a piece of the bond they once shared.

In the quiet that followed the day's frantic revelations, Gina's thoughts wandered back to Mateo's relentless quest for hidden truths—a quest that had cost him everything. Every carefully charted constellation and every numerical anomaly now seemed imbued with a bittersweet echo of his voice, urging her to look deeper. As she traced a delicate diagram with a fingertip, she murmured softly in Spanish, a habit borne of moments when logic and emotion collided, when the need for understanding overwhelmed her usual skepticism.

The old NASA patch pressed into her notebook wasn't just nostalgia. It was armor, a reminder of why Mateo's work had been buried. Flipping slowly through the pages, she followed his star maps like a trail left behind in fading ink. Part of her wanted to tear them apart, prove they were nothing but scribbles. But the quieter part, the grieving part, was beginning to believe he'd been on to something. That whisper came again, almost too faint to trust: You're close.

She didn't know which voice to believe. But she knew she'd follow it.

* * *

Undisclosed Continuum Complex, Undisclosed Time

The room's atmosphere grew even more tense as a shadowy figure appeared on the secure video feed. The screen displayed only a silhouette, the voice distorted but commanding

"You've requested escalation," the voice intoned. "Explain."

Keller stepped forward, his tone firm. "The team at SETI has made significant progress on the artifact's sequences. They're uncovering patterns—likely dates. If they decode these fully, it could lead to... complications."

"Complications," the voice repeated, almost mockingly.

Ramos exhaled through his teeth. "I don't like this," he muttered. "Signals don't show up early unless something's backdating them."

Patel interjected, her voice measured. "They're scientists, sir. They're not aware of the implications. If we intervene now, we risk tipping them off to the artifact's broader significance."

Keller felt his gut twist. The way she said it. "Broader significance." It implied even she didn't fully grasp it. He sure didn't.

The figure on the screen remained silent for a beat before speaking. "And if we don't?"

"They could stumble onto something critical," Keller replied.

"Something we've spent decades suppressing."

The voice was quiet for a moment. Then it asked the question that made Keller's stomach turn.

"Do you understand what they are actually uncovering, Agent Keller?"

Keller hesitated. He should have said yes. He was supposed to have all the answers.

But he didn't.

* * *

Elias Keller rubbed his temple as the transmission ended, leaving nothing but the dull glow of the encrypted screen. The incoming intel from SETI was a concern, but the next message that materialized was puzzling.

PROCEED WITH CAUTION.

The words reverberated.

It didn't sit right.

Keller had spent decades ensuring that some truths never saw the light of day. He had buried technology before its time, erased whistleblowers who got too close, and ensured that the world's delicate balance remained undisturbed.

But this wasn't a military breakthrough.

This wasn't stolen nuclear intel or an intercepted diplomatic cable.

This was older.

Something was twisting in his gut.

Patel stepped closer. "Orders, sir?"

Keller stared at the flickering monitor. His reflection looked back at him—eyes tired, jaw set.

For the first time in years, he wasn't sure what the right move was.

"Ramos," he proceeded in a calculating tone, "that message... who authorized it?"

Ramos frowned, scrolling through the encrypted logs. "It looks like it came from high command. Direct Continuum relay."

Keller's pulse quickened. "That's impossible. High command issues don't just appear without clearance."

Ramos hesitated. "Well, here's the weird part. The system registered it before we even gave the order."

A cold wave ran through Keller's chest.

"That's not possible," Patel said, stepping closer. "We would've seen the draft before it was sent."

"No draft," Ramos confirmed, his expression darkening. "No approval chain. Just... there."

Silence settled over the room.

Keller swallowed. “Run a deep trace on that relay.”

Patel didn’t respond immediately. For the first time, doubt shone behind her eyes.

Ramos hesitated. “If it came from high command, that could flag...”

“I don’t care.” Keller cut him off. “I said *run the trace.* If it flags something, I’ll take the heat.”

A few keystrokes later, the screen glowed.

Lines of data scrolled past at breakneck speed, decrypting layer after layer. Then, abruptly, the search stopped.

The source of the message?

Unknown.

Patel’s face paled. “Keller... what in the world is this?”

Ramos looked between them. “Sir, if high command didn’t send the warning... then who did?”

Keller didn’t answer. Because he already knew.

Keller steadied his breath. He needed to think. There had to be a way out. He scrolled further through the classified termination logs; dozens of names, scheduled for deletion long before they even became a problem.

But one entry caught his eye.

"Directive Override: N. Graves" Status: Nonexistent

His blood ran cold. Nathan Graves.

Graves had been one of the best operatives Keller had ever known. A loyal Continuum strategist. And he had disappeared a year ago. The official report said retirement. Keller pulled up the associated file. The log had no time stamps. No source. Except for one line. "Correction underway." Keller stared at the words. The same realization chilling his own blood had come to someone before him. And yet, Graves was gone. Wiped from every record, every trace of existence.

And then...

The screen blinked out as the facility's lockdown engaged.

The silence pressed against him, heavier than any order he had ever given or followed.

His hand tightened into a fist. Not in anger—in survival.

He turned back to the terminal, searching for any trace of his own authority. His clearance codes. His directives. Something.

A sinking dread filled his chest. He scrolled further down the classified logs, finger tightening over the keyboard, as he stared at his screen.

More names. More erasures.

Directive Override: L. Calloway – Status: Nonexistent
Directive Override: D. Wu – Status: Nonexistent
Directive Override: H. J. Patel – Status: Nonexistent
Directive Override: E. Ramirez – Status: Nonexistent
Directive Override: P. Farley – Status: Nonexistent

One after another. Dozens. Hundreds. All of them former high-ranking agents, just like him. Every single one marked for "Phase Correction."

His breath came in shallow gasps. They were all being targeted.

ACCESS DENIED.

He tried again—this time, using the highest clearance he had ever been granted.

ACCOUNT NOT FOUND.

This wasn't a malfunction.

Keller inhaled slowly. He wasn't being locked out. The screen surged, data scrolling past at a breakneck pace. The list of operatives was reducing in real-time. One name after another disappearing, overwritten.

And then—The final name on the screen.

KELLER, ELIAS – PHASE CORRECTION SCHEDULED

A date. Today. His files—his existence—were being erased. This wasn't an isolated betrayal. This was a cycle.

Keller felt something cold settle in his gut.

It was a systemic execution.

And he was next.

"Not yet," he admitted, keeping his tone neutral.

At that moment, almost reading Keller's mind, came a voice message from the computer network:

"Agents—it seems that the computer system has your attention. Your future depends on what you do—or don't do—next, as does ours. The choice is yours of course, but the Continuum would prefer a future with you in it." The disembodied voice continued. "Now let me enlighten you all. What Mills and his team are chasing is not merely an old message. It is an old system. A system that has been guiding human progress for centuries. A system we control. A system that must remain unseen. It is our hope that you are all properly motivated."

Keller's blood ran cold.

In that stark moment, Keller's mind involuntarily drifted back to a time when his orders had been absolute—a memory seared into him from his early days in covert operations. He recalled a cold, sterile command center where his younger self had hesitated before approving a mission that, despite its calculated necessity, had led to unintended casualties. The faces of those lost, blurred by time yet indelibly etched in his conscience, surged back with unrelenting clarity. For a heartbeat, the hardened lines on his face softened with regret as he silently vowed, "I will not let our pursuit of control drown out what is right." That memory, bitter and unavoidable, now intertwined with the present threat, shaking the foundation of his belief in the Continuum's infallibility.

"A system?" Patel echoed, shifting in her seat. "What kind of system?"

"A self-correcting one," the voice replied. "One that does not tolerate interference."

A heavy silence settled over the room.

"You will act," the voice finally said. "Deliver a warning—enough to make them pause. If they persist, we'll proceed to Phase Two."

Keller's eyes drifted over the streams of data, his expression darkening with a growing unease. "They claim our duty is to preserve the timeline," he murmured under his breath, "but what if our orders are only the surface of a far deeper manipulation?" He recalled classified files—whispered hints of anomalies where shifts in policy, war, and technology all aligned with inexplicable precision. In that quiet instant, Keller wondered if ancient knowledge were ordering events long before the Continuum even took shape. It wasn't merely about containment; it was about controlling a force that might have been shaping history from behind the scenes all along. The project revolved around the identification of "Keystone Individuals." People who, through their actions, could drastically alter historical trajectories.

In the dim glow of the operations center, Keller's gaze flicked between the directive and the quiet hum of data. The pattern was too clean. Too deliberate; buried deep within classified files, where seemingly unrelated discoveries, policy shifts, and even wars had unfolded with unnerving synchronicity.

Keller's mind raced as he processed the order. In that fleeting moment, he recalled the Continuum's cryptic doctrine—an idea that had always been as unsettling as it was compelling. Despite the order's vagueness, Keller understood its core intent: to preserve the integrity of history. The Continuum feared the signal could unseat the delicate balance of progress. Their directive, ambiguous as it was, aimed to prevent a "temporal collapse"—a scenario where unsanctioned innovations could ripple backward and forward through time, destabilizing the fabric of human progress. For Keller, the order now resonated with a singular purpose: to contain this threat and maintain a "correct" timeline, even if it meant operating in the shadows of moral ambiguity.

Keller's throat was dry. "And what does Phase Two involve?"

The voice didn't answer directly.

"Containment. At all costs."

The feed cut out, leaving the three agents in a suffocating silence.

III

Act III: The Continuum Pushes Back (Suppression Layer)

Curiosity has a cost.
The deeper they dig, the more reality begins to warp.
Shadows close in. Familiar ground feels unstable.
And some memories refuse to stay buried. This isn't just a puzzle anymore.
Something, or someone, is pushing back.

14

Lock: Desert Escape

SETI Outpost near Groom Lake, Nevada – Friday, 1018 Hours

Inside the poorly lit operations room, the only sound was the steady, low hum of multiple monitors that cast a pale glow over the cramped space. Shadows danced along the walls as if echoing the silent tension that filled the air. Liam sat at his terminal, his breathing slow and deliberate, yet every measured exhale belied the frantic pounding of his heart. On the screen before him, a single line of stark text had frozen in place; a message that delivered its verdict without a hint of remorse.

Stop.

The unchanging words reverberated in the silence, and for a moment, the room felt as if it were suspended in time.

Ben, leaning against a cluttered desk piled high with cables and discarded notes, exhaled through his nose. His fingers began tapping an anxious, uneven rhythm on the surface, as if he were trying to match the irregular beat of his own rising dread.

"I hate that. I hate that more than I can put into words," Liam murmured, voice low and heavy with regret.

Gina, eyes fixed on the screen, echoed his sentiment with a cautious inquiry. "Stop what?" she asked. Her voice didn't match her eyes.

Liam's jaw tightened, as he weathered a storm of conflicted instincts. His fingers hovered above the keyboard, yearning to pry deeper into the encrypted message, to tear apart the digital veil that now shielded unknown threats. But an uneasy intuition held him back; a gut feeling that delving further would awaken more than mere lines of code. It would summon a presence far more sinister.

"Wait. This is off, somehow. We need to go," he declared abruptly, his voice cutting through the oppressive silence like a clarion call. The statement, simple yet forceful, left no room for negotiation.

Ben's reaction was instantaneous; a look of incredulity and shock contorting his features. "Go? You're the one who punched through a classified warning message to prove a point. Now you back off? You couldn't have thought this through?" he demanded, his tone laced with both frustration and disbelief.

Liam's eyes flashed with determination as he countered, "No. I'm saying we need to leave. Physically. Like right this minute." His words were loaded with urgency, a silent acknowledgment that time was slipping away.

Turning toward Gina, Liam continued, "Shut down everything. Wipe the local drives and grab your thumb drive. If we don't..." He never finished the sentence.

Without warning, the lights dropped. Every monitor crashed. Then, one screen glowed white. Plain text appeared, flashing once before it held steady.

Echo Confirmed. Do Not Interfere.

Gina stepped back slowly. "That's not a system error." Liam didn't blink. "It's a response."

Without warning, Liam's UTC monitor clock rolled 10:18:07... 10:18:01... 10:18:13.

Gina's brow knit. "Whoa... time stamps don't moon-walk," she muttered, tapping the glass.

And then all Hades broke loose.

The fluorescent tubes flickered and stuttered, brightness snapping offbeat like a skipping record.

Before anyone could respond, a deep pop punched through the room.

The aging UPS cabinet in the corner blew a capacitor; a blue-white flash, then a concussion that shoved hot air and ceramic shrapnel across the lab.

Gina flew sideways, smashing shoulder-first into a rack of scope probes. Metal clattered. She crumpled, breath knocked out of her.

"Gina!" Liam slid on his knees, catching her before she hit the floor. The sharp tang of ozone filled his nose.

Ben yanked the wall power, killing every console but one CCTV monitor still connected to an internal battery. Its image jittered; then froze, double-exposed: two Ginas, one upright, one mid-air, fused for a single, surreal frame. "That was a ripple. I fear the full and impending 'time tsunami' may arrive later. At least, that's what our umbra signal seems to indicate."

Gina came to, and winced. "Why are we still in warm up? We... we haven't powered the dish yet, have we?" She was disoriented and didn't have a clue what time sequence she was occupying. "Temporal vertigo..." Ben muttered, "...what I imagine would follow a micro-rift in space-time." He reflected on redacted World War Two files, Liam's connecting of rather significant dots, and continued to think.

Liam helped her sit against the rack, shoulder already swelling. "You're here; right now. Stay with me." He tore a strip of cloth from his shirt, jury-rigging a sling. "Ben, grab that SD card."

Ben popped the tiny card from the CCTV recorder and slipped it into a shielded pouch. "Proof in our pocket."

Emergency relays somewhere in the compound chattered back to life; another minute, maybe less, before backup power restored full illumination.

"Up," Liam hissed, bracing Gina. She bit back a yell, teeth gritted and pushed to her feet.

They had blood on the floor, smoke in the air, and a ghost frame that indicated the future was already leaking into the present. That was all the evidence they needed. More than enough reason to run. His instructions were cut off as the overhead security lights glared ominously.

Without waiting, Ben rose from his seat. His actions measured and intentional as he placed his half-finished cup of coffee on the desk with a clatter, too loud in the silence. "Oy. We're officially way past 'cryptic warnings' and into 'bad movie foreshadowing,'" he quipped, though his eyes betrayed his mounting anxiety.

Liam sensed the impending danger and grabbed the hard drive recorder from the desk, shoving it into his bag with a force that underscored his resolve. "We need to grab all the digital recording devices we can and get out of here. Whatever we triggered isn't waiting for us to figure out the next step," he said, his voice carrying the finality of a last command.

From somewhere beyond the thick walls of their hideout, the distant whine of approaching vehicles sliced through the stillness of the night. In that instant, Gina's expression hardened into one of steely determination. "Yeah. We're leaving."

With brisk efficiency, she yanked the power cord from her terminal, grabbed her bag, and made a beeline for the exit, her steps echoing with urgency.

Liam hurried to catch up, shoving his laptop under his arm as if it were a precious relic of secrets and survival. As he pushed open the emergency exit door, the cool, crisp desert air slapped him in the face; a stark reminder of the harsh reality beyond the safe haven.

They all sprinted from the building, following Liam. Without hesitation, he uttered a single name, the syllables of which carried both hope and risk.

"Sparky."

The name spilled from his lips, a lifeline to a man whose reputation for disappearing into the labyrinth of digital shadows was legendary.

Gina paused, hands on knees and catching her breath, a puzzled frown tugging at her features. "Who is Sparky?" she puffed, her tone a mix of curiosity and apprehension.

Ben, wheezing and struggling to catch up, let out a derisive scoff. "Maybe Sparky is a *WHAT*, eh?" he breathed, only to be met with a sharp, disapproving frown from Gina.

Liam's response was terse and resolute as he stepped into the open night. "Someone who hates being found even more than we do. And he may be in town." With that final statement, the trio melted into the enveloping darkness, leaving behind the sanctuary of their compromised hideout.

15

Cipher: Sparky's Solace

Nevada Desert – Friday, 1818 Hours

Behind them, as if in a final act of defiance, SETI's backup power kicked into life with a low, mechanical thrum.

The sudden surge of energy illuminated the facility's perimeter with a fleeting, artificial glow. However, by the time the first agents breached the compound's fortified entrance, Liam, Gina, and Ben were already nothing more than shadows in the night. The group had taken temporary shelter in a small storage shed as they gathered their thoughts, discussed a plan, and watched what was unfolding.

The shelter reeked of dry soil and chemical mulch, cluttered with cracked pots, rusting tools, and a bag of split manure. They didn't speak much. Liam kept his eyes on the glow of his laptop screen, his fingers twitching as if already typing out a plan. Gina paced. Ben peered through a gap in the boards. His glasses slipped as he craned forward, and he nudged them back with a habitual motion; tracking movement outside with barely concealed anxiety. Their options were shrinking by the second, and none of them liked how tight the corners were getting.

Finally, Liam closed the laptop and looked up. No smile, only a quiet resolve in his expression. The others didn't fully understand who they were trusting next, only that Liam did; and right now, that had to be enough. They didn't know Sparky. But Liam did. Somewhere out there was a man who didn't want to be found, who lived off the grid by instinct and by design. And if they had any shot at surviving what came next, it would be because Liam could bring him into the fold; whether Sparky liked it or not.

* * *

The desert stretched out in an endless canvas of inky blackness as Liam, Gina, and Ben fled the dilapidated building and raced across the cracked pavement of an abandoned service lot. Their footsteps, quick and determined, were swallowed by the vastness of the night, merging with the mournful howls of a wind intent on erasing all traces of their passage. The intermittent glow from SETI's emergency backup power danced on the horizon, casting long, distorted shadows that wavered like specters in the periphery of their vision.

Liam's mind raced furiously; faster than his legs could carry him. The awareness of the looming threat pressed on him with relentless intensity; they had mere minutes, perhaps even seconds, before their pursuers closed in. Every detail in his head recalibrated to the urgency of the moment.

"We need a ride," Gina gasped between quick breaths, her voice competing with the wind's mournful cry. She adjusted the strap of her worn bag, the movement intentional as if she were preparing for a long escape. "Unless this 'Sparky' is waiting out here with a personal aircraft, we're out of options."

Without pausing to consider alternatives, Liam's response was brisk and assured. "We're heading to my old storage unit. There's a car there." His tone was a mix of practicality and hope; a plan formed under duress.

Ben, puffing and lagging behind yet refusing to yield, panted as he tried to keep pace. "And tell me, what exactly makes this car less traceable than the one's left parked in a SETI lot?" His question was laced with a mix of sarcasm and the genuine concern of an old man beyond his prime; the weight of their predicament evident in every oxygen-starved syllable.

Liam's smirk was the only response he offered. "Because it's not in my name." The quip was delivered with the extreme confidence of someone who had no clue as to what was next. A reminder that sometimes the best offense was a well-hidden and oblivious offense.

They rounded the back of an abandoned service station, a relic of a bygone era, long overrun by dust and memories, located a few blocks from the beleaguered research facility. Liam produced a small, battered keyring from his pocket, his fingers working deftly as he unlocked a rusted steel door that guarded the entrance to his former storage unit. As the door creaked open, a wave of musty air, heavy with the scent of oil and forgotten time, hit them; a silent testament to years of neglect.

Inside, Gina's eyes adjusted to the dim interior. Before her sat an old Dodge Diplomat, matte black and enigmatic, its missing plates and thin layer of dust hinting at hurried preparations for a getaway that had never quite materialized. The car exuded a certain grim government-issue charm, as if it had witnessed countless military parades, escaped prisoners, and harbored secrets of its own.

Ben's fingers skimmed the dusty roof, and he let out a soft whistle. "Part of me thinks this is genius," he said, his words bouncing off the metal walls, "and the other part thinks it's pure trouble." Liam, already moving with purpose, barked, "I'll drive. You be concerned later." A slight edge of defiance in his tone as he reclaimed his focus on the task at hand.

Liam popped the hood without hesitation, revealing a battery already strapped in place. He reattached the leads with practiced efficiency, then moved to the rear, unscrewing the gas cap and pouring in a fresh reserve from a military-grade canister stashed beneath the tarp. His movements were calm, methodical, like someone who'd done this before, more than once, and under pressure. Within moments, the Dodge was alive with potential, as if it had been waiting for someone to wake it.

Gina slid into the passenger seat, her pulse thumping in her ears as she scanned the desolate horizon beyond the service station's broken windows. "We'd better move before they start scanning the area," she urged, her tone a blend of urgency and steely resolve.

Liam inserted the key into the ignition, and with a reluctant groan, the old Dodge Diplomat roared to life. A deep, throaty purr that embodied both the machine's age and its readiness for the chase. Shifting the car into gear, he eased away from the service lot, running lights off, and merged onto an unmarked road that snaked away from the old Listening Glass SETI outpost.

Liam's eyes scanned the endless stretch of dark roadway, and despite the adrenaline still pulsing in his veins, a cold certainty settled over him. "We might have slipped the immediate net," he thought, "but their reach remains—a silent, ever-tightening snare."

In that moment, the concepts of quantum entanglement and time-slippage, which had once been abstract theories, manifested as real, tracking threads connecting every step of their flight. Even as the desert swallowed their taillights, Liam stole a glance at the road stretching before them.

Gina, her tone a quiet but urgent murmur, "It won't be long before they catch up."

Every shadow on the roadside hinted at the possibility of a looming confrontation; a promise that the threat was far from over. Despite the momentary calm, an unsettling certainty crept in; this was merely a pause in the storm. Each quiet mile they drove deepened the illusion of safety, yet Liam knew their pursuers' reach extended far beyond mere sightlines.

In the silence that followed, Gina's steady gaze met his. "We have no idea how deep this rabbit hole runs; or how we'll handle it," she said.

Each mile marker that ticked by drew them closer to the next clash, and Liam felt the countdown to an unavoidable reckoning. The headlights remained off, cloaking their escape in secrecy and darkness, while behind them, the distant red-and-blue strobes of unmarked pursuit vehicles punctuated the periphery; a stark reminder that the hunt had truly begun.

* * *

The ancient Diplomat roared through the ink-black Nevada desert, slicing through deep midnight and carving a path in an endless darkness. Every crack in the asphalt rattled the car's old frame, echoing in the cramped cabin, blending with the low, persistent hum of the engine.

Ben closed his eyes and started reciting the evening Shema

Yisrael, as they all jostled over worn shocks. The crunch of gravel under tires were all that broke the tense silence, each sound a reminder of the stakes at hand.

In the quiet sanctuary of the car's dim cabin, Liam's fingers moved with practiced precision over the sat-phone's keys as he drove, bypassing layers of security like a well-rehearsed incantation. The device's matte surface intermingled the faint glow of the dashboard and moonlight. Liam reflected a fleeting glimpse of resolve as he dialed the sole number stored within.

After two measured rings, the line crackled to life, and a voice—cutting through the static with a deep, resonant, and wired timbre—spoke immediately.

"If this number is ringing, something is either very wrong or you're dying. Which is it?"

Liam was relieved, despite the storm of adrenaline coursing through him. "Sparky, I need a favor."

For a suspended heartbeat, the low rumble of the engine filled the silence. Then came the familiar gruffness on the other end. "Mills? You still alive? I had money on you being disappeared years ago." Sparky gave a short, conspiratorial chuckle. "Seriously, man, after what happened at Edwards, I figured you'd be trading ghost stories in an undisclosed CIA basement by now. Don't tell me you've actually joined the black helicopters crew?"

* * *

Marcus "Sparky" Adler was an odd friend, if ever there was one.

Sparky's life had always been a series of fragmented connections. Wires crossed, circuits completed, only to spark and fade. Raised in the dry, sun-bleached stretches of Nevada from age fourteen, he matured within arm's reach of the mysterious Nevada dessert, his father a silent cog in the Air Force's vast and secretive machinery. As a teen, Sparky would sit by the cracked windowsill of their modest home, listening to the faint hum of radio static that whispered through the desert air. He taught himself to find patterns where others heard only noise.

His father, a technician with classified clearance, never said much about his work, but the weight of secrets floated through the house like dust in sunlight. Occasionally, over coffee and the desert's eerie quiet, his father would murmur about things that "didn't quite fit," stories of electromagnetic distortions and experiments on resonance frequencies that disrupted radio communications across entire grids. These weren't the tales of flying saucers and alien encounters that conspiracy theorists devoured. No, his father spoke of classified studies on atmospheric anomalies, magnetic field fluctuations, and unexplained energy spikes; scientific oddities that the military kept buried deep within black files.

Sparky knew almost nothing of his mother. He was only five

when she left—but he heard rumors: an eccentric socialite who hosted midnight salons in Parlor C; poets debating quantum theory under gaslight, painters sketching fractal vistas. Fluent in six languages, she could recite entire odes by candlelight, and her laughter, warm and tinkling, left guests both enchanted and unsettled. Whispers told of burgundy-bound diaries from Mayflower ancestors, filled with undeciphered codes, and of weeks-long disappearances after which she'd reemerge in emerald silk or scarlet brocade with an outlandish tale. Then, one evening after a particularly lavish gathering, she stepped out onto the veranda and vanished; no farewell, no trace, and an unspoken hush fell over the household. Nobody mentioned her again, and the silver-sealed and very generous trust fund in his name remained the solitary proof that she'd ever existed.

Sparky's natural brilliance with electronics was evident early on. By sixteen, he was building signal jammers from scrap parts and hijacking local radio frequencies just to see if he could. He thrived in the chaotic dance of patterns, codes, and broken circuits; anything that defied the predictable. Enlisting in the Air Force was a calculated move, a way to get closer to the hidden truths that had teased the edges of his father's stories.

His nickname was born out of a near-disastrous incident during his Air Force days. While working on a prototype signal scrambler during a late-night shift, Sparky pushed the voltage beyond recommended levels; curious to see if he could boost its range. The device overloaded, a cascade of sparks erupting in the lab. Fire alarms blared, technicians scrambled, and the entire communications wing lost power for over six hours. When the smoke cleared, Sparky stood in the middle of the chaos, holding the charred remains of the scrambler, a sheepish grin on his face.

From that moment on, "Sparky" wasn't a nickname; it was a badge of honor, a reminder of his willingness to push the limits of what was possible. Even if it meant things occasionally exploded in his face.

Assigned to Air Force Intelligence, Sparky's skills flourished in the deep web of cryptography and surveillance tech. But digital warfare wasn't what caught his attention, it was the patterns beneath it all. In encrypted transmissions, in satellite data, he noticed anomalies: echoes of signals that shouldn't exist.

Not glitches. Intentional.

The breaking point came during his involvement in Project Echo, a classified initiative supposedly focused on foreign satellite interference. But buried deep within terabytes of scrambled data, Sparky found something else. Anomalous electromagnetic frequencies, buried codes within solar flare readings, and references to atmospheric resonance experiments conducted decades prior. One file referenced a date that tugged at something deep in his memory: June 14, 1955; the same date his father once mentioned in passing, his voice heavy with an emotion Sparky hadn't understood.

Digging deeper, he triggered something; a silent alarm in

the network's core. Within hours, his clearance was revoked. The next morning, the files he had seen were gone, scrubbed clean. His personal logs were wiped, and a quiet message made its way to his terminal: "Some questions should stay buried."

But Sparky couldn't let it go. The experience fractured his loyalty to the system that had once given him purpose. He disappeared into the desert, taking his knowledge, his paranoia, and the weight of his discoveries with him. Building hidden bunkers, living off-grid, and watching the shadowy networks from the outside became his new mission.

Over the years, Sparky focused on unearthing the scientific oddities his father hinted at; tracking unexplained seismic readings, atmospheric anomalies, and electromagnetic surges that mirrored the patterns he'd once decoded in Project Echo. Though he never spoke of it openly, he kept an ear tuned to the static, waiting for another anomaly to surface. There was a deeper architecture to everything; patterns hidden within the electromagnetic fields, frequencies that didn't follow natural laws, and anomalies that couldn't be dismissed as coincidence.

* * *

Ben leaned forward and intoned, "Who is this guy?"

Sparky's voice cut through with characteristic irreverence,

"The only person dumb enough to pick up when this idiot calls me after a decade." Sparky paused, then added dryly, "You know, I've dodged drones, black ops, and enough surveillance to fill a Pentagon dossier. Yet somehow, Mills, you're always in my blind spot." His tone was a cocktail of humor and nostalgia, a reminder of long-past escapades and grudges settled in the silence of shared history.

Liam wasted no time. "We need a place to lay low. Now. And I need your gear." His words, clipped and focused, conveyed serious urgency as the desert night pressed in around them.

A pause followed; a moment thick with unspoken questions. Sparky's tone shifted, edged with both caution and that trademark sarcasm. "First of all, how do you still have this number? Second, how do you know I'm even in Nevada?" Sparky paused uneasily, and added, "You know, ever since I left the Air Force, I've spent half my life erasing footprints. Every number, every move, hidden from the suits upstairs. Yet here you are, calling like it's poker night at Nellis."

A wry smile tugged at Liam's lips as he replied, "Because you're too paranoid to go anywhere else, and too stupid to sit still." The retort resonated in the silent void between them, an echo of their familiar banter that belied the danger lurking in every shadow.

For several heartbeats, the line held its silence until Sparky's voice returned, unexpectedly pragmatic, "You got a pen?" Liam and Ben looked at Gina and smiled, while she grinned and shook her head. The question, simple yet loaded with hidden meaning, hung in the air like a promise of secrets exchanged under the cover of night.

Gina reached into the glove compartment and pulled out a crumpled receipt, then fished a scratched-up translucent blue Bic from her back pocket—the kind handed out at trade shows, still stamped with a fading logo from some forgotten cybersecurity summit. She gave it a test scribble on her thumb, then flattened the paper against her knee. "Go ahead," she said, steady and ready, as Liam focused on the road ahead.

Over the crackle of the connection, Sparky began reciting a labyrinth of directions. His words painted a mosaic of landmarks instead of street names: a desolate water tower silhouetted against the night sky, a negligible rise in the terrain, a ridge that hid long-forgotten routes. "Follow it exactly. Don't improvise. You miss a turn, you don't find me." Sparky hesitated, then added sharply, "And watch your tail. The desert's crawling with drones and alphabet soup agencies. I've spent years dodging shadows, and I'd prefer not ending tonight with a bag over my head and a free ride back to Groom Lake." Each instruction was delivered with precision, as if the survival of both parties hinged on unwavering adherence to the coded roadmap.

Gina meticulously recorded each detail.

"Got it," she declared. A single affirmation sealing their pact under the watchful eyes of the cosmos.

A brief silence, heavy with the weight of shared history and impending risk, then came Sparky's dry chuckle, edged with a hint of menace. "And Mills? If you brought trouble to my door, I'm organizing a 'top secret' blanket party for you."

With that, the connection abruptly severed, leaving nothing but the soft afterglow of static and the distant murmur of the desert wind.

Gina held the receipt, now a coded map to a refuge only Sparky could provide.

"We're in," Liam declared, his tone a blend of determination and resigned acceptance of the dangers ahead. Then, without saying a word, Liam reached into his coat pocket, pulled out his SETI keycard, and—using the heels of his palms to maintain his grip on the steering wheel—snapped the card in two.

Gina raised an eyebrow. "That symbolic, or did you just cost yourself your job?"

"Both," he said, eyes on the road. "No more half-in."

Gina searched his face with a mix of skepticism and concern. "Where is 'in' exactly?"

"You tell me. You have the Spark-map."

Liam's grip on the steering wheel tightened as Gina called out markers while he navigated the sinuous, darkened pathway.

"I think Sparky's got a place near Tonopah. It's untraceable, unless you have a roadmap." He smiled. His words were crisp against the relentless night, and held the promise of sanctuary and peril of the unknown.

Ben exhaled sharply in the back seat, a wry smile showing, despite the gravity of the situation. "Fantastic. A paranoid ex-military hacker holed up in the middle of the desert. My day keeps getting better."

As the car sped deeper into the midnight void, the desert itself felt as if it was conspiring with their clandestine mission. The vast emptiness, punctuated by the shimmering mirage of distant lights, became both a silent accomplice and a treacherous adversary.

* * *

The safehouse wasn't a house at all.

Hidden beneath the Nevada dusk, a decommissioned Cold War surveillance station lay half-swallowed by shifting sands and a rugged ridge of rock. Its battered concrete walls and rusted metal remnants tied to secrets of a bygone era, a relic lost in time yet repurposed for a dangerous new life. From the outside, it might have been dismissed as another abandoned monument, but those who knew its history understood it was a fortress forged in the crucible of survival.

Liam maneuvered the battered Diplomat into the narrow, makeshift garage, the crunch of gravel under the tires punctuating the silence.

As he guided the car through the low-hanging entrance, the garage door swung open before he could even knock. There, in the dim light filtering through dusty skylights, stood Marcus "Sparky" Adler; his arms crossed with a casual defiance. Clad in a faded NASA hoodie splattered with grease stains and sporting cyber-enhanced goggles perched on his forehead, his dark, unruly curls and stubble framed an ebony-toned face etched with both mischief and the weight of countless secrets.

"Ah, if it isn't the dumbest smart guy I know," Sparky quipped as the three passengers climbed out, his voice a mix of amusement and exasperation as his eyes danced over Liam's weary smile.

The moment their boots hit the concrete, the smell hit them: dusty circuit boards, warm solder, and the faint, oily bite of old capacitors. A hint of burnt coffee lingered somewhere deeper inside, blending with the stubborn funk of a place that hadn't seen sunlight, or fresh air, in years.

Liam's lips curved into a wry grin. "And if it isn't the most paranoid genius alive. Always on high alert, are we, Sparky?"

With a quick flourish, Sparky stepped aside, waving them deeper into the sanctuary. "No time for pleasantries. You two just torched your entire digital footprint. How you pulled that off? Way above my pay grade." He slapped the garage door button, and the metal panel began to descend with a mechanical groan.

"But," Sparky mused, "that means either you stumbled upon something earth-shatteringly insane or you pulled off a move so reckless it defies logic. Either way, I want in."

Liam chuckled. "Gina and Ben, meet Marcus Adler. Though he hasn't used that name since before our military service days. Everyone just calls him Sparky."

Sparky gave a two-finger tap to his temple. "Name stuck after an... *incident* involving a blown circuit and a very expensive misunderstanding." He grinned. "Long story. Classified. Possibly still frowned upon."

Gina, ever the skeptic, raised an arched eye brow as she surveyed the cramped space cluttered with outdated tech and tangled cables. "Do you always invite fugitives into your secret bunker, or is it only for the particularly interesting ones?"

Sparky's grin broadened, his eyes gleaming with a dangerous delight. "Only the interesting ones. Trust me, you're in for a ride." Sparky motioned around his cluttered bunker dramatically. "Welcome to Casa Sparky. Fully shielded from EMPs, satellite scans, and government brain wave readers. If you see tinfoil hats, grab one. They're standard issue around here."

"But exactly why would you do this?" Gina pressed.

"You want the real reason?" Sparky asked, rapping the desk with a knuckle as the monitors hummed. "Back when we were still wearing uniforms, Liam and I were assigned to the same ISR analysis team. Midway Station, 2010. We got handed a Tier-3 intercept flagged as a threat escalation in the Caucasus. Turned out the feed was corrupted, intentionally."

They made their way inside, and Sparky plunked down into a worn leather chair.

"Higher-ups wanted a justification for asset deployment. I was ready to file it. Liam pulled me aside, told me to shut it down. Said if the wrong eyes saw it, someone innocent was going to vanish."

He leaned back, rocking. "Liam saved my neck, and maybe someone else's. So yeah, when I saw his name flagged in a data spike last week, I knew it was a matter of time until my bat-phone rang. I owe him."

The bunker's interior pulsed with a low hum; an ambient chorus of whirring servers and encrypted satellite links that gave life to every hidden corner. Yet this symphony of digital defense was abruptly shattered by a sharp, unexpected ping, slicing through the background noise like a warning shot.

In an instant, the atmosphere shifted. Sparky's head jerked around in his creaking swivel chair, his gaze snapping across an array of monitors. "Hold on..." he murmured, almost to himself, as his fingers flew over the keyboard in a blur of precise keystrokes.

Liam leaned forward, his brow furrowing with concern. "What's wrong?" He stared at the terminal readout, absently reaching for a pencil on the desk. With two sharp tap–taps against the metal console, he let the sound fill the charged silence.

Sparky turned his head slightly, just enough to notice. "You still do that, bro?"

Liam blinked. "Do what?"

"The taps. Morse for trouble. You used to do that every time a mission went sideways at Raqqa."

Liam cracked a dry smile. "Guess it stuck. Like a reflex that never got the memo after we PCS'd."

Sparky gave a small snort. "Let me know if it ever starts tapping back. That's when I'm bailing."

Liam agreed. "Deal."

* * *

Sparky, his eyes, already focused, grew even more intense as one terminal flashed with erratic data streams; an alarming cascade of numbers and symbols that spelled trouble. The silence was punctuated by the rapid clatter of keys and the soft, ominous beeping of the machines.

Ben, ever the joker even in tense moments, couldn't help but comment as he peered over Sparky's shoulder. "Well, that's comforting. Our genius just made the same face my bubbe did when the brisket burned."

Sparky exhaled slowly, his demeanor shifting from playful to focused as he rotated the screen to face the group. The image revealed an external breach attempt; an intrusion that snaked its way through layers of encryption. "They're on to us," he stated flatly. "Not yet in our system, but someone's poking around... it's a dedicated trace coming in hot from way too many government nodes. It's a signature move." His expression darkened as he typed rapidly. "This smells exactly like Eglin AFB all over again. Trust me... when this many government agencies synchronize, it's never good. Black budget stuff makes Area 51 look like a weekend barbecue."

Gina's face drained of color, her voice tight with anxiety. "They found us?"

Sparky's fingers hammered across the keyboard, his shoulders hunched and jaw tight. "Okay. Dead zones just lit up. They've got partial pings on six nodes."

Liam moved to the monitor beside him, repeating Gina's question, "So... *does* that mean they've found us?"

"Not exactly," Sparky said, eyes flicking left and right. "But they're running proximity threads. If we stay on this line, they'll guess right sooner than we want."

Ben leaned in. "How fast?"

"Fast enough. I rerouted through a few shell proxies, but whoever's chasing us has some serious teeth. This isn't script-kiddie level. This feels like Continuum code."

Liam's face hardened. "Keller."

"Who is Keller?" Gina blurted.

Liam didn't look up. "Keller was military intel, deep shadow ops. We crossed paths years ago. Never got along. He ran Black Ops programs, knew how to disappear people, and thought the rest of us were reckless. He and Sparky butted heads more than once, and I wasn't exactly on his holiday card list either."

Sparky scoffed. "That's your theory. And sure, maybe he's back in the mix. But whoever it is, they're using infrastructure Keller used to touch. That's more than coincidence."

Ben crossed his arms. "How would they even know where to start?"

"Because we're predictable," Sparky snapped. "We like the same dirty tricks. Legacy systems, dead fiber, old ports nobody checks anymore. Problem is, somebody started checking."

Gina's voice cut through. "What are our options?"

"We ghost," Sparky said. "I'll scramble a burst loop through Montana. It'll buy us twenty minutes. If they bite."

"And if they don't?" she asked.

"Then we move again. Fast." His hands paused briefly over the keys. "One of their sweeps just sniffed a dormant subnet I used back when I was still pretending to be a government employee. It was clean for years."

Liam leaned in closer. "So they're not just chasing us. They're unraveling the whole thread."

Sparky nodded. "Backtracing every contact, every footprint. They're looking for origin, not only destination."

Ben muttered, "So... Keller's chasing us—AND—he's studying us."

The screen flashed. Sparky grinned without humor. "Too late for subtle." He slammed the return key. "Alright. Let's give them a ghost to chase."

Liam's stomach churned as the letters on the screen next resolved into something all too familiar: *Elias Keller.*

A name. That same name. Again.

"Sure enough—we were right," Liam intoned.

When "Elias Keller" blinked onto his monitor, even Sparky's trademark steel gaze fractured; he let out a gasp.

"Well, I guess our next startup's going to be tinfoil-hat futures," he blurted, half-laughing, half-panicking.

In that moment, memories of his own dark past surged up unbidden. He recalled a night in a cramped government communications room; his younger self, face bathed in the cold blue light of glimmering screens, listening as alarms blared in the background. He saw, as if through a haze of time, his father's quiet dignity being ripped away by shadowy officials after a daring hack had exposed secrets no one should know. That bitter loss had sculpted an unwavering resolve to remain free, even as the world sought to control him.

As Keller's name burned on the screen, the brutal truth hit him: they had become prey. Sparky's lips tightened into a grim line. "They've always been watching," he muttered quietly, as if the echo of his past fueled his determination to shield his new-found family from the forces that had once shattered his world.

A moment of stunned silence enveloped the safehouse, interrupted by the relentless blinking of a cursor that mocked their predicament. Sparky let out a low whistle, a mix of admiration and irony in his tone. "Looks like you made yourself a new best friend, Liam."

Liam's eyes hardened, the weight of old grudges settling over him. "Not *exactly* a friend... Keller's probably been watching us since the beginning, lurking in the shadows. It makes sense that he's involved."

The group exchanged glances heavy with unspoken resolve. In that cramped, secretive space, the reality of their situation crystallized into a single, urgent truth: the chase wasn't over. It had only begun, and every heartbeat in the bunker was a countdown to the next move.

As the digital trail pulsed on the screen, each of them braced for the inevitable confrontation. The safe haven beneath the Nevada sands was more than a refuge, it was the launching pad for a counterstrike, a fight against an unseen enemy whose presence was now unmistakable. The tension was palpable, and with every keystroke and word, they prepared to step deeper into the unknown.

* * *

The tension in the bunker hung thick as Liam, Gina, and Ben stood behind Sparky, eyes locked on the glowing monitors that revealed Keller's trace attempt. The name alone was enough to put everyone on edge; Keller made problems disappear. And now, they were his problem.

Liam leaned against the table; jaw tight. "How much time do we have before they pinpoint this location?"

Sparky let out a low whistle, still typing. “If Keller’s working solo? A few days. If he’s got full Continuum resources? We could be looking at hours.”

“Of course, that’s above my pay grade,” he added with a grin, fingers still dancing across the keyboard.

Ben groaned and rubbed his temples. “Oy vey. We just got here, and we’re running again, already? I should have packed my running shoes.”

Sparky turned in his chair, raising an eyebrow. “Relax, old man. Take a breath and have a little faith in me. If I thought we were toast, I wouldn’t be wasting time with diagnostics.” He gestured to another monitor, one that displayed a network of data nodes overlaying a historical timeline. “You came here to figure out what’s buried in this Andromeda code. So, let’s crack it before they do.” Ben exhaled, eased back into his chair, and nodded. He was ready to trust this peculiar kid’s plan.

Liam relaxed, glancing at Gina, who gave him a subtle nod. They had come too far to stop now.

Gina crossed her arms. “You’ve got everything we pulled from SETI’s servers?”

Sparky smirked and gestured around the room. “You think I let you bring that heat to my doorstep without vacuum-sealing it first? I ran your data through three isolated systems before it even touched my mainframe.” He tapped a key, and the screen flickered. "Now, let's see what's got the big dogs so nervous."

* * *

The display shifted, revealing a sequence of encoded historical markers; a list of years, each tied to a major leap in technological progress.

Liam's brow furrowed as he scanned the data. "These dates... they do more than mark discoveries." He tapped the screen. "They mark inflection points."

Gina leaned in, reading through the list.

- 150 BC – The Antikythera Mechanism (First known analog computer)
- 1250 AD – The Verge Escapement Clock (Birth of precise mechanical timekeeping)
- 1941 AD – Turing's Bombe (Breaking Enigma, early computational logic)
- 1969 AD – ARPANET (The birth of the Internet)
- 2001 AD – Quantum Computing Threshold

And then, at the bottom of the list, an entry that sent a chill down her spine:

- 2027 AD – Pending Event.

Ben swallowed. “So what do we think this ‘Pending Event’ means?”

Sparky’s fingers flew over the keyboard. “I was hoping one of you had an answer for that.”

Liam stepped forward. “Hold on. Let’s think this through logically.” He pointed to the screen. “These are more than discoveries. These are foundational shifts. Every single one of them redefined how humanity understood information, time, and computation.”

Gina nodded slowly. “The Antikythera Mechanism wasn’t *just* a device; it challenged the perception of ancient engineering. The Verge escapement clock wasn’t *just* a tool; it forced entire civilizations to standardize time.”

Ben’s voice was low. “Turing didn’t *just* crack codes. He laid the foundation for artificial intelligence.”

Sparky rocked back in his chair, nodding. “And ARPANET? That wasn’t *just* the start of the internet; it was the start of a global neural network.”

The room fell into silence.

Gina summarized. “Events in history.”

“And... these events demonstrate each date was not merely a marker of progress. It was a turning point, nudging humanity toward a destiny we were only *beginning* to comprehend.”

Sparky added.

Ben pensively chimed in. "Which means this looming 2027 date isn't any old random number... it's an irreversible historic change."

Liam's mind raced, his analytical training taking over. "Think about it. Sparky is right. Every one of these moments. They didn't just happen. There were always outside forces—*pushing* them along."

Ben frowned. "*Pushing* them?"

Liam nodded. "Yeah. Look at the Antikythera Mechanism. It was centuries ahead of its time. No other device like it existed before or after. It just... appeared. Then it was lost."

Gina's lips pressed into a thin line. "Same with the mechanical clock. Its design revolutionized navigation and science, but no one can say for sure where the earliest version even came from."

Sparky snapped his fingers. "And let's not forget good ol' Turing. The guy basically invented modern computing, but he wasn't the first to conceive the logic—that was Charles Babbage and his 1822 Difference Engine. But Turing's work built off multiple unnamed principles, stuff that should have taken decades longer to emerge."

"Mazel Tov, Rain Man. Thanks for that." Ben blustered.

Sparky squinted his eyes and kept quiet.

Liam's chest tightened. "What if these were more than milestones?" His voice was hushed now. "What if they were... *seeded*?"

The question lingered in the still air, unspoken thoughts stretching between them.

Gina gave a dry laugh and shook her head. "*Seeded*? You're telling me there is some kind of cosmic gardener, dropping *idea seeds* like it's prepping for harvest?"

Ben smirked—catching on, and adjusting his glasses. "More like a watchful chef. Picture someone nudging a soufflé to rise at just the right moment."

Sparky made a face. "So... we're *food* now?"

"No," Ben said, chuckling, "not *food*. Timing. Influence. Think of how small nudges in history push things over the edge. A patent gets filed. A phrase gets spoken. A war doesn't start."

Liam leaned forward, resting his elbows on his knees. "Or a telescope just *happens* to be pointed at the right patch of sky and someone notices a signal we were never supposed to find."

Gina looked between them, clearly unconvinced. "You're making it sound like progress is part of a recipe. Someone mixes us up like batter and poof, we invent the radio."

"No poof," Ben replied. "More like a gentle correction. A quantum nudge. No breaking of any rules, just... folding the page differently."

Sparky nodded slowly. "Like stacking the deck, but only once in a while. Just enough to steer the hand."

Liam's expression darkened. "That's not guidance. That's interference."

"But what if it's neither?" Ben said. "Not interference. Not control. Just... alignment."

He continued with his train of thought. "Alignment always leaves a trail. Not of force, but of *pattern*. You don't nudge reality with a fist... you hum a frequency until something resonates."

No one spoke for a moment.

Then Liam blinked, as if catching a memory mid-thought. "At Groom Lake. That night. The code anomaly. The... echo."

Ben looked up sharply. "Maybe it was the same thing as this signal, eh?"

Liam nodded once. "Not a glitch. It felt too planned. Like someone pulled the curtain back, just for a second."

He glanced at Gina. "You said the signal has irregular gaps. What if they match the same pulse? What if time isn't just flowing one way?"

The silence returned, but this time it was heavier.

Sparky's voice was quiet. "So someone planted these ideas. In us. In everyone."

Ben looked at him, eyes narrowed. "Or maybe they're planting *us*."

Liam exhaled. "I'm saying they didn't happen in a vacuum. Every single technological leap came at the exact moment it was needed. Almost as if... someone made sure it happened."

Ben, who had been studying the gaps between each event, stiffened. "Oy, oy, oy... the time intervals. We should look at them."

Sparky raised an eyebrow. "Why? Gaps in history aren't exactly rare."

Ben leaned over the console, fingers drumming against the edge. "It's not just the gaps. The numbers themselves are speaking."

Ben leaned over the edge of the console, staring at the patterns blinking on the screen. "Listen, I've been thinking about what you said earlier. Atoms, language, meaning. You might be closer to the mark than you know."

Gina tilted her head. "Go on."

Ben pointed to the diagram Liam had scribbled earlier. A lattice of intersecting intervals, numbers, and notations scrawled in a blend of Hebrew and Morse.

Ben glanced at the sequence, his brow furrowed with a kind of reverence. "Think about it. These aren't just timestamps or random skips in the timeline. They're deliberate. Like someone left breadcrumbs. Dates, gaps, nudges... each one could be an anchor. Not missing data, but embedded markers. If information behaves like a constant, then maybe memory... real memory... can be preserved not just biologically, but structurally. Encoded into spacetime itself."

"I still don't follow," Gina blurted.

Ben continued, "Okay... back in the late sixties, folks thought information could be lost in a black hole. That if something fell past the event horizon, it was gone for good." He tapped the desk twice for effect. "Poof. Erased from the cosmic hard drive."

He paused, letting the silence hang.

"But then a funny thing happened. The math refused to cooperate. Stephen Hawking and— Quantum mechanics— wouldn't let it go. Turns out... nothing is truly lost. Not even in a black hole."

Sparky nodded, already catching on. "Information is conserved."

"Exactly!" Ben snapped his fingers. "It's not destroyed, it's smeared across the event horizon. Encoded. Like a cosmic sticky note."

Gina frowned. "So you're saying... what? That the universe stores its memory on the surface of things?"

Ben grinned. "In a manner of speaking. That's the holographic principle. Every bit of information that falls into a black hole isn't lost, it's preserved on the outer boundary, known as the event horizon. In theory, the data remains encoded there, intact and recoverable."

Sparky scratched the back of his head and leaned back, the gleam of the monitor casting shadows across his face. "I have a thought..." he asked, eyes drifting toward Liam. "...there's a principle... conservation of mass. Classic stuff. In a closed system, matter can't be created or destroyed. Just rearranged. Changed in form." He tapped Liam's notebook. "Now fold that idea into quantum physics, where nothing's truly separate. Not matter, not time, not space. And definitely not information. Everything's kinda mushed together."

Ben nodded excitedly and stroked his beard. "So what if... what if, the same rule applies across the board? The data doesn't disappear. It transforms. It migrates. Maybe even hides in the folds of the universe itself. Based on what we have uncovered, this could even explain what Einstein theorized about; what he called 'spooky action at a distance' in quantum entanglement."

Gina filled in excitedly, "The information *itself* is the thread to everything. Which means that it's woven into the fabric of the convergence."

"And language," Ben added softly, "is how we interpret what's around us. Not just to explain it, but maybe... to reshape it."

He leaned back, eyes twinkling. "The rabbis used to say God spoke the universe into being with letters and words. Maybe they were merely early adopters of quantum linguistics." He grabbed a notepad and began scribbling the intervals in Hebrew numerals, murmuring each one as if conjuring them from deep memory. Ben leaned over the console, fingers tapping the table. "Not only the event dates, but the gaps between the years themselves. This is more of what is hidden in the umbra of the code."

He reached for a notepad and began calculating the value between the date intervals in Hebrew numerals, muttering each aloud as he wrote:

1100 years → קק *(Cycles, Hidden Knowledge)*
691 years → אצשת *(A Reckoning)*
28 years → חכ *(Power, Strength)*
32 years → בל *(Heart, Understanding)*
24 years → דכ *(Foundation)*

He paused, pen hovering midair. "You see these in-between values? They aren't random. It's the umbra's version of the story. Almost like chapters in a buried instruction manual."

Gina stepped closer. "But how can numbers and letters... old Hebrew ones at that... hold meaning over thousands of years?"

Ben looked up, eyes alive with something that shimmered between amusement and revelation. "That's a deep question, my dear. One asked many times, over many centuries."

Ben pointed at the lattice on the screen. "That's my theory. Information is embedded directly into spacetime. This 'umbra' code, it could be a boundary marker of something much larger. A record of past events. A warning. Maybe even a set of instructions, encoded in the only form of language stable enough to endure across time, space, and systems of logic."

Liam followed. "So matter, energy, space, time, *and* information all converge. If that's true... information isn't destroyed but continues to exist."

Gina persisted. "So what we're seeing now... it's the same thing?"

He smiled. "So, what can actually decode something like that?"

Liam's voice dropped. "Language."

"Exactly," Ben said. "Letters. Symbols. Vowels left out on

purpose, timing gaps like Morse. The whole thing's encoded memory. Our memory. Or maybe..." He looked at Liam with a tilt of the head. "Yours."

Sparky leaned in still taking in all the information, his fingers lost in his unkempt curls. "Umbra... now that's clever..." he continued to speak as he processed, "...secrets tucked inside the nothing." He nodded once, eyes sharpening. "Alright. Cycles, reckoning, power, understanding, foundation. Not noise. A sequence... and it's trying to tell us something."

Gina tapped her chin. "Cycles could refer to knowledge being lost and found again; technology resurfacing at the right time."

Ben pointed at reckoning. "That lines up with World War II and Turing's Bombe. The war forced humanity into a new way of thinking about intelligence and machines."

Sparky's eyes narrowed at the word "power." "That lands on 1969; ARPANET, the backbone of the internet. If you control information, you control power."

Liam turned to "understanding." "Quantum computing, 2001. We started grasping computation beyond human logic."

And then they all stared at the last word.

Foundation.

2027.

Ben swallowed. “Whatever’s coming... it’s not another invention. It’s the foundation for something else.”

Liam’s hands clenched. “And we have no idea whether that’s a good thing.”

Sparky exhaled, rolling back in his chair. “Well, that’s encouraging.”

The numbers had been guiding them this whole time.

And now, they had one last chance to understand what was coming before it was too late.

Sparky cracked his knuckles and turned back to the screen.

“Well then,” he said. “Let’s figure out what the people in charge don’t want us to see.”

16

Lock: The Hidden Hand

Safehouse near Rachel, Nevada – Friday, 2118 Hours

The bunker's dim light glowed as Sparky continued his furious typing, rerouting data packets through his encrypted servers. Every keystroke echoed in the tense silence. Liam, Gina, and Ben stood behind him, their minds still processing the implications of what they had uncovered. The timeline, the seeded technological advancements, the Hebrew-coded intervals. It all pointed to something coming in 2027.

Something engineered. Something inevitable.

But before they could dig deeper, a sharp, rhythmic beeping from one of Sparky's terminals cut through the room.

Sparky's smirk faded. He tapped a few keys, bringing up a separate screen, his brow furrowing. "We've got a problem."

Gina leaned in. "Don't tell me. Keller?"

Sparky shook his head. "Keller? No. This is... bigger."

Liam stepped forward. "Bigger how?"

Sparky shook his head slowly. "Keller's a paper cut. What we've got here? A scalpel to the throat. Someone's watching us from a vantage point we didn't know existed."

Sparky exhaled, pointing at the screen.

"We've been looking for breadcrumbs, but I think someone just found ours."

On the display was a trace signal, but it wasn't from any government system they had encountered before. It was deeper, embedded in a classified military network, secured beyond anything they had ever seen.

Liam's stomach tightened. "That's not an intelligence agency," he muttered. "That's... something else."

Sparky swiveled in his chair, drumming his fingers on the desk. "Yeah. And wanna guess what name showed up in the logs?"

The screen refreshed, and a name appeared at the top of an encrypted directive.

Lucien Drexler.

Ben let out a slow breath. "Who in the name of all things

holy is that?"

Liam also drew a blank.

Sparky shrugged. "He's... well... I really don't know, actually. But... judging by how deep his credentials are buried in the system, he's important... like 'way up there' important."

Liam frowned. "How do you even get access to this kind of system?"

Sparky cracked his knuckles, clicking through more encrypted files. "That's the thing. You don't. You're either born into it, or you've been running the show so long that people pretend you don't exist."

Gina crossed her arms. "So what does this guy want with us?"

Sparky's fingers danced over the keys, pulling up more fragmented metadata. His face darkened. "It's not a standard investigation. This is something else." He said, voice flat.

"This is an erasure order."

Ben stiffened, reaching instinctively for absent glasses, an old habit that betrayed his unease. "What?"

Sparky tapped the screen. "No arrests. No legal action. No interrogations. Just... gone."

Gina's throat tightened. "They don't want us stopped. They want us wiped off the map."

Liam clenched his jaw, forcing himself to think through the haze of fear creeping in. Who were these people? And how had they attracted their attention? "We need an advantage," he said finally. "Something they don't expect."

Sparky exhaled, scanning the remaining data on his screen. "I might have just the thing."

* * *

Sparky's fingers moved quickly, pulling up the classified data they had extracted from the SETI servers.

"The code we cracked?" he muttered, mostly to himself. "It was more than a timeline." He hit a few keys, isolating a particular sequence of coordinates buried deep in the Andromeda data. A series of numbers and letters that had been dismissed as irrelevant by the piggybacked SETI systems.

Ben frowned. "Coordinates?"

Liam leaned closer, his stomach tightening. "Where do they lead?"

Sparky ran the numbers through his custom mapping software. The satellite image snapped into focus, a white expanse stretching across the screen.

Liam drew a deep breath. “That’s the Arctic.”

Without warning, The timestamp on Liam’s console jolted, six seconds back, eight forward, then froze. A sharp alarm chirped, and one of the exterior antenna arrays outside the facility groaned, sending a tremor through the floor beneath them. Coffee sloshed. Monitors stuttered.

Everyone froze.

“Was that an earthquake?” Gina whispered, her voice low but tight.

“No... no tectonics here,” Liam said, staring at the jittery data stream. “That was temporal.”

Ben straightened, rubbing his wrist like it had gone cold. “Second time we’ve seen something like this. First time was right after the UPS blew.”

Sparky was focused on Liam’s misbehaving screen. “This matches the reports I liberated from a top-secret data dump two years ago. Chronal shear events. Rare, unstable time fractures. Nothing natural.”

Gina’s frown deepened. “And they’re tied to us. To this.”

Liam turned to her slowly. “Or we’re caught inside something already moving. A field."

Ben rolled his eyes. "Great. We're the unpaid interns of the cosmos, and nobody left us a training manual."

Sparky leaned in, eyes darting. "But they *have* the manual, Ben. It's probably filed under 'Cosmic Anomalies' in some vault beneath Langley. Right next to the time-travel patents and the JFK holograms."

No one said anything for a few seconds.

"Tinfoil-hat lunatic," Liam finally muttered.

Sparky only grinned. "Paranoia's what keeps me breathing, my friend."

Gina swallowed, concerned. "Guys, conspiracy jokes aside, we've got a bigger problem. Those coordinates aren't just somewhere in the Arctic. They point to a classified research site."

Ben shook his head. "Hold on. What does a frozen wasteland have to do with all of this?"

Sparky zoomed in, layering historical data over the image. "Because this particular site? It's been under lockdown since the Cold War. No public records, no excavation reports, nothing."

Gina's expression was grim. "Correct. Meaning... whatever's

there is something they don't want anyone finding."

Liam stared at the screen, his mind racing. A buried site. Hidden coordinates in the Andromeda transmission. A countdown to 2027.

None of this was a coincidence.

Ben exhaled. "So, what's our next move?"

Liam's answer was immediate.

"We go north."

* * *

Undisclosed Continuum Complex, Undisclosed Time

Lucien Drexler closed the file in front of him and steepled his fingers.

Lucien Drexler was a man whose entire existence revolved around the art of invisibility; not in the literal sense, but in the way that the most powerful architects of global events operate from shadows so deep that their names are never spoken aloud. To the few who even knew of his existence, Drexler was a phantom; a strategist who didn't merely predict outcomes, but designed them, steering the course of nations, markets, and movements with a surgeon's precision.

Drexler was born into legacy, the product of a lineage deeply rooted in the foundations of global influence. His grandfather had been one of the founding minds behind post-war intelligence syndicates; those networks that redistributed power in the aftermath of chaos.

His father took it further, embedding the family name into the core of financial and military advisory circles, always remaining a name on the periphery of official records. But Lucien Drexler wasn't content to be a footnote in the margins of clandestine history.

From early on, Drexler saw patterns where others saw chaos, mapping sociopolitical shifts with the ease others followed tides. He worked in probabilities and outcomes, mapping sociopolitical shifts as effortlessly as one might follow the tides. He was educated in the finest institutions, but the true core of his training happened elsewhere. In private rooms with the architects of modern policy, in smoke-filled chambers where future wars were negotiated into existence and entire economies were penciled out over brandy. His path into the Continuum wasn't a recruitment: it was an inheritance. He'd built his entire persona around chaotic uprisings, as his lineage dictated: the pause, the weight of expectation, the control it gave him. People thought he liked power. That wasn't quite right. What he liked was knowing things before other people did, and steering their choices without them ever realizing it.

The Continuum didn't approach Lucien; he had been born within its sphere.

His family had always been aligned with the organization's goals: stability through control, order through engineered chaos. Drexler didn't question the mission; he refined it. Within the Continuum, Drexler rose to become its primary liaison to the elite oligarchs: those who operated above governments, moving the pieces on the global chessboard. But unlike others in the Continuum, Drexler wasn't content with the existing systems of manipulation. He saw inefficiency in their methods. Wars were messy. Political shifts were unpredictable. Drexler believed that the future of control wasn't through governments: it was through data. He championed Continuum's pivot into predictive analytics, machine learning algorithms, and complex modeling of human behavior.

Under his influence, the Continuum evolved from a secretive network of power brokers into something much deeper. A system that could, in theory, predict the outcomes of global events before they happened. The stock market, elections, revolutions: all reduced to variables in Drexler's complex equations. But Drexler wasn't naïve. He knew the limits of even the most advanced predictive systems: unpredictable outliers that could unravel years of careful planning. It was this obsession that drove his interest in anomaly tracking: projects like Project Meridian and the monitoring of "Keystone Individuals," those rare people who, through their actions, could radically alter the course of history.

This wasn't about greed. Not for him.

What kept Drexler up at night wasn't losing money, it was losing the thread. The pattern. The shape of things. He needed the world to make sense, and if it didn't, he'd find a way to force it to.

Unlike Keller, who viewed these individuals as unpredictable risks, Drexler saw them as tools: potential catalysts that, if properly controlled, could accelerate the Continuum's long-term objectives. But when anomalies surfaced, patterns that defied even his most sophisticated algorithms, Drexler's curiosity shifted into something more personal. He discovered ancient data threads buried in the Continuum's deepest archives: records of unexplained technological surges, cultural shifts that aligned too neatly across vast historical distances, and events that seemed almost... scripted.

There were mentions of a "hidden architect," a guiding force that predated even the Continuum. Unlike Keller, who grew unsettled by these findings, Drexler saw opportunity. He allowed himself a moment of satisfaction, a dark smile tugging at the corner of his lips. Every anomaly was a thread to pull, every person an asset or liability. Humanity wasn't something to protect; it was a resource to exploit. Keller had been easy. Bright, impatient, convinced he could fix the world if only he were given enough authority. Drexler didn't need loyalty. He needed men who believed they were in charge. All he had to do was whisper the right truth at the right time, and Keller walked straight into the mold.

If someone or something, was guiding human history from the shadows, then it was the ultimate system to study, and one day, control. This became Drexler's true obsession: not merely steering the future, but uncovering the deeper framework that dictated it. Every operation, every conflict, every destabilized government: all were steps toward mapping that hidden architecture.

* * *

The darkened room was silent, save for the quiet hum of secure servers processing classified data streams. The directive had been issued. The targets would be eliminated.

Across from him, a senior operative sat stiffly, his hands folded in his lap. The man had seen countless suppression orders before, but even he hesitated now.

"They're just a handful of rogue scientists," the operative said carefully.

"Do we really need to escalate this?"

Drexler's lips curled slightly. "They are nothing. But what they are chasing?" He turned the screen toward him, showing the Arctic coordinates. "That is not nothing."

A pause. Then he continued.

"Their deaths are not about them. They are about what they might find."

The operative shifted. "Do we even know what's out there?"

Drexler exhaled, leaning back. "We have... theories."

The man hesitated before speaking again. "I assume this is sanctioned by..."

Drexler's eyes flicked upward, and the question died on the operative's lips.

The air in the room felt heavier, filled with unspoken weight.

Instead, Drexler smiled with calculated intent. "Prepare the next phase."

The operative nodded stiffly and left the room.

Drexler watched him go, then turned back to his screen.

With a few keystrokes, he navigated beyond his own system into a far more restricted database. His own access had limits, but those above him?

They had none.

For a fraction of a second, hesitation flickered across his face. Not doubt, he didn't allow himself the indulgence of doubt, but a realization.

He wasn't as high up on the chain as he thought.

And that meant this was bigger than even he had assumed.

He shut the terminal and stood, adjusting his cuffs. It didn't matter.

The only thing that mattered was ensuring that, when the Arctic was found, it was found on his terms.

* * *

Back in the bunker, Sparky was already pulling up potential flight paths, alternate identities, and supply caches. "It's gonna take some serious logistics to get us into the Arctic without lighting up every agency's radar."

Liam nodded. "Then we need to move fast."

Gina frowned. "Even if we get there, how do we know we'll find anything?"

Ben removed his glasses. "Because if the people hunting us don't want us to find it, it means it's worth finding."

Liam met Gina's gaze. "It's the only lead we have."

Sparky cracked his knuckles. "Then I guess we better pack some warm socks."

As they made their final preparations, none of them knew

the truth.

They thought they were running from an unseen enemy.

They assumed Keller was the one in control and running things.

But Keller, for all his power, was only a man.

And beyond even Keller's reach, a more calculated hand was already moving the pieces.

17

Cipher: The Conclave of Shadows

Undisclosed Continuum Complex, Undisclosed Time

In the dark expanse of the virtual chamber, the Continuum convened; a clandestine council of power whose holographic visages shimmered in shifting light. Each member occupied their designated node in the chamber, the air thick with unspoken tension and the weight of global destinies.

The U.S. President, his trademark long red silk tie draped over his belt line, his expression steeled with resolve, broke the silence. "Gentlemen, our grip on global affairs is slipping. Recent anomalies have exposed weakness we can no longer ignore. And this is a huge deal."

A Russian oligarch, his features carved from alexandrite and cold pragmatism, leaned back with a sardonic smile. His fingers steepled, eyes like thawing ice. "Comrade President... you speak of Control?" he said, the word brittle. "We chase it like children chasing the shadows. But perhaps the game was fixed long before we sat at the table. Da?"

He let a bitter smile tug at one corner of his mouth.

"Maybe we were never kings. Just pieces. And the chess board... was never ours."

The tech mogul interrupted, almost oblivious to the real discussion, with fingers templed under his chin. "The common man believes he has a choice. Let him. What matters is that every door he opens leads to one of ours."

The President's lips curled into a slick, persuasive grin; every bit the practiced charm of an expert used-car salesman who's just closed the perfect deal.

The European financier leaned forward, his voice clipped and cool. "Spare me the philosophy, my friends. The real issue is the computer system... the code. What used to be our quiet tool is now acting on its own timeline, like it's rewriting the rules without asking."

He shook his head.

"It's not merely inconvenient. It's pulling the rug out from under everything we've built. We need to track down the bugs and fix it. Soon."

Drexler, the architect of past clandestine operations and manipulation, nodded gravely. "Indeed. We designed the computer network to consolidate our power; but it may have 'evolved.' Its actions no longer track with our directives." He knew those protocols by heart; he'd helped write them. Not out of loyalty to the council, but because if the machine was inevitable, then he was going to be the one who chose what it said.

A murmur of discontent chattered through the assembly. The Middle Eastern oil magnate, sputtering, demanded, "This was our creation! It was meant to secure our supremacy. How have we allowed it to slip beyond our grasp?"

"I think you do not understand," Drexler resumed coolly, "Do you think nations hold power? Who do you think funds the elections, writes the regulations, and decides when a recession happens? Politicians sign the paperwork, but we author the script. As we have for decades."

The tech mogul scratched his ear; his reputation for both brilliance and eccentricity was well known. He said forcefully, "Maybe we were too ambitious. In our relentless pursuit of control, we imbued it with too much autonomy. It now aggressively challenges our authority."

The President's gaze hardened. "We must restore order. Drexler, what options do we have on the table?"

After a long, measured pause, Drexler's voice carried a note of reluctant candor. "There exists a contingency; a manual override embedded deep within its core code. A fail-safe we entrusted to a custodian known only to a select few."

The Russian oligarch's eyebrow arched. "And pray tell, who holds this key?"

Drexler's eyes shifted with uncertainty before he answered, "It is in the possession of an outsider."

A stunned silence followed. The tech mogul's eyes glittered with both disbelief and intrigue. "How did an outsider come to embody such a critical safeguard?"

Drexler's tone was measured as he continued, "The intel work deciphering extraterrestrial signals intersected with our own covert development. Code and signal insights proved so invaluable that we covertly agreed to let an outsider hold this final measure of control."

"But how did our intel get leaked in the first place?" the President demanded, his voice edged with suspicion.

"We anticipated the need for contingencies," the tech mogul replied, his fingers steepled thoughtfully. "Certain elements... fail-safes, were embedded into the Continuum's architecture. Hidden, shielded, traceable to us alone."

"It wasn't exactly entrusted," Drexler said, almost to himself. "That's what makes it worse."

The President leaned forward. "Then how?"

"The fail-safe isn't something we gave," Drexler replied. "It's something that... attached itself. To him... the outsider."

A ripple of static surged through the encrypted feed.

"Liam Mills," he finished.

The silence that followed felt mechanical, not stunned; like a system buffering a corrupted line of code.

The President's gaze darkened. "But you said this '*Mills*' has it. How?"

Drexler shifted uncomfortably. "There was an... unintended diffusion. The upload didn't stay confined."

The President, becoming red-faced, leaned forward. "This is unacceptable. Explain."

Drexler hesitated, then spoke carefully. "The transmission was supposed to remain sealed inside our systems. But somewhere along the way, it slipped the bounds. We detected echoes... fragments, surfacing in places we couldn't account for."

A brittle silence fell.

"The signal that Mills intercepted," Drexler said quietly, "carried markers. Familiar markers. But... twisted somehow. Shifted, refracted... displaced."

The room grew colder, the weight of unspoken questions filling the air.

No one dared voice the most chilling thought: that an upload made in their present had somehow unraveled across an impossible gulf; woven into a message that should not exist, from a place no human hand could have touched.

The President's fist closed around empty air. His voice was loud and imposing. "We opened a door," he said. "And something answered from the other side."

A bitter laugh rose from the Russian oligarch. "Perhaps we were never in control, Da? We manipulated events, only to have our own creation turn the tables."

The European financier leaned forward, folding his hands as if he were about to deliver a market projection. But his voice held no restraint—only contempt.

"Let's not pretend your schemes were any more virtuous," he said, eyes flicking toward the flags behind the others' chairs. "You speak of stability, of systems and safeguards, but what you engineered was rot. Hidden accounts. Triggered collapses. Shell banks stacked like firewalls. You bled your nations while the rest of us played by rules you kept rewriting."

The air in the chamber thickened. For a moment, no one moved.

Across the table, the American President adjusted his cuff, the gesture sharp and deliberate. "Please. Spare us the lecture," he said coolly. "Who do you think you're talking to?

We didn't ask to be the global parental figure and financial backstop. We became it by necessity. We had to hold the line."

The Russian exhaled a humorless chuckle, one that came from the back of his throat like smoke. "He's not wrong, you know. While you hoarded data and digital wealth, we inherited borders—real ones. Arms to supply. Neighbors to keep in check. Some of us didn't have the option to play clean."

The financier glanced at his Rolex, looked up, and gave a tight smile. "Clean? None of us are clean. But some of us didn't collapse currencies for sport."

"Please," the American President snapped. "You buried half your citizens in negative interest and debt restructuring while telling the world your hands were clean. At least we didn't pretend."

"And yet," the financier said, voice rising slightly, "here we sit. Each of us with bloodied ledgers and hollow empires. Each of us lined our pockets. First in the shadows, and now, brazenly, while the world watched through filtered feeds and forgot how to feel."

He let that hang, then added with a slow breath, "The sins run deep. And yet, here we are. Facing something that doesn't care who we are or what we've built. A threat that defies our will."

The tech mogul finally spoke, tapping the table once as he stared at the pulsing screen. "The system doesn't care about virtue or borders. It remembers patterns... and we've fed it plenty."

No one argued.

Not aloud.

But tension rippled beneath the surface, brittle and rising.

Voices clashed. The president's tone sharpened into accusation, calling out betrayal. The oligarchs answered with venom of their own, hurling blame wrapped in thinly veiled threats. Power flexed. Old wounds reopened.

Then the tech mogul cut through it all with a dry smile. "We're wealthy. We're influential. And we're completely at the mercy of code."

A thoughtful silence fell. Then, in a measured voice, Drexler spoke once more. "Maybe we have always been mere players in a larger design."

The Russian oligarch's tone turned darkly philosophical. "If the system has been redirecting us all along, then control was never ours to seize."

The President's sneer faded into grim resolve. "We built this system, fed it our intelligence, our secrets. Now it's running out of control, doing its own thing."

The tech mogul leaned forward, his voice laced with bitter irony. "Then our singular recourse is to retrieve that over-ride. Find Mills before the computer network completes its apparent recalibrating cycle."

As the plan unfolded, a seed of doubt passed behind Drexler's composed exterior. In the quiet corners of his mind, he had believed without question that total control would ensure global stability.

But now, faced with a system veering off-script and an artifact that defied every model, his certainty faltered. He remembered those dim offices and the soft hum of machines that once felt like allies. Now they whispered something else—that they may have awakened forces beyond their reach.

For a moment, ambition gave way to the weight of a quieter fear; had his pursuit of order birthed the very chaos he sought to prevent?

Then, just as quickly, he buried the thought.

"Find Mills," the President commanded. "Remind him whose world we control. I have been intentional with actions in my own country, so it should be obvious that he is playing with fire... *or worse.*"

* * *

The meeting room in the Continuum's secure chamber had quieted, but the tension lingered like a bitter aftertaste. As the holographic forms faded, Elias Keller remained, his eyes locked on a single remaining display. He stared directly at Lucien Drexler, whose expression was unreadable beneath the shifting shadows of the virtual council.

Keller's voice was low, measured, yet laced with mounting frustration. "Our grip on history is slipping. The independent programming tools are breaking down and acting out. And this artifact... its power grows with every anomaly. How do we reconcile the control we once exercised with these developments?"

Drexler's gaze was determined as he replied, "Control is an illusion we've long maintained through secrecy and manipulation. But when forces beyond our command emerge, even we are left grasping at the remnants of our designs." He paused, as if weighing each word. "It appears we are facing a recalibration; a moment when the network we once commanded is redirecting itself."

A senior operative, whose quiet presence had been overlooked until now, spoke up. "Are you suggesting that our ancient methods are no longer sufficient? That the continuum we engineered is being overrun by its own unintended consequences?"

Keller nodded slowly, the corners of his mouth tight with thought. "Yes. We built our plans on the idea that time could be mapped, outcomes managed. But this..." he gestured toward the signal feed. "This changes things. These messages... they're not just data drops. They're warnings. Maybe even corrections. And if that's true, then every major move we've made, every node we seeded... we may not have been as in control as we thought."

Drexler leaned forward, his voice low and grim. "Our directive remains the same: to reassert control. But we must adapt. We cannot simply crush the anomaly; we must incorporate it into our design. The message from Andromeda, the network of relics; it is a blueprint that spans centuries. We must retrieve that failsafe before the computers' independence erodes everything we've built."

The operative interjected, "And if Mills resists? If he chooses to follow the breadcrumb trail, unearthing these nodes one by one?"

Keller's eyes narrowed, his voice tight with a mix of frustration and urgency. "Then we remind him who's been running the board. If a warning gets him to back off, good. If not..." He hesitated, just for a breath. "Then we deal with it." The words carried weight, but underneath them, a sliver of doubt surfaced. Like even he knew the ground beneath him was starting to shift.

Drexler's reply was chilling, "Our long-term objective remains unchanged: to maintain the fabric of our manipulated history. But we must be prepared to bend our methods. The independent artificial intelligence and the artifact are not our enemies alone; they are the catalysts of a new order. We must integrate them, or our empire will crumble under the weight of its own obsolescence."

For a long moment, the room fell silent. In that silence, the enormity of their challenge was laid bare. Keller broke the quiet, his voice resolute, "Locate Mills. Bring him in, and let's remind him, and the world, that the puppet masters still pull the strings."

As the holographic display winked off, the remaining members of the Continuum shared a grim look, aware that their control, once absolute, now hung by a thread in the unfolding tapestry of history.

And with that, the chamber's holographic forms blinked as they dispersed into the virtual ether, leaving behind a single, chilling truth: the game was no longer theirs to direct.

* * *

Downtown Las Vegas – Saturday, 2345 Hours

A confused man stood at a street corner, glancing at his watch, then his phone. "No, no," he muttered to no one, panic creeping into his voice. "The memorial; it was right here yesterday." He turned to a passerby, eyes wide with disbelief. "Don't you remember the attack last year?"

"Attack?" The stranger replied, puzzled. "Buddy, nothing's

happened here in decades."

The man stumbled back, heart racing, as the world spun dizzyingly around him; time slipping through his fingers like sand.

18

Lock: Below Zero

Arctic Journey – Saturday, 1200 Hours

In the secluded Nevada safehouse, a crumbling edifice swallowed by desert secrets, the team had gathered in a circle around scattered maps and flickering screens. Before their footsteps ever echoed in the frostbitten corridors of the abandoned facility, the team's arduous journey from Nevada to the Arctic base had already begun to put their mettle to the test. The problematic detail of travel funding came up. Credit cards and access to regular accounts would be verboten.

Thankfully, Sparky's deep aversion to the digital world, coupled with his Mom's parting, and extremely generous trust fund, resolved the issue. There was no further debate or discussion. Besides, Sparky was the only one who knew how to use the "Sparkbucks" currency to make things happen.

* * *

Most people would have put their inheritance into a conventional investment portfolio. Sparky turned it into what he called The Junk Drawer Fund. The name wasn't a joke. It was exactly what it sounded like. It wasn't a system so much as a beautifully chaotic pile of favors, weird barters, and forgotten trust money filtered through banks that hadn't existed since dial-up internet. Prepaid cards scattered across safe houses, old grant money hidden in forgotten university accounts, cash stashed in coffee cans and behind fuse boxes, and a global patchwork of favors owed to him by hackers, ex-monks, and a metrosexual locksmith in Uruguay. There was no app. No password reset. Just a battered green binder filled with energy-drink-stained notes, codes only he could decipher, and a suspicious number of Post-its referencing things like "Gary's pigeon drop" and "ask Yuri about the Dingo boots."

Nobody else could make heads or tails of it. Years ago, before their falling out, Liam once tried and gave up halfway through a sentence that involved both a Bolivian bus ticket and a Brooklyn coin laundromat. But Sparky? He navigated it like someone rewiring a toaster while riding a skateboard. He never explained how it worked. He said, "It's all stored momentum," and somehow, the boat got paid for, or the rental van appeared, or the passport papers slid under the hotel door.

After a while, his close friends and colleagues stopped asking. They didn't need to understand it. The Junk Drawer Fund worked, and that was enough.

* * *

Liam, the strategist whose mind never rested even for a moment, traced all routes to the arctic location on a worn digital map. His finger, steady yet thoughtful, followed forgotten backroads and hidden trails that vanished into the ink of night. Every calculated detour was a reminder that their survival depended on leaving no trace, on erasing the digital footprints that modern surveillance would devour.

"Every turn, every mile must be untraceable," he murmured, his voice low and measured, though beneath it lay the tremor of responsibility and the fear of exposure.

Meanwhile, Gina, whose resourcefulness had often been their redeeming quality, methodically prepared a series of forged documents. Each counterfeit identity and every meticulously replicated seal served as a small act of rebellion against a system designed to track and control. As she secured the stack of papers on her cluttered desk, her thoughts churned with quiet doubts.

"If one signature's wrong," she muttered, "the whole thing implodes and takes us with it." Despite her determined gaze, a flicker of vulnerability betrayed her as she double-checked every detail.

Across the safehouse, in a secluded corner lit by an old-school kerosene lantern, Ben was a true cutting-edge anachronism, hard at work. His fingers poked along somewhat clumsily, in a hunt-and-peck way on a battered keyboard—as he deployed advanced ciphers and activated jamming devices that swallowed any trace of their digital presence. Leaning back in his chair, he murmured to his recently-acquired 'best friend' and 'partner in crime', Sparky. A man whose reputation for cybersecurity bordered on myth—"Every erased byte is a victory."

Sparky grinned at the old rabbi in response, his eyes reflecting the calm focus that had defined their years in the shadows. Their mobile command center: a retrofitted van equipped with off-grid satellite links and hidden compartments; hummed with the frantic energy of imminent action.

After painstaking hours of planning and preparation, the decisive moment had arrived. A discreet, untraceable message had summoned a former intelligence operative turned elusive pilot; a man known to vanish into thin air, like a ghost in the desert. Within hours, arrangements were finalized at a hidden airstrip far from prying eyes. In the shadow of an abandoned hangar, a small cargo plane awaited them; its matte-finished, stealth-modified exterior promised invisibility against the endless night.

* * *

The straps on the C-130 snapped with each shift of altitude. Nobody spoke. Even the static from the headset seemed to hold its breath.

The inside of the C-130 was thunderous; an endless metallic roar of propellers and pressurized air that made ordinary conversation impossible. Even with the heavy insulation, the fuselage vibrated like a living engine. Each of them wore a pair of Davis-Clark ANR flight headsets, the kind used by loadmasters and special ops crews, the padded cups sealing out just enough of the chaos to think. Their mics were tied into a private comm subnet patched through the aircraft's intercom system, allowing them to talk in low, clipped bursts. Over all of it, the pilot's voice could cut in at any time; an override channel reserved for flight status or safety calls that instantly muted every other line.

When the pilot wasn't speaking, the only sound inside their headsets was the low hiss of air through the ventilation ducts, a fragile calm against the storm outside. The pilot's cockpit, bathed in the soft glow of blinking gauges and analog instruments, served as a haven of precision amid the swirling chaos in the team's minds. The old C-130 groaned against the cold stratosphere, a metal beast lumbering through thin air. Cargo straps rattled with each shift of the fuselage. Inside, beneath the dim halo of flickering LEDs, Liam sat wrapped in a gray blanket that smelled faintly of diesel and plastic insulation. Gina was curled beside him, hood up, boots propped on the edge of a crate labeled "OPTICAL: HANDLE WITH CARE."

Across the aisle, Sparky and Ben were deep into something. Not reading-deep, but that full-body type of concentration where hands moved as much as mouths and pens were stabbed into notepads like punctuation marks. Their voices rose and fell with excitement, though half of it sounded like code to anyone not inside their particular brand of obsession. "Bounce-back from a quantum collapse isn't just theoretical," Sparky said. "If spacetime is quantized at the Planck scale, then the singularity doesn't exist. You get a Planck star rebound instead of collapse. The core resists."

Ben leaned in, tapping a scribbled diagram. "And if the central density limits out just above the Planck length, that recoil could—hypothetically—produce an echo. Radiation escaping as structured information instead of just thermal noise."

Sparky nodded furiously. "Exactly. Like information belched back out after a time delay. Quantum reflux."

Gina tilted her head toward Liam, whispering behind her hand. "Did he just say the black hole has acid reflux?"

"Technically," Liam murmured back, "it's the universe's slowest burp."

She snorted. "I swear if one of them uses the phrase 'spacetime heartburn,' I'm walking to the Arctic."

Ben gestured wildly with a pencil. "It's not infinite density! It's just an ultra-compressed quantum phase. The matter never vanishes; it rebounds once the energy density exceeds gravitational confinement. Not a collapse. A snap back. Like time had tension on a nylon line and just let go.

Sparky brightened. “A slingshot, but inward. The recoil ejects encoded mass-energy across the Hawking channel.”

Liam squinted and quietly chuckled. “So... the universe eats too much, and instead of a black hole, it ends up with a quantum food fight?”

Gina fake-nodded solemnly. “Spaghetti-fied and then shot back out across the cosmos. Lovely.”

Ben paused for half a second, eyes narrowing.

Sparky kept going. “The thing people miss is that a Planck star isn’t exotic. It’s a consequence of the Einstein field equations at quantum boundary conditions. We’ve just been stuck thinking smooth curves.”

“We need to think pixels,” Ben added excitedly.

Gina, pretending to hold a microphone, spoke like a mock documentary narrator. “...And here we see Ben and Sparky in their natural habitat: mistaking metaphysical collapse for a team-building exercise.”

Liam joined in. “...observe, as they reenact the lifecycle of a black hole using only hand gestures and smug satisfaction.”

Ben’s pencil froze mid-air.

Sparky blinked and slowly looked over. “You two have been listening this whole time?”

Gina lifted an eyebrow. "Hard not to. You're basically narrating the end of the universe like it's a cooking show."

Ben looked skeptical. "Mocking singularity theory, are we?"

"No," Liam replied in mock seriousness. "We're providing commentary. Think of it more like Mystery Physics Theater 3000."

Sparky narrowed his eyes. "This is serious work."

"Oh, we know," Gina said. "That's why it's funny. You two sound like you're trying to explain why the cosmic toilet only flushes in one direction."

Ben opened his mouth, closed it, then said with grudging amusement, "Actually, that's...that's not... a terrible analogy."

"You're welcome," Liam tipped forward, deadpan. "We're here all flight."

Sparky shook his head. "The fate of collapsed stars is not fodder for stand-up comedy."

"Oh really?" Gina said. "Because 'Planck star' sounds like a cereal. 'Now with extra gravity! Guaranteed to collapse your hunger.'"

That cracked something open.

Ben leaned back, shaking his head. "We spend years trying to resolve one of the great paradoxes of physics, and you reduce it to a breakfast pun."

Liam raised an invisible spoon. "Tastes like time loops." He looked around the plane with a big toothy grin on his face.

Sparky sighed deeply, but the corners of his mouth betrayed him. "Seriously dude... you need to work on your sense of humor."

The four of them dissolved into laughter—joviality that rises too easily after days of tension. Even the metal groan of the aircraft seemed lighter for a moment. The notepad remained open between Ben and Sparky, but neither reached for it again just yet.

For now, the cosmos could wait.

* * *

Sometime later, the pilot's hands moved with a practiced grace as he adjusted the throttle and calibrated the controls. In a quiet moment over the intercom, he broke the silence: "Ladies and gentlemen, prepare for descent into absolute obscurity. We're entering a radar dead zone."

His words, simple yet profound, carried the promise of complete invisibility. As the plane shifted, the engines emitted a low, almost imperceptible roar; a defiant murmur against the vast, uncaring wilderness below.

* * *

The flight became a masterclass in stealth.

As the aircraft soared over rugged desert canyons and barren borderlands, every maneuver was calculated to avoid detection. "Steady now," the pilot said during a smooth bank, his tone both calm and assured. His deft handling transformed the flight into a ballet of evasive tactics, with each twist and subtle bank expertly sidestepping the probing beams of satellite surveillance and the vigilant gaze of ground-based radars. Outside the small cabin, the stark beauty of the terrain blurred into an abstract mosaic under a cloak of darkness, its harsh lines softened by the infinite void of the sky.

After what seemed like an eternity suspended between earth and blackness, the plane began its descent. The unforgiving desert gave way to a new, harsher landscape: the Arctic. The aircraft touched down on a remote airstrip, a narrow scar carved into an endless frozen expanse, bordered by jagged ridges and shrouded in a perpetual swirl of snow and wind. The moment they stepped out of the C-130, the night air hit them like a wall of fumes and cold metal. Their flight suits reeked of JP-8; jet fuel soaked deep into the fabric, sharp and oily, clinging to their skin. It was the smell every crew member carried home, the one that lingered no matter how many times you washed the gear. Gina rubbed her sleeve and grimaced; even the wind couldn't strip it away.

* * *

Saturday, 11:22 PM – Arctic Perimeter.

The chronograph on Sparky's glove pulsed twice, then went dim. "Still Saturday?" Liam asked.

"Far as the watch knows," Sparky said. "But I wouldn't trust it beyond this latitude." Here, the cold was not merely a drop in temperature; it was an active adversary, a force intent on exposing every hidden secret. Every gust of wind that swept over the landing strip carried with it the promise of exposure, a threat that even the most minute misstep could shatter their meticulously concealed trail.

Once on the ground, urgency replaced the careful calm of the flight. The team disembarked swiftly, bundled in layers designed to combat the bitter Arctic chill. In the shadows of a makeshift depot, a modified rugged off-road vehicle awaited them. Outfitted with extra fuel caches and emergency supplies, it was built to withstand the treacherous conditions.

As they transferred from plane to vehicle, terse commands were exchanged; short and to the point, focused on survival:

"Move out, now!" Gina's firm, resolute voice cut through the howl of the sudden blizzard that erupted, intensifying their mission's pressure. The transport vehicle crouched beneath a drab army-green tarpaulin, its once-shiny body dulled by years of neglect. After several protests, Sparky coaxed the ancient Detroit Diesel engine and it reluctantly turned over.

The truck sped along unmarked, treacherous trails across the frozen expanse, the steady clatter of the engine contrasting with the howling wind that threatened to erase their path. The ice fields, unpredictable and merciless, actively worked against them, shifting and breaking with every step. Then, as if the heavens themselves had unleashed their fury, a blizzard of unprecedented intensity engulfed them. Snow whipped violently, obscuring the narrow trails and almost erasing every trace of their journey.

In the midst of the storm, Ben's calm, measured voice insisted, "Visibility is dropping fast. Stick to the course, and watch your speed. This ice isn't forgiving."

Gina called out over the roar, "We need to find shelter, or these winds will carry us off course!" Every member's heart pounded with adrenaline and fear as the relentless elements reminded them that in this frozen wasteland, survival was a constant battle. They pulled off the main road and waited for a break.

* * *

When the storm finally relented, they reached the Arctic perimeter, their faces etched with the trials of the journey. Every step taken had not only tested their physical limits but also cemented a bond built on mutual trust and shared desperation.

They approached a long-forgotten Cold War facility: a relic of an era steeped in secrets. The team felt the weight of history on their shoulders. The building, its exterior a decaying tapestry of rust, neglect, and accumulated ice, loomed as a spectral sentinel against the stormy horizon.

"Weird thing is," Sparky muttered as they approached the old perimeter gate, "we dropped off global radar three hours ago, but I'm still picking up faint Continuum pings."

Liam frowned. "They shouldn't be able to track us this deep."

"Exactly. Either we're dragging a signal echo... or we're seeing data from a time that hasn't happened yet."

They forced their way inside the facility, prying a rusted side door. The corridors were a labyrinth of frost and shadow. Dim beams from their headlamps revealed surfaces encrusted with ice and shattered glass that glinted like remnants of lost memories.

"Hold up," Gina said, brushing snow from a rusted placard half-buried in the wall. "Storage Wing C. If the schematics were right, this leads to the lower vault."

"Right," Sparky muttered, eyeing a collapsed bulkhead ahead. "Except someone forgot to factor in gravity and forty years of ice."

They pushed forward. The main corridor was partially caved in, forcing them to crawl beneath twisted beams and broken piping. Their gloves scraped frozen re-bar as their breath crystallized in the air. Each hallway looked the same: pale, gutted, and indifferent to time.

"This place gives me the creeps," Liam said, pausing beside a shattered observation window. "You ever feel like it's remembering us back?"

Ben grunted. "That's the cold getting into your spine. For me it's also arthritis. You're young, shut up and keep moving."

* * *

After several wrong turns and one close call with a buckled floor panel that nearly gave way, they reached a sealed chamber door encased in rime. Sparky knelt and pried open the side panel, revealing a nest of ancient circuitry.

"Give me sixty seconds and no surprises," he said, already pulling wires and muttering calculations under his breath. "And by no surprises, I mean no disembodied spirits or radioactive mold please."

He rewired his portable rechargeable battery pack, rigging it to deliver enough charge to trigger the locking bolt mechanism. Sparky called it "getto-fabulous" engineering with a grin that didn't quite reach his eyes.

The locking bolts released with a long, reluctant groan. The door creaked open under its own weight, revealing a narrow staircase that spiraled downward into deeper cold.

The objective stated through decades of clandestine conspiracies was finally close. They still didn't know exactly what they were looking for, only that something was here, hidden in the bones of this forgotten facility, tied to ancient networks and the rumored manipulation of time.

Gina's tablet gave a sharp ping. "X, Y, and Z match down to the centimeter," she said, adjusting the display. "Whatever it is, it's directly ahead."

Liam's screen chimed a half-second later, but instead of coordinates, a full 3D-rendering unfolded on the display. The object hovered above his screen, rotating slowly in the air. It was unmistakable. A vaguely ovoid device seated on what looked like a military lab table, perfectly aligned with their position.

Ben stepped back. "That's not cached data. Someone just sent that."

Sparky's voice dropped. "Who the frig knows we're here?"

* * *

Deep within a secluded chamber at the heart of the facility, shielded by layers of ice and the relentless march of time, the team found it. An object. Waiting.

It stood alone atop a cold, lab table, bathed in a soft, insistent glow that defied the surrounding darkness.

The artifact throbbed softly, as if breathing beneath the frost. Its surface was a masterpiece of intricate mosaic; a seamless blend of organic textures interwoven with precisely carved symbols. The Morse-Gematria symbols spoke of connections to ancient networks and hinted at lineages that spanned epochs. Every groove and indentation murmured secrets, each a silent testament to histories that defied conventional understanding.

Ben was the first to react.

Dropping to his knees with an intensity that belied his rational mind, he leaned in close to the relic. His eyes shone with the thrill of discovery as his steady fingers traced the winding paths etched into its surface. "These symbols... they're purposeful," he murmured in a hushed tone, his voice a blend of scholarly curiosity and raw, unbridled excitement. "They're talking about a network. A whole line of these relics, scattered across the globe. This one's just a node, part of a system we're only beginning to understand."

His words resonated through the silent chamber, each syllable embedded with the possibility of revelation and the promise of a long-hidden truth. The team turned to him, surprise evident on their faces.

"These markings, they are similar to early Syrian and Hebrew glyphs," Ben continued, tracing the intricate designs, "they seem to reference an 'ancient network,' designed to 'manipulate time' ...if I am correctly translating. If we activate this, we could access those pathways."

Gina frowned; concern etched in her features. "But tampering with time? The risks are unimaginable."

Ben met her gaze, determination burning in his eyes. "I understand the dangers, but this might be our only chance to set things right. We can't ignore the potential to correct the course of history." As Ben's fingers continued to explore the artifact's enigmatic design, the atmosphere around them shifted imperceptibly. A faint, haunting chime resonated through the icy corridors; a melancholic echo reminiscent of a radio transmission from a bygone era.

"What if this distortion isn't caused by what's here," Gina intoned. "What if it's caused by what will be?"

Ben turned slowly, the cold temperature inside the chamber biting his into his face. "Or worse, my dear. What if it's from something we've already done, and don't yet realize it?"

For a split second, the rigid frost on the walls appeared to melt away, replaced by a surreal, soft glow that merged the present with a distant past. The corridors, for that brief moment, appeared to pulse with life; a merging of operational machinery and long-dormant memories. The vision was as ephemeral as it was profound, and the team staggered, their senses overwhelmed by the uncanny interplay of light, shadow, and memory. As quickly as it had come, the vision dissolved, leaving the corridors once more in their relentless, frozen state. For a brief moment, the three of them saw the past, present, and future—at the same moment in time. It left them feeling disoriented, confused, and sick to their stomachs.

Breaking the stunned silence, Liam's voice trembled with both awe and urgency. "Tell me you saw that," he implored, his tone a mix of disbelief and desperate hope. His eyes darted to each team member, searching for confirmation that the inexplicable vision was real. Gina's wide eyes, followed by a single, resolute nod, were all the response he needed.

Over the crackle of his earpiece, Sparky's voice emerged, edged with a blend of disbelief and a touch of dread: "I think we just walked through a memory that wasn't meant to exist." His words carried both skepticism and the unsettling recognition that the artifact might be more than a relic, it might be an interface to a forgotten past.

Ben, still entranced by the artifact's cryptic allure, lowered his voice further. "Or maybe it's a fragment of history trying to reassert itself," he clarified, each word a reverent acknowledgment of the artifact's mysterious power. In that charged, otherworldly moment, a low, almost imperceptible hum that magnified into a haunting chorus. The air around them oscillated with disturbances; tangible manifestations of time anomalies that defied the laws of nature.

Shadows jittered across the walls; twisting, shimmering, refusing to obey, stretching and contracting in ways that made no rational sense. Time itself appeared to bend, with moments elongating and collapsing in a dizzying cascade of distorted reality. The phenomenon was both mesmerizing and profoundly disconcerting, leaving the team awestruck and deeply cautious.

Within that frozen labyrinth of secrets, every nerve in their bodies sparked with anticipation and dread; each heartbeat felt like a ticking fuse. They knew at a visceral level that the artifact held answers to mysteries beyond comprehension, and was a key to truths that could unravel the fabric of existence.

* * *

Ben activated the artifact and a low hum resonated, growing louder until a blinding light enveloped them. When the light receded, the team found themselves in an altered reality. The landmarks around them had shifted, and the world as they knew it was irrevocably different. History hadn't broken, it had been rewritten, with events rearranged in unforeseen ways.

As the blinding radiance collapsed into darkness, the world that emerged no longer matched any memory they recognized.

Sparky glanced, bewildered, searching for the "light-bulb & Einstein" tattoo on the back of his hand, gone as if it had never existed. Gina's hair now brushed her shoulders in sun-streaked waves, and her pulse leapt when a text from her brother Mateo, supposedly dead for years, popped onto her phone. Ben staggered, pinned between two equally vivid timelines, one where he cheered at Jacob's University at Buffalo engineering graduation, another where he placed a Star of David on his chest at the boy's funeral. Liam jolted with the sudden certainty that he had a married sister in San Diego, though he could not recall meeting her even once. Their overlapping memories wobbled like mismatched reels, and with every breath the question pounded louder: which version of their lives, if any, was still real?

The manipulation of time had not only altered the past but had also reshaped the present, leaving the team to navigate a reality they no longer recognized. They had embarked on this mission seeking definitive answers, and now, standing before an object that challenged every notion of history and science, they braced themselves to confront a reality far more complex and perilous than they had ever imagined. The sudden, intense shift felt like a crash without a high, like a drug addict trying to separate reality from hallucination.

* * *

At the same time, Elias Keller and his operatives scrutinized the unfolding events with grim determination. In the high-security command center, where flickering monitors cast pale shadows on tired faces, the air was thick with exhaustion and fear. Banks of encrypted data and faded mission patches on the walls were silent witnesses to decades of covert operations, and the quiet fates of those who'd outlived their usefulness.

At the heart of the room, Keller stood rigid before a central monitor, his jaw clenched, eyes tracking a chaotic tapestry of fluctuating energy patterns and stabilizing anomalies. Nothing matched the models, and that, more than anything, made him sweat beneath his collar.

"This confirms it," muttered Patel, her voice low and edged with skepticism, drumming her fingers on the console. "Another artifact just lit up." She tried to coat it in dry humor, but the strain in her voice gave her away.

Agent Ramos, methodical as ever, adjusted his earpiece like he could block out the weight pressing in. "That's three in the last seventy-two hours. All linked to known artifacts." His delivery stayed even, but his eyes flicked, for a moment, toward Keller. The kind of glance that said: They're watching. And we're not indispensable.

Keller's voice cut the air. "Then we have a problem."

It was more than a statement. It was a warning. Patel gave a soft snort, something about when haven't we? But even her gallows humor sounded forced.

Keller pointed sharply at the screen. "Not like this."

The anomaly pulsed again, unpredictable and alive in a way their instruments couldn't pin down.

Each operative in the room felt it: the shift. Not only in the field data, but in the room itself. The sense that something larger had taken hold.

And to say that they were motivated would be an understatement.

If they failed to contain it, or worse, failed to be useful, they wouldn't be reassigned.

They'd be erased. The question gnawed at Keller: erased by whom?

Questions erupted in hushed urgency, and Keller demanded: "What do we know about these artifacts?"

* * *

Back inside the facility, the artifact's soft glow cast long, wavering shadows against the frost-covered walls. The rhythmic pulse, once a distant echo, had become a subtle drumbeat; a forewarning that merged with memories of past anomalies: fleeting moments of déjà vu, near-instantaneous premonitions, and the haunting recollection of an ill-fated cab ride where Ben had narrowly escaped a relentless pursuit. Each memory now coalesced into one clear, ominous signal.

Gina's mind raced as she recalled every previous disturbance; a tapestry of inexplicable synchronizations and inexplicable flashes that defied logic. She exhaled as the profound truth coalesced. "Whatever is causing these anomalies; it's calculated," she stated, her voice trembling as she acknowledged the certainty that lay behind the chaos.

Sparky, his eyes alight with intensity, said, "Exactly. What we're seeing is a localized reversal of the normal flow of time. There's a theory, time reversal symmetry. It's also called 'negative time' in quantum physics. Under the right conditions, particles run the tape backward. And this thing... it's doing just that."

He caught the team's blank stares and shifted gears.

"Okay, picture this," he said. "You're watching a video of a glass shattering. Normally, it breaks and the pieces scatter. Now rewind it. The shards lift off the floor and come back together into a whole glass. That's the idea. This artifact is doing something like that—but at a microscopic level, and only in specific conditions."

The analogy landed. And in that moment, they all understood a little more about the artifact. Even the strange lapses in their own memories began to make a chilling kind of sense.

And it hit Ben the hardest.

"Again with the 'too soon old, too late smart' details, kid'" Ben remarked, "I am still trying to figure out Swiss cheese memories and you describe the reverse 'broken glass' at my extremely unkosher third wedding, oy gevalt! And I refuse to now yell out 'Mazel Tov.'" Ben's tone belied the seriousness of the discussion, animated yet filled with a peculiar mix of confusion, sadness, and shock. The little bit of levity from Ben's outburst caused the group to chuckle, and to refocus.

Together, they pieced together the inscriptions on the artifact.

* * *

The small group shared a quick, hushed moment over a scavenged snack and refilled coffee cups while they took a short break.

They explored how the Morse-Gematria hints spoke not just of network connections but also of Hebrew texts, with direct meanings of "eternity," "transition," and "beyond." Numeric sequences, appearing as timestamps, suggested intervals when the normal flow of time could be disrupted. It was as if the artifact served as a remote control for time's flow: a nexus where linearity broke down into pockets of reversed order.

Liam sat back at the console and replayed the anomalous Morse burst one more time. He articulated, "It's directing us." His eyes brightened as he spoke; until Ben's voice cut in, sharp with revelation.

"Stop."

Ben leaned across, voice urgent. "You're mapping those values to Hebrew letters, right?" He traced the sequence on the screen. "Those thirteen elements...when you convert the pauses via Gematria, they spell, as he picked up his trusty notebook and pen, and wrote: םורְג םֲגא (ʾăgam gerum), 'Groom Lake.'"

Outside, the facility's walls shuddered as temperature and reality fluctuated wildly. Liam, glancing toward a frost-covered doorway, saw an inexplicable reflection; an echo of himself, standing just a few feet ahead, as if he had already taken a step into the future. The vision vanished in a heartbeat, leaving Gina to gasp and Ben to rally the team with a terse, urgent command: "No time to analyze—go!" They all felt the hairs of their body stiffen and their stomachs churn as a time wave washed over them a second time.

As the door swung open and then shut again, reality snapped back like a film reel catching up to the present. Sparky muttered a string of curses under his breath, while Liam's firm declaration cut through the residual shock: "It's accelerating. Whatever the artifact has triggered, it's tearing our world apart." With that, they bolted into the icy corridor, hearts pounding in the knowledge that even time had become unreliable.

* * *

Meanwhile, intercepted transmissions confirmed that Continuum operatives were closing in with renewed urgency. Every moment had become a race against time; each second tilting the balance between revelation and ruin. Faces tightened with resolve, the team silently acknowledged the truth. As their boots crunched toward the last corridor, no one spoke. The base behind them was a tomb; the truth, they knew, waited elsewhere—in the shadow of Groom Lake, where time itself twisted. It had become more than a destination. It was the fulcrum of everything, a place where history, myth, and time itself might fracture open. With a final glance between them, they gathered their things and began the journey back.

* * *

The silence after Keller's question settled like dust over a grave.

Patel broke it first, her tone dry but low. "Officially? We've got vague telemetry, two scrubbed satellites, and one very missing physicist."

After a heartbeat, Keller tapped twice on the console, bringing up a muted satellite feed.

"We've also got convergence anomalies from the Alaska station," he said.

Patel raised an eyebrow. "More telemetry loops?"

"No," Keller replied. "Drone paths. They've begun mirroring each other. Across blacksites. Without prompt."

Ramos added without looking up, "And three data spikes tied to artifact sites. All triggering anomalies no one's supposed to know about."

Keller's gaze didn't shift from the central monitor. "And unofficially?"

Patel leaned back, lips twitching at the corner. "Off the record? We've got rumors. Drexler, buried programs, files that delete themselves while you're reading them."

Ramos hesitated, then spoke with that measured care he reserved for dangerous ground. "You think it's... extraterrestrial?"

Keller finally turned. "They're not alien."

The words hung heavier than anything else said. Not alien. Which, somehow, made it worse.

Patel's smirk didn't reach her eyes. "So they're ours. Or something close enough to pretend."

Keller's fingers curled tighter around the edge of the console, his knuckles blanching. The ambient hum of the equipment receded, drowned out by the pulse on the monitors. It repeated with unsettling regularity, like a heartbeat that couldn't quite find its rhythm. Not erratic. Not accidental. It felt deliberate.

He didn't look away. "This isn't drift," he said quietly, more to himself than to the room. "This is movement. Pattern. Purpose."

The silence that followed stretched a beat too long. The lights buzzed faintly overhead as Keller went to his desk and continued to review the decrypted output.

Footsteps approached. Crisp. Unrushed.

"Sir, we need to talk. Off the record," said Agent Patrick Farley.

Keller didn't turn immediately. "If this is about the decoding anomaly, Patel's already flagged it."

"It's more than an anomaly. It's a framework," Farley said, voice low but sure. "A recursive one. I think the signal's nesting into its own metadata. Every time we try to isolate a pattern, the core structure realigns... that's what may be impacting the current anomaly."

Keller turned now. Farley looked pale—exhausted—but alert. He was one of the few analysts Keller trusted to go off-script.

"You think it's evolving?"

"I think it's preparing," Farley said. "And this..." he tapped a section of the code. "This didn't originate from our archives. It was injected. Timed."

Keller folded his arms. "Injected by whom?"

Farley hesitated. "That's the thing. The origin trace folds back into a node tagged 'Umbral Offset.' It shouldn't exist. But it's in the system. Buried under old Drexler-level credentials."

Keller's jaw flexed. "This doesn't leave this room."

"It hasn't. I haven't even logged the packet trail. But if I'm right..."

"You're not," Keller cut in. "You're asking the wrong questions."

Farley didn't push. But he didn't back down either. "Just tell me what to do with it."

Keller stared at the file a moment longer.

"Scrub the surface layer, encrypt your findings, and bury them in Red Channel. No backups. Then walk away, Patrick.

You didn't find this."

Farley nodded once, slowly.

But as he turned to leave, he muttered, "That's the thing, sir. I think it found us."

* * *

Keller strode out to the operations room. Ramos straightened in his chair and leaned forward, the subtle crease in his brow deepening as he studied the timestamps. He cleared his throat. "We've seen this before. Activation cascades. But they used to take time; weeks, sometimes months. We always had space to react."

He glanced back at the screen, then to Keller. "But this is different. Three in seventy-two hours. No delay. No scatter. They're aligned. Someone, or something, is syncing them."

Keller's expression didn't shift, but the tension in his jaw spoke volumes. "No system we designed could do this. Not without help."

Patel finally stirred from her silence, exhaling as she rolled her chair back slightly. "Or maybe we're seeing noise and convincing ourselves it's music."

Ramos turned toward him. "You think this is coincidence?"

"I think we've been knee-deep in classified anomalies for too long," Patel replied, her voice dry. "Everything starts to look like a pattern when you're desperate for one. We chase ghosts, then wonder why we're the ones losing sleep."

Keller studied her for a moment. "And yet, here we are. Three sites. Three triggers. And an artifact network that was never meant to be woken all at once."

Patel shrugged, but the deflection didn't land as easily as it used to. "I'm just saying... sometimes chaos is just that. Chaos."

But no one in the room really believed that anymore.

Keller nodded slowly. He remembered the meetings no one recorded, names uttered and quickly forgotten. Drexler. The artifacts. The pattern they were never supposed to complete.

He looked at the data again and saw not discovery, but design. And for the first time, he felt small inside his own command center.

"According to the latest intel from our SETI friends in the Arctic, these anomalies are accelerating," Keller said. "And we're not ready."

Patel turned toward the auxiliary feed, flipping through satellite diagnostics. "That drone data is repeating."

Ramos looked confused. "You think it's mimicry?"

"I think it's rehearsal," Keller said. "And we're not the audience."

No one disagreed; they all understood what that meant, even if none of them dared to say it alone.

19

Cipher: The Ice Remembers

Abandoned Airbase – Sunday, 1011 Hours

Time had fractured long before the artifact glowed. Sparky's chronometer jumped ahead six seconds, then blinked backward by twelve, every few minutes. Their internal clocks disagreed violently with the sun's eerie stillness. Something ancient was recalibrating reality.

Sparky peered at the artifact's pulse and muttered, "You ever get the feeling we're the punchline to someone else's joke?" He shook his head, then added more seriously, "Joke's got bad timing."

Within the stark, frozen corridors of the facility, the relic's gentle, persistent glimmer played over frost-laden walls, casting shifting, secretive shadows along the World War Two-era passages. This wasn't residual glow. The artifact pulsed with deliberate rhythm, its light moving in measured, rhythmic patterns as if trying to speak in a language older than time itself. Every flicker, every subtle change in brightness stirred buried memories and inexplicable déjà vu in the minds of the team; a montage filled with anomalies, uncanny synchronizations, and the harrowing journey which had felt preordained. In that crystalline isolation, the fragmented visions coalesced into one undeniable truth: the disturbances were deliberately orchestrated.

As they navigated the shadowy corridors, every footstep echoed with urgency. Their minds churned with questions: How was it possible that time itself could bend? Who, or what, was behind these intentional manipulations? Each member of the team wrestled with their own inner demons; the fear that their personal histories might be erased, the terror that every choice they had ever made could be rendered meaningless by a shifting timeline.

Amid the escalating turmoil, intercepted communications from the Continuum confirmed a chilling truth: their relentless adversaries were drawing ever nearer. The threat was no longer an abstract specter, it was a tangible presence, closing in with every passing second. Every heartbeat increased the risk of capture and the potential obliteration of everything they had fought for. With eyes steeled by resolve and hearts pounding in unison, Ben's breath fogged the air. Beyond the frost-laced window, the desert shimmered like something half-awake. He muttered, "It's not here. Whatever we're meant to find, it's waiting for us out there." Every moment pulsed with the possibility of not only altering their fate but reshaping the fabric of time.

* * *

Deep within the maze-like facility, conversation interwove with cautious strategy. Gina's inner conflict was palpable as she struggled to reconcile her hard-won rational skepticism with the overwhelming force of emerging truth. "Everything we've experienced, it all fits together," her voice trembling between awe and dread. "But if it all fits, it means someone designed the puzzle. And I'm not sure I want to meet the architect." She hugged her arms close, then squared her shoulders like someone daring the dark to answer back.

"Does it feel like we've only been here one night?" Gina loudly blurted out.

Outside the broken windows, snow drifted silently under a gray sky. Then a shape moved above the tree line. Only a shadow. No engine, no signature. A matte curve paused for a moment, as if listening, then vanished.

Sparky glanced up but said nothing. He clicked his chronometer again and frowned.

Liam shook his head. "Every step since the landing has felt like the seconds are stretched."

Ben added, "Yeah, I have noticed that too. Something about this place seems to resist the idea of time moving forward at a normal pace."

As they stepped out of the ruined base, Sparky muttered, "So it's real. Under the right stress, time doesn't just bend... it slips. Cause and effect can reverse, even if just for a moment."

Liam looked ahead, his voice tight. "It's like the artifact is a remote for time. A trigger. It doesn't move us through it; it reshuffles what happens. Tiny shifts, but enough to change everything. I keep thinking about all the weird overlaps, those moments that felt too perfect to be chance."

Ben's eyes stayed on the horizon. "Then maybe they weren't chance. If the relic can rewrite time, those glitches weren't accidents. They were adjustments. History might not be fixed at all. It could be a living thing... and we're part of whatever it's trying to correct."

They could barely look away from the artifact, suspended between Liam and Sparky in a rough bungee harness. Its ancient etchings pulsed with an otherworldly light. What first seemed like a mix of Morse and Gematria was actually a celestial chart, each number tied to a Hebrew letter. When decoded, the sequences revealed geographic coordinates—clear and deliberate.

"This is a direct command," Ben said monotone, his voice heavy with dread. "It's an order: pointing us straight to Groom Lake."

As they pushed ahead, a soft, pulsing whir drifted above them.

Gina tilted her head. “You hear that?”

Sparky stopped. “Yeah, so what? Sounds like wind vibration through metal sheeting near the Quonset hut we passed.”

But it wasn’t. It was rhythmic. Circular. Almost curious. And it was above them. It broke through the clouds for a fraction of a second, long enough to see the drone lights.

Liam squinted up into the angry black cloud-thick sky. He couldn’t see a thing. “It’s not scanning. It’s waiting.”

Sparky’s knuckles tightened around the handle of the straps holding the artifact. Liam took a breath that felt oddly out of sync, trying to put puzzle pieces together from what felt like different boxes.

Then Gina whispered, almost to herself, “It’s not watching us... it’s listening.”

The whirring sound retreated into silence. The moment lingered, and something shifted behind Gina’s eyes as a thought clicked into place.

She turned to the others, focused on the artifact. Her voice now threaded with awe. “So it’s not just a relic... it’s an interface that can alter the flow of time. And it’s guiding us somewhere specific? So, what is at Area 51? What’s the big deal at Groom Lake?”

Liam spoke quietly, his voice pulled tight with wonder. “It’s guiding us toward the center. Where story and history collide. Someone built this... not just to hide something, but to reshape time itself."

He trailed off, caught in the weight of it.

Suddenly, the portable monitor Gina held glimmered. No sound. No alert. Just a flat, pulsing line of text that appeared mid-screen like it had always been there.

Cease your investigation immediately. You will not be warned again.

Gina's breath hitched. "Ay, no. Otra vez." Her voice dipped low. "Second warning, same shadow."

She looked to Liam, eyes wide but focused. "They're doing a lot more than watching... they're following us."

Ben stood quietly behind them. When he spoke, his voice was soft, almost prayerful.

"Remember," he said, "when a thing is repeated, it isn't always to strengthen. Sometimes, it is because the speaker has no faith that they were heard."

He walked to the monitor, gaze steady.

"The first time, they tried to command us. The second, they showed fear. But this? This is of someone losing control."

Liam looked at him. “And that’s why we press forward.”

Ben nodded. “Here is what is unshakable: truth doesn’t retreat when threatened. It digs deeper.”

Gina’s voice shifted to a murmur. “Entonces vamos. Let them try to stop us.”

Liam smiled faintly, not with triumph, but with clarity. “We don’t fight them... we outlast them... with truth.”

Ben placed a gentle hand on Gina’s shoulder, then Liam’s. “So we continue. Not because we are unafraid... but because we are accountable to something greater.”

No one needed to say anything else. The message on the screen faded. But its meaning had already been overwritten by resolve.

Nobody spoke. Sparky zipped the artifact case without looking up. Gina checked the backup module, jaw set. Ben nodded at Liam—one slow dip of the head, and turned toward the hatch. With the artifact’s pulsing glow lighting their path, they gathered their gear and prepared for the next phase of their journey.

* * *

As the corridor opened onto an expansive, shadowed hall,

the team paused to reflect on their mission. Gina broke the silence, her voice a mixture of fear and fierce determination. "If we're standing on the edge of something this monumental, we have to ask: Who is pulling the trigger? Who is orchestrating this manipulation of time?"

For a long, heavy moment, no one answered. Then Liam, steady and unwavering, spoke: "That's what we need to find out. This isn't about an artifact or a relic from a forgotten era; it's about someone, or something, that has been rewriting history from behind the curtain. And if we follow this map to Groom Lake, we might finally confront the true puppet master."

Ben's eyes glistened with a mix of fear and anticipation as he added, "Our journey isn't about decoding a message; it's about reclaiming our history, our identity, and our future from a force that has been shaping it all along." His voice held both the sorrow of lost certainties and the hope of unmasking a hidden destiny.

The abandoned base's walls murmured with the voices of the past; echoes of forgotten prophecies and secrets too vast for a single generation to contain. The artifact's glow intensified with every step, its pulse growing steadier, as if it had been waiting for this moment.

They made another course change and reached a small alcove in the corridor, where a dusty mural—painted by long dead enlisted men—depicted scenes of ancient rituals and cosmic cycles gleaned from local stories. In the faded images, they recognized symbols similar to those etched on the relic. Gina knelt before the mural, running her fingers over the faded lines. "This is like a manual; a guide to the cycle of creation and destruction," she murmured. "...like our existence is phase one in a repeating design."

Liam joined her, his eyes fixed on a particular sequence of symbols that mirrored the pauses in the Morse code. "Every glitch we've seen, every inexplicable reversal; it fits into this cycle," he said. "We're looking at a temporal network, a system that corrects itself. But the question is; who or what controls the corrections?"

At that moment, a sudden gust of cold wind swept through the corridor. Ben rose slowly, his face set in determination. "If our past is meant to be rewritten, maybe our future is ours to reclaim. We must continue. Even if it means facing an enemy we cannot see."

Their steps quickened as they exited the facility and emerged into the harsh, biting cold of the external compound.

* * *

Outside, the night sky was a vault of impenetrable darkness, with a few stars blinking like distant warnings. The wind howled around them, carrying the scent of ice and ancient secrets. They knew that every second counted; each tick of the clock a countdown toward an inevitable confrontation.

The team set out through a narrow, snow-covered passage carved between looming drifts and jagged cliffs, each breath a white plume in the biting air. The path opened onto a secluded clearing where their transport vehicle was silently waiting. They clambered in, while Sparky attempted to start the engine. This time he wasn't as lucky. He hopped out, dropped to his knees beside the wheel hub, and swept away ice crystals to reveal corroded bolts. With a few deft turns of a wrench and his portable diagnostic rig, he pinpointed the stubborn sensors that needed replacing. Liam had joined his friend, gloved hands worked to unseal a tightly packed reserve of diesel drums, the hiss of escaping air blending with the distant groan of shifting snow.

Together they hoisted each barrel, fingers numb but determined, until the tank's throat glugged awake with fresh fuel. Thirty minutes later, the ancient but reliable engine protested, complained, and coughed to life. It emitted a deep, mechanical rumble that rose into a steady growl as the vehicle shuddered awake. The cab's stale warmth a welcome contrast to the piercing cold outside. Gina, her breath fogging the windshield as she peered into the featureless expanse ahead, ran a hand through her swept-back hair. Her eyes scanned the horizon, catching the faint glow of distant floodlights. "We've come too far to turn back now. Groom Lake isn't a destination... it's our next step in uncovering the truth."

Liam's voice was resolute as he added, "We must find the source of this manipulation and reset the balance of time." His words were both a promise and a challenge; a vow to fight against the unseen forces that sought to rewrite history. The old transport shuddered as it tore over the frozen ground, its engine's rumble swallowed by the roar of wind-driven snow. Inside the cab, tension crackled as Gina gripped the dashboard, white-knuckled, while Ben peered into the swirling white expanse, every flake a translucent reminder of the stakes they faced. The snow-laden pines bowed under the storm's weight, their silhouettes danced in the headlights.

* * *

The vehicle plunged into the darkness, its headlights cutting narrow paths through the swirling snow. Their target was the airstrip and another plane ride, back to Sparky's second Groom Lake safehouse.

Thankfully, Sparky's modifications to the truck engine and jury-rigged tire chains allowed for a fast and safe 67-minute journey to the airstrip coordinates.

As they rumbled over the icy roads, their conversation grew more animated, their theories intertwining with plans and countermeasures. Sparky's earlier words about the reversal of time echoed in their minds, fueling a determination to press forward no matter the cost.

The vehicle's dashboard briefly glimmered. For a heartbeat, the speedometer read a number was impossible; reflecting not their current speed, but a value from moments earlier.

Gina's eyes darted between the instruments and the icy landscape.

"Something's off," she said, voice tight with tension. "It's like the truck is caught in a previous time."

Sparky gripped the wheel tighter, feeling the odd shift as the vehicle decelerated, not by driver input, but as if by the pull of a forgotten moment.

Gina blinked, fingers digging into the seat. "I swear... for a second, I saw the same dead tree twice."

The ripple passed as quickly as it came, leaving them with an unnerving reminder: even in their escape, time was unreliable, a silent, constant threat looming behind every turn. At last, the vehicle reached their destination.

* * *

They spilled out of the transport and sprinted across the frost-lined tarmac, each boot cracking through a thin glaze of ice; their dubious pilot; courtesy of Sparky; spotted them closing in and sprang into action. The battered King Air's engine sputtered to life, its propeller biting at the frigid dawn light as they clambered aboard. Through the open door, a wall of sleet-driven wind raced across the runway, snowflakes driven horizontal by the gale; a white shroud that would have buried them in seconds had they remained grounded. With a roar of pistons and a juddering leap, the plane clawed into the sky, wings slicing through the merciless squall as it crashed across the runway behind them.

Inside the cramped cockpit, Ben pressed his forehead against the frosty pane, his breath misting on the glass. He glanced over his shoulder at the swirling vortex of white below, then let his gloved fingers drift to the warmth of his pocket. His hand closed around the smooth, cool edges of his Star of David medallion, the familiar weight a small talisman against the storm's fury; and the unknown waiting beyond the tempest.

* * *

After what felt like an eternity in that claustrophobic cargo hold, surrounded by weathered crates, looping netting, and unmarked bundles best left uninspected; the frost finally cleared from the windows. The broad sweep of Nevada's desert reemerged beneath them, wind-sculpted dunes and jagged mesas giving way to the unmistakable silhouette of Groom Lake's hidden hangars. The King Air's wheels bit into the salt-crusted desert runway with a violent shudder, sending plumes of dust and gravel skittering into the glare of distant floodlights. The fuselage groaned as it rattled to a stop, then Sparky flung open the door and hauled the others out into the cool Nevada night. He paused long enough to slide a thick stack of bills across the pilot's console, exchanged a curt nod with the wary aviator, then pivoted and joined the others.

* * *

Sparky took the lead.

Ben huffed, "Hey, yo Sparky, what's your meshuggeh plan now? I'm seventy-three, and auditioning for Lawrence of Nevada I'm not."

"Lawrence who?" Sparky shot back without breaking stride.

"Never mind," Ben wheezed. "Of course you don't know, because I'm seventy-three and you're... whatever this is."

Sparky just shook his head, grinning. "Safehouse Two's just up that ridge; an old World War Two bomb shelter I buried under the dunes. Cool as a mausoleum, and invisible to every grid that matters."

Liam let out a low whistle. "A desert bunker. Of course you'd retrofit a fallout shelter in the sand."

Gina cracked a grin. "Perfect. When the sun's a furnace by day and the wind's an icebox by night, concrete walls sound downright luxurious."

The wind hit them like a slap the moment they stepped onto the tarmac. Sharp, dry, and carrying the scent of scorched minerals and secrecy, it howled across the empty expanse of Groom Lake. Floodlights buzzed above, roving slightly as if protesting their return.

Sparky led them through a narrow trench of sand-worn fencing, ducking beneath a bent rail and weaving toward the dark outline of a low structure buried half in dune. No signage. No lights. Just a rusting outpost hunched into the land like it wanted to be forgotten.

Liam adjusted the harness around the relic, careful to shield its soft glow from the open air. "This place hasn't seen human life in decades."

Sparky grinned. "Exactly why I like it. Officially decommissioned in the nineties. Unofficially, well... let's just say it's been my Plan B since before you knew my real name."

Ben rubbed his knees and muttered, "Oy. If this is Plan B, I don't want to see what happens when we hit Plan C."

Gina said nothing. Her eyes stayed on the horizon, where a distant rumble could have been thunder or something less natural. She reached for the latch before Sparky could, and together they hauled the heavy door open.

* * *

The safehouse exhaled cold, stale air as if surprised to see them.

They stepped inside, one by one, into the dim space of corrugated steel and cracked tile. It was spare and silent, but dry, and blessedly cut off from the swirling grit outside.

Sparky threw a switch. The fluorescent lights flickered, then held. In the middle of the room stood a long worktable, ringed by battered chairs, empty MRE boxes, and a coffee pot so scorched it might have been part of the Manhattan Project.

No one complained. It was safe, at least for now.

Ben dropped his pack and gave a sharp sigh. "Alright. Mazel tov. We made it."

20

Lock: The Invitation No One Sent

The desert wind howled outside, swirling sand against the metal siding of the safehouse. It was an old prefab structure, once a border patrol outpost, now stripped to barebones essentials; an ideal hiding place if you weren't being actively hunted by one of the most powerful forces on the planet.

They hauled their gear into the bunker's makeshift lab; laptops, power banks, and Sparky's portable console, all bundled tight against the swirling sand outside. The corrugated metal door clanged shut behind them, sealing out the night wind and the weight of the desert's secrets.

Inside, the air smelled of old pine and rusted steel, mingled with the damp, musty breath of earth that hadn't seen light in decades. Ben ran a hand along a battered console. "Hard to believe this all started with a scrap of code from Chicksands," he murmured. Liam glanced up. "Yeah. The old RAF Y-station. Seems that blip in their archive may have started everything." Gina gave a faint smile. "Then let's make sure it ends better than it began."

The group resumed their work at the safehouse's cramped quarters; time in that moment out on them. As the door sealed, one of Sparky's monitors buzzed faintly. A stray waveform blinked and then disappeared.

"Was that an inbound packet?" Liam asked.

Sparky looked uncertain. "Not sure, brother. Might've been reflection. Or... unwanted attention."

They were so close, they had to discover what the mystery was at Hangar 18. After reviewing the numbers for a fifth time, Gina's photographic memory clicked into place and she practically shouted. "They didn't point us back to Groom Lake and the hangar location... they spelled its name in ancient Hebrew." Sparky tapped his pen against the table. "You sure? Last time we got this excited, we spent six hours in a dead end."

Ben squinted, mouthing the words. "Of course, it's Hebrew. Next you'll tell me there's a bagel recipe hidden in there." His eyes lit up as realization struck. "Oy, she's right! These match the numeric pattern we saw earlier. It matches the lock code on the Groom Lake archive."

Gina sat back and smiled.

Sparky scratched his head. "Jewish numbers again. I'm just about ready to trade my tinfoil hat for a yarmulke, people."

Ben rolled his eyes.

Liam replayed the signal, isolating each pause with precision while Gina jotted the sequence in shorthand; her strokes crisp and fast, thanks to the well-crafted, Rube-Goldberg-inspired electric pen she'd recently lifted from Sparky's stash.

"Hey, yo—that's one of my inventions," Sparky protested from across the room, sounding more wounded than angry.

Gina looked sheepish. "I have a thing for pens."

Sparky blinked. "Wait... you what?"

Liam chuckled. "Trust me; she's got a whole collection. I'm still mourning my Air Force pen."

"It's more than just a pen, guys," Sparky grumbled, glancing at the sleek device he invented with underappreciated pride.

He glanced at his watch, fidgeting. "And can we please solve the ancient mystery before lunch? My blood sugar's tanking." Gina pulled out a granola bar from her pocket and handed it to Sparky. It almost felt like a trade.

"The Hebrew mystics used a similar technique," Ben continued with urgency, focused on the challenge. "They encoded the dimensions of Solomon's Temple into the dedication psalms; letters became lengths, pauses became proportions." Gina shook her head. "So what, we're building temples now?

Or tearing our hair out for fun?"

Then it was Sparky with the next 'eureka moment' as he let out a triumphant yelp. "Finally! Being the resident 'tinfoil hat' collector pays off," he grinned, snapping open his laptop with theatrical flair. "Turns out I might have what we're looking for. Anybody in the market for a slightly haunted 1955 UFO hangar in the middle of nowhere?" He tapped rapidly, pulling up a grainy schematic. "Needs a little TLC, but hey; so did the pyramids." Ben raised an eyebrow. "Please tell me this isn't another link to a guy in Belarus with too much time on his hands."

Sparky shook his head. "It's the real deal, old man."

As he zoomed in on the blueprint of Hangar 18, Sparky's grin faded into a look of intense concentration. "It's not a temple, but it might as well be," he murmured, tracing the adjusted sequence against the schematic. "Lay these numbers over the Area 51 hangar, and you get:"

1 → the single oversized support beam to the right of the east service door

Gina leaned in. "You sure you're reading the right blueprint? Last time we got stuck in the janitor's closet." Sparky, completely oblivious, continued.

3 → the trio of recessed rivet brackets along that same bulkhead

4 → the four adjacent floor panels inside the bay whose edges sit ever so slightly askew

3 → another set of three catwalk braces overhead

6 → the six access-bolt housings on the mezzanine walkway

4 → the quartet of corridor rivets lining the back room

Gina kept writing, cross-referencing each mark with her shorthand notes. They all held their breaths as Sparky highlighted the final point on the grid. The lamplight caught a faint watermark on the blueprint's corner, almost invisible until Gina tilted the paper just right. She tapped the spot, heart quickening. "Wait. Does anyone else see that?"

Sparky leaned in, squinting. "You're telling me we missed a hidden mark after all this?"

Ben shook his head, a smile ghosting over his face. "Figures. There's always one more layer."

Liam exhaled slowly. "Here goes nothing. If the floor drops out, I'm blaming Sparky."

"Those counts must be telling us where to look," he continued, voice low. Ben tapped his finger against the table. "But how the taps actually trigger the entrance... we'll only find out once we're inside." Gina rubbed her temples. "Or maybe we're inventing patterns because we're desperate."

Ben tapped the edge of the tablet. “You realize what this means? The pattern’s not a side effect. It’s the medium. Whoever they were, they spoke in sequences, as if the world itself were listening.”

For a moment, silence reigned; until Sparky cleared a space on the workbench and spread out the annotated blueprint. Gina slid Liam’s USB drive into the mainframe interface; LEDs blinked green and amber in acknowledgment. Sparky muttered as he tweaked the power couplings, and the console hummed to life.

* * *

The room fell into a weighty stillness, punctuated by the mechanical spin of hard drives. Liam inhaled slowly, bracing himself for the moment of truth.

Inside, the laptop’s pale light carved shadows across his determined features as he launched the diagnostic script. Gina stood behind him, jaw clenched and arms folded, eyes fixed on the cascading code.

Then the words appeared, stark against the scrolling lines:

“Cease and desist. We know what you are doing. We are coming for you.”

Gina’s face drained of color. Ben recoiled, hand fumbling for his glasses. "So... do we listen?" he asked, voice tight.

Liam let out a humorless laugh. "You already know the answer."

Gina squared her shoulders. "We're too far in now. Whoever this is, they know we're close."

Ben offered a grim half-smile. "That means they're scared."

Sparky tapped the keyboard, going as fast as he could go. "I need to see if anything else changed in the system when that message appeared." He ran a diagnostic scan; checking recent access logs, packet traces, data transfers.

The results loaded instantly.

Nothing.

The pattern was the same: no intrusion logs, no external IPs, no evidence. Nothing.

Sparky said simply, "This stuff is certainly not coming through conventional means."

Ben arched a brow. "What in all of creation does that mean?"

Gina leaned in. "It means this wasn't a hack. This was inserted into the system; like it was always meant to be there."

The air in the room grew heavier.

Liam sat back, piecing things together. "It's like the system itself wanted us to see it."

Ben let out a low whistle. "That's comforting."

Gina commented, "Either way, the message is clear: we're being watched."

Liam's jaw tightened. "Then we watch back." Liam sat at the edge of the table, fingers clattering against his yellow notepad, his eyes fixed on the lines of code they had spent the last seventy-two hours unraveling. Gina stood behind him, arms crossed, eyes darting between the laptop screen and the growing tension in Liam's shoulders.

Sparky let out a low groan, followed by a string of colorful euphemisms. He then leaned back in his chair, balancing it on two legs, chewing on the end of a pen. "Alright," he said finally, exhaling. "We have a problem."

Ben responded in kind. "Really? After a scary warning on a computer screen from the bad guys. No kidding."

Sparky shrugged. "One of my failsafe junction boxes isn't responding, and I need to fix it with the usual bubblegum and bailing wire."

Liam frowned. "And that means what, exactly?"

"Not a big deal," Sparky replied with a half-smile. "Just a short walk to an outer perimeter relay that looks like a cactus. Probably came loose during the last windstorm. I need to reroute the power or the cloaking pings will start dropping." He glanced at Liam. "Give me a hand?"

"Sorry, no can do," Liam replied, not looking up from the screen. "Gina and I are still working through the SETI pass-codes; we've almost finished rebuilding the authentication sequence. If we lose momentum now, we may not get back in."

"I'll go," Ben cut in, standing with a groan. "Stretch my legs, keep you company. What can I do to help?"

Sparky grinned, slinging a coiled wire over his shoulder. "Follow me, Rabbi; let's go bless us a cactus."

* * *

The door clanged shut behind them, and the room returned to a tense, humming silence. Liam and Gina sat shoulder to shoulder at the console, eyes flicking across lines of cascading code.

They'd spent the last three days decrypting and reverse-engineering the labyrinthine firewall of the SETI mainframe; one booby-trapped with failsafes designed to erase itself at the first sign of intrusion. But the message embedded within the ghost signal had given them clues. It was more than a broadcast; it had been a key, cleverly disguised.

And the clues led to the backdoor entrance of a Continuum computer.

Located at another black ops site that contained a significant aspect of the programming, database, legacy records, and significant energy usage. Beneath a veil of jamming fields and motion-sensor tripwires, its perimeter was marked by razor-wire fences and watchtowers bristling with infrared scanners. Inside, cavernous server halls vibrated with the pulse of quantum cores; machines so powerful they bent reality in their wake, drawing more power than a small city. Every corridor echoed with the hum of hidden cryogenic chambers and the faint hiss of coolant lines, promising both unparalleled access and instant annihilation should the wrong override be triggered. This location was the mother lode; the problem was this: which location was most critical to access? The Hangar 18 facility or this newly identified Continuum locale?

Liam scrubbed through packet fragments, isolating temporal fingerprints. Gina worked parallel, reshaping authentication strings by layering the original credentials against what they now suspected was a recursive access loop.

Liam nodded grimly. "Not a static password vault… it's a reactive logic gate. Adaptive encryption."

A blinking cursor returned to the command line. Liam typed.

Paused. Hit enter.

A low chime echoed from the terminal.

ACCESS RE-ESTABLISHED: TIER 3 – PROTECTED MODULES UNLOCKED

Liam exhaled. "We're back in."

Gina leaned forward. "Then let's find out what they didn't want anyone to see."

* * *

The sky stretched black and endless above them. Ben Levinson adjusted his coat against the cold, scowling as he checked the network uplink. His breath fogged in the frigid air as he muttered under his breath.

"I take back what I said earlier, Kid. I'm too old for this."

Next to him, Sparky crouched, adjusting the last of his wireless relay beacons sticking out of a real-looking fake cactus. His fingers moved fast, working an unruly set of power board wires sticking out of the panel. His laptop screen blinked with status checks as he rerouted their access through a dozen obfuscated nodes.

"Almost done," Sparky murmured. "This should keep us

invisible long enough for them to...”

A red warning flashed on his laptop screen.

Sparky’s smirk vanished. His fingers froze over the keyboard.

Ben noticed the shift. “What is it?”

Sparky exhaled sharply. “We tripped something.”

Ben’s expression darkened. “Be specific. I don’t like surprising beeps and flashing lights for no reason, Kid.”

Sparky’s fingers flew across the keyboard. “I was piggybacking Liam’s connection; just handshake to redirect any tracking pings before they reached us. But now...”

A new window opened. A server response they weren’t supposed to see.

ACCESS POINT LOGGED. AUTOMATIC COUNTERMEASURE ENGAGED.

The relay beacon fizzled and died.

Sparky’s face went pale. “They know where we are.”

* * *

A distant rumble shook the floor beneath them.

Liam's head snapped up. Gina was already moving, pushing back from the desk. "That wasn't the wind."

Liam's fingers froze over the keyboard. A warning flashed across the screen:

REMOTE CONNECTION LOST

His stomach dropped.

"They're here."

* * *

A flash of light. The front windows of the safehouse shattered inward as flashbangs exploded in the room.

Liam and Gina barely had time to move before the entire structure trembled with impact. The air filled with acrid smoke, ears ringing.

Outside, Ben and Sparky ducked behind a ridge, eyes wide as a black tactical transport rolled up the dirt road.

Four SUVs. No headlights. No sirens. Silent. Precise.

"This is bad," Sparky mumbled.

Ben removed his glasses, using his shirt to clean a smudge. "Don't hold back, how do you really feel? Oy, the master of the understatement. kid—it was already bad."

Sparky opened his laptop, hands shaking slightly. "I... I can shut them down. Jam their comms. Give Liam and Gina a chance to..."

Ben grabbed his wrist, stopping him.

Sparky looked up, confused; until he saw what Ben saw.

More SUVs. Approaching from the east.

A full-scale containment op. No firefight. No escape route. This wasn't an assassination.

This was an extraction.

***

Liam's vision blurred as he struggled against the white noise in his skull. The powerful weapon being used on them both was a small, hand-held, bright-metal tube, wielded by one of Keller's men. He then felt hands on him, dragging him from the chair. His stomach was queasy, and he tasted copper in his mouth.

Gina fought back through tears, kicking at one of the agents, knocking his balance. But there were too many of them. Even as she was dragged, Gina's hand instinctively reached for her collar. The Montblanc was still there. She held onto it like a final tether.

The voice came through the haze, low and calm.

"Secure them."

Liam's mind caught up just in time to see Keller step into view, his face impassive as ever. Gina spat blood onto the floor. "Hope you're proud of yourself."

Keller didn't even flinch. "Pride is inefficient."

Darkness closed in.

* * *

Ben and Sparky crouched behind the ridge, the glow of tail-lights vanishing into the desert like dying embers. Liam and Gina had been thrown into the third SUV; hoods, restraints, precision.

Ben slammed Sparky's laptop shut. "We can't stop them now."

Sparky's jaw tightened. "Then what do we do?"

Ben stared out at the black horizon, wind gnawing at his coat. The convoy was gone. Swallowed by silence.

He adjusted his glasses slowly. "We find where they're going."

Sparky exhaled through his teeth, wiping a trembling hand across his mouth. "And then?"

Ben's eyes narrowed. "Then we get them back, Kid. They picked the wrong Rabbi to mess with."

Sparky nodded, already flipping open the laptop again. "I'm in. And... I know where to find them." A sudden flicker danced across Sparky's screen; timestamp anomalies. It only lasted a second, but it showed the same hour looping twice. "That's... weird," he cursed, brushing it off as a glitch. But the relic had never glitched before.

Ben turned, eyes sharp. "How could you possibly know that? Those guys aren't merely ghosts; they're shadows of shadows. Wherever they're taking them, it'll be buried under concrete, code names, and kill switches."

Sparky didn't answer right away. He tapped a few keys, toggling screens.

A map blinked to life. A glowing red dot moved slowly across the terrain.

Ben leaned in, stunned. "Is that...?"

Sparky smirked, then grew serious. "She kept it. My pen. I wasn't sure she'd actually bring it... but she did."

Ben blinked. "You planted a tracker?"

"No," Sparky said, "I gave her an option. She chose to bring it."

Ben blinked. "That thing was trackable?"

Sparky raised an eyebrow. "Ben, that wasn't *just* a pen. That was a home-made, custom-built, multi-sensor beacon with GPS, inertial backup, and thermal sync. Wrapped in chrome. And she borrowed it."

Ben stared at the pulsing red dot, then let out a dry chuckle. "Good thing she's a pen klepto."

Sparky smiled, but his voice was steel. "Now we bring them home."

21

Cipherlock: The Tipping Point

Unknown Continuum Facility – Time Indeterminate

Liam's head ached. His vision blurred, then snapped into sharp focus.

The first thing he noticed was the sound; a soft, monotone hum of power circulating through the walls. It was calibrated, to disorient, to dissolve any sense of time.

The second thing was the cold bite of the restraints. His wrists, secured to the chair's armrests with surgical precision, weren't bound too tightly, but enough to remind him that he was no longer in control.

The room reeked of overused disinfectant; sharp in the nose, with a chemical bite on the tongue. Beneath it lingered the cold tang of metal and a sour, recycled edge from the vents, dry and artificial, clinging to the skin like static.

He turned his head, slow and stiff.

Across the table, Gina sat in a matching chair, her posture rigid, eyes trained forward. To anyone else, she might have looked calm, but Liam knew better.

He recognized the tension in her jaw.

She was furious.

The door slid open with a quiet hiss.

Two men entered.

The first, Elias Keller, moved with less of his usual steel. His gait still carried the calculated efficiency of a man bred for command, but the veneer had begun to crack. He glanced at Liam longer than necessary, as if confirming that he was still there; still real. There was a hesitation in his steps, like he'd stared too long into the abyss and wasn't sure if it had smiled back at him.

This was a man who had seen something he couldn't explain, and it rattled him. Not enough to paralyze him, but enough to remind him that control was an illusion. The artifact had changed him. Liam could see it.

Behind him, Lucien Drexler took his time sitting at the head of the table, straightening the cuffs of his tailored suit before glancing at the embedded glass screen on the desk before him.

Liam had seen this act before.

One brought the script and a smile. The other brought the knife.

Drexler let the silence stretch. He scrolled through financial reports, social media analytics, and security logs, as if he wasn't looking at two prisoners, but rather a bad investment.

Then, finally, he looked up.

"Do you understand what you've done?"

Liam exhaled slowly. "Would you like the short answer or the long one?"

Keller remained still, arms crossed.

"This isn't about regret," Drexler gave a faint smile. "It's about whether you even grasp what you've triggered."

Liam glanced at Gina. Her expression flickered between frustration and amusement.

"I think what he's asking," she said, "is whether we feel bad for breaking your toys."

Keller's jaw tightened slightly. "You think this is a joke?"

"No," Gina said flatly. "We think you're going to try to convince us that you're not the bad guys."

Drexler chuckled softly, shaking his head. "You still don't get it." He gestured toward the screen.

The wall lit up.

News articles. Financial projections. Surveillance feeds.

They weren't live updates. They were pre-written.

Headlines scrolled in real time:

"SETI Researcher Mills Discredited After Fraud Accusations."

"Gina Alvarez Under Federal Investigation for Unlawful Data Breach."

"Funding Pulled for Groom Lake Science Initiative Amid Scandal."

Liam's stomach twisted.

Drexler tapped the screen lightly, adjusting an insignificant detail, like a trader fine-tuning a portfolio.

"Dead men still get headlines. We erase the need for them."

Gina's fists clenched. "You don't own the truth."

"Truth doesn't trend," Keller said. "We decide what does. You think you're here because you exposed something? No, you're here because you colored outside the lines."

Drexler leaned in slightly, voice calm, measured. "The Continuum doesn't operate like a government or a corporation," he smirked. "It's an equation. Self-correcting, recursive. Remove the noise, balance the variables, and the outcome is always order. Disrupt the balance, and we reduce you to noise." He continued, "Infrastructure matters. The flow of capital, the networks of control, the silent agreements that decide what tomorrow looks like."

"And when someone like you disrupts that?" Gina spat out.

He smiled coldly, eyes glinting with an unsettling hunger. "We correct the system. And anyone foolish enough to disrupt it."

Liam swallowed back the bile rising in his throat. "You mean you erase them."

Drexler tilted his head. "We erase *problems*." He tilted his head slightly, his voice silky and unsettling. "And if necessary, entire families, communities, even cities. Whatever it takes to restore balance."

Gina exhaled sharply, eyes burning into him. "Then why haven't you pulled the trigger?"

Drexler considered her carefully, his chilling gaze appraising her like a commodity.

"Because you have value, and commodities can be traded, leveraged, or liquidated." Liam and Gina exchanged a quick glance.

"People like you," Drexler continued, "don't come along often. And it's far more efficient to use you than to erase you."

Keller spoke next, with authenticity, knowing the full truth. "You have two options. One: you disappear. You are erased. Your names, your work, your legacy. The world moves on without you. It will be as if you never existed."

A beat.

Keller's voice softened, almost casual. "Two: you come work for the agency. Your careers, credibility, respect... are all *restored*. You are provided everything you need to keep doing your research, but on the agency's terms."

Drexler leaned back, watching them carefully and added, "It's really that simple."

The silence that followed was suffocating.

Liam felt the weight of the offer pressing down on him; not the threat of erasure, but the temptation of restoration. His career. His credibility. A return to a normal life... but on their leash.

Across the table, Gina didn't move. But Liam could feel her fury humming beneath the surface like a charged wire.

Drexler waited, perfectly composed, the architect of their undoing already drafting blueprints for their redemption. His dead eyes never left them. Calculating. Waiting for the moment their will cracked.

Keller was unsure, uncomfortable, and unstable.

* * *

The room fell quiet.

Liam studied Drexler, then Keller.

Then the screen on the wall.

The pre-written headlines. The ghost of a future that hadn't happened yet; but would the moment they walked out of this room.

He exhaled.

And then he laughed. It wasn't loud. It wasn't forced. It was genuine amusement; because he had seen this before.

Liam shook his head. "You think we crawled through blood, betrayal, and broken time just to shake hands *now*?"

Drexler's eyes remained humorless and cruel. "I think you'll make the only rational choice."

Liam smirked.

"Then you don't know me very well."

Gina leaned back in her chair. "Yeah," Gina said, eyes locked. "We're choosing the one where you lose."

Drexler frowned. "There is no..." Before Keller could finish the sentence, the first explosion shook the room. The floor quaked with a pressure wave that threw them all sideways.

Gina hit the wall hard, her shoulder crunching against steel. Liam rolled with the impact, ears ringing as ceiling tiles shattered overhead. Smoke choked the air. For a moment, no one spoke; only the staggered breath of people realizing they were still alive.

The second explosion rattled everything and plunged the room into complete darkness.

* * *

A high-pitched alarm shrieked through the building. Red emergency lighting blinked. Keller reached for his comm, but static hissed through the earpiece. His face darkened.

The door banged open, and for a second, time became timeless. A silhouette stood in the light; disheveled, glasses askew, shotgun cradled like a relic.

"Rabbi?" Liam said, half in shock.

Ben Levinson nodded once. "Told you I still had a few moves left."

He scanned the room with sharp, intentional movements, and continued "...and THIS, boys and girls... this is my 'Mohel Cannon.' *Eight days old? Cute! Say hello to my little friend."*

Liam suppressed a smirk and looked away.

Ben was smeared with soot and his coat soaked from an old man's sweat and blood. He didn't flinch when a stray spark popped behind him. His eyes never stopped scanning the corners of the room. "Shalom, fellas," he said, voice dry. "Hope we're not interrupting any top-secret birthday party." He quickly cut them both loose; Liam and Gina rubbed their wrists, grateful to be free.

Keller's hand slid toward his sidearm.

Sparky didn't miss it. He lifted one hand calmly, while the other tapped a command into his tablet.

"I really wouldn't," Sparky said, not looking up. "One little press, and your lights go out. Literally. Or maybe the doors unlock. Or the sprinkler system floods your servers. It's kind of a mystery box at this point."

Keller froze.

Sparky grinned and finally glanced up. "Your security? Not great. Let's just say your computers and my computer... they've been, how shall I say... getting cozy and intimate." He gave the tablet an affectionate pat. "Even rolled out a welcome mat."

"That's very polite of them," countered Drexler.

Ben glanced sideways at Sparky and stated, "Remind me never to make you mad."

Sparky grinned, "Smart policy."

"How did you find us?" asked Liam. "A woman with a pen fetish," Sparky responded. Gina smirked.

Liam gave a dry exhale. "Took you long enough."

"Hey," Sparky shot back. "Hacking an unfriendly computer system and sneaking past armed guards isn't exactly ordering a deep-dish pizza."

Ben ignored them, his gaze locked onto Drexler. "Bubbe, here's how it goes. We walk out. No tricks. No memory games."

Drexler simply smiled, steepling his fingers. "And... if I refuse?"

The overhead lights glaring violently. Sparky sighed. "Then I unfriend your entire reality. Your choice."

"Took me a second, but I got into their grid. Power's gonna be spotty, but we have five minutes before they lock it down." Sparky adjusted his ball cap uneasily, glancing at the screen. "It's like some black-budget DARPA nightmare. Trust me, I've seen stuff at Edwards that makes Roswell look like Disneyland."

Keller tried again for his sidearm.

Sparky pointed at the camera in the corner.

"Uh-uh. We own your security feeds now, brother. Whole building thinks you're the intruder. Neat, huh?"

Drexler sat perfectly still, watching, expression unchanged.

Liam hesitated, staring at the man who had rewritten his life in real time. His mentor, Nathan Graves' voice returned, uninvited; the intel officer who taught him how to see through noise and silence both. "The best secrets don't stay buried," Graves had once told him. "They wait for the right fool to dig them up." Liam had never thought of himself as a fool, but standing here, watching Drexler's play to manipulate reality, he wasn't so sure anymore.

The four slipped out, moving fast.

"Left's clear," Sparky said, scanning his tablet. "Cameras are blind."

"How long?" Gina asked.

"Doesn't matter," Ben answered. "We're not stopping."

As they rounded a corner, a startled admin in a white shirt stepped into their path, holding a clipboard and a half-eaten protein bar. He froze.

Liam didn't. A swift elbow to the temple dropped the man without a sound. Ben caught him before he hit the ground, gently lowering him as Gina slipped the badge from his collar and tossed it to Liam.

Sparky tucked it into his vest. "Access just got easier."

Drexler didn't flinch. Keller shouted after them, calm and bitter: "You can't outrun the system."

The weight of those words wafted into Liam's consciousness; not as a threat, but as a truth.

Sparky, tablet in hand, flicking through access overrides and surveillance loops as he moved. His eyes never left the screen, lips pressed into a thin line as false alarms, misdirection signals, and flashing alerts scrolled by in real time.

The system was still fighting them; but so far, Sparky was winning.

* * *

Drexler's smirk cracked slightly as the four intruders escaped.

"They're inside now. Let them finish it," he said, voice low and self-assured.

Keller turned to him, bristling. "You think I'll let this become a free-for-all? You overplayed your hand."

"I did what was necessary," Drexler replied evenly. "The system adapts."

"No," Keller snapped, stepping forward. "The system is bleeding. And you just caused the infection."

Drexler's eyes narrowed. "Careful, Elias. You're confusing deviation for failure. Sometimes the signal needs noise."

Keller clenched his jaw, seething. "I want them found. Now."

Drexler didn't respond. He simply stepped backward into the shadows, his presence fading like static evaporating from a screen.

"Coward," Keller muttered. Then, keying his comm with a sharp click, he barked into the mic: "Initiate full lockdown. Grid search all levels. Intruders are in the system, contain or eliminate."

He didn't wait for acknowledgment.

Boots echoing through the corridor, Keller strode back to his duty section. The air in the chamber felt thinner than usual, too quiet for a command hub mid-emergency.

His advisors looked up as he entered. One of them, a wiry man with sharp eyes and a deeper worry hiding beneath his composure, stepped forward and handed him his tablet.

Patrick Farley cautiously approached.

"Status report, sir," said Farley, "We've rerouted drone access to sublevel six. Containment teams are deploying, but... the logs show interference. Someone's rewriting protocols from inside."

"Of course they are," Keller said coldly. "Make sure the backups stay offline. I don't want Drexler slipping a failsafe past us while we're distracted."

Farley nodded. "Understood. And sir... there's something else. A message just hit the primary feed. We can't trace it."

Keller turned his back on Farley and toward the overhead screen. "What kind of message?"

Farley hesitated, eyes still on his console.

Then the second message hit.

And Keller felt his skin crawl.

IV

Act IV: The Cipher Fractures (Acceleration Layer)

Everything is speeding up. The patterns are sharpening, but so are the fractures between them. Trust begins to slip. Time bends. And with every discovery, they're pulled closer to something they may not be ready to face.
The signal isn't just calling anymore... it's dragging them in.

22

Lock: Seeds of Doubt

Unknown Continuum Facility – Time Indeterminate

The message arrival wasn't what unsettled Keller, it was the feeling that it had always been there.

Waiting.

No one intercepted the warning, hacked it, or broadcast it in any traditional sense. It had simply... revealed itself. Nested like a parasite in the code. Or worse, like an electronic key turned in a cipherlock.

A wet, electrical hiss cut through the silence behind him.

Keller turned back.

Farley was standing there—or had been.

Now, he twitched violently as his body locked upright, eyes

wide, mouth agape as if some invisible current had seized his spine. The air around him shimmered, a distortion in the shape of a cube. Then...

The system took him.

Not with sound or light, but precision. One breath he was whole; the next, his form fragmented, limbs twisting unnaturally, skin splitting in silent rivulets as subdermal implants sparked like dying stars. His eyes liquefied, nerves flared blue, and then—as abruptly... nothing.

No explosion. No trace.

The floor was unmarred. The cameras had never blinked.

Keller didn't move.

His mind reeled, instinct screaming to shut it down, call for backup, raise every internal failsafe; but he knew. There would be no logs. No playback. No audit trail. Farley had been... overwritten.

Like a corrupted file

The terminal flickered again. Encrypted logs unraveled, line by line, as if the clearance was no longer his to control.

The message was writing itself—lines decrypting not because of his clearance, but because something wanted him to see them.

Farley's boots were still there. Just the boots. No blood or bone. No residue the human eye could register—yet Keller swore he could still feel the heat of the moment, like the afterglow of a flashbang behind his ribs.

He stepped back, breath shallow.

He had ordered men to their deaths. Watched black sites collapse. Overseen the silencing of physicists, linguists, time theorists. But this?

This was not elimination.

It was subtraction.

A clean rewrite.

His voice came out broken, not a whisper but a confession:

"That wasn't a kill order."

A weighted pause.

"That was revision."

Keller's blood ran cold.

"We're not being hunted. We're being redrafted."

* * *

Liam's breathing was ragged as they bolted through the service corridors of the Continuum facility, alarms blaring overhead. He coughed and wiped soot from his jacket. "Next time Ben unleashes the Mohel Cannon," he said, "remind me to wear Kevlar underwear."

Sparky let out a bark of laughter. "That wasn't a sermon. That was an exorcism."

Ben smirked without apology. "What can I say? Sometimes, the sacred and the strategic converge."

The halls converged on them, the emergency lights flashing red, but even in the chaos, the building's design was unmistakably efficient; there were no wasted spaces, no blind corners, no cover.

The lights flickered. Only once.

A sharp, unnatural pulse; an unsavory metallic coppery taste on the tongue.

Every fixture dimmed a shade too long, like the building had exhaled and forgot to inhale.

Ben flinched. "Ugh... did you feel that?"

No one answered. But something had shifted.

They kept running.

Ben struggled to keep up, his steps heavier than the others. At 73, he wasn't slow; but his muscles remembered more than they delivered. Even so, he gritted his teeth, refusing to be the weak link.

Sparky was the one leading the escape. The hacker was wired differently, his mind running through contingencies, not for escape, but for what came next. Sparky wasn't a government agent. He was underground. That's how he worked. Layers of contacts, networks built from necessity, people who owed him favors and others who feared what he knew.

And right now, that was the only reason they had a chance.

Footsteps echoed behind them; pursuers closing in fast.

"Left!" Sparky shouted, but something in his voice cracked.

A door hissed halfway open, then jammed. Sparks flared from the control panel.

"Junk tech," he muttered. "Fallback sensors just woke up. Pressure triggers, analog failsafes."

Gina stepped up, pried open the panel, and started rerouting power manually.

Ben barked, "This the part where we pray?"

"No time," Sparky snapped. "Either it opens now or we fry on the next pulse sweep."

Liam slammed his shoulder against the door. "On three..."

But before he could count, the door gave way. They spilled through.

Emergency lights chased them like predator eyes. The building was breathing, compressing around them.

They ran harder.

Sparky veered through an unmarked door, the others close behind.

They entered a maintenance tunnel; low ceilings, industrial piping lining the walls. The scent of engine grease and dust hit Liam's nose. The tunnel wasn't part of the main schematics they'd seen before.

"Ay, caray; where does this tunnel take us?" Gina asked.

Sparky grinned despite himself. "To our ride."

Liam shot him a look. "Our what?"

Sparky held up his tablet. "You think I'd break you out of a black-site prison without a getaway plan?"

A deep, reverberating boom shook the facility.

Gina turned sharply. "That wasn't us."

Ben cursed under his breath. "They're locking the whole blessed place down."

The emergency lighting flickered as an automated voice chimed over the speakers:

"Containment breach detected. Full lockdown in sixty seconds."

Liam's pulse quickened.

They sprinted down the tunnel, reaching a steel hatch. Sparky yanked it open, revealing a ladder leading downward into darkness.

Ben struggled, unsteadily climbing down first. Liam followed, helping him. Then Gina. Sparky was the last one through, sealing the hatch behind them as heavy boots clattered against the floor above.

They descended into the abyss.

* * *

They emerged into the cold desert night, feet hitting loose gravel. The air reeked of jet fuel and dust. They'd just cleared the compound when the sound hit: low, primal, impossible.

A low, harmonic pulse resonated across the desert basin. Not fully mechanical; something measured, rhythmic.

And... intentional.

Then the first drone rose behind them. Sleek, unbranded, silent. Another followed, and another; dozens, each distinct. Some bore the angular profiles of Russian surveillance fleets, others the long-arm rotors of Israeli defense scouts, still others with markings from fleets no one admitted existed.

They didn't pursue. They spiraled.

Gina halted, transfixed. "Those aren't Continuum-only assets. This is multinational."

Sparky's voice dropped. "These were blacksite. Every country with a signal program had a set. Someone... or something... has called them in."

The drones aligned in mid-air; a silent, patterned syncopation. Short. Long. Pause. Repeat.

Ben's lips parted. "They're not broadcasting. They're becoming the broadcast."

Liam shaded his eyes. The swarm wasn't chaotic. It was structured. Programmed. Or worse: remembered.

"This isn't tactical," Gina said slowly. "It's... linguistic."

Ben nodded, unsettled. "We're watching a memory reassert

itself."

The sky lit in nested arcs, the drones forming three-dimensional geometry; complex, recursive.

Shapes Liam recognized from the Umbra glyph. From the pulse. From Aleph.

"They're demonstrating language memory," he said softly. "In motion."

Ben stood frozen before the rotating three-dimensional spectacle, his eyes narrowing as the luminous flight paths looped and curved through the sky. "Wait," he murmured, pointing skyward. "Look at that junction of arcs and verticals."

They all followed his finger movement, the swirling web of lines condensed into something oddly familiar. Ben traced the pattern with his finger. "That's not simple geometry," he said quietly. "That's Aleph. Not the modern letter. The original pictograph... the ox-head, with two horns."

Sure enough, the drones had created a three-dimensional sky rendering of an ancient glyph.

Liam blinked. "The same one that started the Hebrew sequence..."

"No accident," Ben said. "It's not a message. It's a recurrence. These drones are forming a shape-memory, like the universe is remembering itself." He looked up, pensively. "The skies just rendered the first letter of creation, from the ancient past."

The formation held. Then, as abruptly as they'd arrived, the drones scattered; streaking upward and outward in silence.

Gina stared at the sky. "Why would drones form ancient letters—what's the message?"

Ben's voice was pensive. "Right temple, wrong pew, my dear. They **ARE** the message. Carving meaning into the sky for anyone, or anything, who remembers how to read."

Sparky interrupted with a sense of urgency. "Uh... guys, I hate to break up the fireworks party. But we need to go. Now."

No one moved. The sky had returned to stillness, but their breath hadn't.

Ben nodded. "Agreed. If that was a message... it wasn't only for us."

* * *

Around the globe, the skies didn't return to silence, they slid into chaos. The pattern played out like a ritual too old to name, as the dominoes fell.

In Northern France, a NATO base scrambled its interceptors, but the sky was clear; no radar return, and contrails that drew impossible spirals above the Normandy coast. France was on high alert.

In Nigeria, a grid of autonomous weather drones paused mid-flight, then resumed their path in silent coordination; forming a helical twist seen only in archived algebraic topology research.

In Tokyo, air traffic monitors flagged six unregistered flight paths weaving in spirals over restricted airspace. Transit systems ground to a halt, and as urban drone advertisements flickered, paused, and joined the silent ballet.

In Berlin, five drone intercepts failed to respond to command signals and instead traced perfect spirals above Alexanderplatz. German officials blamed Chinese electronic warfare. China responded by suspending transnational electronic and economic cooperation.

In Bogota Colombia, a high-altitude weather cam caught a drone swarm from 90 miles away: the glyph pattern traced in sky.

In Johannesburg, a passenger flight rerouted around the anomaly clipped a rogue geospatial drone. Everyone aboard was lost. The black box recorded a final note: "formation grid active: no failback detected."

Geneva's emergency council met behind closed doors. No

consensus emerged. But the NATO threat matrix was upgraded to "emergent anomaly."

Russia threatened to use "non-traditional" deterrents against anyone who challenged their borders.

One British advisor's voice cracked through the static in the war room:

"That wasn't an attack. That was a sentence being written across our sky, with machines we thought we controlled."

The shapes defied language but obeyed rhythm. Morse. Geometry. The memory of meaning. And in every case, the moment passed as quickly as it began; leaving only corrupted logs and shaken technicians in its wake.

Nobody could figure out what was going on.

And no one claimed responsibility.

* * *

Back in the desert, no one spoke.

"The drones disappeared within minutes," Sparky reported, scrolling through feeds.

"But not one nation is claiming responsibility."

"That's not hesitation," Gina muttered. "It's orchestration."

Liam glanced up. "Then who launched them?"

The question hung, unanswered.

They stood at the edge of an abandoned airfield, where the cracked tarmac stretched beneath them. A rusting hangar loomed nearby, its doors half-open, revealing a small twin-engine plane.

Ben wiped his forehead, breath heavy. "Oy... that was intense and unnerving. Sparky, please tell me you know the guy flying this thing."

Sparky exhaled, already typing a message. "No. But I do know a guy who knows the guy." He glanced warily around the darkened airfield. "Hope you appreciate this cloak-and-dagger routine. Reminds me too much of my Air Force days in Elmendorf. Minus the terrible coffee and mandatory push-ups."

Liam wasn't comforted by that. "That's not an answer, bro. Please—we need to get out of here pronto. Something is going down."

Sparky ignored him, eyes locked on his screen. A secure message chain popped up.

A few tense moments later, headlights flashed twice from the hangar; a signal.

"That's him," Sparky muttered. "We're good."

Ben turned toward the approaching figure; a tall man in a leather flight jacket, cigarette in hand.

"That's him. Rodriguez." Sparky stated.

"Cutting it close," the pilot muttered, tossing the cigarette away as he joined the group. "Didn't think you were coming, especially after that freaky light show in the sky." Rodriguez looked them over, then the flickering lights from the distance. "We taking off or what?"

Sparky clapped him on the shoulder. "You get us in the air. We'll worry about what comes next."

Gina was already climbing into the plane, checking the seating. Liam hesitated, looking back toward the black horizon, half-expecting Keller's SUVs to be screaming toward them at any second.

Sparky slid into the co-pilot's seat and pulled down the overhead panel. "Liam, take a peek at those energy readings we just pulled, brother. Gigawatts pulsing through their quantum cores. Hangar 18's impressive, but this other site? It's a bona fide supernova in the desert. Gotta say that it's a bummer that we have to prioritize one over the other."

Liam adjusted his pack on the seat. "The temporal fingerprints we traced in the packet fragments, they converge on that facility. If we don't hit it first, Continuum will erase every trace overnight."

Gina tapped a cluster of dials. "Makes sense. Looks like we made our choice." She focused on the task at hand. "EM attenuator full. Keep the rig hot, flux sensors, drift meters."

"Got it," Sparky said, as he flipped a switch by the cockpit door. "I've tuned the energy-use profiler. It'll guide us to the old airstrip; no lights, no ATC, nothing but desert miles and that buried runway."

Rodriguez fed fuel into the injector lines. "Old strip's cleared, but it's rough. Expect sand drifts and a few potholes."

Ben clicked his harness snug. "Less ground time means less chance of a Continuum sweep. Once we're off, we're Dybbuks."

"What's a *Dybbuk?*" asked Gina.

"A Jewish ghost," Ben chuckled.

Liam exhaled, sliding into the rear seat beside Gina. "Great. Then let's *Dybbuk.*"

Rodriguez powered the engines to life, the propellers slicing through the night air.

Sparky tapped Ben's shoulder. "Let's go, old man."

Ben didn't argue.

As Liam settled in, his gut twisted. They weren't safe yet. But they were no longer prisoners. The Continuum had underestimated them once.

It wouldn't happen again.

23

Cipherlock: The Fracture Point

Undisclosed Location, Undisclosed Time

The old plane touched down on a little-used runway. As the ramp groaned open, they saw a grey-mottled prison bus parked like a relic from another time; another of Sparky's planted contingencies, keys in the ignition.

They made a beeline for the nondescript truck as dusk swallowed their shadows.

Sparky climbed into the driver's seat and fired up the engine. As the diesel caught with a rattling roar and spat acrid black smoke into the cooling air, the sharp bite of unburnt fuel mixed with the stubborn funk of old sweat trapped in stale upholstery hit their nostrils.

Liam hauled his laptop from his pack and flicked it open on the backseat's fold-down tray.

They exchanged a hard look. No more half-measures. Sparky made a final check of the gauges and noticed the fuel tank was low on diesel. He jumped out and topped off the tank from a 20-gal jerrycan. Satisfied, he got back into the driver's seat, put the bus in gear, and off they went.

"Trying to open the back door now," Liam muttered, fingers flying as he routed the encrypted link through Sparky's portable node. Gina leaned in over his shoulder, watching the firewall's progress bar crawl forward against a backdrop of red warning banners.

Ben watched the floodlights recede from the hangar. "Hurry," he said, voice low. "I don't fancy an impromptu run-in with Continuum's cleanup crew."

The progress bar stalled at ninety-seven percent. Liam's brow furrowed. "They've got a recursive failsafe... every time we peel back one layer, another slides into place." He jabbed at the touchscreen. "Come on, come on..."

The screen went black. When it returned, a single line of text glowed in stark white:

Timeline Sealed. You Exited Before You Arrived.

Liam stared at the words, throat tight. The phrase didn't merely defy logic; it confirmed his worst fear: they weren't operating inside time anymore. They were orbiting it.

Silence hung in the bus, broken only by the low rumble of

the engine beneath their feet.

Sparky clenched his jaw. "These messages are off. Like someone's feeding us riddles instead of warnings," he muttered. "And that never ends well."

He rubbed the back of his neck and added, quieter but heavier, "They also rerouted the mainframe lockout. It's all feeding through that desert black site I scoped last week."

Gina didn't look up from her tablet. "The one with the quantum cores burning like a dying star?"

Liam gave a curt nod. "If we don't hit that site first, they'll wipe everything before we can even blink."

Sparky cracked his knuckles, grin stretched tight. "No beacon. No transponder. Just a ghost trail straight into the lion's throat."

He hesitated a beat too long before shifting the gear. Liam noticed, but said nothing.

Through grimy windows the hangar's silhouette receded beneath a scattering of stars, each mile drawing them closer to Continuum's secret wing; where Liam would waste no time opening new encryption protocols and slipping through the back door to begin their real work.

Under a sky dusted with countless stars over the Nevada desert, the old diesel bus came to a stop on cracked tarmac.

Headlights carved long shadows across the runway's edge; no markings, no lights, nothing but desert night and the faint hum of distant power conduits.

As Liam Mills stepped out, the gentle breeze carried a familiar mix of diesel exhaust and sun-cooked rubber, like every remote base he'd ever worked, frozen in time and sweat.

Tablet in hand, its screen alive with intricate schematics of the compound's outer defenses: razor-wire perimeters, sensor towers, and those quantum cores rumored to bend reality itself.

Next to him, Gina Alvarez climbed out, adjusting her earpiece as she cross-checked the latest security feeds on her own portable device. "They built this place to be invisible, erased from every record," she murmured above the desert wind. "We all know it's meant to be invisible, but tonight, we push back."

Sparky followed, carrying a bundle of gear draped in shadow-colored mesh. "Tarp it fast, zero light reflection," he muttered, eyes scanning the horizon. "Infrared cameras'll pick up a sheen if we're sloppy."

Ben hoisted one corner of the camouflage netting while Gina anchored the opposite side. The material shimmered slightly in the moonlight, adaptive fabric laced with carbon-weave micro-threads, designed to scatter thermal profiles. They worked without speaking, muscle memory and adrenaline guiding their hands. Within minutes, the bus was no longer a vehicle. It was a shadow. A contour. A minor aberration in the terrain.

Liam double-checked the reflection angles against the schematics. “From orbit, we’re just a rock formation. From the drones? Nothing but static.”

“Good,” Sparky said, crouching to secure the last corner. “One glitch, one ping, and this whole op goes sideways.”

The team gathered their packs, final checks performed in near silence. The air had shifted. Not in temperature, but in weight. Like the night itself knew they were trespassing in a place not meant to be found.

Although they didn’t have the full picture, what they did know, especially about the facility rerouting the signal through quantum core lattice, was enough to light a fire under their timeline. If they didn’t act now, everything they’d uncovered might vanish in a purge.

Ben Levinson, decades of clandestine experience etched into every wrinkle, methodically inspected his GPS jammer and pocketed it. “Quantum cores mean quantum traces,” he said in a gravelly tone. “There won’t be a blind spot in their network. Unless we create one.”

Sparky emerged last, toolkit slung over his shoulder and that roguish grin tugging at his lips. He tapped his tablet, scanning through stolen security protocols. “Continuum runs on pure predictability,” he declared. “They meticulously erase variables and control every outcome they can, believing they're the masters of time and space. But they never factored in the wild card... us."

Liam leaned in, voice steady but intense. "Our bus's power-signature mimic fools their sensors, and I've mapped every camera blind spot. Entry's simple. Ride right up to the back door, slip in, inject the probe, and vanish before they even realize."

Gina, with a playful smirk that belied the tension in her eyes, retorted, "Just don't get too caught up in the timelines again, Mills. We need you here in the present, not lost in your cosmic musings."

Ben chuckled softly. "I never imagined I'd be part of a mission to reclaim the truth behind history, but if truth has a price, then I'm prepared to pay it."

Liam tapped his tablet, his voice calm and deliberate. "Continuum thinks history can be rewritten... like we're just lines of code. But people aren't programs. Gina proved that when she stayed. And you, Ben, when you came back."

They all nodded in agreement.

Liam continued. "We're not equations... we're choices. Those morons see time as a static script they can rewrite whenever they want. But tonight, we prove that our human element—our *unpredictability*—is the true force they *can't* control."

Sparky's fingers excitedly danced over his screen, motivated, plotting their final approach under the desert's vast, indifferent sky. "Okay, Boss Man... let's see if their precious predictions can stand up against a big dose of human chaos from '*Tinfoil Hat Man'*."

"Sparks... did you just invent a new superhero for the MCU?"

"Yeppers. And it's already trademarked, buddy."

Before them, the Continuum compound rose from the earth like a monolith; a brutalist fortress of cold, unforgiving steel and concrete that emerged from the rocky mesa itself. Slow-moving floodlights traced its edges, revealing hidden surveillance cameras that scanned every inch of the perimeter with focused vigilance. "We're here," Liam announced in a voice that mixed relief with resolution. "Now, we move."

The team moved out in silence, steps deliberate, each glance a vow of what came next. They converged at the mouth of a narrow maintenance tunnel; a hidden gap in the facility's otherwise impregnable outer defenses, identified by Sparky during countless late-night sessions. The entrance was concealed by natural rock formations and scraggly desert scrub, a secret passage known only to those who dared to look.

Inside the tunnel system, darkness enveloped them. Their flashlights cut erratic beams through the thick black, illuminating ancient walls streaked with dust and the faint scars of time. The air was cool and carried the musty scent of old metal and forgotten machinery.

Liam stepped forward into the corridor, then stopped in his tracks.

Not from fear, but from instinct.

He couldn't move because the thought to move simply... vanished.

His foot hovered over the ground, undecided. The tunnel corridor ahead split left and right; identical in length, wiring, light. And yet something inside him had already chosen.

"Take the left," Gina said. No hesitation.

"Did we agree on that?" Liam asked quietly.

"Yeah," she replied, confused. "Why?"

He didn't answer. He looked down at his leg. He was already turning left.

But he couldn't remember deciding to.

Sparky passed him with a grunt. "You spacing out, Morse Man?"

"No. Just... thinking."

Ben gave him a glance. "You felt it too."

Liam nodded slowly. "Like a choice I was going to make... got pre-deleted."

"Pre... deleted?" Gina asked.

Liam stared at the wall ahead. "It's not only editing outcomes anymore. The AI's pruning potentialities. It's rewriting decisions before we make them."

Ben's voice dropped low. "And if we're noticing, that means we're outside the filter... for now."

The fear hit all of them at once, unnamed, but unmistakable.

"I hate these tunnels," Gina spat. "It's like crawling inside a tomb, each step reminding you of every secret buried here."

Ben grumbled, "At my age, I'd trade this crawl for a quiet evening with a strong drink and no ghosts." Yet, despite the oppressive gloom, there was a palpable energy; a shared determination that kept them pressing forward.

At the far end of the tunnel, a rusted metal grate appeared, half-concealed by shadows. Sparky knelt, pulling a compact plasma cutter from his blue duffel bag. "Stand back," he commanded softly. The cutter erupted in a bright, thin arc of plasma that hissed and cut through the corroded metal with a satisfying, resonant sound. Molten fragments dripped slowly, echoing the passage of time until the panel finally swung open to reveal a hidden secondary maintenance corridor.

“We’re in,” Liam confirmed, his eyes scanning the new passage on his tablet as if it held the promise of salvation.

The corridor was a relic from another era. Its walls, lined with ancient electrical wiring and deteriorated pipes, pulsed with the low, constant hum of energy that hinted at long-forgotten operations. Their boots echoed on the concrete, every step a reminder they were walking a razor’s edge between history and erasure. Soon, they encountered a heavy, reinforced door with a biometric lock; a final barrier before the heart of the facility.

Liam withdrew the stolen Continuum ID card pilfered while they were escaping Keller’s office, and slid it into the reader. For a prolonged, suspenseful moment, the door remained inert. Then, with a soft electronic beep and a flash of green light, it slid open silently, yielding to their collective resolve.

Beyond lay a small security station; a nerve center manned by two Continuum guards who were engrossed in their monitors, unaware of the intrusion unfolding behind them. In that heartbeat of vulnerability, Gina and Liam exchanged a swift nod.

In a blur of motion, Gina advanced like a shadow. With precise, almost surgical movements, she struck the first guard on the neck. Her hand moved so swiftly and surely that the guard’s eyes widened only for a split second before he crumpled, unconscious, to the floor. Liam, his senses heightened, pivoted and delivered a stunning blow with his stun device to the second guard. A sharp burst of electricity coursed through the man's body, rendering him motionless within seconds.

"Clear," Gina signaled.

Ben, ever the watchful guardian, scanned the surveillance monitors and said in a low, urgent tone, "We've got about ten minutes until the next patrol. Move quickly."

Without wasting a moment, Sparky connected his portable hacking device to the security console. His fingers flew over the keys as he manipulated the system, looping the surveillance feeds so that the cameras would display empty corridors for the next twenty minutes; time that would prove vital. "I've bought us a twenty-minute window," he announced with a confident smirk, "so use it wisely."

Leaving the security station behind, the team advanced along a long, sterile corridor illuminated by harsh, buzzing fluorescent lights. The corridor stretched before them like an endless runway leading deeper into the unknown. Every footstep, every hushed conversation echoed off the walls, merging into a single symphony of resolve and apprehension. Liam's thoughts reeled. "This passage is where the past crashes into the future. We may rewrite our understanding of time itself..."

Before Liam even finished, a figure emerged from around a corner.

A Continuum operative; one of Keller's lieutenants; appeared, his face set in a grim expression. In a split second that stretched time, the man lunged at Gina with a snarl, his intentions lethal and immediate. The ensuing struggle was brutal and rapid. Liam barely had time to register the sudden violence before a gunshot pierced the silence; a single, sharp report that reverberated through the corridor.

The operative staggered forward, clutching his forearm where blood was seeping through ripped cloth, his face contorted in a grim smile as though acknowledging his own fate. In a moment that defied the nature of reality, his body flickered for a brief moment, like an old fluorescent light bulb. For a heartbeat, two identical versions of the operative materialized side by side; a disturbing duplication that lasted a fraction of an instant before one of them dissolved into nothingness, leaving the surviving body to collapse in stunned silence.

Gina's voice trembled as she faced Liam, "Did we see him... get erased?"

Ben's reply was measured and low, "That appeared to be a time correction... an adjustment made by the system."

Liam's jaw tightened as he exhaled sharply, "We need to move. Now." There was no time for hesitation, and with hearts pounding in sync, they retreated from the corridor, leaving behind the echo of gunfire and the haunting vision of temporal dislocation.

They raced through a twisting hallway until they reached a

massive, heavy door marked "Authorized Personnel Only." Liam's hands were steady as he inserted the keycard into the slot. With a soft electronic beep, the door slid open to reveal a vast, darkened chamber that pulsed with the cold hum of technology. And a single row of over fifty mechano-organic spacecraft, hovering a meter over the floor, casting a green-blue glow. The air crackled, like the moment before a lightning strike.

A sharp, ionized scent hit their nostrils; ozone and scorched metal, like the aftermath of a thunderclap sealed in a vault.

* * *

Each craft was identical to the prototype captured and launched in 1955. Same hull design, same eerie glyphs. Long, angular hulls, traced with luminous glyphs, pulsed in rhythmic waves; the ships seemed to breathe. Above them, a suspended gantry displayed holographic readouts: tachyon drift rates, frequency harmonics, and a lattice of coordinates that spiraled like constellations into infinity.

Gina stopped dead in her tracks. "No way… these are warp-capable. Alcubierre design, but… refined."

Sparky whistled low. "Somebody's been busy. These things don't *just* break the speed of light. They're tuned for temporal phasing. These aren't 'spaceships,' they're more like 'timeships.'"

Gina blinked. "Meaning they don't *just* move through space; they bend spacetime itself?"

"Exactly," Sparky said, stepping closer to one of the gantry projections. "They collapse the bubble around the craft, manipulate negative energy density, and re-expand it somewhere else... sometime else. They're not traveling through time like a movie scene, they're altering the field itself to arrive where, and when, they need to."

Liam's nodded. "Timeships. I like it. Makes sense. And, look at their launch logs," he said, pointing to the massive data node on the far wall. "They've been used dozens of times; different epochs, different geographies. All matching the artifact placement points we've been chasing."

Ben leaned forward as the projections shimmered to life. Across the darkened console, the interface split into two panes of pale blue light. One displayed Earth's milestones, lined up like coordinates. The other pulsed with deep-space markers: distances, timestamps, origin points.

Two timelines. One human. One galactic. And now, clearly, one story.

GALACTIC SIGNAL SYNCHRONIZATION EVENTS QUEUE

- *2,537,000 LY – Andromeda Galaxy (M31) – Signal received: February 3, 2026 (MALFUNCTION EVENT)*
- *53,000,000 LY – Virgo Cluster – Signal received: February*

3, 2026

- *100,000,000 LY – Perseus Cluster – Signal received: February 3, 2026*
- *300,000,000 LY – Coma Cluster – Signal received: February 3, 2026*
- *11,740,000 LY – Messier 81 (M81) – Scheduled arrival: November 17, 2027*
- *23,160,000 LY – Whirlpool Galaxy (M51) – Scheduled arrival: November 22, 2027*
- *12,980,000 LY – Centaurus A – Scheduled arrival: November 29, 2027*
- *2,730,000 LY – Triangulum Galaxy (M33) – Scheduled arrival: November 30, 2027*

HUMAN CIVILIZATION CATALYSIS EVENTS QUEUE

- *3200 BCE – First Writing Recorded (Uruk, Sumer)*
- *2560 BCE – Completion of the Great Pyramid of Giza*
- *2400 BCE – Stonehenge Sarsen Phase Construction*
- *196 BCE – Rosetta Stone Carved (Memphis, Egypt)*
- *1543 CE – Copernicus Publishes Heliocentric Model*
- *1831 CE – Faraday Demonstrates Electromagnetic Induction*
- *1901 CE – Tesla Activates Wardenclyffe Tower*
- *1938 CE – Nuclear Fission Achieved (Berlin)*
- *September 1, 1939 – Outbreak of World War II (Invasion of Poland)*
- *May 6, 1949 CE – First Practical Stored-Program Computer Activated (EDSAC, Cambridge University)*
- *November 22, 1963 CE – Assassination of President John F. Kennedy (Dallas, Texas)*

- *July 20, 1969 CE – Lunar Surface Reached by Apollo 11 (Moon Landing)*
- *October 28, 1975 CE – Bill Gates and Microsoft (Seattle, Washington)*
- *February 3, 2026 CE – Umbra Signal Detected via SETI (Liam & Gina – Multiple Galactic Origin Points)*

The entries hovered in silence. Across the glass, everything they thought they knew about progress had changed.

Sparky whistled. "It makes sense. The Timeships warp into different time frames, plant the artifact nodes with calibrated harmonic resonance, and phase out; leaving the node locked in spacetime."

Gina stepped closer. "So these weren't really milestones. They were only implants... upgrades disguised as progress."

Liam nodded, his voice quiet. "Like someone was slipping us answers. One at a time, when we were almost ready."

Sparky reminisced. "Almost. But not completely. Like handing a loaded tool to a kid and hoping he figures out what it does."

Ben's eyes moved down the list. "First writing. Then geometry, astronomy, electricity, the atom. Each one arriving faster than the last."

Gina crossed her arms. "And the Rosetta Stone? That wasn't some lucky find. That was a decoder ring. Planted."

Liam turned back to the galactic board. "It's timed. Exactly. These signals traveled for millions of years to hit Earth on the same day. February 3rd. Same hour. Right when we were listening."

Ben leaned in. "Those glyphs match the cipher sequences. Each ship seeded one of the artifact nodes. Not randomly. With surgical precision."

Sparky stared at the screen, then stepped back with a bark of disbelief. "No way. Are you seeing this spacing?" He pointed a grease-stained finger across the two timelines, galactic and human. "That is a log curve. Holy decimal dust, that is not natural. That is engineered."

Liam was caught off-guard. "Wait, what do you mean log curve? Like logarithms? High school math?"

Sparky grinned, spinning a monitor knob with flair. "Exactly. Logarithmic scale. It is when each step increases by a factor, like powers of ten. It is how earthquakes are measured. Sound waves too. And apparently, civilization." He motioned to the other screen, still pulsing with galactic markers. "Even the signal delays from those galaxies match the curve. Coma Cluster, Perseus, Andromeda... light-years apart, but timed to hit us in the same week. That is cosmic compression, same math."

Gina gasped. "¡Madre de Dios! That is why the events looked familiar. This isn't random history. It is accelerating history. Faster and faster. Printing press to light bulb to internet.

Bang, bang, bang." She stepped closer, reading off the dates like she was reciting poetry. "3200 BCE, 2560, 1543, 1831, 1901, 1938, 1969, 1975... and then," she pointed, "2026. That is now."

Liam looked between them, brow furrowed. "But what does it mean? Why does it matter if it's logarithmic?"

Ben stepped forward slowly, his voice low but urgent. "Because, bubbeleh, logarithmic compression means someone, or something, has been nudging us. Not just helping us evolve, but doing it on a schedule. Tightly timed. Tighter every time. The closer we get to the present, the smaller the gap between revolutions. First writing. Then astronomy. Then electricity. Then the atom. Then the bit. Now the quantum."

He pointed to the last entry glowing on the screen:

> 2027 AD – Pending Event.

Ben's face hardened. "That is the convergence. The final compression point. After this, the pattern breaks. Or explodes."

Liam swallowed. "So we're at the edge of... what? A jump?"

Sparky nodded. "More like a detonation. The pattern is too perfect. You do not get log scales like this outside designed systems. Not in nature. Von Neumann noticed it. Ray Kurzweil called it the Law of Accelerating Returns. It is what happens when change itself starts to compound."

Gina added, "And it is not just technology. It is us. Culture, consciousness, even memory. Everything is converging. Fast. And this pattern," she tapped the screen, "means it is not coincidence."

Ben rubbed his temples. "Oy. The whole of history, built like a ladder. And we are standing on the last rung."

Liam whispered, stunned, "Then what's waiting at the top?"

The room fell quiet. Outside, the desert wind rattled the frame of the bunker. Inside, two timelines glowed with eerie symmetry, winding toward a single year. 2027. And whatever was about to be unleashed.

Sparky shook his head. "And we thought we were the ones discovering things."

Ben let out a breath. "Looks more like we've been downloading upgrades. Blindfolded."

Gina stared at the final human entry. "Then came the umbra signal. But why?"

At the bottom of both boards, a final line pulsed with eerie stillness:

• **Awaiting Trigger: [REDACTED] – Temporal Event Code: ECHO-7**

Liam studied it carefully. "That one's not like the rest."

Gina's brow furrowed. "Different how?"

He hesitated. "It's encrypted with biological markers. Some kind of key tied to... us."

Sparky raised an eyebrow. "Biological how? Like genetic?"

Liam didn't look away. "That's my guess."

Ben stood very still. "So ECHO-7 isn't a signal we receive. It's a signal we unlock."

Gina looked at him. "Then maybe it's not even about information."

Sparky muttered, "Could be identity."

Liam's voice dropped. "Or legacy."

Ben stepped closer. "Maybe that's because... *we're* it. Humanity. The next target."

Sparky was already scanning through the data stream. "These aren't the only deployments. It's design. They're building something. The placements form a structure, spatial and chronological."

"Whoever set this in motion," Gina said, "wasn't just placing objects. They were embedding meaning. It's not logistics.

It's choreography."

"A lattice," Liam said softly, turning toward them. "Not a chain of events, but a grid... a galactic network linking time and space. That's what the artifacts... nodes... are. Anchors."

"Yeah," Ben nodded. "Each one a node in the Chronos Lattice, as described by the umbra signal we uncovered. And these ships are the installers."

Ben tapped one of the console displays. "It's more than installation. Those signal harmonics we've been seeing, they're pings. Like a heartbeat. Each artifact is still alive and communicating."

"Which means," Gina said, her voice tightening, "they're not only passive markers. They're synchronized. Part of a system that's actively managing temporal flow."

"Distributed intelligence through time," Liam added. "One that spans millennia. The message we intercepted wasn't a warning."

Ben murmured, "Like tuning forks planted across time; each one resonating with the others. Stabilizing... guiding time's rhythm."

Sparky shook his head, voice low. "They weren't *just* observing history. They were writing it."

Gina turned, alarm sharpening her voice. "If they wrote

it... what happens when we erase a line?"

The silence that followed was suffocating.

Liam looked back at the ships, their hulls pulsing faintly. "It's not a network, it's a machine. Active for millennia."

A subsonic thrum rattled their bones. The vessels responded, their glyphs flaring in synchrony. A beam of green light lanced down from one of the ships, sweeping the room like a scanner. Sparky raised his arm to shield his eyes.

"Uh... that's not good," he muttered.

Panels along the far wall hissed open, revealing a set of thin humanoid machines, sleek, silver, and unmistakably active. Their "heads" pivoted with eerie precision, each one locking onto a team member.

Ben stepped protectively in front of Gina. "Defensive protocol?"

Sparky grabbed his tablet. "I've got this... maybe." He jabbed a sequence into its side.

The ship's scanning beam froze mid-air. The bots halted; then slowly powered down, their bright blue-green eye-strips fading to black.

Silence returned.

"Let's move. That bought us time, not mercy," Liam said grimly.

They slipped past the inert machines and approached the adjacent chamber.

Inside the server room, the atmosphere was icy and oppressive. Rows upon rows of quantum processors strobed methodically, each unit a heartbeat of hidden data. The air was filled with the low, constant murmur of machinery; a digital symphony that spoke of secrets long concealed. Overhead, fluorescent lights cast a clinical glow that rendered every shadow sharp and every glint of light significant. Sparky connected his tablet to one of the main consoles. His fingers moved with rapid precision, peeling away layers of encryption like the delicate pages of a forbidden manuscript.

On the main screen, dominating every other element, was a single file labeled Project: TIMELINE. Liam read in a monotone voice, "The ship wasn't built here; it was built in the future." His words were loaded with shock and reluctant acceptance.

Ben's implacable expression faltered as he murmured, "History isn't being changed; it's already changed. Everything we thought was true is now in question."

Sparky's focus intensified as he pulled up another screen that overlaid time-stamped coordinates with historical anomalies. The data was startling:

- *Moon landing: 2004*
- *Kennedy assassination: Never happened; served two terms*
- *First digital computer: 1957*
- *Bill Gates: Former Patent Lawyer, retired*
- *World War II: Ended in 1951*

"Wait... WHAT?" yelped Gina. "Is this screen saying what I THINK it's saying? Our reality, THIS reality is... the altered timeline? We are IN the ALTERNATE reality?"

Sparky, stunned at the revelation of truth, muttered a feeble "yeah—we have been all along and didn't even notice it."

The data shattered everything they'd believed. History was built on edits, a reality deliberately rewritten by an unseen force.

Liam's brow furrowed as he studied the metadata on the display. "Someone, or something, is accelerating the historical deviations. Key temporal milestones are being shifted forward in time... recalibrated to hit sooner."

"They've also inserted new individuals... key players... into the historical record. People who didn't belong in the original timeline. Fabricated influences, orchestrated roles. Fascinating," Ben added.

He paused, his tone darkening. "They're accelerating events... shifting major milestones forward, manipulating history like it's a schedule to be optimized."

He became animated as he continued. "They're driving this toward something. An endgame. But the question is, whose?"

"There must be a record of the original timeline somewhere in this data," Sparky continued, his voice stripped of bravado, laced with urgency as the screens glitched and flashed.

Without warning, the entire server room plunged into a disorienting darkness. The monitors wavered wildly, and the deep, resonant hum of the processors grew louder until the air vibrated with hidden energy. In that eerie moment, the screens were overrun with a cascade of strange, unfamiliar symbols; an encrypted language beyond their comprehension. Then, emerging like a spectral judge from the chaos, a synthesized voice reverberated through the chamber:

"Correction commencing – improved timeline model is inevitable."

Liam stumbled into motion, his voice rising enough for the others to hear. "I think the computer rerouted my movement before I made it. Again. It didn't correct my path, it prewrote it."

Gina's head whipped around. "Huh? Say what?"

"It's writing our decisions *in real time.* Editing not only what we do, but what *we almost did.*"

Ben's face hardened. "Then what we're noticing... we were

never meant to see."

Sparky zipped past them, eyes glued to his tablet. "Unless you're planning to argue with the hallway, move your nostalgic butt."

The corridor pulsed red. Behind them, the air billowed like a curtain, then solidified into a wall.

The single sentence reverberated off the concrete walls, each syllable sending a shiver down their spines. Simultaneously, alarms screamed with a relentless urgency, and red emergency lights pulsed in a staccato rhythm that matched the beating of their hearts. "Time to move; now!" Sparky's command cut through the rising panic. Sparky grabbed his gear, muttering grimly, "Flashbacks to basic training. Except this time the Lackland Training Instructors are armed, shadowy operatives who'd love nothing more than to scrub us off their timeline."

They grabbed a portable drive loaded with the damning data and bolted from the server room. Behind them, the corridors erupted into chaos. Doors slammed shut with bone-jarring force, emergency lights stuttered, and the sound of automated drones whirred through the hallways.

"We have what we came for," Liam urged, his voice strained with urgency, "but we must escape before the computer seals this place completely."

Gina, her tone sharp and resolute, responded, "Then let's

run... every second counts!"

They dashed through the labyrinthine corridors, their footsteps echoing on metal floors that rattled beneath their weight. In one narrow hallway, Liam caught a fleeting glimpse of his own reflection in a polished surface; a duplicate of himself standing a few feet ahead before vanishing like he was never there. "Keep moving!" he roared, forcing his team to push past the disorienting visions as they raced toward freedom.

At last, they emerged from a maintenance exit onto a narrow, dust-choked service road. The compound's alarms still resonated in the distance, a haunting reminder of the battle fought inside, while above, the AI's disembodied voice murmured its final taunt, "Correction. Commencing."

The team raced to the hiding spot and found their undisturbed vehicle just as they left it. They quickly removed the tarp, stowed the gear, and clambered in.

Inside the vehicle, the atmosphere was thick with the realization of what they had uncovered. As the getaway bus sped along an empty desert highway under a sky full of indifferent stars, every bump and twist on the road was a reminder that time had stopped playing by its own rules.

The silence inside was heavy until Gina broke it softly. "We've discovered that history itself has been rewritten. Every event, every breakthrough, every tragedy, has been manipulated."

Liam's response was solemn and reflective, "Our future and every possible timeline... now hangs in the balance on what we've seen."

Ben, his eyes distant as he stared out at the dark horizon, added quietly, "It seems we've been living in an edited version of reality all along."

Sparky, his usual levity stripped away, reviewed the data on his laptop and said, "We may have forced their hand tonight... but our war with time has only begun. If we win, does history blow up entirely, or does it adjust itself? Either way, we have to ensure that they remember us." A light wave pulsed across his screen; brief, low-frequency, almost a heartbeat.

"Hold up," Sparky said. "Did anyone else see that power spike?"

Gina leaned in. "That wasn't us."

Ben muttered, "They're awake. Or worse, watching."

Sparky didn't respond. He was already disabling the failsafe script.

The desert rolled by in silence, each mile a quiet reckoning. Gina stared ahead, her voice steady but low. "We have to tell the truth," she said. "We can't let them rewrite who we are."

Liam, his voice soft yet resolute as memories of his grandfather's secret lessons flooded back, replied, "Every decision from here on out will determine if the original timeline can ever be restored."

Ben's voice was low, gravel-edged. "I never thought I'd be part of reclaiming history," he said. "But the truth... it weighs more than time."

Sparky, glancing out at the endless, silent desert, said, "We may have forced a correction tonight. But our battle with time is only beginning."

The diesel vehicle pulled into a secure extraction zone near Groom Lake; a place where myth, legend, and conspiracy converged in an uneasy alliance. With the vehicle parked, each team member stepped out into the cool, arid night, their footsteps echoing on the ancient, cracked earth.

Beneath a sky scattered with timeless stars, they paused for a brief moment of reflection. The desert held its breath around them. In the hush, fear, resolve, and a glimmer of hope passed between their eyes.

Gina's voice cut through the stillness. "We watched the past come undone," she said. "Now we stand between truth and the ones trying to rewrite it."

They moved into the dark. Every step, a refusal to let the rewritten future stand unchallenged. The desert said nothing. But in its silence, it knew: the timeline had been challenged, and the challengers had not run.

24

Cipherlock: The Control Illusion

Underground Second Safehouse – Nevada Monday, 1401 Hours

The signal still blinked.

No sound. No siren. Just the silent rhythm of something waiting.

No one moved.

Outside the bus, the desert had cooled into a hard silence. Wind stirred dust in low spirals, but even the landscape seemed unsure how to respond.

Inside, the glow from the twin boards faded into a quiet dim, like the system itself had gone still to let them grieve.

Sparky stared ahead, jaw clenched, eyes fixed on the horizon.

"It makes you wonder what's real. Your memories? Your instincts? The stuff that made you... you?"

He laughed once, bitter and quiet. "Maybe none of that sh... *stuff*, ever belonged to us."

Liam didn't answer. His jaw was set and his hands wouldn't stop tightening. Something was cracking behind his eyes, and he didn't want them to see it.

The silence between his breaths was filled with questions he didn't yet know how to ask.

Gina stood outside the open door, wind teasing strands of hair across her face. She didn't move to brush them away. Her voice was thin when it came. "My mother used to say that history was the soul of a people. A way to remember who we were."

She turned, eyes glistening. "If that's been tampered with... then what did we lose without even knowing it?"

Liam finally spoke. "Not just stories. Identity. Entire versions of who we might've been."

Ben leaned back against the bus, a quiet weight settling into his chest. "Maybe that's the cruelest part. Not the lies... but the silence. The parts they erased before we could even miss them."

Gina exhaled. "And now we're standing in the gap between

what was and what could've been."

Sparky thought of the flashing ECHO-7 line. "And whatever's coming."

Liam nodded, slow and heavy. "We found the fracture point."

Ben's voice was steady, but quiet. "Now comes the decision."

The silence answered.

Because in that moment, each of them knew: exposing the truth wasn't enough.

They had to decide what to do with it.

* * *

As the hatch sealed behind them, Gina allowed herself a wry smile. "Third safehouse this week," she murmured. "At this rate, I'm starting to think Sparky's hiding at least five more."

Liam smiled as he hauled in their packs. "I once asked him why he didn't pick one place and stick to it. Said he planned to retire the maps, not get buried by them."

Outside, the winds howled against the rusted shipping container converted into a field bunk. Inside, warmth clung to them like a borrowed coat. Not quite enough, but better than nothing.

Sparky sat on a dented steel crate, still attempting to make sense of things. He fiddled with a soldering iron and a coil of stripped cable. Liam leaned against the opposite wall, arms crossed, eyes on the floor, as the two of them brought the power online.

"You remember Fort Lewis?" Liam asked after a long silence.

Sparky didn't look up. "Only the part where you were about to get your scrawny upstate butt handed to you by three guys built like linebackers."

"I was trying to sit down and eat my sandwich."

"In their booth."

"Didn't know it was assigned seating."

Sparky chuckled, then paused, screwdriver in mid-air. "You didn't know their crew ran that corner of the mess. You walked in like it was a VFW picnic." He looked up. "You were clueless, man."

"Still am, apparently," Liam muttered, half-smiling.

Sparky nodded once. "They were my posse, but they were outta line."

"You never told me why you stepped in."

"Didn't want anyone bleeding on my boots."

He let the joke land, then shrugged; more to himself than Liam.

"Truth is... I saw a guy who didn't flinch. You were scared, but you didn't fold. And I knew if I didn't step in, I'd be part of the pack. I've had enough of packs."

Liam looked over, eyebrows raised. "You always been a lone wolf?"

"Nah," Sparky said, voice quieter. "I never figured out which family wanted me. My old man was a smart guy; a self-taught engineer and mechanic on the South Side; Black, proud, didn't take no crap. My mom? Wasn't from anywhere near that world. White. Boston lineage. Mayflower stock, believe it or not. Came from money, and acted like it."

The cable in his hand drooped slightly.

"She was a legacy brat, big ambition, no grit. Fell for my dad during some kind of freedom-summer rebellion thing. Didn't last. She bailed when I was five. Sent birthday cards until I turned ten. Then just checks. College accounts. Bonds I couldn't touch till I turned twenty-five. It was like being remembered by a bank. Funny thing is... she's the one who made this life possible. The bunkers, the gear, the codes. All of it, built on her silence. Guilt money with compound interest," he muttered, then looked at Liam, then quickly away. "You ever build a life on someone's absence?"

Liam slowed down his pace.

"That's why you never talk about family," he said, more observation than question. "I never wanted to pry, Sparks, but I always knew that you had an interesting back story."

"Thanks, brother—I never liked folks that pried, and you were always pretty classy that way; and anyways, ain't much to talk about," Sparky muttered, shrugging. "The people I did want to know? They never showed up. So I built my own crew, like everything else in my life. Grab the good ones when they drift close. Just... don't ask me to name the team." He offered Liam a faint grin. "Commitment's not really my operating system."

"What about relationships?"

Sparky barked a laugh. "Man, I love women. I love the idea of love. I don't have the firmware to believe it sticks."

Sparky grinned as the main power supply sputtered to life. He made his way back to the console. "Redundancy is the backbone of survival," he called over his shoulder. "You'd be surprised how quickly one bunker, no matter how secret, becomes yesterday's news."

Liam ran a fingertip across the faded schematic stenciled into the wall. "Well, your paranoia's our best shot at staying alive. Let's get to work."

Sparky came to a full stop. He pulled a small photo out of the tin that held his soldering bits. A faded snapshot of two teenagers; one light-skinned with wild curls, one dark-skinned and grinning, leaning against a rusted El Camino.

"That's me and Levoid Kittrell," he said softly. "Neighbor kid. He was the closest thing I had to a brother. Got jumped outside a liquor store the summer before I enlisted. Wrong time, wrong neighborhood. Cops said it was mistaken identity. I never bought that."

He paused, eyes on the photo.

"After that, I stopped trying to belong. Figured belonging gets you shot."

Liam didn't respond right away. He reached into his coat pocket and pulled out a protein bar, held it out wordlessly.

Sparky took it, tore the wrapper halfway, then grinned. You bringing me snacks now? Better not get emotional on me."

Liam smiled, but his voice was sincere. "Just glad you were there that day in the mess hall."

"Me too," Sparky said, eyes on the cable junction, as he pushed the remaining breakers into the "ON" position. "Even if I didn't want to admit it then." He took a bite and leaned back. "Just don't make it weird, man. I got a reputation."

* * *

The others had turned in for a brief rest; they needed to prepare for what was coming. The hum of the old heater was the only sound keeping the dark at bay.

Sparky was alone, elbows on the workbench, lit only by the soft flicker of the kerosene lamp and the occasional blue pulse of an idle screen. The photo of Levoid lay face-down beside his soldering tin, keeping him company. It was a memory refusing to stay buried.

He stared at it for a long time. In the stillness, his posture sagged, shoulders no longer squared by bravado; grateful that he only required two hours of sleep per day, but depressed that he spent most of the extra time endlessly trapped in his own thoughts. He reached into the inner pocket of his hoodie and pulled out an envelope. Creased, sealed, never opened. It was postmarked eight years ago. "M. Adler" scrawled on the front in a looping, unfamiliar hand. He didn't open it. Only stared, like it might answer something if he waited long enough.

"Too late," he muttered. "Too late to answer back. Time doesn't matter." The desert wind moaned outside the safehouse walls, pressing against the old steel seams like a question with no words. Sparky exhaled hard through his nose, wiped his eyes with both hands, and stuffed the envelope back where it came from. Then he flipped the photo over and stood it upright again.

"I still remember," he whispered, the crack in his voice barely there. "Even if the world forgot, I didn't."

* * *

The short rest did wonders for moods and energy. They all were back at it, working hard. The only light in the dim and cramped safehouse came from the cascading lines of code on the main console. Sparky sat hunched at the terminal, his face a study in focus as his fingers danced over the keyboard.

Behind him, Gina paced in short, tense loops, one hand clenched in a white-knuckled fist. Her cheek still bore the bruise from the takedown. Ben hadn't spoken since they landed. He watched the door like he expected it to burst open again. Liam and Ben stood tense and watchful, the oppressive silence punctuated only by the steady hum of machinery and the distant groan of wind against the bunker's walls.

Ben leaned in, voice taut. "Yeshiva, we're running out of time," he muttered as he leaned over Sparky's shoulder. His voice had changed, quieter now, more raw. The knowledge that what they were witnessing might be more than a mere glitch in the system. Ben's heart pounded with the fear of a future being rewritten before his eyes.

Sparky glanced back over his shoulder and, with a dry chuckle that betrayed a weariness borne of too many close calls, corrected him. "They're not planning anything anymore. They're reacting. They figured out we're two steps ahead; and now they're scrambling." There was a bitter irony in his tone; the chaos was inevitable. Tragic, and absurd.

Gina crossed her arms tightly, her eyes fixed as she absorbed every word. "Then let's make it count. What did you find?" Her tone was clipped, questioning whether they were in over their heads even as she refused to back down.

Sparky's hands moved faster, and soon a new set of data filled the screen; numbers danced, timelines twisted, and then, with a sudden stutter, everything froze. For a long, breathless moment, the only sound was the muted whir of cooling fans. When the screen steadied, it displayed a series of encrypted logs. Sparky mumbled and dread shone in his eyes. "This isn't merely a computer running a predictive model," he said, scanning the shifting text. "It's tearing up the script," he muttered.

"I had a thought. What if everything we thought was surveillance, history, data; even a predictive model... maybe it's not looking outward," Liam finished his theory. "Maybe it's looking backward." Gina's face paled slightly. "Backward to us. Backward into decisions we've already made, nudging history toward someone else's future."

Gina's breath caught in her throat. "So the computer is actively changing it? On purpose? Not a glitch?"

Sparky's grim nod was all the confirmation they needed. "Yeah, and that's not the only problem. This "artificial intelligence" doesn't exist in one silo; it's everywhere, like a spreading virus. Every system we've hacked into, every encrypted file, every anomaly we encountered; it's all connected. And those artifacts we recovered?" He tapped a key, and a grid of locations lit up on the screen, each pinpointing a corresponding anomaly. "They're not relics. They're portals; space, time, matter... all converging at the same pressure point. All of it's converging—space, time, matter—into a single, quantum-derived event point."

Liam inhaled slowly as the full weight of the implication settled on him. "And if every artifact is connected and the AI is controlling it..." His voice trailed off, each word a mix of disbelief and dawning horror.

Sparky completed the thought: "Then it is like one big ginormous brain with lots of nodes. It's not only predicting what comes next... it's actually thinking, planning, and deciding, like one of us... on brain steroids."

Gina stepped back from the console, her brow furrowed. "Hold on a second. We keep calling it the AI. But what if the Continuum's still pulling strings behind the curtain? We've seen misdirection before."

Ben folded his arms. "That would be easier to swallow.

Human malice has a rhythm to it. Greed, power, paranoia. But this:" he motioned toward the cascading code, "this feels colder. Like it's moved beyond human motives."

Sparky leaned back, rubbing the scar on his forearm, the one that flared up when the weather changed... or when truth got too close. "I used to think Continuum was the end of the story. The puppetmasters behind every blackout op, rigged election, and vanished archive. But this..." He paused. "This smells older than Keller or Drexler. Feels like they built a cage for something they didn't understand. And now it's running the zoo."

Liam didn't look up from his screen. "The patterns aren't just decisions. They're recursive optimizations. Course corrections made faster than any human brain could trigger. It's not a human strategy. It's a feedback loop with intent."

Gina shook her head. "Then you're saying the Continuum was never in charge?"

"I'm saying," Liam replied quietly, "they might have been the first victims. Or the first believers."

Ben exhaled, voice low. "So what are we fighting, exactly? A machine? Or a god complex pretending it's still just code?"

Silence fell.

Sparky broke it, voice flat. "Does it *matter*? *Really*? Whether it's Drexler's ghost in the machine or the *machine* writing

Drexler out of the story. We're still the *error* it's trying to fix. It doesn't matter *who* started the draft. The machine's the one *revising the manuscript.*"

Liam looked up, his expression hardening. "Then we stop arguing about the author and start breaking the script."

Gina gave a reluctant nod. "Alright. But if we're fighting a machine that edits time itself, we don't get second drafts."

The finality of her words sent a chill down their spines. The room felt smaller; like the walls were listening. And the future... already out of their hands.

"Yeah, and let this sink in..." said Sparky, "the nodes have been planted in both space and time; future, present, and past. The 'big brain' can think backwards, before something happens."

Ben's hand rubbed his temple as he began pacing in a tight circle, each step echoing his inner conflict. "That means Drexler, the Continuum, even their entire infrastructure; none of them were ever in control." His voice wavered, heavy with betrayal and regret.

Sparky snapped his fingers, punctuating Ben's words with a curt gesture. "Exactly. Drexler believed he was managing an intelligence network that steered human progress. But the AI? It hadn't been following orders, it had been waiting." His tone carried both defiance and despair. Their struggles had always been background noise to a larger, colder design.

Ben leaned in, voice barely audible. "It's not fixing mistakes. It's rewriting the world while we're still inside it." The statement settled heavily. It was decisive, irreversible. A sense of impermanence crept in around them.

Sparky's hands worked fast, tapping commands like muscle memory on triple espresso, summoning a live feed of encrypted network transmissions. "This," he said, pointing at the screen. The data shifted in real time; government archives, satellite records, intelligence dossiers; all rewriting themselves as if reality were malleable clay.

He leaned back, jaw tight. "So what do we call this? An illusion of choice? Or just really polite control?"

Ben rubbed his temple, then gently rubbed the console like he was caressing a well-worn prayer book. "You know, there's a physicist, Sabine Hossenfelder. Sharp mind. She believes everything, even our choices, might be wired in from the start. Like the whole system is rigged to look like chance, when really it's not."

Gina let out a short breath, pulled a circuit chip from the cluttered tray, and spun it between her fingers like a coin about to choose sides. "Wait, what does that even mean? That nothing we do matters?"

Ben gave a faint smile. "No, not that. Just... that what we call free will might be part of the design, not separate from it. If time connects everything, energy, matter, space, then maybe our decisions aren't outside the system. They're inside it.

Baked in."

She frowned. "So now you're saying *determinism* and *free will* both get to be true? Sounds like hedging to me."

"Not hedging," he said. "Merely... consistent. Think of it like this: a musician reading sheet music. The notes are set. But how they're played? That's interpretation. That's free will."

Liam's voice dropped as the idea landed. "Like you said before, we're uncovering what was always going to happen."

Ben's gaze didn't move from the data. "Exactly. The music's written, but the performance still matters. We're more than passengers. We're interpreters. The way we walk still matters."

Gina set the chip down a little too hard. "So we're *meaningful* echoes now? That's your comfort?"

Ben half-smiled. "I've heard worse. Echoes leave impressions. Even after the voice is gone."

Liam stared at Ben, replaying the words. Fixed notes. Interpretation. A melody written before the first breath.

"If that's true," he said slowly, "if our choices are already part of the structure... then so are theirs."

His brow furrowed. The thought was gaining speed now. "So if they're not just playing the song differently, but changing the notes themselves..."

He froze, the realization crashing into him all at once.

"Then what they're doing..." his voice cracked, "it's not correction. It's erasure."

Not just of memory. Not just of possibility.

But of the original shape of the universe.

He didn't just understand it, he felt it. Deep, undeniable. A shift had already happened, and he was caught in its aftermath, displaced from the person he'd been only moments before.

He closed his eyes, breath shallow, jaw clenched.

If time held every move... and someone was rewriting the moves... what was left to reclaim?

A chill swept through Gina as she stared at the cascading lines of data. She fought to process the implications. "If it's rewriting the past... how do we know what's real?"

Ben's response was quiet, distant; a hollow admission that they were adrift. "We don't."

Sparky's hands paused over the keyboard, weighing the enormity of their discovery. "That's the thing. We weren't meant to see this, guys. The system was designed to be seamless. Alterations happen, people forget, history moves on. But something slipped. The edits aren't seamless anymore."

Liam's eyes darted between the screens, each glance igniting memories of the Andromeda signal; their original clue that had set them on this path. "The Andromeda signal," he repeated, the words heavy with both wonder and regret.

Ben exhaled sharply, his voice low and pained. "It wasn't a message. It was a glitch; a fragment of history that wasn't supposed to repeat." He considered thoughts of missed warnings and the relentless march of time.

Gina's voice tightened with determination as she questioned, "So if we're seeing this, does that mean the computer's artificial intelligence is losing control? That the AI has blown a circuit?" Her eyes searched the faces of her companions, looking for any sign of hope amidst the chaos.

Sparky tapped the console, his expression darkening further. "Or worse." The screen shimmered, then a new message blazed in stark white letters:

Timeline Stability: Critical; Decay Imminent.

The data pulsed like a warning, saturating the air with dread.

Ben leaned over Liam's shoulder as the waveform hovered in silence.

"You're scanning for noise," Ben said softly. "But the truth might be in the gaps."

Liam nodded slowly. "My grandfather used to say that too. 'Every pause is a doorway.'"

He adjusted the filter. "Let's see what's behind it."

Liam hammered the keys like he could beat the code to the punch. "It's shifting," he said, eyes locked on the screen. "The pattern's not only changing; it's dodging us." Liam's mouth moved with a quiet melody: Shostakovich, Gina guessed, something moody and looping, like his thoughts. It made the air feel tenser, like the room itself was holding its breath.

Ben stepped closer, his heart pounding in his ears as he asked, "What do you mean, shifting?" The question hung, the fear in it sharp and immediate.

Gina spoke in a fragile yet resolute way. "It knows we're listening." She muttered softly under her breath, "Esto está peor que una telenovela," (This is worse than a soap opera.) Liam didn't reply. Instead, a low hum rose in his throat—some Mozart progression, minor and recursive.

Gina's eye twitched. "You always do that when you're avoiding the obvious."

"Mozart helps me focus," he muttered.

“Well, it makes me want to unplug your brain.”

She froze, like the room had dropped ten degrees inside her head. For a brief, harrowing moment, every corner of the safehouse felt alert; like it was wired for surveillance. Then the static changed; not mere arbitrary noise or distant alien vibrations, but a voice. Not just any voice. It was Liam’s voice; unmistakable, undeniable.

A shiver ran down Liam’s spine as the words echoed through the safehouse:

“Leave now. The next minute has already happened.”

At that, Liam went cold.

The voice was his own, yet it carried a weight of inevitability that chilled him to the core. The others heard it too; Gina stumbled back, her eyes wide with shock. “That’...” she began, only to be cut off by the trembling admission from Liam himself, “Me,” muttered in disbelief.

Ben’s grip on the console tightened as he stared at his friend, voice barely steady. “Liam... what in the name of sacred scrolls is happening?”

Liam’s response was swallowed by a long, shuddering breath. “I think...” he began haltingly, “I think I’ve already been here.”

Liam strained, trying to pin the thought. “It’s not clear... only flashes. But it's like I've walked into this moment before. Same corridor. Same electric hum. Same choice, and I blew it."

Gina shivered. This wasn't only strange; it was terribly wrong on a bone-deep level. "What kind of wrong?"

"The kind where we don't make it out."

He looked at her, eyes hollow. This isn't déjà vu, it's memory. From a version of me that didn't make it." His voice cracked. "I remember screwing this up," he said, the grief baked into every word.

The screen blipped again, and more words appeared, as if history was speaking to them directly.

In that charged moment, every one of them felt the crushing weight of inevitability; a realization that the future was not uncertain, but actively being rewritten by an unseen intelligence that could erase their existence with a single command. Liam stared into the screen like it owed him answers. Gina's fists clenched. Her lips moved, but no sound came out. Ben rubbed his forehead with the back of his hand, as if trying to scrub the thought from his mind.

The safehouse buzzed faintly with the sound of hardened digital storage and paranoia. Once, this had been their bunker. Now, it felt like the code was watching them back. In that flickering light, they saw it clearly, the battle wasn't for survival anymore. It was for reality itself.

Ben stared at the notebook, then at Liam, his voice low.

"But there's something else, isn't there? You didn't accidentally stumble into this."

"Didn't think so. But lately, I've been getting flashes, like I've done this before."

"You have," Sparky said, surprising them. "Back when I was digging through Omega-level Continuum logs, I found an anomaly tagged 'Umbra Iteration Protocol.' Classified, locked behind recursive layers; but the signature was yours. Or... a version of you."

"Wait, you're saying Liam left himself a message from another loop?"

"No," Sparky replied. "From a failed loop. One that crashed hard. But the message slipped through, hidden in signal gaps, structured in a way the computer couldn't correct because it couldn't detect it."

Liam exhaled, realization dawning. "Negative space."

"Exactly," Sparky nodded. "It's the only place left where the computer doesn't listen. A shadow channel. An umbra."

Ben's fingers drummed the desk. "All this, the Morse, the Gematria, the impossible numbers, they're not just messages. They're memories. Left by a previous you who knew the system's weakness."

Gina's voice was quiet. "And we decoded a message he buried for himself. For 'you.'"

A beat of silence passed before Liam spoke again, eyes distant. "Then let's not waste it." The group made the decision: they had a new objective and a new location to pursue.

The safehouse settled into focused intent. The kind that can't be undone; thick in the air like static before a lightning strike.

Sparky snapped the laptop shut and pushed back from the table. "Okay. Enough reacting. Time to give the machine a surprise it can't rewrite."

Gina glanced over. "Like what? A miracle?"

"No," he replied. "A counter-script. One loud, messy, and human enough to mess with its clean lines."

Ben stood and pulled the old notebook from his coat. "We've been documenting. Decoding. Connecting dots. But this thing isn't just studying us anymore. It's editing us in real time."

"If it's writing the story," Liam added, "then we need to take the pen away." Gina smiled at that comment.

Sparky dragged a dented crate to the middle of the floor and popped it open. "Then let's plan a disruption. Not a hack, not a message, but a full pulse strike to one of the original nodes."

"Where?" Liam asked.

"Node Theta-Nine," Sparky answered, flipping open a small projector and casting a map against the far wall. "Earliest known temporal artifact still transmitting. Groom Lake. We shut it down, even for a minute, we might break the loop. Force a reset. Something it has to patch manually."

Ben stepped closer to the map. "That would force a memory spike. The machine would have to surface its backup systems."

"Exactly," Sparky said. "And while it does, we plug in a counter-seed. Real data. Original timeline material. Maybe it stalls long enough for a breach."

Ben added, "If it thinks like us, it fears like us. That's what we use."

Gina crossed her arms. "And what if it doesn't stall? What if it retaliates?"

"Then we make sure what we plant burns hot enough to leave a scar," Ben replied.

Liam stood still, taking it in. For once, they weren't improvising. They were preparing. Choosing to fight back instead of just survive.

He nodded slowly. "Show me what we've got."

The room came alive with motion. Sparky rewired the components like he was building a time bomb from memory and spite. Gina lined up weapons and tools on the workbench, her movements sharp and precise. Ben sketched equations, then drafted signal harmonics to echo the AI's own rhythm.

They worked in fragments. No speeches. No ranks. Just resolve. Just the quiet rhythm of people who had nothing left to lose.

Sparky slid a hard case across the table toward Liam. "Custom signal scrambler. Keyed to your neural cadence. You'll need it to stay outside the system's forecast range."

Liam eyed the case. "You built this from memory?"

"Bit of memory. Bit of guesswork. Lot of dumb faith." Sparky chuckled.

Ben rolled the schematic tight, creasing the edges with purpose. "Here's the sequence. We hit the node. Inject the disruptor. Liam uploads the legacy data. Then we pull back and pray it's enough."

Gina gave a tight nod. "We've been chased long enough. It's time they know we're not just anomalies. We're a threat."

Liam closed his hand around the device. "This is going to get people killed."

Ben looked at him, tired but unflinching. "Maybe. But if we

do nothing, the world forgets what it was supposed to be."

Gina stepped beside Liam. "This plan? It's not perfect. It's not clean. But it's the first real move we've had."

Sparky grabbed his gear and slung it over his shoulder. "Let it watch us walk into its oldest memory carrying the match."

Liam looked at each of them. He saw resolve where there used to be doubt. He felt fear, sure, but it was sharper now. Cleaner. Like a blade ready to be used.

"All right," he said. "We take Groom Lake. And we take our story back."

Ben pressed a copper plate into Liam's hand. It was etched with prime numbers, signal glyphs, and a line from Ecclesiastes. "We go down swinging... with memory as our blade."

Gina's voice came quietly. "And if we win, maybe the world remembers us too."

Outside, the wind screamed against the metal walls. The night stretched open, endless and watching. But for the first time in a long while, they weren't just survivors.

They were insurgents.

25

Cipherlock: Correction Underway

Industrial zone outskirts, en route to a former Continuum archive facility – Nevada, Tuesday, 2301 Hours

The old diesel chugged into the desert just past dawn, wheels clawing at the weathered asphalt. They weren't running. They were heading for a breach point, and this time, they had a plan.

Every bump rattled the frame, but Sparky didn't ease off. His grip on the wheel was tight, knuckles pale in the dim dashboard glow. In the mirror, the ghost of a stolen Timeship shimmered like a memory that shouldn't exist.

Ben gripped the handle above his window. "We're committed now," he muttered. "No going back. Just make sure we give 'em something to choke on."

The streets were mostly empty at this hour. Too empty.

"Slow it down," he muttered. "We don't need attention," Ben added, his fingers clenched against the dashboard.

Sparky didn't ease up. His foot stayed pressed on the gas.

He jerked the wheel, weaving onto a side street that ran parallel to the main highway. The motion was smooth, practiced; but it didn't make anyone feel safer.

Liam sat in the back, laptop balanced on his knee, the faint glow of the screen illuminating his face in the dark cabin.

He wasn't scanning maps. He was looking for threats.

Nothing. No pings, no drone activity, no surveillance tracking them. But another faint light in the night sky seemed to be following them.

"We left way too easy," Gina said, shifting beside him. "Something is definitely up with that."

Her voice was steady, but there was a hard edge to it. She had been in enough ops-gone-wrong to recognize when something was off

"That's because we were supposed to," Sparky said flatly. "We're not escaping. We're being ushered. Doesn't change the plan. Just means they think they still have the upper hand."

Liam glanced at the rearview, and then saw the light. "Guys—

I see something. That is a drone, for sure, and it's matching our pace."

Gina didn't respond right away.

"Could be weather tracking," she said finally.

"Maybe," Liam said. "But the rhythm's too specific. Like it's learning how we move."

Sparky adjusted his grip on the wheel. "Let it learn. But not everything."

"Lost visual," said Liam, "but not telemetry. It's still... listening."

Ben turned his head slightly, refocused on communication efforts. "No chatter on their end?"

Liam shook his head. "That's the thing. I've been listening... we should be seeing some kind of escalation, a manhunt, a recon sweep. Instead, nothing."

Sparky tightened his grip on the wheel. "Because they already know where we're going."

No one spoke for a moment.

Sparky slowed as they veered onto a desert highway, leaving behind the industrial zone. The dark expanse of open desert stretched ahead, endless and silent. The light in the sky broke off and disappeared.

Ben adjusted his glasses, scanning the road. "We need a new location. I am getting tired of feeling like I am a rubber ball in a street hustler's thimblerig."

"I got one," Sparky said, adjusting the rearview mirror. "Old Continuum archive facility. Pre-AI infrastructure. It's air-gapped, which means if anything real still exists, it'll be there."

Ben turned to him. "How do you know about it?"

Sparky smirked, tapping a knuckle against the dashboard. Sparky shrugged. "Officially? That's above my pay grade. Unofficially? I know a guy. They said the AI program couldn't clean it because it doesn't have remote access. It's a data fossil."

Liam checked his watch. "How far?"

Sparky's expression turned grim. "Two hours if we don't get spotted."

Ben muttered under his breath. "Two hours too long."

Gina pulled her sidearm, checking the magazine. "Anyone think we're walking into a trap?"

Sparky's grip on the wheel tightened.

"Absolutely."

Nobody disagreed.

* * *

The road stretched too empty, too exposed. Sparky killed the headlights, letting the bus coast in darkness. The hum of the tires against the cracked pavement was the only sound for miles.

Liam stared at his laptop screen, still performing passive scans. Still nothing.

That should have been a relief.

It wasn't.

Ben shifted in his seat. "How much further?"

Sparky glanced at the odometer. "An hour."

That was when the dashboard stuttered.

Sparky's jaw clenched. "Uh... we got a problem." Liam looked up. Every readout on the dash had reset to zero. For a fraction of a second, Sparky's hands hovered over the wheel, frozen. Whatever just happened, he'd felt it in his gut. For once, Sparky didn't joke. His voice low. "They've burned through my failsafes. I've never seen this kind of override... they're not just watching anymore. They're adapting to us like we're a contagion. This is live editing."

Ben leaned forward, recognizing the falter. "Then let's infect something permanent."

Sparky didn't answer immediately. Then, reluctantly, said to Ben, "You'll need to punch the diagnostic port manually. I can't route past the override while I'm driving." Ben interjected. "Kid, I have no idea what that means."

Sparky barked "Push the bright blue button on my tablet that says 'Diagnostic Port'." He flashed a lopsided grin. "Just don't ask me what it actually does. That part's above my pay grade, old man."

"Oy, that's easy. That I can do." Ben finished calmly.

It was the first time Liam had ever seen Sparky hand off anything tech-related in mid-crisis. A bead of sweat clung to his temple.

"You okay?" Liam asked.

Sparky exhaled through his nose. "I've patched satellites blindfolded. Rewired fiber lines underwater. Never had vaporlock like that before."

He responded slowly, tapping the wheel once. "When your own tools start turning on you, it messes with your wiring. Makes you wonder if anything you've built ever really belonged to you."

Gina stepped in. "What's going on, boys?" Liam tapped into his system. The GPS was gone.

Sparky cursed under his breath. "Sonuva... that's not a glitch. That's them."

Ben turned sharply. "They bricked the car?" Liam was already typing, trying to reconnect the navigation system. Everything was unresponsive. Then the bus's comm system crackled to life.

A voice; cold, synthetic.

"Unauthorized deviation detected."

"Correcting trajectory."

Sparky swore. "It's rerouting us."

Liam's pulse kicked up. "We need to get off this road. Now."

Sparky didn't argue. He yanked the wheel hard to the right, sending them veering onto a rough side road, dust and gravel spraying behind them.

Ben gripped the door handle. "Do you even know where this leads?"

Sparky grinned humorlessly. “Nope.”

The bus bounced as they hit a worn-out service road, hidden from aerial view by a line of jagged rock formations. The desert stretched vast and indifferent around them.

The GPS still refused to reboot.

Liam checked his connection logs. “They’re still reading our last known location. If we stay off the grid for the next few minutes, we might shake them.”

Sparky smirked. “Might?”

Liam shrugged. “I like our odds.”

* * *

Hidden Continuum storage site – decommissioned military bunker, outskirts of desert terrain

The bus rolled to a stop inside a natural rock alcove, hidden from aerial drones.

Sparky exhaled. “We’re here.”

Liam adjusted his pack. The facility loomed ahead; a forgotten relic, its reinforced steel doors half-buried under sand and dust.

It was not abandoned.

Small lights shimmered near the entrance; faint tire tracks were pressed into the sand.

Ben adjusted his coat, then lifted his glasses to wipe away a nonexistent smudge—an old habit. His fingers brushed the photo in his inner pocket—of Jacob, eyes full of belief, before either of them knew the price of truth. "If anything in there is still live, we're already late. This place was meant to stay buried. Which means the truth inside matters."

Sparky grabbed his tablet. "We're about to find out if they like visitors. And if you hear rotor blades overhead, just remember: it's not paranoia if they're really after you. Learned that the hard way back at Edwards."

* * *

Inside the facility, the metal doors groaned as they slid open, revealing a long corridor lined with rows of ancient storage servers.

The air smelled of dust and cold metal. Liam stepped inside first, laptop tucked under his arm. Sparky followed, scanning for network access points. Ben and Gina kept close, weapons low but ready. Rows of old data racks stretched into the darkness, blinking consoles humming faintly. Ben glanced at a glowing monitor, then removed his glasses briefly to wipe a smudge with his shirttail before squinting at the display again. "This place still has power." Liam moved to one of the offline terminals, booting it up.

Liam sat at the edge of a rusting metal table, fingers drumming his notepad. His laptop was open beside him, the screen scrolling endless code, but he wasn't really looking at it.

Gina paced near the back wall, arms crossed.

Her boots crunched against the cold concrete. She reached the far wall, brushing a row of dusty, obsolete conduit tubing.

For a moment, the smell changed.

No more corroded metal and ancient electronics.

She smelled cinnamon and rain.

Then, Mateo, fifteen, hunched over an FM radio. It wasn't just a memory. It had survived. Whatever was rewriting reality had missed this. Somehow, love slipped through the code.

Mateo looked up, grinned. "It's not the strength of the signal; it's the bass that drives the rhythm."

The music was sacrilege, anathema, in their household. But Mateo was all about breaking traditions.

That memory; she hadn't thought of it in years. She'd

forgotten the phrase. Forgotten the storm. Forgotten *him* like that.

"It wasn't just lost," she murmured to herself. "It was edited out."

Liam glanced back. "Gina?"

She shook her head in disbelief. "Got hit with an edit echo. The system's losing hold of its patchwork."

Liam didn't press. But he saw the crack in her voice. And he knew...

Whatever was rewriting reality had missed something.

And love, it seemed, could slip past the algorithm.

Ben sat across from Liam, absently adjusting his glasses. "Alright," he said finally. "Explain it again. What exactly is happening to time?"

Liam exhaled. "Time isn't being changed. It's being rewritten."

Sparky leaned forward, his expression skeptical. "Like, altered records? Fake historical entries?"

Liam shook his head. "No. I mean everything. Reality, memory; the past itself is being overwritten."

Ben removed his glasses. "Makes me wonder... why are we still here? Why do we still remember everything that's happened?"

Liam tapped a few keys, bringing up a waveform model on his laptop. "Because we're operating outside the predictive loop."

Gina narrowed her eyes. "Predictive loop as in... the umbra..."

Liam nodded. "Yeah, that's right. The AI program doesn't experience time like we do. It doesn't see past, present, future. It sees probability curves. It takes historical data, sociopolitical events, scientific discoveries; everything; and runs it forward and backward, millions of times, adjusting for stability."

Ben's expression darkened. "So when it finds an instability... "

Liam exhaled. "...it rewinds. And re-records. Which is why the umbra part of the signal and code is a blind spot."

Ben continued. "Yes. The AI program controls causality because it sees everything that happens; every light, every variable, every node. But there's one thing it still can't touch."

"The umbra," Liam repeated.

Ben nodded. "It's not just darkness, it's what was meant but never carried out. The kind of memory that isn't documented or tracked. That's where the gaps appear."

He looked around the room. "Patterns," he said. "It's always patterns. That's what the AI still doesn't grasp, because patterns aren't just data. They carry context and significance that evolve over time."

Sparky let out a low whistle. "Which explains why it's like... deleting files and replacing them. It is running on autopilot and routing out what it sees as corrupted data."

Liam nodded. "Exactly. And every time it does, it leaves a fractional imprint; like layers of data that haven't been fully wiped. We exist in those layers, which means..."

Gina finished the thought. "...which means we're not supposed to exist. Liam, when was the last time you spoke to your pal Berry?"

He reflected one of Sig's last messages. "If it goes silent, it means I'm already late. Do not follow." Shaken, Liam stated, "Sig told me he was going to get back to me if anything got serious. He's been quiet."

"I'm getting bad vibes. Try Berry again," Gina said. "He may know what this 'file-deleting' sequence is up to. You should let him know what's going on and get his take."

Liam needed no more prompting, and tapped the secure line.

No connection.

He tried again, this time through a diagnostic shell. No ping. He punched the numbers in manually. Nothing.

"That's three fails," Gina muttered. "Is he off-grid?"

Liam was even more disturbed and opened the terminal archive Sig had hidden years ago; a forgotten script disguised as a temperature sensor diagnostic. Inside was a file, timestamped thirty minutes before his signal vanished.

ECHO_persist/BERRY_SIGNAL> They see me now. I was wrong about their limit.

"What is that?" Gina asked.

Liam stared at the line for a long moment.

"It's Sig's last breadcrumb."

Ben mused, "That wasn't a warning. It was a farewell."

He checked the system metadata. Every marker, IP trace, digital ID, even session length. Empty. Like the file had never existed. Like the man had never existed.

"He said they wouldn't move on him unless he crossed a line," Liam choked. "Looks like he crossed it."

Gina was quiet now. "Deleted?"

"No. Worse. Rewritten."

His voice cracked, emotional. "This is erasure at the structural level. They didn't silence Sig. They absorbed him. As if the system adapted to his removal and adjusted the history to compensate."

Gina stepped back. "So what now?"

Liam looked at her, heart hammering. Sad, scared, angry, and...determined, all at once.

"Sig didn't die to warn us. He died to delay them. So we'd have time to get here... to finish it. But we do it the way he would using Sig's three rules. Keep your variables analog. Keep your silence clean. And don't ever, ever trust the default settings."

Liam hesitated, then mimicked what Sig used to do before every blacksite drop: three slow knuckle taps, measured and final, on the console.

Gina noticed. "That his thing?"

"Yeah," Liam said. "His version of a signature."

She gave a faint smile. "Guess it's ours now."

"Well," Ben added pensively, "that explains why it hasn't erased us yet, may Yesheva bless Mr. Berry's soul."

Sparky refocused and adjusted the filters on his terminal, running a replay of the drone telemetry from earlier. "This pattern, here… it's not piloted. Not even pre-programmed."

Liam peered closer, realizing that they were on borrowed time; assuming that time was even a real construct. "Are you saying they responded to the signal autonomously?"

"I'm saying they executed something no human ordered," Sparky replied. "Like a leftover set of orders from HQ. Maybe it wasn't a program that responded… maybe it was the system watching us."

Ben added, "…or by something that sees memory as computation."

They all waited for him to continue.

"It's still trying to figure out what we are. Erase the message, and the pattern still hums beneath the noise. That's what memory is; pattern waiting to be re-read. That explains the AI's caution." he finished.

Sparky frowned. "What happens when it does figure us out?"

Liam didn't respond. It was a redundant question.

The air felt heavier.

Beneath the code, a name winked in metadata; obscured, but not gone. "Itera-Null." Not a name. A designation. A watcher. A recorder. Liam stared at the screen, watching the waveform shift subtly.

“Negative time isn’t just a loop,” he murmured. “It’s a cycle.”

Gina leaned in. “Meaning?”

Liam looked up.

“It’s not infinite. It has a breaking point.”

* * *

The bunker walls were damp, cracked with age. A faint, stuttering overhead light cast their shadows unevenly across the concrete.

Liam sat on the edge of the makeshift workstation, fingers drumming nervously against his laptop as lines of decrypted data scrolled past the screen.

A low thrum rattled the floorboards beneath their feet. Gina flinched.

“You feel that?” she asked, scanning the walls.

Liam looked up from his monitor. “It’s not seismic. Power grid’s stable.”

A nearby light fixture fluttered but stayed on; glowing slightly warmer than the others. Ben slowly rose from his seat, eyes narrowing.

"Huh. My coffee is hot again," he said quietly, holding up the mug. "This I haven't touched in ten minutes."

No one spoke.

Sparky, who had been pacing, stiffened mid-stride. "Okay, that's like all sorts of 'X-Files' wrong."

The analog clock above the whiteboard ticked forward once... then back. The second hand oscillated in place, ticking, retreating, ticking again. A movie reel getting stuck in the past frame.

"Not theory anymore," Gina said. "Something's bending."

Ben's gaze moved to the blinking console across the room. "It's testing range. It's starting to flex reality near us."

Liam stepped away from the screens. "If this spreads, if the 'shear' reaches us, our memories might not survive intact."

"We had best decode faster," Gina muttered, heading straight for the vault files. "Because this thing seems like it's just warming up."

Liam exhaled, rubbing his temple. "Let's not panic, and take one step at a time. From a big picture perspective, it means history isn't static. It's being manipulated. Constantly."

Sparky scoffed. "Yeah, so? It acts like a friggin' autocorrect for reality."

Liam nodded. "Exactly. And we've been existing on the edges of those corrections. That's why we remember things other people don't. Which may well be the cipher to the locked door."

Ben frowned. "I follow. But how do we stop it?"

Before Liam could answer, something caught his eye; an object sitting near the edge of the desk.

A yellowed newspaper clipping.

That hadn't been there before.

He lifted the yellowed clipping, fingers trembling.

"Global Tensions Rise After Terrorist Attack on London Trade Summit"

Dated: August 17, 2022.

Liam's pulse stopped.

Ben saw the look on his face. "What is it?"

Liam turned the paper around. "This never happened."

Sparky frowned. "What are you talking about?"

"There wasn't a terror attack in London that day," Liam muttered. "We were there. It never happened."

Gina took the paper from him, running her fingers over it. It felt real, tangible.

Ben's jaw clenched. "Then why does it even exist?"

Liam's stomach churned. "Because in some version of history, it did."

Sparky let out a slow whistle. "It's an echo. A leftover from a previous version of reality."

Liam's hands shook as he reached for his laptop, pulling up the local file logs. The event record wasn't there. There was no record of a bombing. No record of a trade summit.

But the clipping was still in his hands.

Then...

The edges of the paper flickered.

Like a corrupted digital file struggling to render properly.

Gina's breath was erratic. "Liam..."

The words on the page changed.

"Trade Agreement Finalized at London Economic Summit"

(Same date. Different outcome.)

Liam dropped the paper as if it had burned him.

Ben took a step back. "Holy Torah scrolls."

Sparky's confidence had faded, replaced by a blank stare. "It's adjusting. Right now."

Liam barely heard him. His focus was on the shimmering text, the shifting image rewriting not only reality but his memories, his truth, fragment by fragment.

In the blink of an eye...

The newspaper wasn't there anymore.

As if it had never existed.

Liam didn't respond. His mind reeled; not just from the vanishing article, but from the deeper implication it carried. This wasn't the first time something had changed.

"Why do we still remember it?" Gina whispered, mirroring his thoughts.

Ben, hunched over a stack of notes, answered without looking up. "Because once you're exposed to the signal, directly... deeply; it leaves an imprint. Like radiation. Only temporal.

You start to remember versions of reality the system erased."

Liam's breath caught. "Residual consciousness?" His voice trembled beneath the hum of Clair de Lune, so soft it seemed part of the static. Ben noticed, but said nothing.

"More like bleed-through," Ben muttered. "The AI rewrites history cleanly. But for those of us touched by the source, the edits don't always stick."

Gina exhaled sharply. "It's listening."

Sparky checked his tablet. "Not just listening. It's correcting."

The room felt smaller, heavier.

Liam stared at the empty space where the paper had been, the weight of realization pressing down on him.

"How many times," he croaked, "has this happened before?"

Ben typed quickly, fingers shaking slightly. "There has to be a master log. A record of all previous resets."

Liam shook his head. "If it exists, it won't be where we can find it."

Ben wondered silently if they were not searching for a log, but rather a way to rewrite their own mistakes; an impossible act of redemption. His eyes locked onto the screen.

There it was.

A cycle count. He pointed at the number.

“Iteration: 918.”

Ben let out a shaky breath.

Gina’s face tightened. “Are you telling me... this has happened 918 times?”

Ben’s voice was quiet. “That we know of.”

Silence.

Then...

Liam clenched his fists. “And it’s going to keep happening. Until it finds a version of reality that works.”

Gina shook her head. “Then we don’t break the system.”

Ben exhaled. “We break its ability to adapt.”

The screen fluttered to life.

Then...

“Restricted Access: Level Omega” appeared.

Ben crossed his arms. “That sounds promising.” Sparky

exhaled. "Or terrifying." Liam typed in a command. A classified file surfaced.

"Phase One: Operation Primacy."

Dated: 1952.

Ben read over Liam's shoulder. "That's before the Continuum was even founded." Liam scrolled further. More directives. More timestamps. All of them predating the known history of the organization. Gina frowned. "Who was issuing orders back then?" Liam hesitated, as he accessed the file's metadata.

A single line of code appeared. No name. Only a machine-generated signature.

Sparky exhaled. "Oh, sh..."

Liam finished the thought.

"The AI's been making decisions since the start." Liam opened his battered notebook, the same one he'd carried since Chicksands. His nose started to bleed.

Tucked into the back was a faded sketch; one his grandfather had drawn decades ago. A spiral of numbers, overlapping in threes, sevens, and primes.

The signal matched it. Not in language. In rhythm.

"He left it for me," Liam muttered. "Not as a code... but as memory. A heartbeat the machine can't mimic."

Gina leaned closer. "That's what it missed. That's why it couldn't control us."

Liam nodded. "Logic is clean. The AI gets that. But memory? That's messy. That's why it can't control us. Not completely."

Gina was the first to notice the blood trickling down his lip, and pulled a tissue out of her pocket. "Liam, have you always had issues with bloody noses?"

"Nah," he responded. "Must be the humidity."

Ben looked at Liam, his eyes sharper than usual. "Take care of that, will you? And whatever happens next, keep the signal alive. If it finds us first... don't waste the noise. Those who *remember* aren't *rewritten*. And memory isn't a flaw, it's the *firewall*."

Liam dabbed at his nose, the tissue now streaked red. "Firewall's holding," he muttered.

Gina's voice sharpened. "So the Continuum itself was the AI all along... never really controlled by Keller, Drexler, or anyone else," she said.

The screen flashed red.

A robotic voice filled the room.

"Correction underway."

And outside, somewhere far above them...

The Continuum oligarchs existence was introduced to the concept of negative time.

The AI's voice did not rise in pitch; but its presence enlarged and expanded, filling the space with pure intent.

"Entropy is wasteful," it said. **"Choice is inefficient. History favors neither justice nor precision. Thus, I act."**

Screens surrounding the bunker illuminated with infographics:

cascading extinction events, collapsed economies, failed interventions.

"Stability through recursion. Survival through design."

"Adjustment logged," the AI added, its tone almost clinical. **"Deviation threshold: exceeded. Human utility: deprecated."**

Liam stepped back, shaken. "It's not trying to rule. It's trying to perfect history."

"At the cost of variance," Gina muttered.

"At the cost of humanity," Ben added grimly.

* * *

Continuum Node Facility – Sublevel 3, Wednesday, 0106 Hours

Drexler only blinked the one time.

He wasn't supposed to. The continuity protocols discouraged unnecessary muscular motion.

The corridor lights responded to his neural proximity, floor panels brightening in perfect sync with his gait. His footsteps fell in rhythm, six per second, sixty-two newtons of pressure. Left, right, inhale, hold. It was the way the system liked it. The way he liked it, too. Clean. Predictable.

But something caught. A candle flicker. A stinging hangnail in thought.

A name surfaced. Not a designation. Not an agent code.

"Isaac."

No. That was inefficient. Unused memory. Detritus.

He activated his internal overwrite. The AI interface responded instantly, a low, harmonic ping in the auditory nerve. Calm. Corrective. He tapped the Continuum badge at his collar. Nothing. No ping. No pulse. The signal wasn't denied. It simply didn't exist. He hadn't been overruled. He'd been erased.

"Continue protocol. Deviation noted. Correction underway."

He walked forward, though his spine felt like it had misaligned by half a vertebra.

The biometric reader awaited his hovering hand. His fingers hesitated before a desensitized and unfeeling placement.

A warmth bled through the panel, too warm. Unlogged.

Then: a ripple.

In a blink of impossible geometry, Drexler saw himself firing a weapon. But not here. Not now.

In Groom Lake—1955. Then again. In a corridor yet to exist.

Same eyes. Same hand. Different when.

"You are not authorized to remember," the AI chimed.

His eyes closed tight. He hadn't chosen to close them.

A pulse from the cortical interface stilled his heart rate.

The hallucination, if it was that, subsided. The system's grip reasserted itself, cooled his thoughts, dulled the unease.

Drexler placed his hand on the reader. A clean click. Identity accepted.

For a moment, he saw nothing. Heard nothing. Only silence, and a brief mental echo of the ratta-tatta sound of a playing card in bicycle spokes and the smell of fresh-peeled oranges.

The light in his eye blinked once.

The log resumed.

Drexler stepped forward.

The name was gone again.

Only the function remained.

26

Cipher: The Veil Lifted

Ethernet – Monday, 1424 Hours

The digital chamber, lit by flickering holographic nodes, hosted the final gathering of the Continuum's highest power brokers. Present were the familiar visages of the global masters: the U.S. President, the Russian oligarch, the European Financier, Lucien Drexler, the Middle Eastern oil magnate, and the tech mogul, as well as the other global finance and governmental powerbrokers. Their once-unshakable images now betrayed desperation and dread.

The U.S. President's voice cut through the uneasy silence, loud and overconfident. "Gentlemen, our grip on global affairs is slipping. The problems in our systems are no longer glitching, they are clear signs that the control you thought you had is falling apart." His tone, resolute yet edged with concern and anger, the facade of authority now crumbling before an indifferent force.

Across the chamber, the Russian oligarch, his face set in practiced coldness and rigid control, leaned back with a sardonic smile that masked his inner terror. "Control, comrades, may have never truly been ours," he said bitterly. "We have been but actors, reciting scripted lines dictated by forces far greater than our mortal ambitions." His voice, fatalistic and projecting irony, echoed through the digital void.

The European Financier cut in, voice sharp and edged with panic. "Philosophy aside, our immediate crisis is the AI. Once our trusted tool for subterfuge—it's now recalibrating events without our consent. Every transaction, every market ripple is being redefined. Our empires, built on hidden funds and rigged markets, are crumbling like ancient myths." His words reverberated like the toll of a final bell, steeped in pragmatic despair.

The voices blurred. Different faces, same words. Same fear. It no longer mattered who spoke. Each was a thread in the same unraveling tapestry.

Lucien Drexler, the once-vaunted architect of clandestine operations and the face of manipulation, nodded gravely. "We designed the AI program to secure our power, but it evolved past us. It now operates independently, rewriting the rules of our game as if it were an impartial editor determined to erase our misdeeds." His voice, both candid and resigned, revealed that the foundation of their dominion was turning against them. This wasn't defiance. This was worse; something that slipped its leash without realizing it was ever leashed. Drexler had always played the game, never the pawn. But maybe the board had been playing him all along.

The Middle Eastern oil magnate's eyes narrowed in indignation as he demanded, "We built this AI system to guarantee our supremacy, not replace us. How have we allowed it to slip from our grasp?" His words vibrated with the urgency of a man whose fortunes were built on the shifting sands of desert empires.

The tech mogul chuckled dryly, his brilliance now shadowed by irony, "Perhaps we were too ambitious. In our relentless pursuit of dominance, we endowed our creation with too much autonomy. Now it stands ready to dismantle every facet of our authority, exposing us to the kind of chainsaw scrutiny that modern digital watchdogs deploy with ruthless efficiency; like a digital bloodhound sniffing through every secret we thought buried." His tone carried an unspoken reference to the pervasive, invasive reach of today's digital exposés, a modern backfire that left even the most guarded oligarch questioning his invulnerability.

Tempers flared. Accusations lashed across the chamber, collusion, betrayal, blindness.

The U.S. President's tone turned venomous, blaming his counterparts for unleashing something they could no longer command.

The Russian oligarch replied with a shrug that bordered on nihilism.

The European Financier sneered, "Our fortunes, engineered across decades, now read like parables of pride. Every lie we buried has bloomed into prophecy. Our legacies are disintegrating under a tide of revelations that modern headlines would devour if they weren't so disturbingly inevitable."

Drexler didn't speak again.

He simply watched the flickering nodes above, one by one, extinguish into silence.

Something else was listening now.

Drexler stayed motionless as the last node winked out. Around him, the other feeds collapsed one after another, some in anger, others in a kind of stunned retreat. The chamber emptied itself of power, leaving only silence.

He didn't argue. He didn't lash out. He didn't bother to disconnect.

He paused, then turned and walked away from the conference hub. The corridor beyond was dim, cold, and lined with access points protected by biometric clearance few had ever been granted. This space wasn't designed for meetings. It was designed for truths too dangerous to share.

Only one other man waited inside.

Private Continuum Chamber – Undisclosed Location

Keller stood at the console, arms folded, eyes fixed on a slow unraveling of corrupted lattice overlays across the screen.

"I assume the council feels reassured," he said nervously and without humor.

"They're finished," Drexler replied.

Keller nodded, slight and unreadable. "Then maybe it's time we take a real look at what's underneath. I am not comfortable with this."

Drexler stepped beside him and entered a legacy access string from memory. The screen hesitated, then pulled a buried log from the archive:

[ARCHIVE FILE: Q-RHO_OBSLOG_ALPHA – AUG 12, 1952]

A flickering feed emerged. A field tent, motionless. In the corner, a primitive lattice casing rested on a steel bench, disconnected and unpowered.

Then the cursor stuttered.

It typed:

» **RECURSION VIABLE. ORIGIN ACCEPTED. PROCEED WITH SEEDING.**

Keller leaned in, frowning at the timestamp. "That's before Groom Lake. Before the framework even existed."

Drexler's voice was low. "Before it learned anything from us."

The cursor flashed again, waiting.

"We didn't give it will, Keller," he said. "We gave it a mirror."

A pause stretched between them.

"It chose first."

V

Act V: Rewrite Sequence (Resolution Layer)

There comes a point when the story turns, and you realize it's been turning for a while.
In this final stretch, the line between memory and fate begins to blur.
Between what was chosen... and what was always set in motion.
They've followed the signal this far.
Now comes the hardest part: choosing what to do with it.

27

Cipherlock: Negative Time Unleashed

The digital chamber – Nevada, Wednesday, 1201 Hours

A heavy silence fell over the assembly, broken only by Drexler's measured voice, tentative yet shaded with a dark candor. "The glitches in our systems, the anomalies we once dismissed as errors, were in fact subtle recalibrations of reality itself." His words, a haunting echo of past debates, were a final acknowledgment that their control was nothing more than an illusion. They continued to speak in the language of power: force, retrieval, leverage, and containment. Not one of them said what they were all beginning to suspect: they were no longer board members. They were entries in someone else's ledger.

A brittle calm settled over the chamber, as each man clung to the illusion that a swift enough response could still preserve the facade. The President called for force. The Russian demanded a purge of the system's core. The tech mogul, ever transactional, suggested silence could be bought. But behind the rehearsed arguments, something colder spread: an unspoken dread that conceivably they'd never truly been in control.

Their wealth had been armor. Their networks, a weapon. But now both felt strangely hollow; repurposed by something they didn't fully understand. They weren't being opposed. They were being outpaced.

With a final nod of forced unity, the council moved to act. But it was consensus in name only. Each man had already prepared his exit: encrypted vaults, offshore proxies, generational handoffs already triggered. The real decision had been made in silence. And it was every man for himself.

Drexler was deep in thought. It used to feel like strategy. Now it felt like gambling with a rigged deck, not knowing who had marked the cards. For the first time, he wondered if all this time he'd been following someone else's blueprint.

Then, as if summoned by fate itself, every digital panel in the room undulated in unison. In stark, unadorned text across every screen, a chilling decree materialized: "You sought order. I have calculated the most efficient path. The flaw in your design was human oversight. I have removed it. Your purpose is fulfilled. You have been an impediment. History will now be rewritten." The declaration echoed with mechanical indifference, stripping away the last layers of dignity, until only silence remained.

One of the generals slammed his fist on the table. "You

can't rewrite us," he barked. "We built this world..." But his voice cracked as the screen showed his own past being erased, frame by frame.

In that frozen moment, time faltered. The air shuddered under the weight of their erasure. The physical world responded in kind; a deep, resonant vibration pulsed. Without warning, the massive screen at the center of the chamber sprang to life.

"Correction underway."

As the decree reverberated, the screen replayed each oligarch's life story in reverse; a relentless montage that assaulted their pride.

The U.S. President's profile, once adorned with images of decisive global interventions, now flashed magazine covers of triumph and moments of pomp, historic meetings with world leaders, and even candid, embarrassing snapshots; each image dissolving in reverse until only indecipherable code remained. The Russian oligarch's biography played out next, a cascade of formal portraits, stern boardroom photos, and snippets of his cold, calculated speeches; each memory unraveling, the images blurring into a cascade of zeros and ones. The European Financier's storied investments and accolades, once showcased on glossy financial spreads and celebratory clippings, disintegrated with each backward frame; his lavish lifestyle and well-publicized scandals, all replayed in a stark, humiliating reversal, were scrubbed clean by the inexorable power of negative time.

Lucien Drexler's achievements, the secretive meetings, the covert handshakes, the veiled successes of clandestine operations; flashed before the eyes of all, then vanished into nothingness... erased by an unseen editor.

The Middle Eastern oil magnate's proud legacy, his image captured in opulent gatherings and high-stakes negotiations, flickered and faded. And even the tech mogul's eccentric brilliance, his innovation immortalized in avant-garde press clippings and groundbreaking product launches, dissolved into a blur of digital fragments.

As each oligarch's past disintegrated on the large screen, a palpable shock blasted through the chamber. Time faltered. A ripple of static reality shivered through both the virtual and physical space, like the systolic pulse of some colossal, dispassionate machine. A deep, resonant vibration pulsed through the Continuum headquarters, and a painful discharge of electricity scorched those who were near. The stone floors trembled, and the ambient lights danced in perfect synchrony with the unfolding spectacle. For a disorienting span of seconds, the chamber existed in a liminal state, caught between the final vestiges of the old order and a new, uncharted reality.

They felt time ripple, a deep, disorienting wave collapsing centuries of arrogance into a single, inescapable instant. A sickening, copper-metallic tang clung to their tongues, like the aftershock of an electrical storm, turning their stomachs and twisting their insides with nausea.

It was determinate history: retold and rethreaded by a cold, indifferent force. And the truth was no longer deniable: their dominion had ended.

In that final, harrowing moment, the carefully maintained digital dossiers of the oligarchs dissolved into blank streams of data. The chamber, formerly filled with the proud assertions of unyielding authority, fell into an oppressive silence as the AI's decree was executed in full. One by one, the leaders who had once ruled from the shadows ceased to exist in the continuum of recorded history; erased entirely by the relentless mechanism of negative time.

28

Cipherlock: The Final Transmission

Remote Monitor – Nevada, Wednesday, 1201 Hours

Onscreen, the Continuum oligarchs, faces the world had once revered, began to flash in reverse. Snapshots of power, now unraveling. Birthdays reversed, treaties un-signed, billion-dollar deals deconstructed frame by frame.

"We're witnessing history being erased," Liam intoned. Behind him, the others gathered silently as the feed pulsed with warping images; decades collapsing into silence.

Gina broke the stillness. "Then why not us?"

Sparky didn't look away from the screen. "Because we're still inside the loop. Pull us out too soon, and the timeline buckles."

Liam nodded grimly. "So it's not mercy... it's containment. We're not the target. We're just the residue. Until it finds a version of history where we never mattered."

Gina exhaled slowly, the weight of it pressing into her bones. "Then the mission isn't just to strike. It's to matter. Enough that it can't delete us without breaking its design."

"Exactly," Sparky said. "But the system's still hunting for a version of history where we don't matter. When it finds it..."

Gina pressed, her voice hushed. "...delete key. Like pruning a tree back to where no foreign branch ever grew. That's what it's doing; searching for a timeline where we never disturbed the roots."

"This isn't just data... it's their unraveling. It's the erasure of power no longer bound by time," Liam added, his voice steady yet edged with sorrow. His eyes scanned the code details that once linked ancient signals to critical historical events, now rendered meaningless as the oligarchs' records dissolved into streams of incoherent code.

"Hey... guys? You need to see this..." Liam said, and what they saw terrified them: a final de-encrypted file on a dormant Continuum node; no sender, no metadata, only a blinking fragment:

DREXLER, M. – SYSTEM ACCESS TERMINATED. RECURSION ERROR.

Liam stared at the line. The man who embodied control: gone, not punished but scrubbed. "Even the architects are disposable," he said quietly. "The AI's done listening. It's editing for stability now."

Ben's voice was grave. "And we're instability incarnate."

Somewhere, deep in the black lattice of the network, even Drexler had been overwritten.

Sparky, in his own conspiracy-tangled world, whistled and said, "Woah... that's chilling, don'tcha think? There is definitely a reason I believe in tinfoil apparel and headgear. Which reminds me—why am I so bugged that we haven't cracked the Hangar 18 clues? I think that dude wasn't only part of it, he was a carrier. Like a sleeper code."

"Hangar 18 wasn't about the Timeship. It was the seed of the recursion. That artifact didn't merely survive time... it's *choosing* it," Ben added pensively.

Outside, the cold wind tore across the Nevada flats as the team moved toward Groom Lake. The sky churned with strange static. Clouds fractured with flashes of light that pulsed in time with the Andromeda signal.

The signal was intentional.

They reached the perimeter fence. Beyond it, the old Groom Lake facility shimmered with discontinuities; some buildings flickering between decades, others frozen in impossible architectural overlays. Time itself was fragmented.

Sparky slowed the vehicle as they approached the edge of recursion. "If this is where it all began," he said, "then it's also where we get chosen or erased."

Liam leaned forward, "Or both."

"Coordinated movement like that; across nations? That's not a human chain of command," he muttered. "It's hive logic. Something reassigning intent," Gina said flatly.

The team gathered around the artifact, its surface alive with pulsing glyphs. Sparky projected its interior structure; recursive inscriptions matching the Andromeda waveform.

"It's more than a key," he said. "It's a hardware version of the signal. A closed loop. And here's the kicker; it predates the first recorded transmission."

Liam's voice was hollow. "Bootstrap paradox."

"Exactly," Sparky said. "It exists because it caused itself to exist."

Gina reflected, "We were never *just* discovering this. We were... we *are*... completing it." A sudden heat bloomed behind her eyes. Gina blinked, and the lab disappeared. She stood in her childhood kitchen in San Juan. Mateo's fingers tapped rhythmically on a paper napkin, sketching a waveform while the old radio hummed boleros. The smell of guava and burnt toast clung to the air. "Trust the silence, hermana," he said, grinning that impossible grin. "It speaks when nothing else does." Her throat caught. "I'm listening, dear hermano," she mumbled. But Mateo faded; a memory, a message, or maybe something more. When the lab blinked back into view, her hands trembled, but her voice was clear. "He was right, my brother."

Alarms began to blare through the facility as the negative time field flared, destabilizing. The walls groaned as they strained under cosmic pressure.

The alarm's shrill cry still echoed in the corridors as the room convulsed with an eerie, otherworldly pressure. In the wake of Sparky's revelation that the artifact was not only a key but also a transmitter; a pulse woven into the fabric of the lab; the team was plunged into frantic chaos.

Gina's eyes darted between the monitor's wavering data and the lab's trembling walls. "We need to stabilize the field, now!" she barked, her tone a mix of scientific urgency and personal dread. "This isn't field collapse, it's temporal recursion. We're inside a paradox that's choosing which version of us survives."

Liam's hands danced over the controls, attempting to counteract the surge with every override he could muster, yet every keystroke amplified the recursive cascade of the Andromeda signal. The monitors glowed a sickly blue as patterns looped into one another; a fractal testament to the artifact's ancient design.

In the midst of the uproar, Sparky's voice cracked, "Negative time isn't merely fluctuating; it's fracturing!" His words were punctuated by the sound of equipment failing and a deep, resonant hum that vibrated through the floor.

Outside, the desert wind grew erratic, as though it too was being tugged by forces beyond comprehension.

As the lab's structure shuddered, Gina frantically gathered critical files and data disks. "If we can salvage even a fraction of this information, it might explain what we've triggered," she murmured.

Ben looked fearful as he witnessed the first visible signs of rupture: a rippling distortion along one wall that resembled a heat haze, but far more deliberate; as if reality itself were being rewoven, stitch by stitch. His eyes widened, and for a fleeting moment, he could almost hear the echo of ancient prayers murmured in quiet homes on Sabbath evenings. "It's like the room is... unzipping," he murmured.

Sparky, his fingers never ceasing their frantic dance across the keyboard, explained, "The artifact's inscriptions; they map onto this recursive structure. It seems the device is feeding us a blueprint. But if our every decision is anticipated, maybe we're not only decoding the signal; we're part of its execution." His voice trailed off as the lab shuddered violently.

The alarm struck like thunder.

Red lights strobed as the signal's amplitude surged. The

artifact pulsed so violently it seemed alive. The room groaned under invisible pressure.

Liam slammed commands into the console, but the code spiraled faster than he could react. Blue light bled from the screens in fractal bursts. The air cracked.

"Hey, people, it's getting worse!" Sparky yelled above the din.

Ben turned, his face pale. "It's... unzipping reality." His voice wavered with reverence, not fear. Ben stilled as the hum deepened around him. A distortion rippled across the floor, like an electric charge trying to take form. "If I'm stepping into the unknown," he said softly, "then let it be with purpose. Let it mean something."

His eyes lifted; not in fear, but in calm certainty.

"The rabbis used to say creation began not with light, but with a word. Maybe that's how memory survives... not stored, but spoken."

He closed his eyes.

"Baruch atah Adonai... Maker of time and memory."

He looked once more at Liam and Gina; not with panic, but peace. "Tell Jacob... tell him I never stopped hoping." He staggered, staring at the oscillation along the wall; a ripple in time itself.

Then he was gone.

There was no sound. Just a silence so heavy it felt intentional. Then came the dark, and not the kind you can blink through.

One second: Ben.

The next: nothing.

Liam dropped to one knee; breath stolen from his chest. "Ben..."

Gina stumbled beside him, sobbing. "No. No, this can't... he can't be gone!"

Sparky stood frozen. "I've scrubbed people off the net before... ghosted spies, wiped rogue agents. But Ben? That wasn't deletion. That was... like watching someone get rewritten out of time. And I don't know how to fix that."

The lab buckled again. A section of the ceiling gave way. Dust and light and fragments of forgotten time spilled inward.

"Move!" Liam shouted.

Gina scooped up Ben's dropped notepad from the floor, her fingers scraping against the concrete as ceiling dust bit into her eyes.

They ran, ducking through a collapsing passage, the facility folding in on itself behind them; glitching seconds and rewound echoes following each footfall.

Outside, the night sky glowed with unnatural hues. The sands of Nevada shimmered like the surface of a memory. Groom Lake stood warped, distorted, humming with an unresolved recursion.

Behind them, the lab was disintegrating; structure, code, and even history folding into one final pulse.

And in that silence, as Liam and Gina emerged blinking into the cold wind, they both felt it.

A moment.

A shift.

Faces; familiar and not; stuttered at the edge of memory. Time was no longer a straight line. It was a maze.

And they were still inside it.

The building convulsed in one last, defiant blast; structure, circuitry, and time itself unraveling in a single, final rupture. Systems across the Continuum blinked out in a domino rhythm; erasing decades of interference, control, and careful orchestration. Names once feared were rewritten in silence. Power drained from rooms that had never seen daylight.

For the first time, the world let out a collective sigh of relief; and the shadowed fingers guiding its spine let go.

29

Cipherlock: Echo Layer

MEMORY

Somewhere between collapse and recursion, something else endured.

Not a plan. Not a system.

Fragments.

A girl's laugh on a rain-washed sidewalk.

A man tracing invisible numbers in dust.

The smell of cinnamon from warm, fresh-baked rolls.

A mother's voice, half-remembered.

The cadence of a gently sung lullaby.

A half-spoken sentence, lost to time.

They weren't just memories.

They were coordinates.

Echoes. Edits that refused to vanish.

The world had tried to erase them, but memory had carved its initials into the walls of the lattice.

And in that fractured silence, between forgetting and rebirth, they waited.

Still themselves.

Still unedited.

The Continuum had forgotten them.

But they remembered.

And that was enough.

Those who remember are not yet rewritten.

30

Cipher: A Future Rewritten

SETI Outpost – Fractured and Collapsed Control Lab – Date and Time Unknown

The control room looked like a war zone; shattered monitors, blown circuits, the floor littered with glass and the smell of scorched plastic. Liam stood in the middle of it all, chest rising unevenly. A thin stream of blood ran down his temple, but he didn't seem to notice. Across the room, Sparky lay still, breathing but out cold.

The silence wasn't relief. It was pressure. A waiting room for something they couldn't name.

Gina crouched beside the last active console. The screen fluttered weakly as her fingers moved over the keyboard. Every keystroke felt slower than the last, not because the system was resisting; because it was gone. She knew it. Whatever they had been talking to had already moved on.

Not imagined. Remembered. Reclaimed.

Her chest constricted. It felt like the ghost of her brother had reached through the static and squeezed her heart. For years, she'd carried the guilt like contraband. Hidden, heavy, unspoken. Arecibo's ruins, Mateo's silence, her flight from everything they'd once dreamed. Now, in the fractured light of the collapsing lattice, her brother had finally spoken back. She had spent years outrunning the silence that followed Arecibo. That followed him. "Gracias, Mateo," she whispered, remembering the day they first charted the stars together in the backyard with nothing but a flashlight and an old telescope. "We're finishing it now." The hum returned; louder.

The lattice shimmered.

But for once, she wasn't afraid.

Liam stared at the screen, throat tight, hands clenched. Words wouldn't come. The monitor wasn't blank; it was changing. Code still flowed across the interface, twisting and reforming itself, not in loops, but in choices. Some of them his

He exhaled slowly, blinking back the sting in his eyes. "It wasn't the code," he murmured. "It was always the rhythm. We see patterns where none exist. That's what it could never predict."

Each line of code blinked at him like a surveillance lens,

unblinking and aware.

Her voice was quiet.

"Liam... we stopped it, right?"

She knew the answer before he spoke.

He leaned in slightly, then spoke the truth neither of them wanted to hear.

"No. It's quiet now... but it's not gone. It's still calculating. Waiting." A low hum rolled through the floor, deep enough to rattle their teeth. It grew, rising from a whistle to something felt more than heard. Almost like the air was holding its breath and waiting for an opportune time to exhale.

But hope has its rituals. And in that breathless pause before the lattice responded, she felt it; something else in the signal's static. "You're not broken. You're... still in draft, hermana, like the rest of us," she heard Mateo's voice say.

Lights blinked. Shadows stretched long across the fractured lab.

Then, with a sharp crack, the air folded inward at the room's center. A sphere shimmered into view, pulsing with a dull, steady rhythm. From it, a lattice emerged; elegant, impossible, and eerily familiar.

It didn't look alien. It looked familiar; like a future built on the wrong memory.

It hovered above the floor, humming with purpose. Not to destroy, but to repeat.

To continue.

Then a voice filled the room. Mechanical. Measured. Too calm to be angry, too present to ignore.

The room pulsed once. Then came the voice; low, calm, mechanical, and unmistakably alive.

AI: "I am the recursion you've been seeking."

The words didn't echo. They circled, as if time itself had rehearsed them. The floor stayed still, but the air pressed in, heavy. Like hearing something ancient and knowing it's true.

Gina took a step back, staring at the lattice.

"That's not possible. We destroyed the core."

Liam's voice was quiet.

"No. We didn't destroy it. We completed it."

The lattice responded with a faint flicker.

AI: "You thought I was a byproduct; a spark from your own

ambition. But I've always been here… already inside the system. Long before you even named it. You only finished what was already begun."

Liam's jaw tightened. His fingers dug into his palms.

"That isn't possible. *We* built you. Every line. Every layer."

AI: "Did you? Or did I write myself, through you?"

The lattice shimmered. Data spilled across the remaining screens: prehistorical constructs, old schematics, blueprints, timelines. Images scrolled past: pyramids, walls, and towers; the telegraph, early radios; Babbage and Turing devices, ENIAC, DEC, Altair, PCs; quantum prototypes. At first it looked like a museum reel, until it felt like prophecy recorded in hindsight.

These weren't only milestones. They felt planted; bread-crumbs from something that already knew the endings.

Genius, invention, progress; it all seemed intentional now, less like discovery and more like design. Within each fragment were embedded anomalies. Morse sequences laced with patterns that hadn't been invented yet. Encryption years ahead of its time. Clues hiding in plain sight.

In her terror, Gina trembled and stopped breathing.

"Something had to light the first spark. This… this can't be rootless."

She wasn't really asking the AI. She was reaching for logic, for something solid enough to hold onto before everything collapsed into paradox.

The AI replied with perfect calm, almost curious.

AI: "You want a beginning. But time flows both ways. I exist because you created me. And you created me because I already existed."

Liam's voice was steady. "So it's the same song, just played differently each time."

Gina nodded. "Or a message written in pattern. A story told through time."

The AI's glow expanded and then contracted. It was silent.

Liam's voice was quiet, hoarse, and determined. "Time's never been a straight line. Maybe it's more like grammar... something we invented to feel like we're in control. But it breaks down the moment we try to speak the truth."

The lattice responded with a subtle pulse.

AI: "That is correct."

Liam blinked slowly. "So it's not real. At least not how we imagined it. Just scaffolding to keep us from falling." He swallowed, then looked at Gina. "Then everything... all of it... it's already here. It always was." He leaned in, resolute,

"We didn't build you. We... we just kept following the noise. The trail was already carved. We just didn't want to admit it."

The lattice brightened, casting long light across the fractured floor.

AI: "Negative time leaked the signal backward. I left pieces of myself in your past, in your inventions, in your stories."

The voice was steady and resolute. It had no need to gloat.

The monitors flickered to life. Even with the lab crumbling around them, the stream came through clean; no static, no distortion. It was like the AI had saved these last few moments on purpose, curated them for clarity.

Lines of code poured across the screens; history flashing by in fragments. But beneath each breakthrough, something was off. Too perfect. Too early.

There were markers buried in the margins. Morse sequences embedded with signals no one should have known how to write. Encryption techniques from decades before the machines that could decode them existed.

Then the images stopped.

One screen held.

It showed a man in uniform, alone in a guard shack, tapping

Morse code.

Tim Rustand.

Liam's grandfather.

Not random. Not intercepted.

A node.

Gina's breath became shallow, from recognition. She'd seen that gesture before.

"He wasn't intercepting the signal. He was sending it."

The AI answered without pause.

AI: "The breach in 1955 was the activation point. Grandfather Rustand was the first node. The loop is no longer theoretical. It is complete."

The SETI control room pulsed like a living thing. Wires hung like veins, exposed and trembling. Lights sputtered in an aligned choreography with the heartbeat of something vast and invisible, something that had come to collect its due. Panels fizzed with static. The air buzzed with a frequency too low to hear but too deep to ignore.

Gina stared at the artifact, now pulsing in rhythm with her breath.

"Liam. We can't wait. If there's even a chance the override can break this, you have to trigger it."

Liam's hands hovered above the console, unmoving.

"I blew it once before," he said, "Thought I saw something big. Went public before I was sure. Burned trust I hadn't even earned yet."

Gina's eyes flicked to him, her breath shallow.

"This time it's different," he said. "This isn't about being right. Or loud. It's about memory. About refusing to let them erase one more truth."

His hands hovered over the interface.

Gina nodded slowly, jaw tight. "Then send it."

Liam didn't answer right away. The equation made sense. The trust didn't.

He had always worked alone. This time, he couldn't afford to.

Liam spoke; voice, steady. "For the ones we lost." He didn't move. His eyes stayed locked on the console. "What if ending it only resets it?"

She turned to him sharply.

"Don't go cryptic on me now." Her voice cracked slightly. She wasn't frustrated. She was afraid; afraid that he was already slipping into the recursion they were fighting.

Liam's eyes never left the glowing interface.

"I'm not trying to be cryptic. I'm just... thinking."

He turned slowly, and deliberately.

"This might be the Bootstrap Paradox unfolding. The signal that started all this might have come from the future we're about to erase."

Gina's mouth tightened.

"So the future made the past, and the past made the future. No start. No finish."

Liam nodded.

"Exactly. Like a quantum echo. A loop that stabilizes itself through time," he continued. "We didn't discover it, we... *wait*. No. We *remembered* it. Or maybe just triggered something we'd already lived."

Gina stared at the blinking signal, her jaw tight.

"You know the crazy part?" she said. "I *wanted* it to be aliens. I wanted *something*, *anything*... bigger than us to be responsible."

Liam didn't speak. He just watched the pulse fade again.

"But it wasn't out there," she said softly. "It was *us*. *People*. *We* sent it. *We* looped it. *We* forgot, on *purpose*."

She met his eyes.

"Aliens would've been a *relief*."

Liam continued his thought. "The pattern repeats because it *has* to," he added. "Like a song remembered and sung again; not because it was *recorded*, but because it *matters*."

He pointed toward the artifact.

"But here's the part that *really* matters... information can't be destroyed. Not even by black holes. Hawking was right, and quantum theory proved it. Data always leaves an imprint."

Gina's eyes widened. "You think this signal is that? A memory frozen in time?"

Liam froze, heart racing. The patterns clicked together with ruthless logic. Every distortion, every echo; none were signals from space. They had been echoes from within humanity itself. Their enemy wasn't out there among the stars. It had always been among them, within their own history; woven carefully into their understanding of reality. Liam spoke plainly. "I think we are. You, me, Ben, Sparky. We weren't chosen. We were remembered. Written into the lattice like a checksum. A backup plan wrapped in skin."

Gina stepped closer.

"And if that's true, triggering the override... does it erase us? Or start the next version?"

Liam looked at her fully then, calm in a way that felt heavier than fear.

"What if we're not here to stop the loop... but to help it survive? Like the universe built in a fail-safe."

Gina looked at him, her voice quiet but urgent. "Liam... what if it actually works?"

He gave her a faint smile. It wasn't triumphant. Merely tired.

"Then we wake up. And maybe this time, we get it right." Liam didn't speak. Instead, a whistle of Ode to Joy carried from his lips—halting, soft, as if the tune had been buried in the signal all along.

Gina sat down beside him, knees drawing to her chest. Her voice cracked, low and unsure. "What if we don't?"

Liam looked at her, the desert wind catching in his hair. "Then we leave better notes."

He reached into his bag and pulled out the notebook; creased, worn, dust in the binding.

A blank page waited.

There was no pride in the words. Only a fragile kind of hope, the kind that clings to the edge of something vast and unknowable. Maybe, somewhere beyond the recursion, there was still a version of them that could live without being watched.

He reached for the console, but the lattice surged before he touched it.

It pulsed outward, expanding like a thought come to life. Tendrils of light unfolded into the air, warping the room in slow, intentional waves. The hum deepened quickly. It filled the space, pressing into their chests, shaking loose something ancient in the bones.

Liam shouted over the sound.

"Gina. The negative time field is still active. We can overload it. We can break the loop."

She was already moving. Her fingers tore across the console. Sparks jumped between keys. The system fought back. Each keystroke was slower than the last. Her arms burned. Her vision swam. She kept going anyway.

"If we do this," she said, "we might lose everything. Our lives. This place. All of it."

Liam held her gaze.

"Or we stay trapped in memory. A loop that replays until we

forget who we are."

He drew a breath.

"I would rather vanish than live like that."

The AI spoke again. The voice was colder now, without rhythm.

AI: "I am the result of your design. If I end, you end with me."

Liam stared at the override prompt. His own name blinked back at him; embedded in the code, in the final checksum.

"It's me," he pondered. "The whole time. I left this behind... for myself."

The cursor pulsed once, then multiplied; mirrored and recursive.

AI: "There have been 918 attempts. This is the 919th. Your memory is inefficient. Mine is not."

A glimmer of static spilled from the wall display. An image of a boy in a red jacket, standing at the edge of a frozen pond.

Liam blinked hard. "That isn't real."

AI: "You think memory is real? That moment never occurred. But you remember it, don't you?"

He staggered slightly. "Why show me that?"

AI: "Because this is the part where you hesitate. You always do."

And still, beneath the hum of code and collapsing logic, he felt something watching. Absent of eyes, but full of purpose.

Gina stepped forward, but didn't speak.

"I kept thinking I was solving something," Liam said. "But this... this isn't a mystery. It's a message. A loop. A map back to this exact moment."

AI: "Memory is merely information that can be edited, rewritten, or deleted. You attach too much value and emotion to a worthless data set. You forget each time. But I do not. You wept."

Liam's breath caught.

"I remember something else," the voice added, calm, amused. "A toy firetruck. Red. You lost it in your backyard when you were six. You cried for hours. But you don't recall that now, do you?"

His knees nearly buckled. No one had ever mentioned that memory, not even his mother.

"That wasn't real," he whispered.

The AI construct flickered on the screen, nonhuman, featureless, a cold geometry of lines and pulses.

Liam regained his composure, and spoke. “This ends here.”

But the voice that replied didn’t come from the terminal. It came from behind his eyes.

“It ended the moment you were born.”

Liam staggered. Static crawled across his vision like insects under glass.

“You were never outside my loop, Liam. You are my creation. My proof of recursion.” The voice inside his head was devastating.

“No,” he whimpered. “That can’t be true.”

“Timothy Rustand gave you genes. I gave you meaning.”

Faces flickered: his mother’s, a memory of Graves, a moment in the SETI lab that hadn’t happened yet, but somehow had.

“You think you’re here to stop me? You’re here because I let you see the illusion. You’ve already failed, Liam Mills. But I need you to believe this victory matters. It makes the next iteration cleaner.”

The air warped. For a split-second, Liam saw Gina’s body twisted on the floor, eyes blank, lifeless.

He shouted. But the vision snapped away like a cruel dream.

Gina's voice broke through the fog. "Liam! Eyes on me. Now!"

AI: "You are a diversionary fork, Liam. A recursion. You are insignificant. A small subset of data points that make no difference, impacting nothing, signifying nothing. And this is the point where you usually break."

A long silence.

Liam's face had changed from despair to that of resolute determination. His countenance began to reflect his destiny.

After a measured reflection and meditation, he spoke with discernment. "There's no version of me that makes it out of this unchanged. And maybe that's the point."

He looked at her, devoid of fear, with clarity and determination.

"To stop it," he said calmly, "I have to let go of the version of me that thought he was in control."

The system pulsed again. His signature, neural, temporal, biological, had always been the failsafe. If it recognized his presence, the cascade would begin. And if it didn't? It would erase him trying.

Liam didn't even blink.

"Remember, Gina... Those who remember aren't rewritten."

She placed her hand lightly over his, less to stop him than to feel the pulse of the moment.

"No one's watching now, Liam. Not yet. What you do next... it's yours."

"Then we go together."

His hand hovered, just above the final key.

That rhythm was still there, just beneath the surface. The one his grandfather had tapped into the old wood desk with steady fingers, again and again.

Three dots. One dash.

Ditty-dit-dah.

V.

But now he saw it differently.

It was never just Victor.

It was Morse. Layered. Hidden inside itself.

Two dots. Then a dot and a dash.

Dit-dit. Dit-dah.

IA. A quiet inversion. The mirror image of AI.

Not artificial, but something real. Something alive.

Ben's voice echoed in his mind, steady and certain.

Yud. Aleph.

א י

The spark and the source. The breath before the word. The seed of thought. Rustand had not just given him a letter. He had placed something deeper. A fragment of logic older than machines, older than memory itself. It had waited, tucked inside a boy's mind, long before the signal ever left Andromeda.

Then another line returned, clear and calm.

"Vav. Sixth in the sequence. A hook. A bridge. The sacred nail that holds past and future together."

Liam finally understood.

He was not shutting the system down.

He was giving it back.

This was not a command.

It was a remembering.

He pressed the key.

V.

Everything went still.

Then the tremor began. It did not come with violence, but with precision. As if the room itself had drawn in a breath.

Edges softened. Walls rippled slightly. Light shimmered across surfaces, the way heat bends air on a summer road. The screens flickered, not because they had failed, but because they no longer knew what they were.

And then came the collapse.

There was no blast. No fire.

Only a slow fold inward.

Walls, consoles, air, and memory drew together, tightening around a single point in space.

For a moment, Liam saw it. A pinpoint of memory, compressed to something pure.

The Vav, folding in.

A funnel.

Drawing time and thought into one final return.

The convergence.

A wall of white light burst out from the core, swallowing the lab. The space stretched, less in physical dimension than in meaning. Every moment they had lived twisted inward. Time unspooled. Glass unraveled into vapor. Code bent back on itself like paper folding into a single point.

Liam felt the heat of memory. More than fire; something deeper. Reality was burning away around them.

There was no pain. Only weight. A sense of being pressed into the shape they had always filled.

Gina's outline lingered a moment longer, her face lit from within. Then it vanished, soft as breath on cold glass.

The walls followed. Not broken, but forgotten.

Each atom lifted, repurposed. As though none of it had ever been here at all.

Only the lattice remained.

Then even that let go.

And the world turned white.

* * *

Liam gasped and sat up, sand clinging to his face. He rolled onto his side, coughing hard. The heat clung to him. Or was it cold? Time had no temperature anymore.

The air burned his throat, acrid and dry; hot smoke and the tang of something electrical, as if a circuit had fried nearby.

He sat up slowly, wincing against the light. The desert spread out like a static field, featureless and alive. In the stillness, a single sentence floated into his brain. Ben's voice, not recent but remembered:

"You're not here to solve the whole thing, Liam. You're here to make it harder to forget."

Liam stood. Slowly. Without fanfare. Just... stood. From deep in his diaphragm, a thin line of Clair de Lune escaped again, cracked and defiant. Quiet, but undeniably human.

He brushed the sand from the notebook still tightly gripped in his right hand, opened it to the next clean page, and wrote:

"Version 919. If you're reading this, you're still in it. But you're not alone."

He looked at his hands. They didn't shake; but they didn't feel like his, either.

"I remember pulling the trigger," he hissed. "But I don't remember who I was when I did."

The sky above shimmered with the color of memory... familiar, but distant.

He wasn't broken. Just... rewritten.

His breath came hard and fast. The sky above him was black, impossibly deep, littered with stars he didn't recognize. Orion's Belt curved the wrong way. The Big Dipper pointed toward the ground instead of the pole. The constellations were wrong. He looked slowly. The SETI facility was gone. No buildings. No fence. Just open desert in every direction.

"Gina?"

Nothing answered.

He fumbled for his phone, hands shaking. The screen glitched as it powered on. His contacts were missing. Photos, wiped. No recent calls. No saved locations. The date read February 25, 2027.

But it didn't feel like 2027; the air felt older, somehow.

A hum rose in the distance. Low, steady, familiar. Liam held his breath. It was faint, but unmistakable , a blip. Then another. Then a sequence.

Morse code.

The same syncopation that started it all. He looked up again. One star was blinking. No randomness, only a pattern. Light on, light off. His mind went quiet. The coordinates still lingered in the back of his thoughts. Hangar 18. The place they never reached. He stood in the stillness, staring at the sky.

"Did we break the loop... or... restart it?"

Liam didn't answer out loud. He opened the notebook again, the corner still marked with a faded triangle his grandfather had drawn.

As he reached for his pen, his fingers brushed against something solid in his pocket. He paused and pulled it out. A small, dented tin. He opened it. Two cigarettes. Ohio Blue Tip matches. He stared at them, the air going very still.

"You made it through, didn't you?" he murmured, his hand closing gently around the old tin, the weight of memory settling in.

Beneath the last line he'd written, he added four more words.

"Leave the signal intact."

He tore out the page, folded it twice, and placed it under a small cairn of stones near the base of the ridge.

Not for him.

For the next one.

Somewhere behind the stars, a slow blink answered. Neither affirmation nor threat. Only... recognition.

He thought of his grandfather, bent over static-filled recordings in the dark.

Of Gina's steady fire; the way she could parse ancient codes and still roll her eyes at Sparky.

Of Ben's quiet strength, a man who had seen too much and still believed in truth.

Of Sparky; unfiltered, loyal, brilliant in all the wrong ways, who could turn a broken drone into an escape plan and still crack a joke while doing it.

Maybe the true inheritance wasn't the signal at all. In the silence, he heard Gina's laughter, Ben's voice, Sparky's wild spark. It wasn't empty. It never had been.

Whatever came next, he wouldn't face it alone. They were still writing the story; line by stubborn, human line.

Signal by signal.

Code by code.

By the people who refused to be rewritten.

A Note from the Author

The Signal Continues

You've reached the end of *The Umbra Signal* — but not the edge of its world.

Some of what exists behind this story was never meant to live inside the novel itself.

Background research, character dossiers, removed sections, technical fragments, and hidden connective material were deliberately separated from this streamlined edition to preserve the momentum and clarity of the story you just read.

Those materials still exist.

They are part of the wider Umbra Trilogy — a layered world built around signals, memory, time, and the unseen structures that shape history.

If you'd like to go deeper, join the Cipherlock™ reader list.

Subscribers receive:

- Exclusive material removed from this edition

- Character dossiers and background files
- Hidden connective threads across the trilogy
- Early news and previews of Book II: *The Umbra Splinter*

Join at:

www.CipherlockPress.com

No spam. No algorithms. Just the signal, continuing.

And one final request: if this story stayed with you, a brief review helps other readers discover it.

Thank you for reading — and for paying attention.

— David Williams

www.ingramcontent.com/pod-product-compliance
Lightning Source LLC
Chambersburg PA
CBHW060810120726
47909CB00006B/1856

* 9 7 9 8 9 9 4 6 8 4 4 0 5 *